"If anyone is the complete master of the grand-scale sf novel, it's Bear. . . . [*Moving Mars*] is also told extremely well with nothing lacking in ... ... rary excellence." —*Booklist*

"Greg Bear's *Mov...* ... ... g society struggling against ... ... ors of its own inhospitable ... ... rupulous in its details regarding the nature of Mars and the difficulties in settling the planet. . . . The novel's best moments involve Bear's ingenious biological and physical speculations, which do not simply color the narrative but (it is one of Bear's characteristic strengths) shape and inform its texture." —*The Washington Post*

"Bear's Mars is one of the most vividly realized of the recent body of areological novels . . . He has the gift of implying a whole background with high-resolution but subtly-signaled background details, again built into the language of the milieu rather than in more obtrusive devices." —*Locus*

"Mars fans are in for a real treat with the publication of *Moving Mars* by Greg Bear. A young Martian scientist makes an astounding discovery that plays a key element in the deteriorating relationship between Earth and its colony. After a deceptively slow start in which Mr. Bear sows the seeds of his piquant premise with delicate precision, this grand adventure in hard science fiction surges forward to a powerful resolution." —*Romantic Times*

"Greg Bear is a writer's writer, and *Moving Mars* is another winner. It's chock full of physics, metaphysics, nano-biology and gritty politics, set amid a dazzling high-tech 22nd century cold war between Earth and Mars. This is as good as hard science fiction gets." —*Portland Oregonian*

"*Moving Mars* is an accomplished, thoroughly mature novel that should be placed at the top of anyone's 'to be read' stack." —*Science Fiction Age*

Other books by Greg Bear

Hegira
Psychlone
Beyond Heaven's River
Strength of Stones
The Wind from a Burning Woman
Blood Music
Eon
The Forge of God
Eternity
Hardfought
Tangents
Heads
Songs of Earth and Power
Anvil of Stars
Queen of Angels

MOVING MARS

GREG BEAR

A TOM DOHERTY ASSOCIATES BOOK
NEW YORK

MOVING MARS

Cover art by Wayne Barlowe
Stepback art by Eric Peterson

A Tor Book
Published by Tom Doherty Associates, Inc.
175 Fifth Avenue
New York, N.Y. 10010

Tor® is a registered trademark of Tom Doherty Associates, Inc.

ISBN: 0-812-52480-2
Library of Congress Catalog Card Number: 93-26546

First edition: November 1993
First mass market edition: December 1994

Printed in the United States of America

0 9 8 7 6 5 4 3 2

For Ray Bradbury

MOVING MARS

A day on Mars is a little longer than a day on Earth: 24 hours and 40 minutes. A year on Mars is less than two Earth years: 686 Earth days, or 668 Martian days. Mars is 6,787 kilometers in diameter, compared to Earth's 12,756 kilometers. Its gravitational acceleration is 3.71 meters per second squared, or just over one-third of Earth's. The atmospheric pressure at the surface of Mars averages 5.6 millibars, about one-half of one percent of Earth's. The atmosphere is largely composed of carbon dioxide. Temperatures at the "datum" or reference surface level (there is no "sea level," as there are presently no seas) vary from −130° to +27° Celsius. An unprotected human on the surface of Mars would very likely freeze within minutes, but first would die of exposure to the near-vacuum. If this unfortunate human survived freezing and low pressure, and found a supply of oxygen to breathe, she would still be endangered by high levels of radiation from the sun and elsewhere.

After Earth, Mars is the most hospitable planet in the Solar System.

Part One

~

The young may not remember Mars of old, under the yellow Sun, its cloud-streaked skies dusted pink, its soil rusty and fine, its inhabitants living in pressurized burrows and venturing Up only as a rite of passage or to do maintenance or tend the ropy crops spread like nests of intensely green snakes over the wind-scoured farms. That Mars, an old and tired Mars filled with young lives, is gone forever.

Now I am old and tired, and Mars is young again.

Our lives are not our own, but by God, we must behave as if they are. When I was young, what I did seemed too small to be of any consequence; but the shiver of dust, we are told, expands in time to the planet-sweeping storm . . .

2171, M.Y. 53

An age was coming to an end. I had studied the signs half-innocently in my classes, there had even been dire hints from a few perceptive professors, but I had never thought the situation would affect me personally ... Until now.

I had been voided from the University of Mars, Sinai. Two hundred classmates and professors in the same predicament lined the brilliant white floor of the depot, faces crossed by shadows from sun shining through the webwork of beams and girders supporting the depot canopy. We were waiting for the Solis Dorsa train to come and swift us away to our planums, planitias, fossas, and valleys.

Diane Johara, my roommate, stood with her booted foot on one small bag, tapping the tip of the boot on the handle, lips pursed as if whistling but making no sound. She kept her face pointed toward the northern curtains, waiting for the train to nose through. Though we were good friends, Diane and I had never talked politics. That was basic etiquette on Mars.

"Assassination," she said.

"Impractical," I murmured. I had not known until a few days ago how strongly Diane felt. "Besides, who would you shoot?"

"The governor. The chancellor."

I shook my head.

Over eighty percent of the UMS students had been voided, a gross violation of contract. That struck me as very damned unfair, but my family had never been activist. Daughter of BM finance people, born to a long tradition of caution, I straddled the fence.

The political structure set up during settlement a century before still creaked along, but its days were numbered. The original settlers, arriving in groups of ten or more families, had dug warrens in water-rich lands all over Mars, from pole to pole, but mostly in the smooth lowland plains and the deep valleys. Following the Lunar model, the first families had formed syndicates called Binding Multiples or BMs. The Binding Multiples acted like economic super-families; indeed, "family" and "BM" were almost synonymous. Later settlers had a choice of joining established BMs or starting new ones; few families stayed independent.

Many BMs merged and in time agreed to divide Mars into areological districts and develop resources in cooperation. By and large, Binding Multiples regarded each other as partners in the midst of Martian bounty, not competitors.

"The train's late. Fascists are supposed to make them run on time," Diane said, still tapping her boot.

"They never did on Earth," I said.

"You mean it's a myth?"

I nodded.

"So fascists aren't good for anything?" Diane asked.

"Uniforms," I said.

"Ours don't even have good uniforms."

Elected by district ballot, the governors answered only to the inhabitants of their districts, regardless of BM affiliations. The governors licensed mining and settlement rights to the BMs and represented the districts in a joint Council of Binding Multiples. Syndics chosen within BMs by vote of senior advocates and managers represented the interests of the BMs themselves in the Council. Governors and syndics did not often see eye to eye. It was all very formal and polite—Martians are almost always polite—but many procedures were uncodified. Some said it was grossly inefficient, and attempts were being made to unify Mars under a central government, as had already happened on the Moon.

The governor of Syria-Sinai, Freechild Dauble, a tough, chisel-chinned administrator, had pushed hard for several years to get the BMs to agree to a Statist constitution and central government authority. She wanted them to give up their syndics in favor of representation by district. This meant the breakup of BM power, of course.

Dauble's name has since become synonymous with corruption, but at the time, she had been governor of Mars's largest district for eight Martian years and was at the peak of her long friendship with power. By cajoling, pressuring, and threatening, she had forged—some said forced—agreements between the largest BMs. Dauble had become the focus of

Martian Unity and was on the sly spin for president of the planet.

Some said Dauble's own career was the best argument for change, but few dared contradict her.

A vote was due within days in the Council to make permanent the new Martian constitution. We had lived under the Dauble government's "trial run" for six months, and many grumbled loudly. The hard-won agreement was fragile. Dauble had rammed it down too many throats, with too much underhanded dealing.

Lawsuits were pending from at least five families opposed to unity, mostly smaller BMs afraid of being absorbed and nullified. They were called Gobacks by the Statists, who regarded them as a real threat. The Statists would not tolerate a return to what they saw as disorganized Binding Multiples rule.

"If assassination is so impractical," Diane said, "we could rough up a few of the favorites—"

"Shh," I said.

She shook her short, shagged hair and turned away, soundlessly whistling again. Diane did that when she was too angry to speak politely. Red rabbits who had lived for decades in close quarters placed a high value on politeness, and impressed that on their offspring.

The Statists feared incidents. Student protests were unacceptable to Dauble. Even if the students did not represent the Gobacks, they might make enough noise to bring down the agreement.

So Dauble sent word to Caroline Connor, an old friend she had appointed chancellor of the largest university, University of Mars Sinai. An authoritarian with too much energy and too little sense, Connor obliged her crony by closing most of the campus and compiling a list of those who might be in sympathy with protesters.

I had majored in government and management. Though I had signed no petitions and participated in no marches— unlike Diane, who had taken to the movement vigorously—my name crept onto a list of suspects. The Govmanagement Department was notoriously independent; who could trust any of us?

We had paid our tuition but couldn't go to classes. Most of the voided faculty and students had little choice but to go home. The university generously gave us free tickets on state chartered trains. Some, including Diane, declined the tickets and vowed to fight the illegal voiding. That earned her—and, guilty by association, me, simply slow to pack my belongings—an escort of UMS security out of the university warrens.

Diane walked stiffly, slowly, defiantly. The guards—most of them new emigrants from Earth, large and strong—firmly gripped our elbows and hustled us down the tunnels. The rough treatment watered my quick-growing seed of doubt; how could I give in to this injustice without a cry? My family was cautious; it had never been known for cowardice.

Surrounded by Connor's guards, packed in with the last remaining voided students, we were marched in quickstep past a cluster of other students lounging in a garden atrium. They wore their family grays and blues, scions of BMs with strong economic ties to Earth, darlings of those most favoring Dauble's plans; all still in school. They talked quietly and calmly among themselves and turned to watch us go, faces blank. They offered no support, no encouragement; their inaction built walls. Diane nudged me. "Pigs," she whispered.

I agreed. I thought them worse than traitors—they behaved as if they were cynical and *old*, violators of the earnest ideals of youth.

We had been loaded into a single tunnel van and driven to the depot, still escorted by campus guards.

The depot hummed.

A few students wandered down a side corridor, then came back and passed the word. The loop train to the junction at Solis Dorsa approached. Diane licked her lips and looked around nervously.

The last escorting guard, assured that we were on our way, gave us a tip of his cap and stepped into a depot cafe, out of sight.

"Are you coming with us?" Diane asked.

I could not answer. My head buzzed with contradictions, anger at injustice fighting family expectations. My mother and father hated the turmoil caused by unification. They strongly believed that staying out of it was best. They had told me so, without laying down any laws.

Diane gave me a pitying look. She shook my hand and said, "Casseia, you *think* too much." She edged along the platform and turned a corner. In groups of five or less, students went to the lav, for coffee, to check the weather at their home depots . . . Ninety students in all sidled away from the main group.

I hesitated. Those who remained seemed studiously neutral. Sidewise glances met faces quickly turned away.

An eerie silence fell over the platform. One last student, a female first-form junior carrying three heavy duffels, did a little shimmy, short brown hair fanning around her neck. She let one duffel slip from her shoulder. The shimmy vibrated down to her leg and she kicked the bag two meters. She dropped her other bags and walked north on the platform and around the corner.

My whole body quivered. I looked at the solemn faces around me and wondered how they could be so *bovine*. How could they just stand there, waiting for the train to slow, and accept Dauble's punishment for political views they might not even support?

The train pushed a plug of air along the platform as it passed through the seals and curtains. Icons flashed above the platform—station ID, train designator, destinations—and a mature woman's voice told us, with all the politeness in the world and no discernible emotion, "Solis Dorsa to Bosporus, Nereidum, Argyre, Noachis, with transfers to Meridiani and Hellas, now arriving, gate four."

I muttered, "Shit *shit shit*," under my breath. Before I

knew what I had decided, before I could paralyze myself with more thought, my legs took me around the corner and up to a blank white service bay: dead end. The only exit was a low steel door covered with chipped white enamel. It had been left open just a crack. I bent down, opened the door wide, glanced behind me, and stepped through.

It took me several minutes of fast walking to catch up with Diane. I passed ten or fifteen students in a dark arbeiter service tunnel and found her. "Where are we going?" I asked in a whisper.

"Are you with us?"

"I am now."

She winked and shook my hand with a bold and happy swing. "Someone has a key and knows the way to the old pioneer domes."

Muffling laughter and clapping each other on the back, full of enthusiasm and impressed by our courage, we passed one by one through an ancient steel hatch and crept along narrow, stuffy old tunnels lined with crumbling foamed rock. As the last of us left the UMS environs, stepping over a dimly lighted boundary marker into a wider and even older tunnel, we clasped hands on shoulders and half-marched, half-danced in lockstep.

Someone at the end of the line harshly whispered for us to be quiet. We stopped, hardly daring to breathe. Seconds of silence, then from behind came low voices and the mechanical hum of service arbeiters, a heavy, solid clank and a painful twinge in our ears. Someone had sealed the tunnel hatch behind us.

"Do they know we're in here?" I asked Diane.

"I doubt it," she said. "That was a pressure crew."

They had closed the door and sealed it. No turning back.

The tunnels took us five kilometers beyond the university borders, through a decades-old maze unused since before my birth, threaded unerringly by whoever led the group.

"We're in old times now," Diane said, looking back at me. Forty orbits ago—over seventy-five Terrestrial years—these tunnels had connected several small pioneer stations. We filed past warrens once used by the earliest families, dark and bitterly cold, kept pressurized in reserve only for dire emergency . . .

Our few torches and tunnel service lamps illuminated scraps of old furniture, pieces of outdated electronics, stacked drums of emergency reserve rations and vacuum survival gear.

Hours before, we had eaten our last university meal and had a warm vapor shower in the dorms. That was all behind us. Up ahead, we faced Spartan conditions.

I felt wonderful. I was doing something significant, and without my family's approval.

I thought I was finally growing up.

The ninety students gathered in a dark hollow at the end of the tunnel, a pioneer trench dome. All sounds—nervous and excited laughter, questioning voices, scraping of feet on the cold floor, scattered outbreaks of song—blunted against the black poly interior. Diane broke Martian reserve and hugged me. Then a few voices rose above the dull murmurs. Several students started taking down names and BM affiliations. The mass began to take shape.

Two students from third-form engineering—a conservative and hard-dug department—stood before us and announced their names: Sean Dickinson, Gretyl Laughton. Within the day, after forming groups and appointing captains, we confirmed Sean and Gretyl as our leaders, expressed our solidarity and zeal, and learned we had something like a plan.

I found Sean Dickinson extremely handsome: of middle height, slight build, wispy brown hair above a prominent forehead, brows elegantly slim and animated. Though less attractive, Gretyl had been struck from the same mold: a slim young woman with large, accusing blue eyes and straw hair pulled into a tight bun.

Sean stood on an old crate and gazed down upon us, establishing us as real people with a real mission. "We all know why we're here," he said. Expression stern, eyes liquid and compassionate, he raised his hands, long and callused fingers reaching for the poly dome above, and said, "The old betray us. Experience breeds corruption. It's time to bring a moral balance to Mars, and show *them* what an individual stands for, and what our rights really mean. They've forgotten us, friends. They've forgotten their contractual obligations. True Martians don't forget such things, any more than they'd forget to breathe or plug a leak. So what are we going to do? What can we do? What *must* we do?"

"Remind them!" many of us shouted. Some said, *"Kill them,"* and I said, "Tell them what we—" But I was not given a chance to finish, my voice lost in the roar.

Sean laid out his plan. We listened avidly; he fed our anger and our indignation. I had never been so excited. We who had kept the freshness of youth, and would not stand for corruption, intended to storm UMS *overland* and assert our contractual rights. We were righteous, and our cause was just.

Sean ordered that we all be covered with skinseal, pumped from big plastic drums. We danced in the skinseal showers naked, laughing, pointing, shrieking at the sudden cold, embarrassed but greatly enjoying ourselves. We put our clothes back on over the flexible tight-fitting nanomer. Skinseal was designed for emergency pressure problems and not for comfort. Going to the bathroom became an elaborate ritual; in skinseal, a female took about four minutes to pee, a male two minutes, and shitting was particularly tricky.

We dusted our skinseal with red ochre to hide us should we decide to worm out during daylight. We all looked like cartoon devils.

By the end of the third day, we were tired and hungry and dirty and impatient. We huddled in the pressurized poly dome, ninety in a space meant for thirty, our rusty water tapped from an old well, having eaten little or no food, exercising to ward off the cold.

* * *

I brushed past a pale thoughtful fellow a few times on the way to the food line or the lav. Lean and hawk-nosed and dark-haired, with wide, puzzled eyes, a wry smile and a hesitant, nervously joking manner, he seemed less angry and less sure than the rest of us. Just looking at him irritated me. I stalked him, watching his mannerisms, tracking his growing list of inadequacies. I was not in the best temper and needed to vent a little frustration. I took it upon myself to educate him.

At first, if he noticed my attention at all, he seemed to try to avoid me, moving through little groups of people under the gloomy old poly, making small talk. Everybody was testy; his attempts at conversation fizzled. Finally he stood in line near an antique electric wall heater, waiting his turn to bask in the currents of warm dry air.

I stood behind him. He glanced at me, smiled politely, and hunkered down with his back against the wall. I sat beside him. He clamped his hands on his knees, set his lips primly, and avoided eye contact; obviously, he had had enough of trying to make conversation and failing.

"Having second thoughts?" I asked after a decent interval.

"What?" he asked, confused.

"You look sour. Is your heart in this?"

He flashed the same irritating smile and lifted his hands, placating. "I'm here," he said.

"Then show a little enthusiasm, dammit."

Some other students shook their heads and shuffled away, too tired to get involved in a private fracas. Diane joined us at the rear of the line.

"I don't know your name," he said.

"She's Casseia Majumdar," said Diane.

"Oh," he said. I was angry that he recognized the name. Of all things, I didn't want to be known for my currently useless family connections.

"Her third uncle founded Majumdar BM," Diane continued. I shot her a look and she puckered her lips, eyes dancing. She was enjoying a little relief from the earnest preparations and boredom.

"You have to be with us in heart *and* mind," I lectured him.

"Sorry. I'm just tired. My name is Charles Franklin." He offered a hand.

I thought that was incredibly insensitive and gauche, considering the circumstance. We had made it to the heater, but I turned away as if I didn't care and walked toward the stacks of masks and cyclers being tested by our student leader.

Neither a Statist nor a Goback, Sean Dickinson seemed to me the epitome of what our impromptu organization stood for. Son of a track engineer, Sean had earned his scholarship by sheer brainwork. In the UMS engineering department, he had moved up quickly, only to be diverted into attempts to organize trans-BM unions. That had earned him the displeasure of Connor and Dauble.

Sean worked with an expression of complete concentration, hair disheveled, spidery, strong fingers pulling at mask poly. His mouth twitched with each newfound leak. He hardly knew I existed. Had he known, he probably would have shunned me for my name. That didn't stop me from being impressed.

Charles followed me and stood beside the growing pile of rejects. "Please don't misunderstand," he said. "I'm really behind all this."

"Glad to hear it," I said. I observed the preparations and shivered. Nobody likes the thought of vacuum rose. None of us had been trained in insurrection. We would be up against campus security, augmented by the governor's own thugs and maybe some of our former classmates, and I had no idea how far they—or the situation—would go.

We watched news vids intently on our slates. Sean had posted on the ex nets that students had gone on strike to protest Connor's illegal voiding. But he hadn't told about our dramatic plans, for obvious reasons. The citizens of the Triple—the linked economies of Earth, Mars, and Moon—

hadn't turned toward us. Even the LitVids on Mars seemed uninterested.

"I thought I could help," Charles said, pointing to the masks and drums. "I've done this before . . ."

"Gone Up?" I asked.

"My hobby is hunting fossils. I asked to be on the equipment committee, but they said they didn't need me."

"Hobby?" I asked.

"Fossils. Outside. During the summer, of course."

Here was my chance to be helpful to Sean, and maybe apologize to Charles for showing my nerves. I squatted beside the pile and said, "Sean, Charles here says he's worked outside."

"Good," Sean said. He tossed a ripped mask to Gretyl. I wondered innocently if she and Sean were lovers. Gretyl scowled at the mask—a safety-box surplus antique—and dropped it on the reject pile, which threatened to spill out around our feet.

"I can fix those," Charles said. "There are tubes of quick poly in the safety boxes. It works."

"I won't send anybody outside in a ripped mask," Sean said. "Excuse me, but I have to *focus* here."

"Sorry," Charles said. He shrugged at me.

"We may not have enough masks," I said, looking at the diminishing stacks of good equipment.

Sean glared over his shoulder, pressed for time and very unhappy. "Your advice is not necessary," Gretyl told me sharply.

"It's nothing," Charles said, tugging my arm. "Let them work."

I shrugged his fingers loose and backed away, face flushed with embarrassment. Charles returned with me to the heater, but we had lost our places there.

The lights had been cut to half. The air became thicker and colder each day. I thought of my warren rooms at home, a thousand kilometers away, of how worried my folks might be, and of how they would take it if I died out in the thin air, or

if some Statist thug pierced my young frame with a flechette . . . God, what a scandal that would make! It seemed almost worth it.

I fantasized Dauble and Connor dragged away *under
arrest*, glorious and magnificent disgrace, perhaps worth my
death . . . but probably not.

"I'm a physics major," Charles said, joining me at the end
of the line.

"Good for you," I said.

"You're in govmanagement?"

"That's why I'm here."

"I'm here because my parents voted against the Statists.
That's all I can figure. They were in Klein BM. Klein's holding out to the last, you know."

I nodded without making eye contact, wanting him to go
away.

"The Statists are suicidal," Charles said mildly. "They'll
bring themselves down . . . even if we don't accelerate the
process."

"We can't afford to wait," I said. The skinseal wouldn't
last much longer. The nakedness and embarrassment had
bonded us. We *knew* each other; we thought we had no secrets. But we itched and stank and our indignation might soon
give way to general disgruntlement. I felt sure Sean and the
other leaders were aware of this.

"I was trying to get a scholarship for Earth study and a
grant for thinker time," he said. "Now I'm off the list, I'm
behind on my research—" He paused, eyes downcast, as if
embarrassed at babbling. "You know," he said, "we've got to
do something in the next twenty hours. The skinseal will rot."

"Right." I looked at him more closely. He was not homely.
His voice was mellow and pleasant, and what I had first
judged as lack of enthusiasm now looked more like *calm*,
which I was certainly not.

Sean had finished weeding out the bad helmets. He stood
and Gretyl called shrilly for our attention. "Listen," Sean
said, shaking out his stiff arms and shoulders. "We've had a

response from Connor's office. They refuse to meet with us, and they demand to know where we are. I think even Connor will figure out where we are in a few more days. So it's now or never. We have twenty-six good outfits and eight or ten problem pieces. I can salvage two from those. The rest are junk."

"I could fix some of them if he'd let me," Charles said under his breath.

"Gretyl and I will wear the problem pieces," Sean said. My heart pumped faster at his selfless courage. "But that means most of us will have to stay here. We'll draw sticks to see who crosses the plain."

"What if they're armed?" asked a nervous young woman.

Sean smiled. "Red rabbits down, cause up like a rocket," he said. That was clear enough. Martians shoot Martians, and glory to us all, the Statists would fall. He was right, of course. News would cross the Triple by day's end, probably even reach the planetoid communities.

Sean sounded as if he thought martyrdom might be useful. I looked at the young faces around me, eight, nine, or ten—my age—almost nineteen Terrestrial years—and then at Sean's face, seemingly old and experienced at twelve. Quietly, as a group, we raised our hands with fingers spread wide—the old Lunar Independence Symbol for the free expression of human abilities and ideas, tolerance against oppression, handshake instead of fist.

But as Sean brought his hand down, it closed reflexively into a fist. I realized then how earnest he was, and how serious this was, and what I was putting on the line.

We drew fibers from a frayed length of old optic cord an hour after the mask count. Twenty-six had been cut long. I drew a long, as did Charles. Diane was very disappointed to get a short. We were issued masks and set our personal slates to encrypt signals tied to Sean's and Gretyl's code numbers.

We had already gone over and over the plan. Twenty

would cross the surface directly above the tunnels leading back to UMS. I was in this group.

There were aboveground university structures about five kilometers from our trench domes. The remaining students—two teams of four each, Charles among them, under Sean's command—would fan out to key points and wait for a signal from Gretyl, the leader of our team of twenty, that we had made it to the administration chambers.

If we met resistance and were not allowed to present demands to Connor personally, then Sean's teams would do their stuff. First, they would broadcast an illegal preemptive signal to the satcom at Marsynch, forcing on all bands the news that action in the name of contractual fulfillment was being taken by the voided students of UMS. Contractual fulfillment meant a lot even under the Statist experiment; it was the foundation of every family's existence, a sacred kind of thing. Where Sean had gotten the expertise and equipment to send a preemptive signal, he would not say; I found his deepening mystery even more attractive.

Sean would personally take one team of four to the rail links at UMS junction. They would blow up a few custom-curved maglev rods; trains wouldn't be able to go to the UMS terminal until a repair car had manufactured new rods, which would take several hours. UMS would be isolated.

Simultaneously, the second team of four—to which Charles was assigned—would break seals and pump oxidant sizzle—a corrosive flopsand common in this region—into the university's net optic and satcom uplink facilities. That would break all the broad com between UMS and the rest of Mars. Private com would go through, but all broadband research and data links and library rentals would stop dead . . .

UMS might lose three or four million Triple dollars before the links could be repaired.

That of course would make them angry.

We waited in two lines spiraling from the center of the main trench dome. At the outside of the spiral lines, Sean and

Gretyl stood silent, jaws clenched. Some students shook their red-sealed hands to get ready for the cold. Skinseal wasn't made to keep you cozy. It only protected against hypothermia and frostbite.

My own skinseal had come loose at the joints and sweat was pooling before being processed by the nanomer. I had to go to the bathroom, more out of nerves than necessity; my feet and legs had swollen, but only a little; I was not miserable but the petty discomforts distracted me from the focus I needed to keep from turning into a quivering heap.

"Listen," Sean said loudly, standing on a box to peer over our heads. "None of us knew what we'd be getting into when we started all this. We don't know what's going to happen in the next few hours. But we all share a common goal—freedom to pursue our education without political interference—freedom to stand clear of the sins of our parents and grandparents. That's what Mars is all about—something new, a grand experiment. We'll be a part of that experiment now, or by God, we'll die trying."

I swallowed hard and looked for Charles, but he was too far away. I wondered if he still had his calm smile.

"May it not come to that," Gretyl said.

"Amen," said someone behind me.

Sean looked fully charged, face muscles sharply defined within a little oval of unsealed skin around his eyes, nose and mouth. "Let's go," he said.

In groups of five, we removed our clothes, folding them neatly or just dropping them. The first to go entered the airlock, cycled through, and climbed the ladder. When my turn came, I crowded into the lock with four others, held my breath against the swirling red smear, and slipped on my mask and cycler. The old mask smelled doggy. Its edges adhered to the skinseal with the sound of a prim kiss. I heard the whine of pumps pulling back the air. The skinseal puffed as gas pressures equalized. Moving became more difficult.

My companions in the lock began climbing. My turn came and I took hold of the ladder rungs and poked through the hatch, above the rust-and-ochre tumble and smear. With a kick, I cleared the lip, clambered out onto the rocky surface of the plain, and stood under the early morning sky. The sun topped a ridge of hills lying east, surrounded by a dull pink glow. I blinked at the glare.

We'd have to hike over those hills to get to UMS. It had taken us half an hour simply to climb to the surface.

We stood a few meters east of the trench dome, waiting for Gretyl to join us. In just minutes, smear clung to us all; we'd have to destat for half an hour when all this was over.

Gretyl emerged from the hole. Her voice decoded in my right ear, slightly muffled. "Let's get together behind Sean's group," she said.

We could breathe, we could talk to each other. All was working well so far.

"We're off," Sean said, and his teams began to walk away from the trench. Some of them waved. I caught a glimpse of Charles from behind as his group marched in broken formation toward the hills, a little south of the track we would follow. I wondered why I was paying any attention to him at all. Skinseal hid little. He had a cute butt. Ever so slightly steatopygous.

I bit my lip to bring my thoughts together. *I'm a red rabbit,* I told myself. *I'm on the Up for the first time in two years, and there are no scout supervisors or trailmasters in charge, checking all our gear, making sure we get back to our mommies. Now focus, damn you!*

"Let's go," Gretyl said, and we began our trek.

It was a typical Martian morning, springtime balmy at minus twenty Celsius. The wind had slowed to almost nothing. The air was clear for two hundred kilometers. Thousands of stars pricked through at zenith like tiny jewels. The horizon glimmered shell-pink.

All my thoughts aligned. Something magical about the moment. I felt I possessed a completely realistic awareness of our situation . . . and of our chances of surviving.

The surface of Mars was usually deadly cold. This close to

the equator, however, the temps were relatively mild—seldom less than minus sixty. Normal storms could push winds up to four hundred kiphs, driving clouds of fine smear and flopsand high enough and wide enough to be seen from Earth. Rarely, a big surge of jetstream activity could send a high-pressure curl over several thousand kilometers, visible from orbit as a snaking dark line, and that could raise clouds that would quickly cover most of Mars. But the air on high Sinai Planum, at five millibars, was too thin to worry about most of the time. The usual winds were gentle puffs, barely felt.

My booted feet pounded over the crusted sand and tumble. Martian soil gets a thin crust after a few months of lying undisturbed; the grains fall into a kind of mechanical cement that feels a lot like hoarfrost. I could dimly hear the others crunching, sound traveling through the negligible atmosphere making them seem dozens of meters away.

"Let's not get too scattered," Gretyl said.

I passed an old glacier-rounded boulder bigger than the main trench dome. Ancient ice floes had sculpted the crustal basalt into a rounded gnome with its arms splayed across the ground, flat head resting on its arms in sleep . . . pretended sleep.

Somehow, red rabbits never became superstitious about the Up. It was too orange and red and brown, too obviously dead, to appeal to our morbid instincts.

"If they're smart and somebody's anticipating us, there may be pickets out this far to keep track of the periphery of the university," Sean said over the radio.

"Or if somebody's tattled," Gretyl added. I was starting to like Gretyl. Despite having an unpleasant voice and an unaltered, shrewlike face, Gretyl seemed to have a balanced perspective. I wondered why she had kept that face. Maybe it was a family face, something to be proud of where she came from, like English royalty's unaltered features, mandated by law. The long nose of King Henry of England.

Damn.

Focus gone.

I decided it didn't matter. Maybe focusing on keeping a focus was a bad thing.

The sun hung above the ridge now, torch-white with the merest pink tinge. Around it whirled the thinnest of opal hazes, high silicate and ice clouds laced against the brightening orange of day. The rock shadows started to fill in, making each step a little easier. Sometimes wind hollows hid behind boulders, waiting for unwary feet.

Gretyl's group had spread out. I walked near the front, a few steps to her right.

"Picket," said Garlin Smith on my right, raising his arm. He had been my classmate in mass psych, quiet and tall, what ignorant Earth folks thought a Martian should look like.

We all followed Garlin's pointing finger to the east and saw a lone figure standing on a rise about two hundred meters away. It carried a rifle.

"Armed," Gretyl said under her breath. "I don't believe it."

The figure wore a full pressure suit—a professional job, the type worn by areologists, farm inspectors, Statist police. It reached up to tap its helmet. It hadn't seen us yet, apparently, but it was picking up the jumbled buzz of our coded signals.

"Keep going," Gretyl said. "We haven't come this far to be scared off by a single picket."

"If it *is* a picket," Sean commented, listening to our chat. "Don't assume anything."

"It has to be a picket," Gretyl said.

"All right," Sean said with measured restraint.

The figure caught sight of us about four minutes after we first noticed it. We were separated by a hundred meters. It looked like a normal male physique from that distance.

My breath quickened. I tried to slow it.

"Report," Sean demanded.

"Armed male in full pressure suit. He sees us. Not reacting yet," Gretyl said.

We didn't deviate from our path. We would pass within fifty meters of the picket.

The helmeted head turned, watching us. He held up a hand. "Hey, what is this?" a masculine voice asked. "What in hell are you doing up here? Do you folks have ID?"

"We're from UMS," Gretyl said. We didn't slow our pace.

"What are you doing up here?" the picket repeated.

"Surveying, what's it look like?" Gretyl responded. We carried no instruments. "What are *you* doing up here?"

"Don't bunny with me," he said. "You know there's been trouble. Just tell me what department you're from and . . . have you been using code?"

"No," Gretyl said.

We had closed another twenty yards. He started to hike down the rise to inspect us.

"What in hell are you wearing?"

"Red suits," Gretyl answered.

"Shit, it's *skinseal*. It's against the law to wear that stuff except in emergencies. How many of you are there?"

"Forty-five," Gretyl lied.

"I've been told to keep intruders off university property," he said. "I'll need to see IDs. You should have UMS passes to even be up here."

"Is that a gun?" Gretyl asked, faking a lilt of surprise.

"Hey, get over here, all of you."

"Why do you need a *gun*?"

"Unauthorized intruders. Stop now."

"We're from the Areology Department, and we've only got a few hours up here . . . Didn't you get a waiver from Professor Sunder?"

"No, dammit, *stop right now*."

"Listen, friend, who do you answer to?"

"UMS is secure property. You'd better give me your student ID numbers now."

"Fap off," Gretyl said.

The picket raised his rifle, a long-barreled, slender automatic flechette. My anger and fear were almost indistinguishable. Dauble and Connor must have lost their minds. No student on Mars had ever been shot by police, not in fifty-

three years of settlement. Hadn't they ever heard of
Tienanmen or Kent State?

"Use it," Gretyl said. "You'll be all over the Triple for
shooting areology students on a field trip. Great for your career. Really spin you in with our families, too. What kind of
work you looking for, rabbit?"

Our receivers jabbered with the picket's own coded outgo-
ing message. More jabber returned.

The man lowered his rifle and followed us. "Are you
armed?" he asked.

"Where would students get guns?" Gretyl asked. "Who in
hell is giving you orders to scare us?"

"Listen, this is serious. I need your IDs now."

"We've got his code," Sean said. "He's been told to block
you however he can."

"Great," Gretyl said.

"Who are you talking to? Stop using code," the picket demanded.

"Maybe they're not clueing you, rabbit," Gretyl taunted.

Gretyl's bravado, her talent for delay and confusion, astonished me. Perhaps she and Sean and a few of the others had
been training for this. I wished I knew more about *revolution*.

The word came to me like a small blow on my back. This
was a kind of *revolution*. "Jesus," I said with my transmitter
off.

"What's he doing?" Sean asked.

"He's following us," Gretyl said. "He doesn't seem to
want to shoot."

"Not with *flechettes*, sure enough," Sean said. "What a
banner that would be!" I filled in the details involuntarily:
STUDENTS RIPPED BY BURROWING DARTS.

More code whined in our ears like angry insects.

We marched over another rise, the guard following close
behind, and saw the low poke-ups of UMS. The UMS warrens extended to the northeast for perhaps a kilometer, half
levels above, ten levels deep. The administration chambers
were closest to the surface entrance and the nearby train de-

pot. Train guides hovered on slender poles, arcing gently over
another rise to link with the station.

Sean's teams were probably there now.

More guards emerged from the UMS buildings, armed and
in full pressure suits.

"All right," came a gruff female voice. "State your business. Then get the hell out of here or you'll be arrested."

Gretyl stepped forward, a scrawny little red devil with a
black masked head. "We want an audience with Chancellor
Connor. We are students who have been illegally voided and
whose contracts have been flagrantly broken. We demand—"

"Who in hell do you think you are? A bunch of fapping rodents?" The woman's voice scared me. She sounded out-
raged, on the edge of something drastic. I couldn't tell which
of the suited figures she was, or if she was outside at all.
"You've crossed regional property. Goddamned Gobacks
should know what that means."

"I'm not going to argue," Gretyl said. "We demand to
speak with—"

"You're *talking* to her, you ignorant shithead! I'm right
here." The foremost figure raised an arm and shook a gloved
fist. "And I'm in no mood to negotiate with trespassers and
Gobacks."

"We're here to deliver a petition." Gretyl removed a metal
cylinder from her belt and extended it. One of the guards
started forward, but Connor grabbed his elbow and shook it
once, firmly. He backed away and folded his arms.

"Politics of confrontation," Connor said, voice harsh as old
razors. "Agitprop and civil disobedience. You'd think you
were on Earth. Politics doesn't work that way here. I have a
mandate to protect this university and keep order."

"You refuse to meet with us and discuss our demands?"

"I'm meeting with you now. Nobody demands anything of
lawful authority except through legal channels. Who's behind
you?"

I looked over my shoulder, misunderstanding.

"There's no conspiracy," Gretyl said.

"Lies, my dear. Genuine lies."

"Under Martian contract law, we have the right to meet with you and discuss why we have been voided and our contracts broken."

"State law superseded BM law last month."

"Actually, it doesn't. If you want to check with your lawyers—" Gretyl began. I cringed. We were bickering and time was running out.

"You have one minute to turn around and go back to where you came from, or we'll arrest you," Connor said. "Let the legals sort it out. Do your families know where you are? How about your advocates? Do *they* know and approve?"

Gretyl's words bristled. "I can't believe you are being so stubborn. I'm asking for the last time—"

"Right. Arrest them, my authority, statute two-five-one, Syria-Sinai district books."

Some of the students began to talk, asking worried questions. "Quiet!" Gretyl shouted. She turned to Connor. "Is this your last answer?"

"You poor dumb rodents," Connor said. She swiveled to enter the open lock door. Connor behaved even more rudely than she had been portrayed to us in the briefings, supremely confident, intractable and ready to provoke an incident. Guards moved forward. I turned and saw three guards behind us, also closing. We had to submit.

Gretyl stepped away from the first guard. Another flanked her on the right, coming between us, and she stepped back. There were twenty of us and ten guards.

"Let them take you," Gretyl said. "Let them arrest you." Then why was she resisting?

A guard took my arm and applied sticky rope to my skinsealed wrist. "You're lucky we're bringing you in," he said, grinning. "You wouldn't last another hour out here."

Two of the guards devoted themselves exclusively to Gretyl. They advanced with hands and sticky ropes held out. She backed away, held up her arm as if waving to them, and touched her mask.

Time got stiff.

Gretyl turned to look at the rest of us. Her eyes looked scared. My heart sank. *Don't do anything just to impress Sean,* I wanted to shout to her.

"Tell them what you saw here," Gretyl said. *"Freedom conquers!"* Her fingers plucked at and then slipped beneath the seam of the mask. A guard grabbed at her arm but he wasn't quick enough.

Gretyl ripped away the mask and sprang to one side, sending it flying with a wide toss. Her long-nosed face flashed pale and narrow against the pink sky. She squeezed her eyes shut and clamped her mouth instinctively. Her arms reached out, fingers extended, as if she were a tightrope walker and might lose her balance.

Simultaneously, I heard small thumps and felt the ground vibrate.

Connor hadn't had time to enter the poke-up airlock. "Get her inside! Get her inside!" she screeched, pushing through her associates.

The guards stood still as statues for what seemed like minutes, then reached for Gretyl and dragged her as fast as they could to the airlock. She struggled in their arms. I saw her face pinking, blood vessels near the surface rupturing as the plasma boiled. Vacuum rose.

Gretyl opened her eyes and reached up with one hand to grab at her chin. She pulled her own jaw open. The air in her lungs rushed out, moisture freezing in a cloud in the still air.

"They've blown track," someone shouted.

"Get her INSIDE!"

Gretyl looked at the sky through rime-clouded eyes.

The guard in front of me jerked the sticky rope forward and I fell into the dirt. For an instant it seemed he might kick me. I looked up and saw narrow grim eyes behind the helmet visor, mouth open, face slack. He stopped and blinked, waiting for orders.

I twisted my head around to see how my companions were being treated. Several lay in the dirt. The guards systematically pushed us down and planted boots on our backs. When all nineteen lay flat, the guards stood back. The door to the lock opened again and someone stepped out, not Connor.

"They're under arrest," a man's voice said over the radio. "Get them inside. Strip that stuff off and put them in a dorm. Delouse them."

There have never been lice on Mars.

They separated us quickly. Three guards pulled five of us away from the airlock and marched us through chilly tunnels to the old dorms, seldom used now. The new dorms had been equipped with more modern conveniences, but these were maintained for an emergency or future overload of students.

"Can you get this off by yourself?" the tallest of the three asked, gesturing at our skinseal. She removed her helmet beneath the dimmed lights of the hall, lips downturned, eyes miserable.

"What did he mean, delouse?" another guard asked, a young, muscular male with West Indian features and accent.

The guards were all fresh Martians. That made sense. The new United Mars state would be their sponsor, their BM and family.

"You can't just hold us here," I said. "What happened to Gretyl?" My four companions turned on the guards, pointing fingers and shouting. We all demanded our rights— communication, freedom, advocates.

It became an open rebellion until the third guard pulled a flechette from his pack. He was the shortest, a slim man with plain, short-cut brown hair and perfect, saintly features. His eyes narrowed, very cold. I thought, *Here's a Statist sympathizer.* The others were merely hired hands.

"Blow it down, right now," he demanded.

"You injured Gretyl!" I shouted. "We need to know what happened to her!"

"Sabotage is treason. We could shoot you in self-defense."

He raised the pistol. All of us backed away, including the two other guards.

"That wouldn't be smart," I said.

"Not for you." The slim fellow gave us a cold thin smile and pushed us down the hall.

We entered a stripped-down double room, immediately sprawling on the bare cot and chairs, another small gesture of useless defiance.

"You're going to be here for a while, so get comfortable."

I didn't like him pushing his pistol and didn't want to provoke him any further. We peeled off our skinseal—it was a blessed relief to be free of it, actually. The West Indian tossed the shreds into dust bags. Enough smear floated loose to make us sneeze.

As if meeting for the first time, the five of us nodded and made introductions where necessary. We knew each other only slightly; one had been a classmate of mine, Felicia Overgard, about a year younger and two steps behind. I did not know Oliver Peskin well, a step higher and an agro major, and I had only met Tom Callin and Chao Ming Jung in the trench dome.

The slim fellow averted his eyes. Bizarre, waving a gun at us but ashamed of our bare flesh. He thrust the gun at the vapor sacks in the washroom. "I don't know if you have lice, but you smell pretty rank."

The vapor bags hadn't been refilled or filtered in some time and we didn't smell much better after the showers. Water was inadequate to get rid of smear, and we carried itchy patches of red and orange all over. We'd have welts by tomorrow.

Three hours passed and we learned nothing. The guards stayed in their suits to avoid the dust. They had removed any identifiers and would not tell us their names. The sympathizer grew more and more grim as the hours crawled, and then ramped up to nervous, fidgeting with his gun. He whistled and pantomimed breaking it down and reassembling it. Finally, his slate chimed and he answered.

After a couple of brief acknowledgments, he sent the female guard out of the room. I wondered what they would do next, why they didn't want the woman there.

Surely they weren't *that* stupid.

Conversation with my companions became thin and quiet. Fear had worn off—we no longer thought we were going to be shot—but the numbing sense of isolation that replaced it was no better. We settled into shivering silence.

The rooms were kept at minimum heat and we still didn't have any clothes. The three men suffered worse than Felicia and I.

"It's cold in here," I said to the sympathizer. He agreed but did nothing.

"It's cold enough to make us sick," said Oliver.

"All right," said the sympathizer.

"We should find them some clothes," said the West Indian.

"No," said the sympathizer.

"Why not?" Chao asked. Felicia had given up covering herself with her hands.

"You caused a hell of a lot of trouble. Why make it any easier on you?"

"They're human, man," the West Indian said. He was not very old, twelve or thirteen, and he had to be a recent immigrant. His West Indies accent was still obvious.

The sympathizer squinted and shook his head dubiously.

We've won, I thought. *With fools like this, the Statists don't have a chance.* I couldn't quite convince myself, however.

We spent ten hours in that dorm room, cold and naked, skin itching furiously.

I fell asleep and dreamed of trees too tall to fit into any dome, rooted unprotected in the red dirt of Mars: redwoods in red flopsand, lofting a hundred meters, tended by naked children. I had had the dream before and it left me for a moment with an intense feeling of well-being. Then I remembered I was a prisoner.

The West Indian prodded my shoulder. I rolled on the thinly carpeted floor. He averted his eyes from my nakedness and drew his lips tightly together. "I want you to know I am not all in this," he said. "My heart, I mean. I am truly a Martian, and this is my first work here, you know?"

I looked around. The sympathizer was out of the room. "Get us some clothes," I said.

"You blew up the train lines and these people, they are very angry. I just tell you, don't blame me when the shit sprays. People go up and down the halls—the tunnels. I look out, there is so much going on. They are afraid, I think."

What did they have to be afraid of? Had the LitVids grabbed Gretyl's injury or death and put our cause on the sly spin?

"Can you send a message to my parents?"

"The fellow Rick has gone," the West Indian said, shaking his head. "He meets with others, and he leaves me here."

"What happened to Gretyl?"

He shook his head again. "I hear nothing about her. What I saw, it made me sick. Everybody is so crazy. Why did she do it?"

"To make a point," I said.

"Not worth losing your life," the West Indian said, frowning deeply. "This is small history, petty people. On Earth—"

My temper flared. "Look, we've only been here a hundred Earth years, and our history is small stuff by Earth standards, but you're a Martian now, remember? This is corruption and dirty politics—and if you ask me, it's directly connected with Earth, and the hell with all of you!"

You really sound committed, I thought. Abuse could do wonders.

I awakened the others with my outburst. Felicia sat up. "He isn't armed," she observed. Oliver and Chao stood warily and brushed dust off their backsides, muscles tensed as if they were giving thought to jumping the man.

The West Indian looked, if possible, even more abjectly miserable. "Do not try something," he said, standing his ground with arms out, shaking his head.

The door opened and the sympathizer returned. He and the

West Indian exchanged glances and the West Indian tilted and shook his head, saying, "Oh, *man*." Behind the sympathizer came a fellow with short black hair. He wore a tight-fitting, expensive, and fashionable green longsuit.

"We're kept here against our will—" Oliver complained immediately.

"Under arrest," the man in the fashionable green suit said jovially.

"For more than a day, and we demand to be released," Oliver finished, folding his arms. The man in the suit smiled at this literally naked presumption.

"I'm Achmed Crown Niger," he said. His voice was high Mars, imitative of the flat English of Earth, an accent rarely heard in the regional BMs. I presumed he would be from Lal Qila or some other independent station, perhaps a Muslim. "I represent the state interests in the university. I'm going from room to room getting names. I'll need your family names, BM connections, and the names of people you'll want to talk to in the next hour."

"What happened to Gretyl?" I asked.

Achmed Crown Niger raised his eyebrows. "She's alive. She has acute facial rose and her eyes and lungs need to be rebuilt. But we have other things to talk about. Under district book laws, you are all charged with criminal trespass and sabotage—"

"What happened to the others?" I pursued.

He ignored me. "That's serious stuff. You're going to need advocates." He turned to the sympathizer and barked, "Damn it, get these people something to wear." He looked back at us and his ingratiating smile returned. "It's tough being legal in front of naked people."

Thirty armed men and women, as many LitVid agents, Chancellor Connor, and Governor Dauble herself stood in the dining hall, Connor and Dauble and their entourage well away from the offending students. We clustered in bathrobes near the serving gates, the twenty-eight who had gone out with

Sean and Gretyl, criminals caught in the act of sabotage. Those left behind in the trench domes had been collected as well. Dauble and Connor were about to celebrate their victory on LitVid across the Triple.

Medias and Pressians, my father called them: the hordes of LitVid reporters that seemed rise out of the ground at the merest hint of a stink. On Mars reporters were a hearty breed; they learned early to get around the tight lips of BM families. Ten of the quickest and hardiest—several familiar to me— stood with arbeiter attendants near the Statist cluster, ear loops recording all they saw, images edited hot for transmission to the satcoms.

Diane stood in a group across the hall. She waved to me surreptitiously. I did not see Sean. Charles was five or six meters from me in our pack and did not appear injured. He saw me and nodded. Some from his group had sustained bruises and even broken bones. Blue boneknits graced three.

We said nothing, stood meek and pitiful. This was our time to be victims of the oppressive state.

Dauble came forward flanked by two advisors. A louder curled on her shoulder like a thin snake. "Folks, this has gone much too far. Chancellor Connor has been courteous enough to supply the families of these students—"

"Banned students!" Oliver Peskin shouted next to me. Others took up the cry, and another chorus followed on with, "Contract rights! Obligations!"

Dauble listened, face fixed in gentle disapproval. The cries died down.

"To supply all of their families with information on their whereabouts, and their status as arrested saboteurs," she finished.

"Where's Gretyl?" I shouted, hardly aware I'd opened my mouth.

"Where's Sean?" someone else called. "Where's Gretyl?"

"Family advocates are flying in now. The train service has been cut, thanks to these students, and our ability to uplink on broadband has been severely curtailed. These acts of sabotage—"

"Illegal voiding!" another student shouted.

"Constitute high felonies under the district book and United Martian codes—"

"Where's *SEAN*? Where's *GRETYL*?" Oliver shouted, hair awry, flinging up his hand, fingers splayed.

Guards moved in, shoving through us none too gently, and grabbed him. Connor stepped forward and raised her arm. Achmed Crown Niger ordered the guards to release him. Oliver shrugged their arms away and smiled back at us triumphantly.

Dauble seemed unaffected by the confusion. "These acts will be fully prosecuted."

"Where's *SEAN*? Where's *GRETYL*?" several students yelled again.

"Sean's *dead*! Gretyl's *dead*!" shouted one high, shrill voice. The effect was electric.

"Who says? Who knows?" others called. The students cried out and milled like sheep.

"Nobody has been killed," Dauble said, her composure suddenly less solid.

"Bring *SEAN*!"

Dauble conferred with her advisors, then turned back to us. "Sean Dickinson is in the university infirmary with self-inflicted wounds. Everything possible is being done to help him. Gretyl Laughton is in the infirmary as well, with injuries from self-exposure."

The reporters hadn't heard this yet; their interest was immediate, and all focused on Dauble.

"How were the students injured?" asked one reporter, her pickup pointed at Dauble.

"There have been several small injuries—"

"Inflicted by the guards?"

"No," Connor said.

"Is it true the guards have been armed all along? Even before the sabotage?" another reporter asked.

"We anticipated trouble from the beginning," Dauble said. "These student have proven us correct."

"But the guards aren't authorized police or regulars—how do you justify that under district charter?"

"Justify all of it!" Diane shouted.

"I don't understand your attitude," Dauble said to us after a few moments of careful consideration in the full gaze of hot LitVid. "You sabotage life-support equipment—"

"That's a lie!" a student shouted.

"Disrupt the lawful conduct of this university, and now you resort to attempted suicide. What kind of Martians are you? Do your parents approve of this treachery?"

Dauble screwed her face into an expression between parental exasperation and deep concern. "What in the hell is wrong with you? Who raised you—*thugs*?"

The meeting came to an abrupt end. Dauble and her entourage departed, followed by the reporters. When several reporters tried to talk to us, they were unceremoniously ejected from the dining hall.

How very, very stupid, I thought.

I felt a bit faint from hunger; we hadn't eaten in twenty hours. A few university staff, clearly uncomfortable, served us bowls of quick paste from trays. The nutritional nano was tasteless but still seemed heaven-sent. We had been provided with sleeping pads and blankets and were told winds were up and dust was blowing, grounding shuttles. No advocates or parents had yet come in to see us.

While being fed, we had been divided into groups of six, each assigned two guards. The guards actively discouraged talk between the groups, moving us farther and farther apart until we spread out through the hall. Oliver, considered a loudmouth activist, was prodded into a selected group of other loudmouths that included Diane. Charles sat with five others across the hall, about twenty meters away.

When we still tried to talk, the dining hall sound system blared out loud pioneer music, old-fashioned soul-stirring crap I had enjoyed as a kid, but found bitterly inappropriate now.

When I was free to speak with the Medias and Pressians, I thought, what a story I'd tell . . . I had seen and done things in the past few days that my entire life had not prepared me for, and I had felt emotions unknown to me: righteous anger, political confraternity and solidarity, deep fear.

I worried for Sean. All our information came through Achmed Crown Niger, who visited every few hours to hand out scraps of generally useless news. I took a real dislike to him: professional, collected, he was every gram the guvvie man. I focused on his pale, fine-featured face for a time, blaming him for all our troubles. He must have advised the chancellor and governor . . . *He* must have outlined their strategy, maybe even planned the banning and voiding of students . . .

I thought dreamily about a possible life with Sean, if he paid any attention to me after his recovery.

Nothing to do. Nothing to think. The lights in the dining hall went out. The music stopped.

I slept on the floor, nestled like a puppy against Felicia's back.

Someone touched my shoulder. I opened my eyes from a light doze. Charles leaned over me, his face thinner and older, but his smile the same: too calm, somehow, like a young Buddha. His cheeks had pinked as if smirched with poorly applied makeup: a mild case of vacuum rose. Most of the students around us still slept.

"Are you okay?" he asked.

I sat up and looked around. The lights were still dim, but it was obvious the guards had gone.

"Tired," I said. I swallowed hard. My throat was parched and I could feel the oxidant welts itching fiercely. "Where's our food and water?"

"I don't think we're going to get any unless we go for it ourselves."

I stood and stretched my arms. "Are you all right?" I asked, squinting at him, reaching up to his cheeks.

"My mask leaked. I'm fine. My eyes are okay. You look strong," Charles said.

"I feel shitty," I said. "Where are the guards?"

"Probably trying to get out of here any way they can."

"Why?"

He lifted his hands. "I don't know. They backed out about an hour ago."

Oliver Peskin and Diane walked over and we squatted on the floor in whispered confab. Felicia stirred and poked Chao in the ribs.

"What happened to Sean?" Diane asked Charles.

"He was planting a charge when it went off," Charles said. "They say he set it off on purpose."

"He wouldn't do that," Felicia said, face screwed up in disgust.

"Gretyl pulled her mask off," I said.

"Insane," Charles said.

"She had her reasons," Chao said.

"Anyway," Diane went on. "We need leaders."

"We're not going to be here much longer," Oliver said.

"Oliver's right. We're not guarded. Something's changed," Charles said.

"We have to stick together," Diane insisted.

"If something's changed, it has to have changed in *our* favor," Oliver said. "It couldn't get any worse."

"We still need leaders," I said. "We should wake people up now and see what the group thinks."

"What if we've won?" Felicia asked. "What do we do?"

"Find out how much we've won, and why," Charles said.

We explored the tunnels around the dining hall, venturing back to the old dorms, all quite empty now. We encountered a few arbeiters about their maintenance business, but no humans. After an hour, we begin to worry—the situation was spooky.

Fanning out, we began a systematic exploration of the upper levels of the entire university, reporting to each other on local links. Charles volunteered to join me. We took the north tunnels, closest to emergency external shafts and farthest from the administration chambers. The tunnels were dark but warm; the air smelled stale, but it was breathable. Our feet made hollow scuffing echoes in the deserted halls. The university seemed to be in an emergency power-down.

Charles walked a step ahead. I watched him closely, wondering why he wanted to be so friendly when I had given him so little encouragement.

We didn't say much, simply stating the obvious, signaling to each other with whistles after splitting to try separate tunnels, nodding cordially when we rejoined and moved on. Gradually we moved south again, expecting to meet up with other students.

We explored a dark corridor connecting the old dorm branch with UMS's newer tunnels. A bright light flashed ahead. We stood our ground. A woman in an ill-fitting pressure suit shined her light directly into our faces.

"University staff?" she asked.

"Hell, no. Who are you?" Charles asked.

"I'm an advocate," the woman said. "Pardon the stolen suit. I flew in through the storm about half an hour ago. Landed during a dust lull and found a few of these abandoned near the locks. We were told there was no air in here."

"Who told you that?"

"The last man out, and he went in a hurry, too. Are you all right?"

"I'm fine," I said. "Where is everybody?"

The advocate lifted her face plate and sniffed noisily. "Sorry. My nose hates flopsand. The university was evacuated seven hours ago. Bomb threat. They said a bunch of Gobacks had dumped air and planted charges in the administration chambers. Everybody left in ground vehicles. They took them overland by tractor to an intact train line."

"You're brave to come this far," Charles said. "You don't think there *is* a bomb, do you?"

The woman removed her helmet and smiled wolfishly. "Probably not. They didn't tell us anybody was here. They must not like you. How many are here?"

"Ninety."

"They voided the reporters before they evacuated. I saw you on LitVid. Press conference didn't go well. So where are the rest of you?"

We led her to the dining hall. All the far-flung explorers were called in.

The advocate stood in the middle of the assembly, asking and answering questions. "I presume I'm the first advocate to get here. First off, my name is Maria Sanchez Ochoa. I'm an independent employed by Grigio BM from Tharsis."

Felicia stepped forward. "That's my family," she said. Two others came forward as well.

"Good to see you," Maria Sanchez Ochoa said. "The family's worried. I'd like to get your names and report that you're all safe."

"What's happened?" Diane asked. "I'm very confused." Others joined in.

"What happened to Sean and Gretyl?" I asked, interrupting the babble.

"University security handed them over to Sinai district police early yesterday morning. Both were injured, but I don't know to what extent. The university claimed they were injured by their own hands."

"They're alive?" I continued.

"I presume so. They're at Time's River Canyon Hospital." She started recording names, lifting her slate and letting each speak and be recognized in turn.

I looked to my right and saw Charles standing beside me. He smiled, and I returned his smile and put a hand on his shoulder.

"Will someone take this outside and shoot it up to a satcom? None of the cables or repeaters are working, thanks to you folks." Ochoa gave her slate to a student, who left the dining area to get to the glass roof of the administration upper levels.

"Now, some background, since I doubt you've heard much news recently."

"Nothing useful," Oliver said.

"Right. I hate to tell you this, but you didn't do a thing for your cause by acting like a bunch of Parisian Communards. The Statist government planted its own bombs months ago, political and legal, far away from UMS, and they exploded just two days ago. We have a bad situation here, folks, and that explains some of the delay in getting to you. The constitutional accord is off. The Statists have resigned, and the old BM Charter government has been called back into session."

The battle was over. But we were small potatoes.

Ochoa concluded by saying, "You folks have wrecked university property, you've violated laws in every Martian book I can think of, and you've put yourselves in a great deal of danger. What has it gotten you?

"Fortunately, it probably won't get you any time in jail. I've heard that former Statist politicos are shipping out by dozens—and that probably includes Connor and Dauble. Nobody in their right mind is going to charge you under Statist law."

"What did they do?" Charles asked.

"Nobody's sure about *all* that they've done, but it looks like the government invited Earth participation in Mars politics, sought kickbacks from Belter BMs to let them mine Hellas—"

Gasps from the assembly. We had thought *we* were radical.

"And planned to nationalize all BM holdings by year's end."

We met these pronouncements with stunned silence.

We stayed in the old dorms while security crews from Gorrie Mars BM checked out the entire university grounds. New rails were manufactured, trains came in, and most of us went

home. I stayed, as did Oliver, Felicia, and Charles. I was beginning to think that Charles wanted to be near me.

I met my family in the station two days after our release,
Father and Mother and my older brother Stan. My parents
looked pale and shaken by both fear and anger. My father
told me, in no uncertain terms, that I had violated his most
sacred principles in joining the radicals. I tried to explain my
reasons, but didn't get through to him, and no wonder: they
weren't entirely clear to me.

Stan, perpetually amused by the attitudes and actions of his
younger sister, simply stood back with a calm smile. That
smile reminded me of Charles.

Charles, Oliver, Felicia and I bought our tickets at the
autobox and walked across the UMS depot platform. We all
felt more than a little like outlaws, or at least pariahs.

It was late morning and a few dozen interim university administrators had come in on the same train we would be taking out. Dressed in formal grays and browns, they stood
under the glass skylights shuffling their feet, clutching their
small bags and waiting for their security escort, glancing at us
suspiciously.

Rail staff didn't *know* we were part of the group responsible for breaking the UMS line, but they suspected. All credit
to the railway that it honored charter and did not refuse service.

The four of us sat in the rearmost car, fastening ourselves
into the narrow seats. The rest of the train was empty.

In 2171, five hundred thousand kilometers of maglev train
tracks spread over Mars, thousands more being added by
arbeiters each year. The trains were the best way to travel:
sitting in comfort and silence as the silver millipedes flew
centimeters above their thick black rails, rhythmically
boosting every three or four hundred meters and reaching
speeds of several hundred kiphs. I loved watching vast
stretches of boulder-strewn flatlands rush by, seeing fans of

dust topped by thin curling puffs as static blowers in the train's nose cleared the tracks ahead.

I did not much enjoy the train ride to Time's River Canyon Hospital, however.

We didn't have much to say. We had been elected by the scattered remnants of the protest group to visit Sean and Gretyl.

We accelerated out of the UMS station just before noon, pressed into our seats, absorbing the soothing rumble of the carriage. Within a few minutes, we were up to three hundred kiphs, and the great plain below our ports became an ochre blur. In a window seat, I stared at the land and asked myself where I really was, and who.

Charles had taken the seat beside me, but mercifully, said little. Since my father's stern lecture, I had felt empty or worse. The days of having nothing to do but sign releases and talk to temp security had worn me down to a negative.

Oliver tried to break the gloom by suggesting we play a word game. Felicia shook her head. Charles glanced at me, read my lack of interest, and said, "Maybe later." Oliver shrugged and held up his slate to speck the latest LitVid.

I dozed off for a few minutes. Charles pressed my shoulder gently. We were slowing. "You keep waking me up," I said.

"You keep napping off in the boring parts," he said.

"You are so fapping *pleasant*, you know?" I said.

"Sorry." His face fell.

"And why are you . . ." I was about to say *following me* but I could hardly support that accusation with much evidence. The train had slowed and was now sliding into Time's River Depot. Outside, the sky was deep brown, black at zenith. The Milky Way dropped between high canyon walls as if seeking to fill the ancient flood channel.

"I think you're interesting," Charles said, unharnessing and stepping into the aisle.

I shook my head and led the way to the forward lock. "We're stressed," I murmured.

"It's okay," Charles said.

Felicia looked at us with a bemused smile.

In the hospital waiting room, an earnest young public defender thrust a slateful of release forms at us. "Which government are you sending these to?" Oliver asked. The man's uniform had conspicuous outlines of thread where patches had been removed.

"Whoever," he answered. "You're from UMS, right? Friends and colleagues of the patients?"

"Fellow students," Felicia said.

"Right. Now listen. I have to say this, in case one of you is going to shoot off to a LitVid. 'The Time's River District neither condones nor condemns the actions taken by these patients. We follow historical Martian charter and treat any and all patients, regardless of legal circumstance or political belief. Any statements they make do not represent—' "

"Jesus," Felicia said.

" '—the policy or attitudes of this hospital, nor the policy of Time's River District.' End of sermon." The public defender stepped back and waved us through.

I was shocked by what we saw when we entered Sean's room. He had been tilted into a corner at forty-five degrees, wrapped in white surgical nano and tied to a steel recovery board. Monitors guided his reconstruction through fluid and optic fibers. Only now did we realize how badly he had been injured.

As we entered his room, he turned his head and stared at us impassively through distant green-gray eyes. We made our awkward openings, and he responded with a casual, "How's the outside world?"

"In an uproar," Oliver said. Sean glanced at me as if I were only there in part, not a fully developed human being, but a ghost of mild interest. I specked the moments of passionate speech when he had riveted the crowded students and compared it to this lackluster shell and was immensely saddened.

"Good," Sean said, measuring the word with silent lips before repeating it aloud. He looked at a projected paleoscape of Mars on the wall opposite: soaring aqueduct bridges, long gleaming pipes suspended from tree-like pedestals and fruited with clusters of green globes, some thirty or forty meters across . . . A convincing mural of our world before the planet sucked in its water, shed its atmosphere, and withered.

"The Council's taken over everything again," I said. "The syndics of all the BMs are meeting to patch things together."

Sean did not react.

"Nobody's told us how you were hurt," Felicia said. We looked at her, astonished at this untruth. Ochoa had checked into all the security reports, including those filed by university guards, and pieced together the story.

"The charges," Sean said, hesitating not a moment, and I thought, *Whatever Felicia is up to, he'll tell the truth . . . and why expect him not to?*

"The charges went off prematurely, before I had a chance to get out of the way. I set the charges alone. Of course."

"Of course," Oliver said.

Charles stayed in the rear, hands folded before him like a small boy at a funeral.

"Blew me out of my skinseal. I kept my helmet on, oddly enough. Exposed my guts. Everything boiled. I remember quite a lot, strangely. Watching my blood boil. Somebody had the presence of mind to throw a patch over me. It wrapped me up and slowed me down and they pulled me into the infirmary about an hour later. I don't remember much after that."

"Jesus," Felicia said, in exactly the same tone she had used for the public defender in the waiting room.

"We did it to them, didn't we? Got the ball rolling," Sean said.

"Actually—" Oliver began, but Felicia, with a tender expression, broke in.

"We did it," she said. Oliver raised his eyebrows.

"I'm going to be okay. About half of me will need replac-

ing. I don't know who's paying for it. My family, I suppose.
I've been thinking."

"Yeah?" Felicia said.

"I know what set the charge off," Sean said. "Somebody
broke the timer before I planted it. I'd like one or all of you
to find out who."

Nobody spoke for a moment. "You think somebody did it
deliberately?" I asked.

Sean nodded. "We checked the equipment a hundred times
and everything worked."

"Who would have done something like that?" Oliver
asked, horrified.

"Somebody," Sean said. "Keep the students together. This
isn't over yet." He turned to face me, suddenly focusing.
"Take a message to Gretyl. Tell her she was a goddamned
fool and I love her madly." He bit into the words *goddamned
fool* as if they were a savory cake that gave him great satis-
faction. I had never seen such a join of pain and bitter pride.

I nodded.

"Tell her she and I will take the reins again and guide this
mess home *right*. Tell her just that."

"Guide the mess home *right*," I repeated, still under his
spell.

"We have a larger purpose," Sean said. "We have to break
this planet out of its goddamned business-as-usual, corrupt,
bow-down-to-the-Triple, struggle-along mentality. We can do
that. We can make our own party. It's a beginning." His eyes
fixed on each of us in turn, as if to brand us. Felicia held out
her splayed fingers and Sean lifted his free arm to awkwardly
press his hand against hers. Oliver did the same. Charles
stood back; too much for him. I was about to raise my hand
and match Sean's. But Sean saw my hesitation, my change of
expression when Charles stepped back, and he dropped his
hand before I could decide.

"Heart and mind, heart and mind," Sean said softly. "You
are . . . Casseia, right? Casseia Majumdar?"

"Yes."

"How did your family fare in all this?"

"I don't know," I said.

"They're fixed to prosper. The Gobacks will do well in the next government. It was funny, Connor thinking we were Gobacks. Are you a Goback, Casseia?"

I shook my head, throat tight. His tone was so stiff and distant, so *reproving*.

"Show it to me, Casseia. Heart and mind."

"I don't think you have any right to question my loyalty because of my family," I said.

Sean's gaze went cold. "If you're not dedicated, you could turn on us . . . just like whoever broke the timer."

"Gretyl handled the charge," Charles said. "Nobody else touched it. Certainly not Casseia."

"We all *slept*, didn't we?" Sean said. "But it's irrelevant, really. That part's over."

He closed his eyes and licked his lips. A cup came up from the wallmount arbeiter and a stream of liquid poured into his mouth. He sucked it up with the expertise of days in the hospital.

"What do you mean?" Felicia asked in a little voice.

"I'll have to pick all over again. Most of you went home, didn't you?"

"Some did," Felicia said. "We stayed."

"We needed students to occupy and hold, to take the administration chambers and dictate terms. We could work from the university as a base, claim it as a forfeit for illegal voiding, claim it for damages . . . If I had been there, that's what we would have done."

I felt like crying. The injustice of Sean's veiled accusations, mixed with my very real infatuation and guilt at not serving the cause better, turned my stomach.

"Go talk to Gretyl. And you two . . ." He pointed to Charles and me. "Think it over. Who are you? Where do you want to be in ten years?"

* * *

Gretyl was less severely injured, but looked worse. Her head had been wrapped in a bulky breather, leaving only a gap for her eyes. She had been laid back at forty-five degrees on a steel recovery plate as well, and tubes ran from mazes of nano clumps on her chest and neck. An arbeiter had discreetly draped the rest of her with a white sheet for our visit. She watched us enter, and her silky artificial voice said, "How's Sean? You've been to see him?"

"He's fine," Oliver said. I was too unhappy to talk.

"We haven't been allowed to visit. This hospital shits protocol. What's being said outside? Did we get any attention?"

Felicia explained as gently as possible that we really hadn't accomplished much. She was ready to be a little harder with Gretyl than with Sean; perhaps she was infatuated with Sean as well. I had a sudden insight into people and revolutions, and did not like what I saw.

"Sean has a plan to change *that*," Gretyl said.

"I'm sure he does," Oliver said.

"What's on at UMS?"

"They're moving in a new administration. All the Statist appointees have resigned or been put on leave."

"Sounds like they're being punished."

"It's routine. All appointments are being reviewed," Oliver said.

Gretyl sighed—an artificial note of great beauty—and extended her hand. Felicia squeezed it. Charles and I remained in the background. "He thinks the charge that blew up was tampered with," Oliver said.

"It may have been," Gretyl said. "It must have been."

"But only you and he handled it," Charles said.

Gretyl sighed again. "It was just a standard Excavex two-kilo tube. We didn't pay a lot of money. The people who stole it for us may have tampered with it. They could have done something to make it go off. That's possible."

"We don't know that," Oliver said.

"Listen, friends, if we haven't attracted any attention yet, it's because—" She stopped and her eyes tracked the room zipzip, then narrowed.

"I have new eyes," she said. "Do you like the color? You'd better go now. We'll talk later, after I'm released."

On our way out of the hospital, in the tunnel connecting us to Time's River Station's main tube, a hungry-looking, poorly-dressed and very young male LitVid agent tried to interview us. He followed us for thirty meters, glancing at his slate between what he thought were pointed questions. We were too glum and too smart to give any answers, but despite our reticence, we ended up in a ten-second flash on a side channel for Mars Tharsis local.

Sean, on the other hand, was interviewed the next day for an hour by an agent for New Mars Committee Scan, and that was picked up and broadcast by General Solar to the Triple. He told our story to the planets, and by and large, what he told was not what I remembered.

Nobody else was interviewed.

My sadness grew; my fresh young idealism waned rapidly, replaced by no wisdom to speak of, nothing emotionally concrete.

I thought about Sean's words to us, his accusations, his pointed suspicion of me, his interview spreading distortions around the Triple. Now, I would say that he lied, but it's possible Sean Dickinson even then was too good a rabbler to respect the truth. And Gretyl, I think, was about to pass on some sound advice about political need dictating how we see—and use—history.

When we returned to our dorms at UMS, we found notices posted and doors locked. Diane met me and explained that UMS had been closed for the foreseeable future due to "curriculum revisions." Flashing icons beneath the ID plates told us we could enter our quarters once and remove our belongings. Train fare to our homes or any other destination would not be provided. Our slates received bulletins on when and

where the public hearings would be held to determine the
university's future course.

We were arguably worse off than we had been with Dauble
and Connor.

Charles helped Diane and me pull our belongings from the
room and stack them in the tunnel. There weren't many—I
had sent most of my effects home after being voided. I helped
Charles remove his goods, about ten kilos of equipment and
research materials.

We ate a quick lunch in the train station. We didn't have
much to say. Diane, Oliver and Felicia departed on the north-
bound, and Charles saw me to the eastbound.

As I lugged my bag into the airlock, he held out his hand,
and we shook firmly. "Will I see you again?" he asked.

"Why not?" I said. "When our lives are straightened out."

He held onto my hand a little longer and I gently removed
it. "I'd like to see you before that," he said. "For me, at least,
that might be a long way off."

"All right," I said, squeezing through the door. I didn't
commit myself to when. I was in no mood to establish a relationship.

My father forgave me. Mother secretly admired all that I had
done, I think—and they personally footed the bill for expensive autoclasses, to keep me up-to-date on my studies. They
could have charged it to the BM education expenses, as part
of the larger Goback revival. Father was a firm believer in
BM rule, but too honorable to squeeze BM-appropriated
guvvie funds, or take the victor's advantage.

When next I saw Connor, it was on General Solar LitVid.
She was on the long dive to Earth, issuing pronouncements
from the WHTCIPS (Western Hemisphere Transport Coali-
tion Interplanetary Ship) *Barrier Reef*, returning, she was at
pains to make Martians understand, to a kind of hero's welcome. Dauble was with her but said nothing, since day by
day the awful truth of her failed Statist administration was
coming out.

It so happened that there was a Majumdar BM advocate on that very ship, and he took it upon himself to represent all the BMs and other interests hoping to settle with Connor and Dauble. He served them papers, day after day after day, throughout the voyage . . .

By the time both of them got to Earth, ten months later, they would be poor as Jackson's Lode, born on Mars, exiled to Earth, doomed to dodging Triple suits for the rest of their days.

2172, M.Y. 53

What was happening on Mars was an excellent example of politics in action in a "young" culture, my special area of study with respect to Earth history, and I should have been fascinated, but in fact I ignored much of the daily news.

My youthful ideals had been trodden on none too delicately, and I didn't know what to make of it. Before I could speck out the eventual course of my education and decide how to serve my family, I had to re-establish who I was. My mother supported my youthful indecision; my father gave in to my mother. I had some time away from commitments.

When UM restarted classes, I switched campuses and majors, going to Durrey Station, the third-largest town on Mars and home of UM's second-largest branch. I studied high humanities—text lit from the nineteenth and twentieth centuries, philosophy before quantum mechanics, and the most practical subject in my list, morals and ethics as a business art. Four hapless souls shared my major, studying things most pioneering, practical Martians could not have given a damn about.

I needed a rest. So I decided to have fun.

* * *

I hadn't thought about Charles for months. I did not know he had gone to Durrey Station as well. When classes started, we did not run into each other immediately. I saw him in Shinktown over student break.

Seven hundred and ninety students fled UM Durrey at Solstice and either went to work on their farms, if from the local, more sober and well-established families of Mariner Valley, or took refuge in Shinktown. Some, already married, spread out to their half-built warrens, soon to become new stations, and did what married people do.

My family kept no farms and required little of me in the way of overt filial piety. They loved me but let me choose my own paths.

Shinktown was a not very charming maze of shops, small and discreet hotels, game rooms, and gyms, seventeen kilometers from Durrey Station, where students went to get away from their studies, their obligations to family and town; to blow it all out and kick red.

Mars has never been a planet of prudes. Still, its attitudes toward sex befitted a frontier culture. The goals of sex are procreation and the establishment of strong connections between individuals and families; sex leads to (or should lead to) love and lasting relationships; sex without love may not be sinful, but it is almost certainly wasteful. To the ideal Martian man or woman, as portrayed in popular LitVids, sex was never a matter of just scratching an itch; it was devilishly *complicated*, fraught with significance and drama for individual and family, a potential liaison (one seldom married within one's BM) and the beginning of a new entity, the stronger and dedicated dyad of perfectly matched partners.

That was the myth and I admit I found it attractive. I still do. It's been said that a romantic is someone who never accepts the evidence of her eyes and ears.

In this age, few were physically unattractive. There was no need and little inclination among most Martians to let nature take its uncertain course. That particular question had been hammered into a viable public policy for most citizens of the Triple seventy Martian years and more ago. I was attractive enough, my genetic heritage requiring little adjustment if any—I'd never asked my mother and father, really—and men were not reluctant to talk to me.

But I had never taken a lover, mostly because I found young men either far too earnest or far too frivolous or, most commonly, far too dull. What I wanted for my first (and perhaps only) love was not physical splendor alone, but something deeply significant, something that would make Mars itself—if not the entire Triple—sigh with envy when my imagined lover and I published our memoirs, in ripe old age . . .

I was no more a prude than any other Martian. I did not enjoy going to bed alone. I often wished I could lower my standards just enough to learn more about men; handsome men, of course, men with a little grit, supremely self-confident. For that sort of experimentation, beauty and physical splendor would be more important than brains, but if one could have both—wit and beauty and prowess—

So fevered my dreams.

Shinktown was a place of temptations for a young Martian, and that was why so many of us went there. I enjoyed myself at the dances, flirted and kissed often enough, but shied from the more intimate meetings I knew I could have. The one continuing truth of male and female relations—that the man attempts and the woman chooses—was in my favor. I could attract, test, play the doubtless cruel and (I thought) entirely fair game of sampling the herd.

In the middle of the break, on an early spring evening, a local university club held a small mixer following a jai alai game in the arena. I'd attended the game and was enjoying a buzz of frustration at lithe male bodies leaping and slamming the heavy little ball, uneasy with a mix of strong Shinktown double-ferment tea and a little wine, and I hoped to dance it off and flirt and then go home and think.

I spotted Charles first, from across the room, while dancing with a Durrey third-form. Charles was talking to ("chatting up" I said to myself) a tall, big-eyed exotique who seemed to me way out of his league. When the dance ended, I edged through the crowd and bumped into him by accident from behind. He turned from the exotique, saw me, and to my dismay, his face lit up like a child's. He fell all over himself to disentangle from the big-eyed other.

I had thought about the UMS action for months and wanted to talk about it, and Charles seemed perfect to fulfill that function.

"We could get dinner," Charles suggested as we strolled off the dance floor.

"I've already eaten," I said.

"Then a snack."

"I wanted to talk about last summer."

"Perfect opportunity, over a late dessert."

I frowned as if the suggestion were somehow improper, then gave in. Charles took my arm—that seemed safe enough—and we found a small, quiet autocafe in an outer tunnel arc. The arc branched north of Shinktown quarters for permanent residents and offered little convenience shops, most tended by arbeiters. We passed through the central quadrangle, a hectare of tailored green surrounded by six stories of stacked balconies. The quadrangle architecture tried to imitate the worst of old Earth, retrograde, oppressive. The shop arc, however, was comparatively stylish and benign.

We sat in the cafe and sipped Valley coffee while waiting for our cakes to arrive. Charles said little at first, his nerves evident. He smiled broadly at my own few words, eager to be accommodating.

Tiring rapidly of this verbjam, I leaned forward. "Why did you come to Shinktown?" I asked.

"Bored and lonely. I've been up to my neck in Bell Continuum topoi. You ... don't know what this is, I presume."

"No," I said.

"Well, it's fascinating. It could be important someday, but right now it's on the fringe. Why did *you* come?"

I shrugged. "I don't know. For company, I suppose." I re-alized, with some concern, that this was my way of being co-quettish. My mother would have called it bitchy, and she knew me well enough.

"Looking for a good dance partner? I'm probably not your best choice."

I waved that off. "Do you remember what Sean Dickinson said?"

He grimaced. "I'd like to forget."

"What was wrong with him?"

"I'm not much of a student of human nature." Charles ex-amined his tiny cup. The cakes arrived and Charles slapped palm on the arbeiter. "My treat," he said. "I'm old-fashioned."

I let that pass as well. "I think he was *monstrous*," I said.

"I'm not sure I'd go that far."

My lips wrapped around the word again, savoring it. "Monstrous. A political monster."

"He really stung you, didn't he? Remember, he was hurt."

"I've tried to understand the whole situation, why we didn't accomplish anything. Why I was willing to follow Sean and Gretyl almost anywhere . . ."

"Follow *them*? Or the cause?"

"I believed—believe in the cause, but I was following *them*," I said. "I'm trying to understand why."

"They seemed to know what they were doing."

We talked for an hour, going in circles, getting no closer to understanding what had happened to us. Charles seemed to accept it as a youthful escapade, but I'd never allowed myself the luxury of such japes. Failure gave me a deep sensation of guilt, of time wasted and opportunities missed.

When we finished our cakes, it seemed natural that we should go someplace quiet and continue talking. Charles sug-gested the quad. I shook my head and explained that I thought it looked like an insula. Charles was not a student of history. I said, "An insula. An apartment building in ancient Rome."

"The city?" Charles asked.

"Yeah," I said. "The city."

His next suggestion, preceded by a moment of perplexed reflection, was that we should go to his room. "I could order tea or wine."

"I've had enough of both," I said. "Can we get some mineral water?"

"Probably," Charles said. "Durrey sits on a pretty fine aquifer. This whole area lies on pre-Tharsis karst."

We took a small cab to the opposite arc, hotels and temp quarters for Shinktown's real source of income, the students.

I don't remember anticipating much of anything as we entered Charles's room. There was nothing distinguished about the decor—inexpensive, clean, maintained by arbeiters, with no nano fixtures; pleasant shades of beige, soft green, and gray. The bed could hold only one person comfortably. I sat on the bed's corner. It occurred to me suddenly that by going this far, Charles might expect something more. We hadn't even kissed yet, however, and the agreement had been that we come here to talk.

Still, I wondered how I would react if Charles made a move.

"I'll order the water," he said. He took two steps beside the desk, unsure whether to seat himself on the swing-out chair or the edge of the bed beside me. "Gassed or plain?"

"Plain," I said.

He set his slate on the desk port and placed an order. "They're slow. Should take about five minutes. Old arbeiters," he said.

"Creaky," I said.

He smiled, sat on the chair, and looked around. "Not much luxury," he said. "Can't afford more." The one chair, a small net and com desk, single drop-down bed with its thin blanket, vapor bag behind a narrow door, sink and toilet folded into the wall behind a curtain—all squeezed into three meters by four.

I casually wondered how many people had had sex in this room, and under what circumstances.

"We could spend years trying to figure out Sean and Gretyl," Charles said. "I don't want you to think I've forgotten what happened."

"Oh, no," I said.

"But I've got too much else to *ponder*, really." He used the word in a kind of self-parody, to deflate the burden it might carry. "I can't worry about the mistakes we made."

"Did we make mistakes?" I asked. I smoothed some wrinkles in the thin blanket.

"I think so."

"What mistakes?" I led him on, angry again but hiding it.

Charles finally pulled out the chair and sat with his elbows on his knees, hands clasped in front of him. "We should choose our leaders more carefully," he said.

"Do you think Sean was a bad leader?"

"You said he was 'monstrous,' " Charles reminded me.

"Things went wrong for all of us," I said. "If they had gone better, everything might have turned out differently."

"You mean, if Connor and Dauble hadn't hung themselves, we might have provided the noose."

"It seems likely."

"I suppose that's what Sean and Gretyl were trying to do," Charles said.

"All of us," I added.

"Right. But what would we have done after that? What did Sean really want to accomplish?"

"In the long run?" I asked.

"Right," Charles said. He was revealing a capacity I hadn't seen before. I was curious to see how far this new depth extended. "I think they wanted anarchy."

I frowned abruptly.

He looked at me and his face stiffened. "But I didn't really—"

"Why would they want anarchy?"

"Sean wants to be a leader. But he can never be a consensus leader."

"Why not?"

"He has the appeal of a LitVid image," Charles said. How could he not see how much he was irritating me? I felt a perversity again; I wanted him to anger me, so I could deny him what he had come here to gain, that is, my favors.

"Shallow?"

"I'm sorry, this is upsetting you," Charles said softly, kneading his hands. "I know you liked Sean. It makes me . . . I didn't want to bring you here to—"

The door chimed. Charles opened it and an arbeiter entered, carrying a bottle of *Durrey Region Prime Drinking Water, Mineral*. Charles handed me a glass and sat again.

"I really don't want to talk politics," he said. "I'm not very good at it."

"We came here to talk about what went wrong," I persisted. "I'm curious to hear you out."

"You disagree with me."

"Maybe," I said. "But I want to hear what you have to say."

Charles's misery became obvious in the set of his jaw, drawn in defensively toward his neck, and the way he clenched his hands. "All right," he said. I could sense him giving up, assuming I was out of his reach, and that added to my irritation. Such presumption!

"What kind of leader would Sean be?"

"A tyrant," Charles said softly. "Not a very good one. I don't think he has what it takes. Not enough charm at the right time, and he can't keep his feelings under control."

My anger evaporated. It was the strangest feeling; I *agreed* with Charles. That was the monstrousness I was trying to understand.

"You're a better judge of human nature than you think," I said with a sigh. I leaned back on the bed.

He shrugged sadly. "But I've fapped up," he said.

"How?"

"I want to know you better. I feel something really special when I see you."

Intrigued, I was about to continue with my infernal questioning—*How? What do you mean?*—when Charles stood up. "But it's useless. You haven't liked me from the start."

I gaped at him.

"You think I'm awkward, I'm not in the least like Sean, and that was who you'd set your sights on ... And now I seem to be putting him down."

"Sean doesn't appeal to me," I said, eyes downcast in what I hoped was demure honesty. "Certainly not after what he said."

"I'm sorry," Charles said.

"Why are you always apologizing? Sit down, please."

Neither of us had touched our mineral water.

Charles sat. He lifted his glass. "You know, this water has been sitting for a billion years, locked in limestone ... Old life. That's what I'd *really* like to be doing. Besides getting the physics grants and starting research, I mean. Going Up and exploring the old sea beds. Not talking politics. I need someone to come with me and keep me company. I thought maybe you'd like to do that." Charles looked up, then rushed his proposal out breathlessly. "Klein BM has an old vineyard about twenty kilometers from here. I could borrow a tractor, show you the—"

"A winery?" I asked, startled.

"Failed. Converted to a water station. Not much more than a trench dome, but there are good fossil beds. Maybe the old discarded vintage has mellowed by now and we could try to gag it down."

"Are you asking?" I felt a sudden warmth so immediate and unexpected that it brought moisture to my eyes. "Charles, you surprise me." I surprised myself. Then, eyes downcast again, "What are you expecting?"

"You might like me better away from this place. I don't fit into Shinktown, and I don't know why I came here. I'm glad I did, of course, because you're here, but ..."

"An old winery. And ... going Up again?"

"In proper pressure suits. I've done it often enough. I'm

pretty safe to be with." He pointed his finger Up. "I'm no LitVid idol, Casseia. I can't sweep you off your feet."

I pretended not to hear that. "I've never gone fossiling," I said. "It's a lovely idea."

Charles swallowed and quickly decided to press on. "We could leave now. Spend a few days. Wouldn't cost much— my BM isn't rich, but we'd borrow equipment nobody's using now. No problem with the oxygen budget. We can bring hydrogen back for a net gain. I can call and tell the station to warm up for us."

This was something slightly wicked and hugely unexpected and quite lovely. Charles would never pressure me to go one step farther than I wanted. It was perfect.

"I'll try not to bore you with physics," he said.

"I can take it," I said. "What makes you think I was ever interested in Sean, romantically?"

Wisely, he didn't answer, and immediately set about making late-night preparations.

Martians saw the surface of their world most often through the windows of a train. Perhaps nine or ten times in a life, a Martian would go Up and walk the surface in a pressure suit—usually in crowds and under close supervision, tourists on their own planet.

Call it fear, call it reason, most Martians preferred tunnels, and dubbed themselves rabbits, quite comfortably; red rabbits, to distinguish from the gray rabbits on Earth's moon.

I think I was more nervous sitting in the tractor beside Charles than I had been in my skinseal months earlier. I trusted Charles not to lose us in the ravines and ancient glacier tongues; he radiated self-confidence. What unnerved me was the proximity to emotions I had safely kept locked away behind philosophy.

I will not explain my turnaround. I was becoming attracted to Charles, but the process was slow. As he drove, I sneaked looks at him and studied his lean features, his long, straight nose, slow-blinking eyes large and brown and observant, upper lip delicately sensuous, lower lip a trifle weak, chin prominent, neck corded and scrawny—a heady mix of features I found attractive and features I wasn't sure I approved of. Unaesthetic, not perfection. Long fingers with square nails, broad bony shoulders, chest slightly sunken . . .

I knit my brows and turned my attention to the landscape. I was not inclined to physical science, but no Martian can escape the past; we are told tales in our infant beds.

Mars was dead; once, it had been alive. On the lowland plains, beneath the ubiquitous flopsands and viscous smear lay a thick layer of calcareous rock, limestone, the death litter of unaccounted tiny living things on the floor of an ancient sea that had once covered this entire region and, indeed, sixty percent of northern Mars.

The seas, half a billion Martian years before, had fallen victim to Mars's aging and cooling. The interior flows of Mars slowed and stabilized just as Mars began to develop— and push aside—its continents, thus cutting short the migration of its four young crustal plates, ending the lives of chains of gas-belching volcanoes. The atmosphere began its long flight into space. Within six hundred million Martian years, life itself retreated, evolving to more hardy forms, leaving behind fossil sea beds and karsts and, last of all, the Mother Ecos and the magnificent aqueduct bridges. ("Ecos" is singular; "ecoi" plural.)

All around us, ridges of yellow-white limestone poked from the red-ochre flopsand. Rusted, broken boulders scattered from impact craters topped this mix like chocolate sprinkles on rhubarb sauce over vanilla ice cream. Against the pink sky, the effect was severe and heart-achingly beautiful, a chastening reminder that even planets are mortal.

"Like it?" Charles asked. We hadn't talked much since leaving Durrey in the borrowed Klein tractor.

"It's magnificent," I said.

"Wait till we get to the open karsts—like prairie dog holes. Sure signs of aquifers, but it takes an expert to know how deep, and whether they're whited." Whited aquifers carried high concentrations of arsenic, which made the water a little more expensive to mine. "Whited seas had entirely different life forms. That's probably where the mothers came from."

I knew little about the mother cysts—single-organism repositories of the post-Tharsis Omega Ecos, a world's life in a patient nutshell, parents of the aqueduct bridges. Their fossils had been discovered only in the past few years, and I hadn't paid much attention to news about them. "Have you ever seen a mother?" Charles asked.

"Only in pictures."

"They're magnificent. Bigger than a tractor, heavy shells a foot thick—buried in the sands, waiting for one of the ancient wet cycles to come around again . . . The last of their kind." His eyes shone and his mouth curved up in an awed half-smile. His enthusiasm distanced me for a moment. "Some might have lasted tens of millions of years. But eventually the wets never came." He shook his head and his lips turned down sadly, as if he were talking about family tragedy. "Some hunters think we'll find a live one someday. The holy grail of fossil hunters."

"Is that possible?"

"I don't think so."

"Are there any fossil mothers where we're going?"

He shook his head. "They're very rare. And they're not found in karsts. Most have been found in the sulci."

"Oh."

"But we can look." He smiled a lovely little boy's smile, open and trusting.

The Klein BM winery, a noble experiment that hadn't panned out, lay buried in the lee of a desiccated frost-heave plateau twenty kilometers west of Durrey Station. Now it was maintained by arbeiters, and fitfully at that, judging from the buildup of static flopsands on the exposed entrance. A gate carried a bright green sign, "Trés Haut Médoc." Charles urged the tractor beneath the sign. The garage opened slowly and balkily, gears jammed with dust, and Charles parked the tractor in its dark enclosure.

We sealed our suits and climbed down from the cabin. Charles palmed the lock port and turned to face me. "I haven't been here since the codes were changed. Hope I've been logged on the old general Klein net."

"You didn't check?" I asked, alarmed.

"Joking," he said. The lock opened, and we stepped in.

Over the years, the arbeiters had repaired themselves into ugly lumps. They reminded me of dutiful little hunchbacks, moving obsequiously out of our way as we explored the narrow tunnels leading to the main living quarters. "I've never seen arbeiters this old," I said.

"Waste not, want not. Klein's a thrifty family. They took the best machines with them and left a skeleton crew, just enough to tend the water."

"Poor things," I said dubiously.

"Voilá," Charles announced, opening the door to the main quarters. Beyond lay a madman's idea of order, air mattresses piled into a kind of shelter in one corner, sheets covering a table as if it were a bed, decayed equipment lovingly stacked in the middle of the floor for human attention, smelling of iodine. The machines had been bored. A large arbeiter, about a meter tall and half as wide, a big barrel of a machine with prominent arms, stood proudly in the middle of its domain. "Welcome," it greeted in a scratchy voice. "There have been no guests at this estate for four years. How may we serve you?"

Charles laughed.

"Don't," I said. "You'll hurt its feelings."

The arbeiter hummed constantly, a sign of imminent collapse. "This unit will require replacements, if any are available," it told us after a moment of introspective quiet.

"You'll have to make do," Charles said. "What we need is a place fit for habitation, by two humans . . . separate quarters, as soon as possible."

"This is not adequate?" the arbeiter asked with mechanical dismay.

"Close, but it needs a little rearrangement."

We couldn't help giggling.

The arbeiter considered us with that peculiar way older machines have of seeming balky and sentient when in fact they are merely slow. "Arrangements will be made. I beg your pardon, but this unit will require replacement parts and nano recharge, if that is possible."

Four hours later, with the living quarters in reasonable shape and our provisions for several days stored and logged in with the arbeiters, Charles and I stopped our rushing about and faced each other. Charles glanced away first, pretending to critically examine the interior furnishings. "Looks like a bunkhouse," he said.

"It's fine," I said.

"Well, it's not luxury."

"I didn't expect it to be."

"I came here once when I was ten, with my dad," Charles said, rubbing his hands nervously on his pants. "A kind of getaway for a couple of days while traveling from Amnesia to Jefferson, through Durrey . . . Klein holdings intrude into the old Erskine BM lands here. I don't know how that happened."

Another moment of uneasy silence. Clearly, Charles did not know how to begin, nor what was expected; neither did I, but as the female in this pairing, it was not my responsibility to initiate, and I did not want to try.

"Shall we see the winery?" he inquired suddenly, holding out his hand.

I took the hand and we began our formal tour of Trés Haut Médoc.

Charles was disarmingly nervous. Disarming, because I had to say little and do nothing but follow him; he gave a gentle, constant commentary on things Martian, most of which I knew. His voice was soothing even as he ran through technical details. In time, I listened more to the tone than the content, enjoying the masculine music of fact laid upon fact, an architecture to shield us for the moment against being alone together.

Ninety percent or more of any Martian station lay underground. Pressurization requirements and protection against radiation flux through the thin atmosphere made this the most economical method of construction. Some attempts had been made in the first ten years to push high-rises and multi-story uplooks through the dirt, but Mars had been settled on a shoestring. Buried or bermed construction was much cheaper. Heat exchangers, sensors, pokeups, entrances and exits, a few low buildings, broke the surface, but even now we remained, by and large, troglodytes.

Half of the aquifers on Mars were solid—mineral aquifers—and half liquid. Solid aquifers came in many varieties. Some were permafrosts and heaves, which produced hummocky terrain. Some ice domes on Mars were ten kilometers across, but nearly all heaves had long since lost the water that produced them. The evaporated water either re-condensed at the poles, or was lost across the ages to space. The thin atmosphere was nearly moisture-free.

Trés Haut Médoc sat half a kilometer above a liquid flow, probably the same flow that supplied Durrey. Water seeped through the limestone and pooled in deeper fissures and caves extending as much as ten kilometers below the karst.

Our first stop was the pumping station. The pump, a massive cluster of steel-blue cylinders and spheres melded together like an abstract sculpture, had been working steadily for fifteen Martian years. It extracted its own fuel, deuterium, from the water it pulled out of the ground.

"We hooked this up to the Durrey pipes about nineteen years ago, Earth years," Charles explained, walking around the pump. "Just after the winery shut down and the station was automated and evacuated. A source of revenue to offset our failure." Our footsteps echoed hollow on the frosted stone floor. Air whispered through wall-mounted vents, cool and tangy-musty. "It's the station's only reason to exist now. Durrey wants it, pays for it, so we keep the pump going. While I'm here, I'll justify our visit by filing a report . . ."

"And get some replacement arbeiters," I suggested.

"Maybe. The folks who set up the winery were a California family . . . Or were they Australian? I forget now."

"Big difference," I suggested.

"Not really. I know a lot of Australians and Californians now. Except for accent, they're pretty alike. My own family is from New Zealand, actually. How about yours?"

"I'm not sure. German/Indian, I think."

"That explains your lovely skin," Charles said.

"I don't pay much attention to heritage."

Charles led me into the water-settling chambers. The dark pools sat still as glass in their quarried limestone basins, filling two chambers each a hectare in extent and ten meters deep. Somewhere beneath our feet, transfer pumps thumped faintly, sending the water to Durrey's buried pipelines. I breathed in the cold moist air, touched the damp limestone walls.

"Like old bones, that rock," Charles said.

"Right. Sea bottoms."

"Half our towns and stations couldn't exist without limestone flats."

"Why didn't it get turned into marble or something?" I asked, partly to demonstrate I was not totally ignorant of areology.

Charles shook his head. "No major areological activity for the past billion years. Marble takes heat and pressure to form. Mars is asleep. It can't do the job any more."

"Oh." I had not demonstrated anything except my ignorance. Still, that didn't bother me; I was giving Charles every chance to show off, just to see who he really was, what kind of man I had chosen to spend a few days with, alone.

We took a bridge over the farthest pool and down a sloping tunnel. The next chamber held row upon row of corrugated mirror-bright stainless-steel tanks wrapped in coils of orange ceramic pipes. Here the musty-tangy smell was almost over-powering. It stimulated something like racial memory, and I thought of cool dank root cellars on warm summer days, filled with sweet-smelling wooden crates of apples and pota-toes, hard-packed dirt floors . . .

"The old vats," Charles said. "*Cuve*, they were called. Juice from the grapes—"

"I can guess," I interrupted. "I'm something of a wine con-noisseur, actually." That was stretching the truth considerably.

"Oh, really?" Charles asked, genuinely pleased. "Then maybe you can explain more to me. I've always wondered why the winery didn't work out."

"Where'd they get their grapes?" I asked, adopting an ex-pert air.

"*Cuvée in situ*. Grew them in the vats, grape cell suspen-sion . . . Inoculated it, fermented it right where it grew."

"That's why it failed," I said with a sniff. "Worst wine imaginable." So I had heard, at any rate; I had never tried it myself.

"My folks tell me it was pretty bad. Some of it's stored around here, I think . . . Just abandoned."

"For how long?"

"Twenty years at least."

"Terrestrial years," I said.

"Right."

"I prefer Martian years, myself."

Charles took my little feints and jabs pretty well, I thought, not getting irritated, yet not backtracking to flatter me, either.

"Shall we look for them?"

"Yeah," he said. "I remember seeing them when I was a child . . . somewhere down here." He led the way. I lagged a few steps and peered into a glass window in the side of one *cuve*. Empty blackness. The whole place saddened me. How often had Martians attempted to do something the way it had been done on Earth, half inventing something, half following ancient tradition, and failing miserably?

"You know how we make wine now, don't you?" I asked, catching up with him.

"Pure nano, all artificial, right?"

"Some of it's not bad, either."

"Have you ever tasted Earth wine?" Charles asked.

"Good heavens, no," I said. "My family's not rich."

"I tasted some a few years ago. Madeira. Cost a friend four hundred Triple dollars."

"Lucky man," I said. "Madeira used to be aged in the holds of ships, sent around the Horn." That just about plumbed my knowledge of wine.

"It was pretty good. A little sweet, though."

We pushed aside a thin fiberglass door and entered a storage area behind the vat room. Hidden behind neatly folded piles of filter cloth, a single lonely drum sat in one corner. Charles stooped beside the drum and peered at its label. "Vintage 2152," he said. "M.Y. 43. Never bottled, never released." He glanced up at me with a comic look of fearful anxiety. "Might kill us both."

"Let's try it," I said.

The spigot plug had been turned to the wall. Charles called one of the maintenance arbeiters to bring in a forklift and move the drum. The arbeiter did its work, and we were able to tap the barrel. Charles went off to find glasses, leaving me with my thoughts in the cold, empty room.

I stared at the foamed rock walls, then said, out loud, "What in hell am I doing?" I was far from any station or town, with a young man I knew little about, putting myself into what could be a very compromising situation, going against my better judgment, much less my previous plans for just such an occasion ... when I would have tested and picked out a very suitable candidate for a *serious* relationship, a *significant* love-matching.

Clearly, I didn't know my own mind. I liked Charles, he was certainly pleasant, but he was no ...

Sean Dickinson.

I frowned and pinched my upper arm as a kind of punishment. If Sean Dickinson were here, I thought, we might already be in bed together ... But I could see Sean waking in the morning, glancing at me with disapproval, taciturn after a night of passion. Was that what I wanted? Experience of *sex* with the added spice of an illusion of romance, with someone I could never have a future with, and therefore no strings attached?

My face heated.

Charles returned with two thick glasses and I pretended to examine the arbeiter for a moment, blinking myself back into control. "Anything wrong?" Charles asked.

I shook my head, smiling falsely. "It just looks so pitiful." I took one of the glasses.

Charles stretched his neck between nervous shoulders, clearly more unsure about me than I was about him. But he made a brave show, and with a magician's hocus-pocus gesture, turned the stopcock and poured a thin stream of deep red liquid into his glass.

"It wouldn't be polite to offer you some first," he said, and lifted the glass. "It's my family's mistake, after all."

He sniffed the glass, swirled it, smiled at the pretension, and took a sip. I watched his face curiously, wondering how bad it could be.

He showed genuine surprise.

"Well?" I asked.

"Not fatal," he said. "Not fatal at all. It's drinkable."

He poured a glass for me. The wine was rough, demanding a little more throat control to get it down than I really preferred, but it was not nearly as bad as it could have been.

"We're young," Charles decided. "We'll survive. Should we decant a liter or two, have it with dinner?"

"Depends on what dinner is," I said.

"What we brought with us, and whatever I can scrounge from the emergency reserves."

"Maybe I can cook," I said.

"That would be great."

* * *

We ate in the station boss's dining room on an old metal table and chairs that nobody had seen fit to remove. Ten-year-old music played softly over the louder system, rapid hammer-beat kinjee tunes that might have put my parents in a romantic mood, but did nothing for me. I preferred development, not drugdrum.

I will not say the wine liberated me from my cares, but it did induce calm, and for that I was grateful. The food was tractable—gray paste at least five years old—Martian years—that fortunately shaped itself into something palatable, if not gourmet. Charles was embarrassingly appreciative. I had to bite my tongue not to point out that the paste did most of the work. He was trying to be nice, to make me feel good. My ambivalence was a puzzle to both of us.

The air system in the old warren creaked and groaned as we finished our dinner. Outside, the boss's station display told us, the surface temp had dropped to minus eighty Celsius and the wind was whining at a steady one hundred kiphs. I wasn't worried for our safety—we had enough supplies to keep us for a couple of weeks. If we wished to leave, the tractor could get us through anything but a major storm, which wasn't in the offing, according to satcom weather reports.

We weren't in any danger, nobody knew where we were, the wine illumined a Charles more and more handsome with every sip, and still my neck ached with tension.

"Tomorrow we'll go out to the shaved flats in an old melt river canyon," Charles said, lifting his glass and staring at the wine within as if it were rare vintage. He closed one eye to squint at the color, caught my dubious expression, and laughed. His laugh might have been the first thing I fell in love with—easy and gentle, self-deprecating but not humble, accompanied by a roll of his eyes and a lift of his chin.

"What are shaved flats?" I asked.

"Natural fractures in the limestone. Upper layers separate from lower, maybe because of vibration from the wind, and the upper layer begins to fragment. Soon—well, in a hundred million years—frost forms in the cracks, and the upper layer erodes into sand and dust, which blow away, leaving the next layer down . . . Shaved, so to speak."

"Where does the frost come from, this far south?" I asked.

"The shaving stopped about three hundred million years ago. Not enough water frost to matter any more. Some CO_2 in the winter. But that's where fossils are. This used to be a pretty good area for ancient tests."

"Tests?"

"Shells. Most no bigger than your finger, but my great uncle found an intact Archimedes snapper about three meters long. Right here, while digging out the tunnels for this station."

"What's an Archimedes snapper?" I knew something about old Martian biology, enough to remember the largest creature of the tertiary Tharsis period, but I wanted to listen to Charles some more. His voice was very pretty, actually, and I had come to enjoy hearing him explain things.

"Big screw-shaped jointed worm with razor-sharp spines. Spun through sea-bottom muds chopping up smaller animals, then sent out stomach tendrils to digest the bits and suck them in."

I grued delicately. Charles appreciated the effect.

"Pretty grim if you were, say, a triple test jelly during mating season," he added, finishing his glass. He lifted it toward me, inquiring without words if I wanted more.

"But I'm not," I said. "So why does it sound awful?"

"More wine, awful?" Charles asked.

"I'm not a triple test jelly, so why does an Archimedes snapper sound horrible?"

"Not used to fresh meat," Charles said.

"I've never had meat," I said. "It's supposed to . . . sharpen your drives. Your instincts."

Charles lifted his glass again toward me. I wondered if he wanted me drunk. That would not be a very sporting desire, a supine woman nearly out of her senses; would that satisfy him, or would he try for all of me, mind as well as body?

"No thank you," I said. "It looks like blood."

"Venous blood," Charles agreed, putting his half-full glass down. "I've had enough, too. I'm not used to it."

"I think it's time to sleep," I suggested.

Charles stared at the floor. I focused on his smile and specked an image of Charles and me without blankets, without clothes, in blood-warm rooms, and felt more heat rise that was not due to the wine. I wanted to encourage him, but something still held me back.

If he did not make a move now, he might miss me, and I would not have to decide whether to accept. I wondered how many women had put heavy action on Charles, and how often he had accepted—if ever. It would be awful if we were both inexperienced—wouldn't it?

"We have a lot to do tomorrow," Charles said, turning his eyes away. "I'm pleased you decided to come with me. It's a real boost to my ego."

"Why?"

"I'd hate to rush anything now," he said, so softly I could hardly hear.

"Rush what?"

He filled his glass of wine, then frowned and stuck out his tongue. "I don't know why I did that. I don't want any more. You're very tolerant." His next words came in a rush, accompanied by quick hand gestures as if in a debate. "I'm shy and I'm clumsy and I don't know what to do, or whether to do anything, and the thing I want most right now is to just *talk* with you, and find out why I'm so attracted to you. But I think I should be doing something else, too, trying to kiss you or . . . Of course, I wouldn't mind that." He looked squarely at me, distressed. "Would you?"

I had hoped to be guided through this by someone who could educate *me*.

"Talking is good," I said.

Charles came forward a little too quickly, and we kissed.

He put his hand on my shoulder, hugged me without squeezing, and then, instinct shoving in, began to get more insistent. I gently pushed him back, then leaned forward and kissed him again to show I wasn't rejecting him. His face flushed and his eyes unfocused. "Let's take it easy," I said.

We slept in separate rooms. Through the wall, I heard Charles pace and mumble. I don't think he got much sleep that night. Surprisingly, I slept well.

The next morning, I dressed, came into the kitchen and found the main arbeiter frozen in the middle of the floor. I touched it tentatively. A faint recorded voice said, "I am no longer functional. I need to be repaired or replaced." Then it shut down completely.

I made my own cup of tea and waited for Charles. He came in a few minutes later, trying not to look tired, and I warmed a cup for him.

"Sleep well?" I asked.

He shook his head. "And you?"

"I slept okay. I'm sorry you were upset."

"You're not a Shinktown sweet. Not to me."

"I'm glad," I said.

"But I don't know what you expect."

I took his hand and said, "We are going to spend a wonderful day sightseeing and looking for fossils. We'll talk more and get to know each other. Isn't that enough?"

"It's a start," Charles said.

We ate breakfast and suited up.

"None of this was scrubbed by glaciers," Charles said, pointing to the plain with his gloved hand. We both wore full pressure suits in the tractor cab, but our helmet visors were raised. The tractor motors ramped to a low whine as we climbed a bump in the flat expanse. "They swept by about a hundred kilometers east and fifty west. They left a melt river canyon not far from here, though. It cuts down through a couple of billion years.

"We'll pass through three layers of life descending into the canyon. The topmost layer is about a half a billion years old. The glaciers came about a hundred million years after they died. The middle layer is two billion years old. That's the Secondary and Tertiary, Pre-shield and Tharsis One Ecos. At the bottom, in the shaved flats, is the silica deposit."

"The Glass Sea," I said. Every Martian was given a Glass Sea fossil at some point in their childhood.

Charles steered us around a basalt-capped turban of limestone. Basalt fragments from an ancient meteor impact lay scattered over the area. I tried to imagine the meteor striking the middle of the shallow ocean, spraying debris for hundreds of kilometers and throwing up a cloud of muddy rain and steam . . . Devastation for an already fragile ecology. "Makes me twitchy," I said.

"What does?"

"Time. Age. Makes our lives look so trivial."

"We *are* trivial," Charles said.

I set my face firmly and shook my head. "I don't think so. Empty time isn't very . . ." I searched for the right word. What came to mind were *warm, alive, interesting*, but these words all seemed to reveal my *feminine* perspective, and Charles's knee-jerk response had been decidedly masculine and above-it-all intellectual. "Active. No observers," I concluded lamely.

"Given that, we're still here for just an instant, and the changes we make on the landscape will be wiped out in a few thousand years."

"I disagree," I continued. "I think we're going to make a real mark on things. We observe, we plan ahead, we're organized—"

"Some of us are," Charles said, laughing.

"No, I mean it. We can make a big difference. All the flora and fauna on Mars were wiped out because they . . ." I still couldn't clearly express what I wanted to say.

"They weren't organized," Charles offered.

"Right."

"Wait until you see," Charles said.

I shivered. "I don't want to be convinced of my triviality."

"Let the land speak," Charles said.

I had never been very comfortable with large ideas—astrophysics, areology, all seemed cavernous and dismal compared to the bright briefness of human history. In my studies I focused on the intricacies of politics and culture, human interaction; Charles I think preferred the wide-open territories of nature without humanity.

"We interpret what we see to suit our own mindset," I said pompously.

For a moment, his expression—downturned corners of his mouth, narrowed eyes, a little shake of his head—made me regret those words. If I was playing him like a fish on a line, I might have just snapped the line, and I suddenly felt terribly insecure. The touch of my glove on his thick sleeve did not seem adequate. "I still want to go and see," I said.

Charles let go of the guide stick. The tractor smoothed to a stop and jerked. He half-turned in his seat. "Do I irritate you?" he asked.

"No, why?"

"I feel like you're testing me. Asking me key questions to see if I'm suitable."

I bit my lip and looked into my lap, trying for some contrition. "I'm nervous," I said.

"Well, so am I. Maybe we should just let up a bit and relax."

"I was just expressing an opinion," I said, my own temper flaring. "I apologize for being clumsy. I haven't been here before, I don't know you very well, I don't know what—"

Charles held up his hands. "Let's forget all of it. I mean, let's forget everything that stands between us, and just try to be two friends out on a trip. I'll relax if you will. Okay?"

I came dangerously close to tears at the anger in his tone. I looked out the window but did not see the ancient carved grotesques outside.

"Okay?" he asked.

"I don't know how to be different," I said. "I'm not good at masks."

"I'm not either, and I don't like trying. If I'm not the right person for you, let's put it all aside and just enjoy the trip."

"I don't know what's making you so angry."

"I don't know, either. I'm sorry."

He pulled the stick forward and we drove in silence for several minutes. "Sometimes I dream about this," he said. "I dream I'm some sort of native Martian, able to stand naked in the Up and feel everything. Able to travel back in time to when Mars was alive."

"Coin-eyed, slender, nut-brown or bronze. 'Dark they were, and golden-eyed.' "

"Exactly," Charles said. "We live on three Marses, don't we? The Mars they made up back on Earth centuries ago. LitVid Mars. And this."

The tension seemed to have cleared. My mood shifted wildly. I felt like crying again, but this time with relief. "You're very tolerant," I said.

"We're both difficult," Charles said. He leaned to one side and bumped helmets with me. Our lips could get no closer, so we settled for that.

"Show me your Mars," I told him.

The melt river canyon stretched for thirty kilometers, carving a wavering line across the flats. A service path had been carved into the cliffs on both sides, cheaper than a bridge, marring the natural beauty but making the canyon bottom accessible to tractors.

"The areology here is really obvious," Charles said. "First comes the Glass Sea, then Tharsis One with deep ocean deposits, building up over a billion years, limestone ... Then ice sheets and eskers ... Then the really big winds at the end of the last glaciation."

We rolled down the gentle packed tumble slope into the canyon. The walls on each side were layered with iron-rich hematite sands and darker strata of clumped till. "Wind and ice," I said.

"You got it. Flopsand and jetsand, smear, cling and grind . . . There's a pretty thick layer of northern chrome clay." Charles pointed to a gray-green band on our right, at least a meter deep. He swerved the tractor around a recent boulder fall, squeezed through a space barely large enough to admit us, and we came out twenty meters below the flats. Our treads pushed aside flopsand to reveal paler grades of grind and heavy till.

"We have as many words for sand and dust as the Inuit have for snow," Charles said.

"Used to be a school quiz," I said. " 'Remember all the grades of dust and sand and name them in alphabetical order.' I only remember twenty."

"Here we are," Charles said, letting the stick go. The tractor slowed and stopped with a soft whine. Outside the cabin, silence. The high wind of the night before had settled and the air was still. A dust-free sky stretched wall-to-wall pitch-black. We might have been on Earth's moon but for the color of the canyon and the rippled red and yellow bed of the ancient melt river.

Charles enjoyed the silence. His face had a look of relaxed concentration. "There's a rock kit in the boot. We'll dig for an hour and return to the tractor." He hesitated, thinking something over. "Then we'll head home. I mean, back to the station."

We checked our gear thoroughly, topped up our air supply from the tractor's tanks, pumped the cabin pressure into storage, and stepped through the curtain lock with a small puff of ice crystals. The crystals fell like stones to the canyon floor.

"I remember this," Charles said over the suit radio. "It hasn't changed. The sand patterns are different, of course, and there have been a few slumps . . . but it looks real familiar. I had a favorite fossil bed about a hundred meters from here. My father showed it to me."

Charles portioned out my share of tools to carry, took my

gloved hand, and we walked away from the tractor. I saw two deposition layers clearly outlined in a stretch of canyon wall that had not slumped: a meter of brown and gray atop several meters of pale yellow limestone, and below that, half a meter of grays and blacks.

We walked across shaved flats now, covered with sand; the oldest limestones, and beneath, the Glass Sea bottom. I drew in my breath sharply, a kind of hiccup, startled at how this realization affected me. Old Mars, back when it had been a living planet . . . Alive for a mere billion and a half years.

Where life arose first was still at issue; Martians claimed primacy, and Terrestrials disputed them. But Earth had been a more violent and energetic world, closer to the sun, bombarded by more destructive radiation . . . Mars, farther away from its youthful star, cooling more rapidly, had condensed its vapor clouds into seas a quarter of a billion years earlier.

I believed—like most loyal Martians—that this was where life had first appeared in the Solar System. My feet pressed thin flopsand five or six centimeters above the graveyard of those early living things.

"Here," Charles said, taking us into the inky shadow of a precarious overhang. I looked up, worried by the prominence. Charles saw my expression as he stooped and brought out his pick hammer. "It's okay," he said. "It was here when I was a kid. Can you shine a light?"

We worked by torch. Charles pried up a slab of dense crumbling limestone. I helped lift the slab away, twenty or thirty kilos of rock, piling it to one side. Charles handed me the pick.

"Your turn," he said. "Under this layer. About a centimeter down."

I swung the pick gently, then harder, until the layer cracked and I was able to finger and brush away the fragments, clearing a space a couple of hands wide. Charles held the torch.

I peered back through two billion Martian years and saw the jewel box of the past, pressed thin as a coat of paint, opalescent against the dark strata of those siliceous oceans.

Round, cubic, pyramidal, elongated, every shape imaginable, surrounded by glorious feathery filters, long stalks ter-
minating in slender, gnarled roots: the ancient Glass Sea
creatures appeared like illustrations in an old book, glittering
rainbows of diffraction as the torch moved. I specked them
waving in the soup-thick seas, sieving and eating their
smaller cousins.

"Sometimes they'd lift from their stalks and float free,"
Charles said. I knew that, but I didn't mind him telling me.
"The biggest colonies were maybe a klick wide, clustered
floats, raising purple fans out of the water to soak up
sunlight . . ."

I reached down with my gloved hand to touch them. They
had been glued firmly against their deathbed; they were
tough, even across the eons.

"They're gorgeous," I said.

"The first examples of a Foster co-genotypic bauplan,"
Charles said. "These are pretty common specimens. No spe-
ciation, all working from one genetic blueprint, making a few
hundred different forms. All one creature, really. Some folks
think Mars never had more than nine or ten species living at
a time. Couldn't call them species, actually—co-genotypic
phyla is more like it. No surprise this kind of biology would
give rise to the mother cysts."

He took a deep breath and stood. "I'm going to make a
pretty important decision here. I'm trusting you."

I looked up from the Glass Sea, puzzled. "What?"

"I'd like to show you something, if you're interested. A
short walk, another couple of hundred meters. A billion and
a half years up. Earth years. First and last."

"Sounds mysterious," I said. "You hiding a mother deposit
here?"

He shook his head. "It's on a secure registry, and we license it to scholars only. Father took me there. Made me
swear to keep it secret."

"Maybe we should skip it," I said, afraid of leading
Charles into violating family confidences.

"It's okay," he said. "Father would have approved."

"Would have?"

"He died on the *Jefferson*."

"Oh." The interplanetary passenger ship *Jefferson* had suffered engine failure boosting from around the Moon five Martian years before. Seventy people had died.

Charles had made a judgment on behalf of his dead father. I could not refuse. I stood and hefted my bag of tools.

The canyon snaked south for almost a hundred meters before veering west. At the bend, we took a rest and Charles chipped idly at a sheet of hard clay. "We've got about an hour more," he said. "We need fifteen minutes to get to where we're going, and that means we can only spend about ten minutes there."

"Should be enough," I said, and immediately felt like kicking myself.

"I could spend a year there and it wouldn't be enough," Charles said.

We climbed a gentle slope forty or fifty meters and abruptly came upon a deep fissure. The fissure cut across the canyon diagonally, its edges windworn smooth with age.

"The whole flatland is fragile," Charles said. "Quake, meteor strike ... Something shook it, and it cracked. This is about six hundred million years old."

"It's magnificent."

He lifted his glove and pointed to a narrow path from the canyon floor, across the near wall of the fissure. "It's stable," he said. "Just don't slip on the gravel."

I hesitated before following Charles. The ledge was irregular, uneven, no wider than half a meter. I pictured a slip, a fall, a rip or prick in my suit.

Charles looked at me over his shoulder, already well down the ledge. "Come on," he said. "It's not dangerous if you're careful."

"I'm not a rock climber," I said. "I'm a rabbit, remember?"

"This is easy. It's worth it, believe me."

I chose each step with nervous deliberation, mumbling to myself below the microphone pickup. We descended into the crevice. Suddenly, I couldn't see Charles. I couldn't hear him on radio, either. We were out of line of sight and he was not getting through to a satcom transponder. I called his name several times, clinging to the wall, each moment closer to panic and fury.

I was looking back over my left shoulder, creeping to my right, when my hand fell into emptiness. I stopped with a low moan, trying to keep my balance on the ledge, waving for a grip, and felt a gloved hand take hold of my arm.

I turned and saw Charles right beside me. "Sorry," he said. "I forgot we wouldn't be able to talk through the rock. You're fine. Just step in . . ."

We stood in the entrance to a cave. I hugged Charles tightly, saying nothing until my hammering heart had settled.

The cavern stabbed deep into the fissure wall, ending in black obscurity. Its ceiling rose five or six meters above our heads. The fissure's opposite wall reflected enough afternoon sunlight into the cavern that we could see each other clearly. Charles lifted the torch and handed it to me. "It's the last gasp," he said.

"What?" I still hadn't recovered my wits.

"We've gone from alpha to omega."

I scowled at him for his deliberate mystery, but he wasn't looking at me.

Gradually, I realized the cavern was not areological. The glass-smooth walls reflected the backwash of light with an oily green sheen. Gossamer, web-like filaments hard as rock stretched across the interior and flashed in my wavering torch beam. Shards of filament littered the floor like lost fairy knives. I stood in the silence, absorbing the obvious: the tunnel had once been part of something alive.

"It's an aqueduct bridge," Charles said. "Omega and Mother Ecos."

This wasn't a cavern at all, but part of a colossal pipeline,

a fossil fragment of Mars's largest and last living things. I
had never heard of an aqueduct bridge surviving intact.

"This section grew into the fissure about half a billion
years ago. Loess and flopsand filled the branch because it ran
counter to the prevailing winds. Cling and jetsand covered the
aqueduct, but didn't stop it from pumping water to the south.
When the Ecos failed and the water stopped, this part died
along with all the other pipes, but it was protected. Come
on."

Charles urged me deeper. We stepped around and under the
internal supports for the vast organic pipe. Water once carried
by this aqueduct had fed billions of hectares of green and
purple lands, a natural irrigation system greater than anything
humans had ever built.

These had been the true canals of Mars, but they had died
long before they could have been seen by Schiaparelli or Per-
cival Lowell.

I swallowed a lump in my throat. "It's beautiful," I said as
we walked deeper. "Is it safe?"

"It's been here for five hundred million years," Charles
said. "The walls are almost pure silica, built up in layers half
a meter thick. I doubt it will fall on us now."

Light ghosted ahead. Charles paused for me to pick my
way through a lattice of thick green-black filaments, then extended his arm for me to go first. My breath sounded harsh
in the confines of the helmet.

"It's easier up ahead. Sandy floor, good walking."

The pipe opened onto a murky chamber. For a moment, I
couldn't get any clear notion of size, but high above, a hole
opened to black sky and I saw stars. The glow that diffused
across the chamber came from a patch of golden sunlight
gliding clockslow across the rippled sand floor.

"It's a storage tank," Charles said. "And a pumping station.
Kind of like Trés Haut Médoc."

"It's immense," I said.

"About fifty meters across. Not quite a sphere. The hole
probably eroded through a few hundred years ago."

"Earth years."

"Right," he said, grinning.

I looked at the concentric ripples in the sand, imagining the puff and blow of the winds coming through the ceiling breach. I nudged loose dust and flopsand with my boot. This went beyond confidence. Charles had guided me into genuine privilege, vouchsafed to very few. "I can't believe it."

"What?" Charles asked expectantly, pleased with himself.

I shrugged, unable to explain.

"I suppose eventually we'll bring in LitVid, maybe even open it to tourists," he said. "My father wanted it kept in the family for a few decades, but I don't think any of my aunts or uncles or the Klein BM managers agreed. They've kept it closed all these years in his memory, I suspect, but they think that's long enough, and there is the resource disclosure treaty to consider."

"Why did he want it closed?"

"He wanted to bring Klein kids here for a history lesson. Exclusively. Give them a sense of deep time."

Charles walked to the spot of sun and stood there, arms folded, his suit and helmet dazzling white and gold against the dull blue-green shadows beyond. He looked wonderfully arrogant, at home with eternity.

That sense of deep time Charles's father had coveted for his BM's children stole over me and brought on a bright, sparkling shock unlike anything I had ever experienced. My eyes adjusted to the gloom. Delicate traceries lined the glassy walls of the buried bubble. I remembered the paleoscape mural in Sean's hospital room. The natural cathedrals of Mars. All broken and flat now . . . except here.

I tried to imagine the godly calm of a planet where an immense, soap-bubble structure like this could remain undisturbed over hundreds of millions of years.

"Have you shown anybody else?" I asked.

"No," Charles said.

"I'm the first?"

"You're the first."

"Why?"

"Because I thought you'd love it," he said.

"Charles, I don't have half the experience or the . . . awareness necessary to appreciate this."

"I think you do."

"There must be hundreds of others—"

"You asked to see my Mars," Charles said. "No one's ever asked before."

I could only shake my head. I was unprepared to understand such a gift, much less appreciate it, but Charles had given it with the sweetest of intentions, and there was no sense resisting. "Thank you," I said. "You overwhelm me."

"I love you," he said, turning his helmet. His face lay in shadow. All I could see were his eyes glittering.

"You can't," I answered, shaking my head.

"Look at this," Charles said, lifting his arms like a priest beneath a cathedral dome. His voice quavered. "I work on my instincts. We don't have much time to make important decisions. We're fireflies, a brief glow then gone. I say I love you and I mean it."

"You don't give me time to make up my own mind!" I cried.

We fell silent for a moment. "You're right," Charles said.

I took a deep breath, sucking back my wash of emotions, clutching my hands to keep them from trembling. "Charles, I never expected any of this. You have to give me room to breathe."

"I'm sorry," he said, almost below pickup range for his helmet. "We should go back now."

I didn't want to go back. All of my life I would remember this, the sort of romantic moment and scene I had secretly dreamed of, though stretched beyond what I could have possibly imagined; the kind of setting and sweeping, impassioned declarations I had hoped for since such ideas had even glimmered in me. That it aroused so much conflict baffled me.

Charles was giving me everything he had.

* * *

On the way back to the tractor, with ten minutes before we started using reserves, Charles knelt and chipped a square from the Glass Sea bed. He handed it to me. "I know you probably already have some," he said. "But this is from me."

Leave it to Charles, I thought, *to give me flowers made of stone.* I slipped the small slab of rock into my pouch. We climbed into the tractor, pressurized, and helped each other suck dust from our suits with a hose.

Charles seemed almost grim as he took the stick and propelled the tractor forward. We circled and climbed out of the canyon in painful silence.

I made my decision. Charles was passionate and dedicated. He *cared* about things. We had been through a lot together, and he had proven himself courageous and reliable and sensible. He felt strongly about me.

I would be a fool not to return his feelings. I had already convinced myself that my qualms before had come from cowardice and inexperience. As I looked at him then—he refused to look at me, and his face was flushed—I said, "Thank you, Charles. I'll treasure this."

He nodded, intent on dodging a field of boulders.

"In a special place in my heart, I love you, too," I said. "I really do."

The stiffness in his face melted then, and I saw how terrified he had been. I laughed and reached out to hug him. "We are so—*weird*," I said.

He laughed as well and there were tears in his eyes. I was impressed by my power to please.

That evening, as the temperature outside the station dipped to minus eighty, the walls and tunnel linings of the warrens creaked and groaned, and we dragged our beds together in the boss's sleeping quarters. Charles and I kissed, undressed, and we made love.

I don't know to this day whether I was his first woman. It didn't matter then, and it certainly doesn't matter now. He did not seem inexperienced, but Charles showed an aptitude for catching on quickly, and he excited and pleased me, and I was sure that what I felt was love. It had to be; it was right, it was mutual ... and it gave me a great deal of pleasure.

I delighted in his excitement, and after, we talked with an ease and directness impossible before.

"What are you going to do?" I asked him, nested in the crook of his arm. I felt secure.

"When I grow up, you mean?"

"Yeah."

He shook his head and his brows came together. He had thick, expressive eyebrows and long lashes. "I want to understand," he said.

"Understand what?" I asked, smoothing the silky black hair on his forearm.

"Everything," he said.

"You think that's possible?"

"Yeah."

"What would it be like? Understanding everything—how everything works, physics, I guess you mean."

"I'd like to know that, too," he said. I thought he might be joking with me, but lifting my eyes, I saw he was dead serious. "How about you?" he asked, blinking and shivering slightly.

I scowled. "God, I've been trying to figure that out for years now. I'm really interested in management—politics, I guess would be the Earth word. Mars is really weak that way."

"President of Mars," Charles said solemnly. "I'll vote for you."

I cuffed his arm. "Statist," I said.

Waiting for sleep, I thought this part of my life had a clear direction. For the first time as an adult, I slept with someone and did not feel the inner bite of adolescent loneliness, but instead, a familial sense of belonging, the ease of desire satisfied by a dear friend.

I had a lover. I couldn't understand why I had felt so much confusion and hesitation.

The next day, we made love again—of course—and after, strolling through the tunnels with mugs of breakfast soup, I helped Charles inspect the station. Every few years, an active station—whether deserted or not—had to be surveyed by humans and the findings submitted to the Binding Multiples Habitat Board. All habitable stations were listed on charts, and had to be ready for emergency use by anybody. Trés Haut Médoc needed new arbeiters and fresh emergency supplies. Emergency medical nano had gone stale. The pumps probably needed an engineering refit to fix deep structural wear that could not be self-repaired.

After finishing diagnostics on the main pumps, still caught up in yesterday's trip and my deep-time shock, I asked Charles what puzzled him most about the universe.

"It's a problem of management," he said, smiling.

"That's it," I said huffily. "Talk down to my level."

"Not at all. How does everything know where and what it is? How does everything talk to every other thing, and what or who listens?"

"Sounds spooky," I said.

"Very spooky," he agreed.

"You think the universe is a giant brain."

"Not at all, madam," he said, letting a diagnostic lead curl itself into his slate. He tucked the slate into his belt. "But it's stranger than anyone ever imagined. It's a kind of computational system ... nothing but information talking to itself. That much seems clear. I want to know how it talks to itself, and how we can listen in ... and maybe add to the conversation. Tell it what to do."

"You mean, we can persuade the universe to change?"

"Yeah," he said blandly.

"That's possible?" I asked.

"I'd bet my life on it," Charles said. "At least my future. Have you ever wondered why we're locked in status quo?"

Cultural critics and even prominent thinkers in the Triple had speculated on the lack of major advances in recent decades. There had been progress—on Earth, the escalation of the dataflow revolution—that had produced surface changes, extreme refinements, but there had not been a paradigm shift for almost a century. Some said that a citizen of Earth in 2071 could be transported to 2171 and recognize almost everything she saw ... This, after centuries of extraordinary change.

"If we could access the Bell Continuum, the forbidden channels where all the universe does its bookkeeping ..." He smiled sheepishly. "We'd break the status quo wide open. It would be the biggest revolution of all time ... much bigger than nano. Do you ever watch cartoons?"

"What are those?"

"Animations from the twentieth century. Disney cartoons, Bugs Bunny, Road Runner, Tom and Jerry."

"I've seen a few," I said.

"I used to watch them all the time when I was a kid. They were cheap—public domain—and they fascinated me. Still do. I watched them and tried to understand how a universe like theirs would make sense. I even worked up some math. Observer-biased reality—nobody falls until he knows he's over the edge of a cliff ... Instant regeneration of damaged bodies, no consequences, continuous flows of energy, limited time, inconsistent effects from similar causes. Pretty silly stuff, but it made me think."

"Is that how our universe works?" I asked.

"Maybe more than we realize! I'm fascinated by concepts of other realities, other ways of doing things. Nothing is fixed, nothing sacred, nothing metaphysically determined—it's all contingent on process and evolution. That's perfect. It means we might be able to understand, if we can just *relax* and shed our preconceptions."

When we finished the survey, we had no further excuses to stay, and only a few hours before we had to return the tractor to Shrinktown.

Charles seemed dispirited.

"I really don't want to go back. This place is ideal for being alone."

"Not exactly ideal," I said, sliding an arm around his waist. We bumped hips down the tunnel from the pump to the *cuvée*.

"Nobody bothers us, there's things to see and places to go . . ."

"There's always the wine," I said.

He looked at me as if I were the most important person in the world. "It'll be tough going home and not seeing you for a while."

I hadn't given much thought to that. "We're supposed to be responsible adults now."

"I feel pretty damned responsible," Charles said. We paused outside the *cuvée* hatch. "I want to partner with you."

I was shocked by how fast things were moving. "Lawbond?"

"I'd strike a contract."

That was the Martian term, but somehow it seemed less romantic—and for that reason barely less dangerous—than saying, "Get married."

He felt me shiver and held me tighter, as if I might run away. "Pretty damned big and fast," I said.

"Time," Charles said with sepulchral seriousness. He smiled. "I don't have the patience of rocks. And you are incredible. You are what I need."

I put my hands on his shoulders and held him at elbow's length, examining his face, my heart thumping again. "You scare me, Charles Franklin. It isn't nice to scare people."

He apologized but did not loosen his grip.

"I don't think I'm old enough to get married," I said.

"I don't expect an answer right away," Charles said. "I'm just telling you that my intentions are *honorable*." He hammed the word to take away its stodgy, formal sense, but didn't succeed. *Honorable* was something that might concern my father, possibly my mother, but I wasn't sure it concerned me.

Again, confusion, inner contradictions coming to the surface. But I wasn't about to let them spoil what we had here. I touched my finger to his lips. "Patience," I said, as lovingly as possible. "Whether we're rock or not. This is big stuff for mere people."

"You're right," he said. "I'm pushing again."

"I wouldn't have known how good a lover you are," I said, "if you hadn't been a little pushy."

I napped on the trip back to Shrinktown. The tractor found its way home like a faithful horse. Charles nudged me two hours before our arrival and I came awake apologizing. I didn't want him to feel neglected. I turned to watch the short rooster tail of dust behind, then faced Charles in the driver's seat. "Thank you," I said.

"For what?"

"For being pushy." I was about to say, "For making a woman out of me," but the humor might not have been obvious, and I didn't want him to think I was being flippant about what had happened.

"I'm good at that," he said.

"You're good at a lot of things."

I had promised my family I would spend time at Ylla, my home station, before returning to school. There was a week left for that, but I had to go to Durrey to catch the main loop trains north. Charles would stay in Shrinktown a few more days.

We parked the tractor in the motor pool garage and kissed passionately, then walked to the Shrinktown station, promising to get together when school resumed.

When I got back to Durrey, Diane Johara—again my roommate—opened the door and smiled expectantly at me. "How was he?" she asked.

"Who?"

"Charles Franklin."

I had told her I was going on a trip Up but hadn't given any specifics. "Have you been snooping?" I asked.

"Not at all. While I was out at the family farm, our room took messages. One of them is from a Charles at Shrinktown depot. Where's your slate?"

I grimaced, remembering I had left my slate in the tractor by accident. Maybe that was why Charles was calling. "I've misplaced it," I said.

Diane lifted an eyebrow. "I looked at the list when we got back. The same Charles we suffered with at UMS, I assume."

"We went fossil-hunting," I said.

"For three days . . . ?"

"Your nose is sharp, Diane," I said.

She followed me into my curtained area. I pulled the cot from the wall and flopped my case on the blanket.

"He seemed very nice," Diane said.

"You want gory details?" I asked, exasperated.

Diane shrugged. "Confession is good for the soul."

"You must have had a boring time at the farm."

"The farm is always a dusting bore. Nothing but brothers and married cousins. But a great swimming hole. You should come with me sometime. Might meet someone you like. You'd be good for our family, Casseia."

"What makes you think I'd transfer my contract?"

"We have so much to offer," she said brightly.

"You're a top pain, Diane." I unpacked quickly and folded everything into drawers. The thought of being alone for the rest of the vacation seemed bleak.

"Any good males in your family?" she asked. "I'd transfer contracts . . . for someone like *Charles*."

A few months before, I would have stuck my tongue out at her, or thrown a pillow. Somehow that seemed undignified. I had a lover—*was* a lover—and that demanded maturity in some ways even more than being in the UMS action did.

"All right. I went with Charles to a family station," I admitted. "He's nice."

"He's pretty," Diane said wistfully. "I'm happy for you, Casseia."

I rolled up my bag. "Can I listen to my messages in private?"

"Now you can," Diane said.

The message from Charles made my heart pound. He was still pushing.

An hour after arriving at Shrinktown, Charles had recorded, "You left your slate in my bag. I'm sending in to your home station now. I just wanted to make sure you understand that I'm serious. I love you and I don't think I'll ever find another woman like you. I know you need time. But I know we can share our dreams. I miss you already."

He was more impressed with me than I was. I sat on the edge of the cot, scared out of my wits.

I lay awake that night, aroused by the floating memories of Charles. It had been so confusing and so wonderful, but I knew I was too young to get married. Some did lawbond at my age: those who had morphed their futures since second form, who knew what they wanted and how to get it.

If I told Charles I did not wish to marry now, he would smile and say, "You have all the time you need." And that wasn't the answer I wanted to hear. The truth was, what needed to mature in me was my whole approach to mixing the inner life with the outer. What if Charles was not ideally suited for me? Why settle for something less than the best?

I shook my head bitterly, feeling so very selfish and even treasonous. Charles had given me everything. How could I refuse?

How could I think such thoughts and yet still profess, even to myself, that I loved him?

I sent a text message back, not trusting my voice: *The time at Trés Haut Médoc was lovely. I'll treasure it always. I can't talk about going lawbond because I am much less sure of myself than you seem to be. I want to see you as soon as possible. We need to get together with our friends and do all sorts of things before we can even think about commitment, don't you agree?*

I signed off with *Love, Casseia Majumdar.* I had signed letters to distant relatives that way. Not *I love you,* a strong declaration, but simply, tersely, *Love.* Charles would be hurt by that. It hurt me to write it and not change it . . .

But I sent the message. I left a farewell message on the room for Diane, who was staying at Durrey to study in privacy.

Then I boarded the train to North Solis. I leaned my head against the double-paned glass and looked out at nighttime Mars, at Phobos like a dull searchlight above the glooming hills west of Durrey.

I am frightened, I told myself. *I can never again be what I was. I can never be to another what I was to Charles. Something has ended and I am afraid.*

I made the trip across Claritas Fossae back to Jiddah Planum and Ylla, the bosom of my family, greeting my parents and brother with affection, falsely trying to convey a jaunty air of self-assurance, everything's fine here, I'm just the same as always. *But I'm a lover now, Father. Mom, I've had a man, and it was wonderful . . . I mean,* he *was wonderful, and I think I'm in love, but it's going very fast, and God I wish I could talk to you, really talk . . .*

Charles did not respond for three days.

Perhaps he had plumbed the depths of my character and decided he had made a serious mistake. Perhaps he had seen through to my basic immaturity and insincerity and decided to write me off as a Shinktown sweet after all.

My slate was delivered by postal arbeiter, but I had already ordered another, not trusting the room to record all my messages. I could not concentrate on planning my next octant's curriculum. I was a nervous wreck.

I hated the suspense and uncertainty. I had felt I was in control and had lost that control and now it was my turn to be played on the line like a fish. Irritation turned to numb sadness. But I did not call him.

At the end of three days, as I undressed for a very lonely bed, Charles called me direct.

I robed and took his call in my room. His image came clear as life over my bed. He looked exhausted and sounded devastated and his face was ghostly pale. "I'm really sorry I've been out of touch," he said. "I wish we could talk in person. It's been a nightmare here."

"What's wrong?" I asked.

"Our BM has had all of its Earth contracts severed. I had to fly to McAuliff Valley for a family meeting. I'm there now. God, I'm sorry, you must have thought—"

"I'm fine," I said. "I didn't hear anything on the nets."

"It's not public yet. Don't tell anybody, Casseia. I think we're being voided because our Lunar branch is starting up major prochine operations in Lagrange. Earth doesn't like it. The Greater East-West Alliance, actually, but it might as well be the whole Earth."

GEWA—pronounced *Jee-wah*, an economic union of Asia, North America, India and Pakistan, the Philippines, and parts of the Malay Archipelago—had been causing problems for a number of BMs, including Majumdar.

"Is it really that bad?"

"We can't ship any goods to Earth, and we can't exchange process data with GEWA signatories."

"How does that affect you?" I asked.

"We're looking at an across-the-board loss for the next five Earth years. My scholarship is down the tubes," Charles said. "I had hoped to join the Trans-Mars Physics Co-op for my fifth-form studies. If Klein can't ante up, I can't pay my share, and I don't even go to fifth form."

"Damn," I said. "I know how much that means—"

"It puts everything on hold, Casseia. What you said . . . about taking time to think things through . . ." His voice shook and he worked to control it. "Casseia, I can't possibly go lawbond, I don't have any prospects for scholarship—"

"It's okay," I said.

"I feel like an idiot. Everything was going so well, maybe, I thought, maybe we can—"

"Yeah." I hurt for him.

"I'm sorry."

"You don't need to be."

"I love you so much."

"Yeah," I said.

"I want to see you. As soon as I'm free here—we have some family decisions to make, consensus on BM direction, response, and so on—"

"Serious. I know."

"I want to get together. At Durrey, when we go back, or at Ylla, wherever. No pressure, just . . . see you."

"I want to see you, too."

He reaffirmed that he loved me, and we mumbled our way through farewells. His image faded and I took a deep breath and got a drink of water.

Charles was in trouble and that took pressure off me, and I felt guilty relief. I knew I had to talk to someone, soon, but my Mother and Father certainly would not do . . .

I called Diane.

She answered with vid off, then switched it on. She wore a ragged blue robe she had treasured since girlhood. She had caked her hair with Vivid, a mud-colored treatment she was addicted to. It rolled slowly on her scalp. "I know, I know, I'm ugly," she said. "What's up?"

I told her about Charles's situation. I told her he had asked me to lawbond and that we couldn't now. That I was and had been very confused.

She whistled and dropped onto her cot. "Lightspeed kind of guy, isn't he?" she asked, narrowing her eyes. Talking remote was never the same as being in the same room, especially for a good heartfelt, but Diane's manner cut the distance. "You told him to go slow, I hope."

"I don't think he can. He sounds so in love."

"That's either wonderful, or he's grit. How do you feel?"

"He is so sincere and . . . he's so sweet, I feel guilty not dropping my tanks and digging in."

"Well, he's your first, and that's sweet alone. But you're not telling Aunt Di how you feel. Do you love him?"

"I'm worried I'm going to hurt him."

"Ah. I mean, uh-oh."

"You sound *experienced*," I said testily, knotting my fingers.

"I wish I were. Casseia, stop pacing and relax. You're giving me an ache."

I sat.

"You went with him to Trés Haut Médoc. He wasn't just climbing into your suit. You must have seen something special in him. Do you love him?"

"Yes," I said.

"But you don't want to lawbond."

"Not right away."

"Ever?"

I shook my head, neither yes nor no. "Don't tell me I'm a fool not to, because he's pretty and kind. I know that already."

"No such, Casseia. Although I'm a bit envious. He *is* smart, he *was* good—I assume—"

"He was *very good*," I cried.

"And he's willing to wait. So wait."

I pressed my lips together and stared at her. "What if I decide not to lawbond? Would that be fair? He'd have wasted time on me . . ."

"God, Casseia, I hope no sophisticated Terrie ever hears this. We Martians are such *serious* folk. Love is never wasted. Do you want to dump him now and try someone else?"

"No!" I said angrily.

"Hey, it *is* an option. Nobody's forcing you to do anything. Don't forget that."

Talking with her simply dropped me deeper. "I feel really terrible now," I said. "I'd better go."

"Not on your life. Why are you so charged about this?"

"Because if I love him, I should feel differently. I should feel all one way, not three ways. I should be happy and giving."

"You're ten years old, Casseia. Young love is never perfect."

"He uses Earth years," I lamented.

"Ah, a fault! What other faults does he have?"

"He's so smart. I can't understand anything about his work."

"Take a course. He doesn't want you for a lab assistant or fraulein arbeiter, does he?"

"When I'm away from him, I don't know what to feel."

Diane wrinkled her face is disgust. "All right, we're running in circles. Who's waiting in a side tunnel?"

"Nobody," I said.

"You know how men react to you. You're attractive. Charles isn't the only slim and randy buck on Mars. You can afford to relax a bit. What do you know about him? You know his family isn't rich . . . his BM is in trouble with Earth . . . he wants to be a physicist and understand everything. He's pretty he's gentle, he's rugged on the Up . . . God, Casseia, I'm going to hit you if you just *void* him!"

I shook my hanging head. "I've got to go, Diane."

"Sorry I'm not helping."

"It's okay."

"Do you love him, Casseia?" she asked again, eyes sharp.

"No!" I fumbled to hit the vid off. I missed.

"Don't cut me now, roomie," Diane said. "You don't love him at all?"

"I can't. Not now. Not one hundred per."

"You're positive?"

I nodded.

"Could you come to love him, someday?"

I stared at her blankly. "He's very persuasive," I said.

"One hundred per?"

"Probably not. No. I don't think so."

"Be kind, then. Tell him honestly how you feel right now."

"I will."

She looked away for a moment, then brought up her slate. "You know me," she said. "Always squirreling. Well, I have something interesting here, if you want to know about it."

"What?" I asked.

"Charles may be rugged on the Up and good in bed, but he has plans, Casseia. Have you checked up on your friend?"

"No."

"I always make sure I know as much as possible about my male friends. Men can be so tortuous."

I wondered what she was going to throw at me now, and my shoulders tensed: that he was actually a Statist, that he had been spying for Caroline Connor in the trench domes.

"This doesn't toss any sand on how nice a guy he is, but our good Charles wants to be a *real* physicist, Casseia. He's applied to be a subject for enhancement research."

"So? It's the pro thing. Even Majumdar accepts it."

"Yeah. And on Earth, everybody does it. But Charles has applied to be hooked to a Quantum Logic thinker."

I fell silent for a moment. "Where d-did you learn that?"

"Open records, medically oriented research applications, UMS. He put in the request early last summer, before the trench domes."

My insides sank. "Oh, God," I said.

"Hey, we don't know much about such a link."

"Nobody can even *talk* to a QL thinker!" I said.

"I didn't want to puddle your dust, Casseia, but I thought you'd want to know."

"Oh."

"When will you be back?"

I mumbled an answer and cut the vid. My head seemed filled with foam. I didn't know whether to be angry or to cry.

On Mars, we had escaped most of the ferment of enhancements and transforms and nanomorphing commonplace on Earth. We were used to low-level enhancements, genetic correction, and therapy for serious mental disorders, but most

Martians eschewed the extreme possibilities. Some weren't available off Earth; some just didn't suit our pragmatic, pioneer tastes. I think the cultural consensus was that Mars would let Earth and, to a lesser extent, the Moon try the radical treatments, and Mars would sit the revolution out for a decade or two and await the results.

If what Diane had learned was true—and I couldn't think of any reason to doubt her—Charles seemed ready to zip right to the cutting edge.

What had been youthful ambivalence before ramped to near-panic now. How could I maintain any kind of normal relationship with Charles when he would spend much of his mental life listening to the vagaries of Quantum Logic? Why would he want that in the first place?

The answer was clear—to make him a better physicist. Quantum Logic reflected the way the universe operated at a deep level. Human logic—and the mathematical neural logic of most thinkers—worked best on the slippery surface of reality.

What I knew of these topics, I had picked from school studies and mass LitVid, where physically and mentally enhanced heroes dominated Terrie youth programming. But in truth, I understood very little about Quantum Logic or QL thinkers.

One last question chased me through the rest of the day, through dinner with my parents and brother, through the BM social hour and tea dance later in the evening, into a sleepless bed: *Why didn't Charles tell me?*

He hadn't given me everything, after all.

Early the next morning, my mother and I planned my education through the next few years. I wasn't in the mood, but it had to be done, so I put on as brave and cheerful a face as I could manage. Father and Stan had gone to an inter-BM conference on off-Mars asset control; our branch of the family had traditionally served the Majumdar BM by directing the family's involvement in Triple finances, and Stan was following that road. I was still interested in management and political theory, even more now that I had spend a few months away from such courses. The UMS action, and my time with Charles, had sharpened my resolve.

Mother was a patient woman, too patient I thought, but I was grateful to have her sympathy now. She had never approved of political process; my grandmother had left the Moon in protest when it had reshaped its constitution, and her daughter had retained a typical Lunar sense of rugged individualism.

Both Mother and I knew what I owed to the family: that beginning in another year or so, I would become useful to the BM, or get lawbonded, transfer, and become useful to another BM. Political studies did not seem particularly useful to anybody at this time.

Still, if I wanted to study state theory and large-scale govmanagement, she would go along ... after voicing a quiet, polite protest.

That took about five minutes, and I sat stolidly, hearing her through. She discussed the difficulties of politics in BM-centered economies; she told me that the best and most lasting contributions could be made within one's own BM, or as a BM-elected representative to the Council, and even that was something of a chore and not a privilege.

She made her points, a restrained but heartfelt version of Grandmother's Lunar cry of "Cut the politics!" and I said in reply, "It's the only thing that really interests me, Mother. Somebody has to study the process; the BMs have to interact with each other and with the Triple. That's just common sense."

She leaned her head to one side and gave me what Father called her enigma look, which I had seen many times before, and never been able to describe. A loving, suffering, patiently expectant expression, I can say now after decades of thought, but that still doesn't do it justice. This time, it might have meant, "Yes, and it's the world's third-oldest profession, but I wouldn't want *my* daughter doing it."

"You're not going to change your mind, are you?"

"I don't think so."

"Then let's do it right," she said.

We sat in the dining room, poring over prospectuses as they flitted around us in stylish picts and texts, symbols and previews of various curriculums vying to draw us in deeper. Mother sighed and shook her head. "None of these are very enticing," she said. "All entry-level stuff."

"A few look interesting."

"You say you're serious about this?"

"Yes."

"Then Martian political theory won't be enough. It's small grit compared to Terrie boulders."

"But Terrie eds are expensive—"

"And probably biased toward Earth history and practices, God forbid," she added. "But they're still the best for what you seem to want."

"I don't want to ask for something nobody else in the family has gotten."

"Why not?" she asked brightly, enjoying the chance to seem perverse.

"It doesn't seem right."

"Nobody in our branch of Majumdar has gone out for govmanagement. Finance, economics, but never system-wide politics."

"I'm a freak," I said.

She shook her head. "Recognizably my daughter, however. I'll clear for it if you really want it."

"Mother, we couldn't afford more than a year—"

"I'm not talking about autocourse eds," she said. "If you aim for the stars, pick the bright ones. The least you should settle for is a Majumdar scholarship and apprenticeship."

I hadn't even dreamed of such a thing. "Apprenticed to whom?"

She made a wry face. "Who in our family knows the most about politics, particularly Earth politics? Your third uncle."

"Bithras?"

"If your father and the BM pedagogues approve. I couldn't get that for you by myself; I'm still a bit of an outsider at that level. I'm not sure your father could pull enough strings and call in enough favors. We've only met Bithras three times since you were born—and he's never met you—"

"What would I do?"

"Inter-BM affairs, and of course Triple affairs. Attend the Council meetings, I assume, and study the Charter and the business law books."

"It would be perfect," I mused.

"Next best thing to a real government to study. We tend to neglect that kind of management at the station level, and for that I'm thankful."

"But I'd still need Terrie autocourses to fill out my currie."

She smiled cagily. "Of course." She touched my nose lightly with her finger. "But they wouldn't go on *our* tab. All educational costs for apprenticeship are billed to the high family budget."

"You've been giving this some thought behind my back," I accused.

"I've put up with your eccentricities," she said with a lift of her chin and stretch of her neck, "because we try to encourage independent thinking in our young folks. We hope they'll experiment. But I honestly never thought I'd see a daughter of mine go into politics—"

"Govmanagement," I amended.

"For a career," she said. "I'm put off by it, of course, and I'm also intrigued. After a few years studying the Council, what can you teach *me* when we argue?"

"We never argue," I said, hugging her.

"Never," she affirmed. "But your father thinks we do."

I let her go and stood back. With this much resolved, I needed to solve another problem. "Mother, I'd like to ask somebody to visit Ylla. Somebody from Durrey. He needs a vacation—he's had some pretty bad news—"

"Charles Franklin from Klein," my mother said.

I hadn't mentioned him.

She smiled and gave me another enigma look. "His mother called to see if you were worthy of her son."

My shock must have showed. "How could she?" And behind that question, *How could he talk about me with his parents?*

"Her only child is very important to her."

"But we're adults!"

"She seemed nice and she didn't ask any leading questions. She thinks Charles is a wonderful young man, of course, and from what she tells me, I don't disagree. I assume you think he's wonderful. Is he?"

I sputtered, trying to express my indignation. She put a finger to my lips. "It's traditional for us to drive you crazy," she said. "Think of it as revenge for when you were two years old. Charles is welcome any time."

Mars supported four million citizens and about half a million prospective citizens, a little less the population of the old United States in 1800.

Some prospective citizens were Eloi emigrating from Earth, starting fresh on Mars, where going for Ten Cubed—a life span of at least one thousand Earth years—was not just accepted, but ignored. Earth forbade life spans artificially extended much over two hundred years, forcing the Eloi to emigrate elsewhere or reverse their treatments. Mars accepted a hefty fee from Earth for taking in each and every Eloi—though it was not widely advertised.

Some immigrating to Mars were pioneers pure and simple, heading out from Earth or Moon to find a simpler and more basic existence. They must have found Mars a disappointment—we had long since spun beyond the era of foamed rock insulation and narrow tunnels between trench domes.

I met Charles at the Kowloon depot, ten kilometers from our home warrens at Ylla. As Charles took his bag from the arbeiter, I spotted Sean Dickinson in a train window. Even with less than five million humans (and perhaps three hundred legally recognized thinkers) spread out over a land area equal to Earth's, Mars was positively cozy. You couldn't help running into people you knew, wherever you went. Sean and I exchanged cordial nods. I pointedly embraced Charles. Sean watched us impassively as the train slid out of the depot.

"I am *incredibly* glad to see you," Charles said.

I made a warm sound and squeezed his hand. "That was Sean," I said. "Did you see him?"

"Sat with him," Charles said. "He seems more cheerful than when we last met. He told me to apologize for making stupid accusations against you. He's going south. I didn't ask where."

"That's nice," I said, and my face warmed. "Welcome to Jiddah Planum. Accountants, investment analysts, small engineering firms. No fossils to speak of, even Glass Sea."

"You're here, and that's enough," Charles said. We crossed the walkways to the lounge and booked tickets for the return. Ylla dug into the northern outskirts of Jiddah Planum. Smaller, slower trains fanned from Kowloon to Jiddah and Ylla and even smaller stations east.

Charles's face seemed thinner. We had been apart for just over a week, yet he had changed drastically in both feature and mood. He held me close as we boarded our train, and fell back into his seat with a sigh. "God, it is good to see you," he said. "Tell me what you've been doing."

"I told you in my letters," I said.

"Tell me in person. I worried, just getting letters."

"Letters require much more effort," I said.

"Tell me."

I told him about applying for a Majumdar apprenticeship. He approved without reservation. "Brave and noble Casseia," he said. "Go right to the top in the face of tradition."

"Just my father," I said. "My mother's actually pretty neutral about politics."

"We're none of us going to be neutral for long," Charles said. "Klein is wounded. Others are going to be hit next."

"By Earth? By GEWA?"

He shrugged and looked out the window at the dull ochre prairies and shallow, kilometer-wide valleys and ditches called fossas. "We're some sort of threat. Nobody seems to know what sort, but they're using obvious muscle on us. We're going to the Charter Council next week to ask for solidarity and relief."

"Relief?" I was incredulous; Martian BMs rarely asked for relief. So much had to be conceded with competing BMs to get inter-family guarantees.

"We're in big trouble, as I said. I hope Majumdar misses all this."

"What will you do if you get the Council to call for solidarity? That's the step before appealing for unified action by all the BMs—"

"Shh," he said, holding up a finger. "Don't use that word, *united*." He smiled, but the smile was not convincing.

"How did you get time off to come here?"

"I've done my share and more in the planning phase. I have three days before I return."

"The next eighth at Durrey starts in four days," I said.

"I'll have to miss it."

"You're quitting school?"

"Family emergency sabbatical," he said. "I'll be on call until the crisis passes."

"That could put you a year behind . . ."

"Martian year," Charles said, patting my arm. "I'll make it. Just my luck to be in a vulnerable BM. If you're going into high-level govmanagement, maybe we can transfer your contract . . ."

Suddenly that wasn't funny. I turned away, unable to hide my irritation, and Charles was dismayed. "I'm sorry," he said. "I'm not being disrespectful. I really wanted to come here and persuade you to . . . and you said . . . I know, Casseia, I'm sorry."

"Never mind." He was missing the cause of my anger, couldn't possibly understand—not yet. "We have a lot to talk about, Charles."

"So serious," he said. He closed his eyes and leaned against the headrest. "This isn't going to be a vacation?"

"Of course it is," I said. That wasn't quite a lie.

Charles arrived in the middle of a most unusual paucity—most of my blood relations and relations by marriage, who normally trooped through Ylla and our warrens like a herd of friendly cats, had trooped elsewhere, spreading out across Mars on errands or vacations. We would have a rare time of privacy, and neither Charles nor I would have to suffer the staring eyes of curious urchins, impolite questions from my aunts, hints of liaisons from my elder cousins. Even my brother was away. Ylla Station would be empty and quiet, and for this I was supremely grateful.

Ylla occupied sixty hectares of an almost featureless prairie of little interest but for aquifers and solid ice lenses. Prospectors had mapped out a chain of stations along the Athene Aquifer in the first decade of the Mars expansion, thirty years ago; three of a possible six had been built, Ylla the first. It had originally been known as Where's Ylla.

The lack of sentient Martians had disappointed few. Martian settlers landing on their new home, and taking station assignments, quickly became hard-bitten and practical; it was no picnic. Keeping a station open and staying alive was tough enough in those decades without having to deal with unhappy natives. Still, I had played Ylla as a girl, and my brother had played the defensive Mr. Ttt with his gun of golden bees, stalking human astronauts ...

I related much of this nervously to Charles as the small train whined over the ditches and onto the main prairie, trying to keep an appearance of calm when in fact I was miserable. I had asked Charles to come to Ylla to ask him a question I now thought rude and unnecessary; rude, because he would have mentioned his desire to be enhanced had he wished to, and unnecessary, because I was determined to end our brief relationship. But I couldn't simply tell him on the train.

And I couldn't tell him at dinner. My parents of course

went all-out with this meal, celebrating the first time I had brought a young man to our station.

Father was particularly interested in Charles, asking endless questions about the Terrie embargoes on Klein. Charles answered politely and to the best of his knowledge; there was no reason to keep any of this secret from someone as highly placed as Father.

My parents generally eschewed nano food, preferring garden growth and syn products. We ate potato and syn cheese pie and fruit salad and for desert, my father's syn prime cheesecake with hot tea. After dinner, we sat in the memory room, small and tightly decorated as most old Mars station rooms are, with the inevitable living shadow box from Earth, the self-cycling fish tank, the small, antique wall-mount projectors for LitVid.

I loved my parents, and what they felt was important to me, but their immediate and natural affection for Charles was distressing. Charles fit right in. He and my father leaned forward in their chairs, almost knocking heads, talking about the possibility of hard financial times ahead, like old friends.

Inevitably, Father asked him what he planned to do with himself.

"A lot of things," Charles answered. "I'm much too ambitious for a Martian."

Mother offered him more tea. "We don't see any reason why Martians shouldn't be ambitious," she said, lips pursed as if mildly chiding.

"It's simply impractical to do what I want to do, here, at this time," Charles said. He shook his head and grinned awkwardly. "I'm not very practical."

"Why?" Father asked.

He has come all this way to be with me, I thought, *and he spends this time talking with my parents . . . about what he is going to do in* physics.

"Mars doesn't have the research tools necessary, not yet, perhaps not for decades," Charles said. "There are only two thinkers on the planet dedicated to physics, and a few dozen barely adequate computers tied up in universities with long waiting lists. I'm too young to get on any of the lists. My work is too primitive. But ..." He stopped, hands held in mid-air, parallel to each other, emphasizing his point with a little jerking gesture. "The work I hope to do would take all of Earth's resources."

"Then why not go to Earth?" my father asked.

"Why not?" I put in. "It would be a marvelous experience."

"No chance," Charles said. "My grades aren't perfect, my psych evaluations aren't promising, to work on Earth they make outsiders pass rigid tests ... We have to be ten times better than any Terrie."

My father smelled a young man with ambitions but insufficient drive. "You have to do what you have to do," he said gruffly.

Instantly I was on Charles's side, saying abruptly, "Charles knows what to do. He knows more than most Terrestrials."

My father lifted an eyebrow at the vehemence of my defense. Charles took my hand in appreciation.

"Worse scholars than you have filtered through," Father said. "You just have to know how to handle people."

"I don't know anything about handling people," Charles said. "I've never known anything but how to be straight with them."

He looked at me as if that were a trait I might admire, and though I thought it disingenuous, not admirable, I smiled. Concern passed from his face in a flash, replaced by adoration. His brown eyes even crossed a little, like a puppy's. I turned away, not wanting to have such an effect on him. I wanted to be away from my parents, alone with Charles, to express my affection but tell him this was not the time. I felt horrible and a little queasy.

"Casseia would go to Earth in a moment if the opportunity arose," my mother said. "Wouldn't you?" She grinned at me proudly.

I stared at the fish tank, sealed decades ago on Earth, lovingly tended by my father and given to my mother on the day of their nuptials. "Nobody's offered," I said.

"You're good, though," Charles said. "You can jump the hurdles. You have a way with people."

"Our sentiments exactly," Father said, smiling proudly. "She just needs a little self-confidence. Support from people other than her parents."

Father took me aside while Mother and Charles talked. "You're not happy, Casseia," he said. "I see it, your mother sees it—Charles must see it. Why?"

I shook my head. "This is going all wrong," I said. "You *like* him."

"Why shouldn't we?"

"I asked him here . . . to talk with him. And I can't be alone with him to talk . . ."

Father smiled. "You can be alone later."

"That isn't why I'm unhappy. You're examining him as if I'm going to *lawbond* him."

My father narrowed one eye and stared at me like a prospector examining a vein in rock. "He meets my approval so far."

"He's a friend, and he's here to talk. I'm not asking for your approval."

"We're embarrassing you?"

"I just have some important things to talk about with him, and this is taking so much *time*."

"Sorry," Father said. "I'll try to keep the inquisition short."

We returned to the memory room. Slowly, my father pried Mother away from the conversation and suggested they inspect the tea garden. When they were gone, Charles settled back contentedly, well-fed and relaxed. "They're good people," he said. "I can see where you come from."

He could have said anything and it would have irritated me. This irritated me more. "I'm my own woman," I said.

He lifted his hands helplessly and sighed. "Casseia, you're

going to tell me something. Tell me now. You're driving me muddy."

"Why didn't you say you applied for a link?"

He frowned. "Pardon?"

"You've applied to link with a QL thinker."

"Of course," he said, face blank. "So has a third of my physics fourth form."

"I know what a QL thinker is, Charles. I've heard what it can do to people . . ."

"It doesn't make them into monsters."

"It doesn't do them any good as human beings," I said.

"Is that what's going wrong between us?"

"No."

"Something *is* going wrong, though."

"What kind of life would there be for someone . . ." I was getting myself into a mire and couldn't find a solid path out.

"Married to a QL?" He seemed to think that was funny. "It was a whim, Casseia. It's been talked about on Earth. Some of our senior physicists think it could help break tough conceptual problems. It would be temporary."

"You didn't tell me," I said.

He tried to skirt the issue. "I'll never get the chance now," Charles said.

"But you didn't *tell* me."

"Is that what's upsetting you?"

"You didn't trust me enough to tell me." I couldn't believe we were getting stuck in the wrong topic . . . all to avoid the words I knew would be hurtful, words I actually had no clear reason for saying.

Here was Charles directly in front of me. Part of me—an energetic and substantial part—wanted to apologize to him, to take him to the tea garden and make love with him again. I would not allow that. I had reached my decision and I would follow through, no matter how painful for both of us.

"I have a lot of growing to do," I said.

"So do I. We—"

"But not together."

His mouth went slack and his eyes half-lidded. He looked down, closed his mouth, and said, "All right."

"We're both too young. I've enjoyed our time together."

"You invited me to meet your parents before telling me this? That's hardly fair. You've wasted their time."

"They like you as much as I do," I said. "I wanted to talk to you in a place I was familiar with, because this isn't easy for me to say. I *do* love you."

"Um hm." He wouldn't look at me directly. He kept searching the walls as if for a way to escape. "You wanted me to tell you about future plans that might never have happened, to get you upset over something . . . probably impossible. And you're disappointed."

"No." I thrust my jaw forward, pushing ahead despite the confusion, only now understanding the core of my response. "I'm telling you straight. Later, perhaps, when we've achieved something, when our minds are settled, when we know what we want to do—"

"I've known that since I was a boy," Charles said.

"Then you should have picked somebody more like you. I don't know what I'm going to do, or where it's going to take me."

Charles nodded. "I pushed too hard," he said.

"Damn it, stop that," I said. "You sound like a . . ."

"What?"

"Never mind." I just looked at him, eyes wide, trying to show the real affection I felt for him by the way my eyes tracked the points on his very fine face.

"You're not happy, are you?" he asked.

"We can't grow up in a couple of months," I said.

He held up his hands. "I want to be with you, make love with you, reach out to you . . . watch you when you go to sleep." I found that a particularly frightening picture: domestic coziness. Not what I imagined I needed at all. Youth is a time for adventure, for many changes, not for commitment and life spent on a fixed path. "You could teach me so much about politics and the way people work together. I need that.

I think so far into the abstract I get lost. You could balance me."

"I wonder if I'll ever be ready for that," I said. "It might be better if we stayed friends."

"We must always be friends," he said.

"Just friends, for now," I added gently.

"Wise Casseia," he said after a few seconds of silence. "I apologize for being so clumsy."

"Not at all," I said. "It's charming, really."

"Charming. Not convincing."

"I don't know what I want, Charles," I said. "I have to find out for myself."

"Do you believe in me?" he asked. "If you do, you'd know life with me will never be dull."

I have him a glance partly puzzled, partly irritated.

"I'm going to do important things. I don't know how long it will take me, Casseia, but I have glimmers even now. Places where I can contribute. The work I do on my own—I don't show it at the university—it's pretty good stuff. Not seminal, not yet, but pretty good, and it's only the warm-up."

I saw now, for the first time, another side of Charles, and I did not like it. His face wrinkled into a determined frown.

"You don't have to convince me you're smart," I said peevishly.

He took my shoulders, hands light but insistent. "It isn't just being smart," he said. "It's as if I can see into the future. I'll be doing really fine work, great work, and I sometimes think, whoever my partner is, she helps me do that work. I have to choose my partner, my friend, my lover, very carefully, because it isn't going to be easy."

I could have finished the conversation then with a handshake and a firm good-bye. I did not like this aspect of Charles. He was not half as smart as my father, I thought, yet he was full of himself, a raging egotist, full of such big ideas. "I have my own work to do," I said. "I need to be more than just somebody's partner, just a support for their work."

"Of course," he said, a little too quickly.

"I have to follow my own path, not just glue myself to someone and be dragged along," I said.

"Oh, of course." His face wrinkled again.

Charles, please don't cry, damn it, I thought.

"There's so much inside," he said. "I feel so strongly. I can't express myself adequately, and if I can't do that, I certainly can't convince you. But I've never met a woman like you."

You haven't met many women, I thought, not very kindly.

"Wherever you go, whatever we end up doing, I'll be waiting for you," he said.

I took his hand then, feeling this was an appropriate if not perfect way to get out of a tough situation. "I really feel strongly about you, Charles," I said. "I'll always care for you."

"You don't want to get married, something I can't do now anyway, and you knew that . . . So you don't want me to consider you a steady partner, or anything else, either. You don't want to see me again."

"I want the freedom to choose," I said. "I don't have that now."

"I'm in your way."

"Yes," I said.

"Casseia, I have never been so embarrassed and ashamed."

I stared at him without comprehending.

"You have a lot to learn about men."

"Of course."

"About people."

"No doubt."

"And you don't want to learn it from me. What did I do to you to make this end so soon?"

"Nothing!" I cried. I wouldn't be able to control myself much longer. It was agony to realize that after this, Charles would have to stay the night; there were no trains to the Kowloon depot at this hour. We would have to face each other in the morning, with my parents about.

"I would like to live alone, on my own, and make my own

life and see what I'm capable of," I said, half-mumbling. My eyes filled with tears and I lifted my head to keep them from spilling down my cheeks. "Don't wait for me. That isn't freedom."

He shook his head rapidly. "I did something wrong."

"No!" I shouted.

We hadn't left the memory room. I took his arm and led him to the warren hub, then opened the door to the tea garden tunnel. I pushed him through, teeth clenched.

The tea garden lay in a cylinder-shaped cell ten meters below the surface. Dense green bushes thrust from walls, ceiling, and floor toward a rippling sheet of portable sun. The leaves rustled in the circulating air. I held his arm and stopped at the south end of the cell.

"I'm the one who's done something wrong," I said. "It's me, not you."

"It felt so obvious. So true," Charles said.

"Maybe it would have been, three years from now, or five. But we've missed the timing. Who knows what we'll be doing then."

Charles sat on a bench. I sat beside him, wiping my eyes quickly with a sleeve. Only a few years ago I had given up playing with dolls and burying myself in LitVids about girlhood in Terrie Victorian times. How could this have come so fast?

"On Earth," Charles said, "they teach their kids all about sex and courtship and marriage."

"We're old-fashioned here," I said.

"We make mistakes out of ignorance."

"I'm ignorant, all right," I said. Our voices had returned to a normal tone of conversation. We might have been discussing a tea competition. *Martians dearly love their tea; I prefer pekoe. And you?*

"I won't apologize any more," he said, and he took my hand. I squeezed his fingers. "I meant what I said. And I tell you now . . . whenever you're ready, wherever we may be, I'll be there for you. I won't go away. I chose you, Casseia, and I won't be happy with anyone else. Until then, I'll be a friend. I won't expect anything from you."

I wanted to jump up and scream, *Charles, that is just so dumb, you don't get what I'm saying* ... But I didn't. Suddenly, I saw Charles very clearly as an arrow shot straight to the mark, with no time to lie or even to relax and play; a straight and honest man who would in fact be a wonderful and loving husband.

But not for me. My course could not follow his. I might never hit my mark, and I doubted our two marks would ever be the same.

I realized that I would miss him, and the pain became more intense than I could bear.

I left the tea garden. My father showed Charles the guest room.

After, Father came to my room. The door was sealed and I had turned the com off, but I heard his knock through the steel and foam. I let him in and he sat on the edge of my cot. "What is going on?" he asked.

I cried steadily and silently.

"Has he hurt you?"

"God, no," I said.

"Have you hurt him?"

"Yes."

Father shook his head and curled his lip before assuming a flat expression. "I won't ask anything more. You're my daughter. But I'm going to tell you something and you can take it for what it's worth. Charles seems to be in love with you, and you've done something to attract that love ..."

"Please," I said.

"I took him to the guest room and he looked at me like a lost puppy."

I turned away, heartsick.

"Did you invite him here to meet with us?"

"No."

"He thought that was your reason."

"No."

"All right." He lifted one knee and folded his hands on it, very masculine, very fatherly. "I've wondered for years what I would do if anybody hurt you—how I'd react when you started courting. You know how much I love you. Maybe I was naïve, but I never gave much thought to the effect you might have on others. We've raised you well . . ."

"*Please*, Father."

He took a deep breath. "I'm going to tell you something about your mother and me that you don't know. Just think of it as fulfilling a duty to my sex. Women can hurt men terribly."

"I *know that*." I hated the whine in my voice.

"Hear me out. Some women think men are pretty hard characters and should get as good as they give. But I don't approve of your carelessly hurting men, any more than I'd approve if Stan started hurting women."

I shook my head helplessly. I just wanted to be alone.

"Family history. Take it for what it's worth. Your mother spent a year choosing between me and another man. She said she loved us both and couldn't make up her mind. I couldn't stand the thought of sharing her, but I couldn't let go, either. Eventually, she drifted away from the other man, and told me I was the one, but . . . it hurt a lot, and I'm still not over it, thirteen years later. I wish I could be gallant and understanding and forgiving, but I still can't hear his name without cringing. Life isn't simple for people like us. We'd like to think our lives are our own, but they're not, Casseia. They're not. I wish to God they were."

I could not believe Father was telling me such things. I certainly did not want to hear them. Mother and Father had always been in absolute love, would always be in love; I was not the product of whims and unstable emotions, not the product of something so chaotic as what was happening between Charles and me.

For a few seconds I could hardly talk. "Please go," I said, sobbing uncontrollably, and he did, with a muttered apology.

* * *

The next morning, after a breakfast that lasted forever, I accompanied Charles to Kowloon depot. We kissed almost as brother and sister, too much in pain to say anything. We held hands for a moment, staring at each other with self-conscious drama. Then Charles got on the train and I turned and ran.

The forces were building.

Klein asked for but did not receive guarantees of solidarity, and there was a split in the BM Charter Council. Earth and GEWA asked more Martian BMs to sign more stringent agreements favorable to Earth. There were more embargoes against bigger BMs, and some folded into each other, facing pernicious exhaustion of funds—bankruptcy. Even the largest unaffected BMs realized that the systems of independent families was headed for a breakdown; that solidarity in the face of outside pressure would soon not be a choice, but a necessity.

The first time around, my application for a syndic apprenticeship was turned down. I switched from Durrey back to UMS and resumed studies at the much-reduced govmanagement school. I applied for the apprenticeship again six months later, and was rejected again.

Bithras Majumdar, syndic of Majumdar BM and my third uncle, had been summoned to Earth in late 2172, M.Y. 53, to testify before the Senate of the United States of the Western Hemisphere. Bithras's testimony could have been transmitted and saved us all a lot of money. Politicians and syndics seldom do much unrehearsed talking in public. But the arrogance of Earth was legendary.

GEWA—the Greater East-West Alliance—had emerged as the greatest economic and political power on Earth. Within GEWA, the United States had kept its position as first among equals. Still, it was generally accepted on Mars that GEWA was using the United States to express its strong disappointment with Mars's lack of progress toward unification. Thus, the United States wanted to hold direct talks with, and take direct testimony from, an influential Martian.

It seemed in a perverse way all very romantic and adventurous; and if everybody had been practical, I probably would never have been offered the chance to go to Earth. Even the most dedicated red rabbit looked upon Earth with awe. Whatever our opinions of her heavy-handed politics, her feverish love of overwhelming technology, her smothering welter of biological experiment, her incredible *worldliness*, on Earth you could walk naked in the open air, and that was something we all wanted to try at least once.

So, having failed twice, I applied again, and this time, I believe—though she never confessed—that my mother pulled strings. My application went further than it had ever gone, my level of interviewing rose several ranks—and finally I was led to understand that I was being seriously considered.

The last time Charles and I saw each other, in that decade, was in 2173. While waiting for a decision on my application, I served a quarter as a Council page at Ulysses and worked in the office of Bette Irvine Sharpe, mediator for Greater Tharsis. Working for Sharpe was great experience; being given that job, my mother thought, was a sign of high BM favor.

I attended a barn dance held to raise funds for Tharsis Research University, newly established and already the bright spot for Martian theoretical science, as well as the center of Martian thinker research.

Charles was there, in the company of a young woman whose looks I did not approve of. We saw each other under the beribboned transparent dome erected for the occasion on a fallow rope field.

I wore a deliberately provocative gown, emphasizing what did not need emphasizing. Charles wore university drab, a green turtleneck and dark gray pants. Charles managed to separate from the clutches of his friend, and we faced each other over a table covered with fresh, newly-designed vegetables. He told me I looked wonderful. I complimented his clothes, not honestly; they were dreadful. He seemed calm, but I was nervous. I still felt guilt over what had happened between us; guilt, and something else. Being near him made me uncomfortable, but I still thought of him as a friend.

"I've applied for a syndic apprenticeship. I'd like to go to Earth," I said. "There's a good chance I'll get it. I might go to Earth with my Uncle Bithras."

Charles said he was pleased for me, but added glumly, "If you get it, you'll be gone for two years. A Martian year."

"It'll flash," I said.

He looked dubious. "I told you I'd always be willing to be your partner," he said.

"You haven't exactly been waiting," I said, a sudden wash of anger and embarrassment coloring my face, sharpening my tone.

Charles was quicker on his feet now and more experienced with people. "You haven't been very encouraging."

"You never called," I said.

He shook his head. "You were the one who said good-bye, remember? I have a few tatters of pride. If you changed your mind, I figured you would call me."

"That's pretty arrogant," I said. "Relationships are mutual."

He braced himself to say something he didn't want to say and looked away. "Your world has grown too large for me. Waiting doesn't seem practical."

I just stared at him.

"You've matured, you're becoming everything I knew you would be. I wish you all the best. I will love you always."

He bowed, turned, and walked away, leaving me totally flustered. I had approached him as an old friend, and he had brought up this uncomfortable thing that I thought we had both left behind, just as I told him about what promised to be the greatest accomplishment of my young life. Such pure emotional blackmail deserved my deepest contempt.

I walked briskly across the tarp-covered field and palmed into a rest kiosk. There I stood by a gently flowing resink and

stared into the single round mirror, angrily asking why I felt
so terrible, so sad.

"Good riddance," I tried to convince myself.

I never disliked Charles, never found in him anything I did
not admire. Yet even now, with a century of living between
me and her, I can't bring myself to call that young woman a
fool.

I tell all this as trivial prelude to things neither Charles nor
I could imagine. I look back now and see the relentless roll
of events, building across the next seven Martian years to the
greatest event in human history.

Trivial pain, trivial lives. The shiver of specks of dust
ramping to the storm.

Part Two
~

You can go home again, but it will cost you.

In the late twenty-second century, travel between Mars and Earth remained a corporate or government luxury, or a jape of the very rich. A passenger of average mass traveling from Earth to Mars, or Mars to Earth, would pay some two million Triple dollars for the privilege.

The rest had to settle for sending their messages by light-speed dataflow, and that put a natural wall between one-on-one conversations.

From Earth to the Moon, reply delay is about two and two-thirds seconds, just enough to catch your breath and not quite enough to lose your chain of thought. To Mars, delay varied with the planetary dance from forty-four minutes to just under seven.

The art of conversation lapsed early between Earth and Mars.

As soon as I heard I was a finalist for the apprenticeship, I began furiously re-studying Earth politics and cultural history. I had already gone far beyond what most Martians are taught in the course of normal education; I had become, somewhat unusually on Mars, a *Terraphile*. Now I needed to be an expert.

I had some idea of the kinds of questions I would be asked; I knew there would be interviews and tough scrutiny; but I did not know who would be conducting the examinations. When I learned, I couldn't decide whether to be relieved or nervous. Ultimately, I think I was relieved. The first interview would be with Alice, Majumdar's chief thinker.

The interview was conducted in Ylla, in an office reserved for more formal, inter-family business meetings. I dressed slowly that morning, taking extra care with the fresh clothes as they formed beneath the mat on my bed. I scrutinized myself in a mirror and in vid projection, looking for flaws inside and out.

I tried to calm myself on the hundred-meter walk to the business chambers, deliberately choosing a longer route through family display gardens, offset from the main tunnels, filled with flowers and vegetables and small trees growing beneath sheets of artificial sun.

Thinkers were invariably polite, infinitely patient, with pleasant personalities. Also smarter than humans and faster by a considerable margin. I had never spoken with Alice before, but I knew my uncle had established a specific set of criteria for his apprentice. I had little doubt that she would speck me soundly and fairly. But taking into account my age and lack of experience, that little doubt quickly magnified into a bad case of nerves.

A few minutes early, I presented myself to the provost of selection, an unassuming, monk-faced, middle-aged man from Jiddah named Peck. I had met Peck while going through scholarship prep. He tried to put me at ease.

"Alice's hookup is clean and wide," he said. "She's in a good mood today." That was a small joke. Thinkers did not exhibit moods; they could model them, but they were never dominated by them. Unlike myself. The mood dominating me came close to panic.

I murmured I was ready to begin. Peck smiled, patted my shoulder as if dealing with a child, and opened the door to the office.

I had never been here before. Dark rosewood paneling, thick forest-green metabolic carpet, lights lurking serenely behind brass fixtures.

A young girl with long black hair, wearing a frilly white dress—Alice's image—seemed to sit behind the opal-matrix desk, hands folded on the polished black and fire-colored stone. Alice had been named after Lewis Carroll's inspiration, Alice Liddell, and favored Liddell's vividly animated portrait as an interface. The image flickered to reveal its unreality, then stabilized. "Good morning," she said. She used a dulcet young woman's voice.

"Good morning." I smiled. My smile, like Alice, flickered to announce its illusory nature.

"We've worked together once before, but you probably don't remember," Alice said.

"No," I admitted.

"When you were six years old, I conducted a series of history LitVids from Jiddah. You were a good pupil."

"Thank you."

"For some months now, Bithras and Majumdar BM have been preparing to journey to Earth to deal directly with various partners and officials there."

"Yes." I listened intently, trying to focus on the words and not on the image.

"Bithras will take two promising young people from the family to Earth with him, as apprentice assistants. The apprentices will have important duties. Please sit."

I sat.

"Does my appearance make you uncomfortable?"

"I don't think so." It *was* odd, facing a young girl, but I decided—forced myself to decide—that it did not bother me excessively. I would have to learn to work closely with thinkers.

"Your ed program is ideal for what Bithras will require in an apprentice. You've strongly favored government and management, and you studied theory of management in dataflow cultures."

"I've tried," I said.

"You've also investigated Earth customs, history, and politics in some detail. How do you feel about Earth?"

"It's fascinating," I said.

"Do you find it appealing?"

"I dream about it. I'd love to see it real."

"And Earth society?"

"Makes Mars look like a backwater," I said. I did not know—have never known—how to dissemble. I doubted Alice would be impressed by dissembling, anyway.

"I think that's generally agreed. What are Earth's strengths, regarded as a unit?"

"I'm not sure Earth can be thought of as a *unit*."

"Why?"

"Even with com and link and ex nets, common ed and instant plebiscite . . . there's still a lot of diversity. Between the alliances, the unallied states, the minorities of untherapied . . . a lot of differences."

"Is Mars more or less diverse?"

"Less diverse and less coherent, I'd say."

"Why?"

"Earth's people are over eighty percent therapied or high

natural. They've had a majority of designer births for sixty Earth years. There's probably never been a more select, intelligent, physically and mentally healthy population in human history."

"And Mars?"

I smiled. "We value our kinks."

"Are we less coherent in our management and decisions?"

"No question," I said. "Look at our so-called politics—at our attempts to unify."

"How do you think that will affect Bithras's negotiations?"

"I can't begin to guess. I don't even know what he—what the BM or the Council plans to do."

"How do you perceive the character of the United States and the alliances?"

I cautiously threaded my way through a brief history, conscious of Alice's immense memory, and my necessarily simple appraisal of a complex subject.

By the end of the twentieth century, international corporations had as much influence in Earth's affairs as governments. Earth was undergoing its first dataflow revolution; information had become as important as raw materials and manufacturing potential. By mid-twenty-one, nanotechnology factories were inexpensive; nano recyclers could provide raw materials from garbage; data and design reigned supreme.

The fiction of separate nations and government control was maintained, but increasingly, political decisions were made on the basis of economic benefit, not national pride. Wars declined, the labor market fluctuated wildly as developing countries joined in—exacerbated by nano and other forms of automation—and through most of the dataflow world a class of therapied, superfit workers arose, highly skilled and self-confident professionals who demanded an equal say with corporate boards.

In the early teens of twenty-one, new techniques of effective psychological therapy began to transform Earth culture and politics. Therapied individuals, as a new mental rather than economic class, behaved differently. Beyond the expected reduction in extreme and destructive behaviors, the therapied proved more facile and adaptable, effectively more intelligent, and therefore more skeptical. They evaluated political, philosophical, and religious claims according to their own standards·of evidence. They were not "true believers." Nevertheless, they worked with others—even the untherapied—easily and efficiently. The slogan of those who advocated therapy was, "A sane society is a polite society."

With the economic unification of most nations by 2070, pressure on the untherapied to remove the kinks and dysfunctions of nature and nurture became almost unbearable. Those with inadequate psychological profiles found full employment more and more elusive.

By the end of twenty-one, the underclass of untherapied made up about half the human race, yet created less than a tenth of the world economic product.

Nations, cultures, political groups, had to accommodate the therapied to survive. The changes were drastic, even cruel for some, but far less cruel than previous tides in history. As Alice reminded me, the result was not the death of political or religious organization, as some had anticipated—it was a rebirth of sorts. New, higher standards, philosophies, and religions developed.

As individuals changed, so did group behavior change. At the same time, in a feedback relationship, the character of world commerce changed. At first, nations and major corporations tried to keep their old, separate privileges and independence. But by the last decades of twenty-one, international corporations, owned and directed by therapied labor and closely allied managers, controlled the world economy beneath a thin veneer of national democratic governments. Out of *tradition*—the accumulated mass of cultural wishful thinking—certain masques were maintained; but clear-seeing individuals and groups had no difficulty recognizing the obvious.

The worker-owned corporations recognized common economic spheres. Trade and taxation were regulated across borders, currencies standardized, credit nets extended world-wide. Economics became politics. The new reality was form-alized in the supra-national *alliances*.

GEWA—the Greater East-West Alliance—encompassed North America, most of Asia and Southeast Asia, India, and Pakistan. The Greater Southern Hemisphere Alliance, or GSHA—pronounced *Jee-shah*—absorbed Australia, South America, New Zealand, and most of Africa. Eurocon grew out of the European Economic Community, with the addition of the Baltic and Balkan States, Russia, and the Turkic Union.

Non-aligned countries were found mostly in the Middle East and North Africa, in nations that had slipped past both the industrial and dataflow revolutions.

By the beginning of the twenty-second century, many Earth governments forbade the untherapied to work in sensitive jobs, unless they qualified as *high naturals*—people who did not require therapy to meet new standards. And the definition of a sensitive job became more and more inclusive.

There were only rudimentary Lunar and Martian settle-ments then, with stringent requirements for settlers; no places for misfits to hide. The romance of settling Mars proved so attractive that organizers could be extremely selective, re-jecting even the therapied in favor of high naturals. They made up the bulk of settlers.

All settlements in the young Triple accepted therapy; most rejected *mandatory* therapy, the new tyranny of Earth.

Alice and I gradually moved from the stuffy air of an exam to a looser conversation. Alice made the change so skillfully I hardly noticed.

I wondered what it had been like to live in a world of kinks and mental dust. I asked Alice how she visualized such a world.

"Very interesting, and far more dangerous," she answered. "In a way there was greater variety in human nature. Unfor-tunately, much of the variety was ineffective or destructive."

"Have *you* been therapied?" I asked.

She laughed. "Many times. It is a routine function of a thinker to undergo analysis and therapy. Have you?"

"Never," I said. "I don't seem to have any destructive kinks. May I ask *you* a question?"

"Certainly."

I was beginning to feel at ease. If Alice found me inadequate, she wasn't giving any signs. "If Earth is so fit and healthy, why are they putting so much pressure on Mars? Doesn't therapy improve negotiating skills?"

"It allows better understanding of other individuals and organizations. But goals must still be established and judgments made."

"Okay." I felt the heat of argument rise in me. "Say we are both operating from the same set of facts, and I disagree with you."

"Do we share the same goals?"

"No. Say our goals differ. Why can't we pool our resources and compromise, or just leave each other alone?"

"That may be possible as long as the goals are not mutually exclusive."

"Earth is pressuring Mars, and conflict is possible. That implies we're involved in a game with only one winner, winner take all."

"That is one possibility, a zero-sum game. Yet it is not the only type of game in which conflict may result."

I sniffed dubiously. "I don't understand," I said, meaning, *I don't agree.*

"Hypothetical situation allowed?"

"Go ahead."

"I will model the Earth-Mars conflict without complex mathematics."

"I have the feeling you've modeled this at a much higher level . . ."

"Yes," Alice answered.

I laughed. "Then I'm outclassed."

"I don't mean to offend."

"No," I said. "I just wonder why I'm bothering to argue."

"Because you are never satisfied with your present condition."

"I beg your pardon?"

"You must never cease from improving yourself. From my point of view, you are an ideal human partner in a discussion, because you never close me off. Others do."

"Does Bithras close you off?"

"Never, though I have made him furious at times."

"Then go on," I said. *If Bithras can take it, so can I.*

Alice described in words and graphic projections an Earth rapidly approaching ninety percent agreement in spot plebiscites—the integration of most individual goals. Dataflow would give individuals equal access to key information. Humans would be redefined as units within a greater thinking organism, the individuals being at once *integrated*—reaching agreement rapidly on solutions to common problems—but *autonomous*, accepting diversity of opinion and outlook.

I wanted to ask *What diversity? Everybody agrees!* but Alice clearly had higher, mathematical definitions for which these words were mere approximations. The freedom to disagree would be strongly defended, on the grounds that even an integrated and informed society could make mistakes. However, rational people were more likely to choose direct and uncluttered pathways to solutions. My Martian outlook cried out in protest. "Sounds like beehive political oppression," I said.

"Perhaps, but remember, we are modeling a dataflow culture. Diversity and autonomy within political unity."

"Smaller governments respond to individuals more efficiently. If everybody is unified, and you disagree with the status quo, but can't escape to another system of government—is that really freedom?"

"In the world-wide culture of Earth, dataflow allows even large governments to respond quickly to the wishes of individuals. Communication between the tiers of the organizations is nearly instantaneous, and constant."

I said that seemed a bit optimistic.

"Still, plebiscites are rapid. Dataflow encourages humans to be informed and to discuss problems. Augmented by their own enhancements, which will soon be as powerful as thinkers, and by connections with even more advanced thinkers, every tier of the human organization acts as a massive processor for evaluating and determining world policy. Dataflow links individuals in parallel, so to speak. Eventually, human groups and thinkers could be so integrated as to be indistinguishable.

"At that point, such a society exceeds my modeling ability," Alice concluded.

"Group mind," I said sardonically. "I don't want to be there when that happens."

"It would be intriguing," Alice said. "There would always remain the choice to simulate isolation as an individual."

"But then you'd be lonely," I said, with a sudden hitch in my voice. Perversely, I yearned for some sort of connection with agreement and certainty—to truly belong to a larger truth, a greater, unified effort. My Martian upbringing, my youth and personality, kept me isolated and in constant though not extreme emotional pain, with little sense of belonging. I deeply wished to belong to a just and higher cause, to have people—friends—who understood me. To not *be lonely*. In a few clumsy, halting sentences, I expressed this to Alice as if she were a confidant and not an examiner.

"You understand the urge," Alice told me. "Possibly, being younger, you understand it better than Bithras."

I shuddered. "Do you want to belong heart and soul to something greater, something *significant*?"

"No," Alice said. "It is merely a curiosity to me."

I laughed to relieve my embarrassment and tension. "But for people on Earth . . ."

"The wish to belong to something greater is an historical force, recognized, sometimes fought against, but regarded by many as inevitable."

"Scary."

"For Mars in its present condition, very scary," Alice agreed. "Earth's alliances disapprove of our 'kinks,' as you call them. They desire rational and efficient partners, of equal social stability, in an economically united Solar System."

"So they put pressure on us, because we're a rogue planet . . . You don't think Martians want to belong to something greater?"

"Many Martians place a high premium on their privacy and individuality," Alice said.

"Frontier philosophy?" I asked.

"Mars is remarkably urbanized. Individuals are tightly knit into economic groups across the planet. This does not much resemble families or individuals isolated on a frontier."

"Have you and Bithras discussed Earth's goals?"

"That is for him to tell you."

"All right," I said. "Then I'll tell you what *I* think, all right?"

Alice nodded.

"I think Earth has some greater plan, and autonomy of any part of the Triple stands in their way. Eventually, they'll want to tame and control Mars as they've already done with the Moon. And then they'll work on the Belters, the asteroids and space settlements . . . bring us all into the fold, until their central authority controls all the resources in the Solar System."

"That is close to my evaluation," Alice said. "Have you spent much time in simulated Earth environment?"

"No," I confessed.

"There is much to be learned by doing so. You may also wish to put on a simulated Terrestrial personality, just to understand."

"I'm really not into that much . . . technical intimacy," I said.

"May I say this is also typical of Martians? You must understand your counterparts intimately to engage in effective negotiations. I guarantee they will have studied Martian attitudes in detail."

"If they *become* us, won't they think like us?"

"This is a curious misconception, that to understand how someone else thinks is to agree with their thinking. Understanding is not *becoming*, is not agreeing."

"All right," I said. "So what happens if the entire Earth links up and we deal with a group mind? Why should that increase their need for resources?"

"Because the goals of a highly integrated mentality will almost certainly be more ambitious than those of a more disparate organization."

"Nobody's ever satisfied with what they have?"

"Not in human experience; not at the level of governments, nations, or planets."

I shook my head sadly. "What about you?" I asked. "You're more powerful and integrated than I am. Are you more ambitious?"

"By design, I serve human needs, and am content to do so."

"But legally you're a citizen, with rights like me. That should include the right to want more."

"Equal in law is not equal in nature."

I worked this over in silence for a moment. Alice's image smiled. "I've enjoyed our conversation very much, Casseia."

"Thank you," I said, suddenly remembering why this meeting had been arranged. I sobered. "It's been great . . . fun."

"That is a compliment to me."

I itched to ask the obvious question.

"I will relay my evaluation to Bithras."

"Thank you," I said meekly.

"There will of course be interviews with humans."

"Of course."

"Bithras usually does not interview."

I had heard that before, and found it odd.

"He places high trust in his associates, and in me, actually," Alice said, still smiling.

And not much trust in his own judgment? "Oh."

"We will talk again later," she said. Her image stood and

the provost, Peck, opened the door to the office and entered.
I said good-bye.

"How did I do?" I asked Peck as he escorted me out.

"I haven't grit of an idea," he said.

I waited anxiously for six days. I remember being more than
testy—I was intolerable. Mother defended me before my irritated father; my brother, Stan, simply stayed out of my way.
More relatives crowded the warrens, my aunt's family and
her four adolescent children. I tried to hide as much as possible, unable to decide whether I was some sort of social
leper or a chrysalis about to become a butterfly.

I spoke once with Diane, now an apprentice instructor at
UM Durrey, but didn't tell her about the interview. I half-
believed in jinx. The support of friends and family, I thought,
might attract the attention of vicious deities, looking for all-
too-fortunate young women who needed to be cut down to
size.

On the sixth day, my slate chimed its melody for an official
message. I retreated from the hall outside our family quarters
to my room, sealed the door, lay on my side on the cot, and
pulled the slate from my pocket, propping it up before me. I
took a deep breath and scrolled the words.

Dear Casseia Majumdar,

*Your application to serve as an apprentice to Syndic
Bithras Majumdar of Majumdar BM has been approved. You
will act as his assistant on the upcoming journey to Earth.
You will meet with Bithras soon. Please prepare your affairs
quickly.*

(signed)
Helen Dougal
Secretary to the Syndic, Majumdar BM

A shiver took me. I lay back on the bed, wondering whether I would laugh or throw up.

I was spinning right to the center of power, if only to observe.

The other lucky apprentice was an earnest fellow from Majumdar's station in Vastitas Borealis, Allen Pak-Lee. Allen was two years older than me. I had met him briefly at UMS. He seemed quiet and sincere.

We were also taking a registered copy of Alice. Majumdar BM was paying, at discount, about seven and a half million to ferry the four of us—Alice Two counting as one passenger, though she weighed less than twenty kilos.

As secretary and apprentice negotiator I would spend a lot of time with my third uncle. Bithras, a perpetual bachelor almost three times my age, was legendary for his tendency to seek the female. Our family relationship presented no absolute obstacle to him; I was not blood, and while liaisons within BMs were mildly discouraged, they were common enough. I knew this going into the job—I thought I could handle the situation.

I had been told his advances were reasonably diplomatic and that he took rebuffs without loss of face or resentment; I was also told that in public he would act fatherly and protective, and that in many respects he was honorable, intelligent, and kind.

"But if you go to bed with him," my mother told me as she helped me pack, "you're sunk."

"Why?" I asked.

"Because he's a conservative old sodder," she said. "He professes to love women dearly, and he does in his own way. But—and this I learned from one of his partners—he _hates_ sex."

"_I'm_ confused," I said, packing a cylinder of raw cloth into the single steel case allowed for the journey.

"He's like a dog that adores the hunt but doesn't enjoy killing the fox."

I laughed, but Mother raised her eyebrows and pinched her lips. "Believe me. He lives for his work, and for an unmarried man of his stature, sex can be messy, irrational, and potentially dangerous. He has to live with this other self, a self he has never been able to control. But this is a prime opportunity for you."

I made a face and folded my medicine kit into the case.

"Poke it," mother said. I poked the kit and it squirmed.

"It's fresh," I said. "I didn't know he was such a monster. Why does anybody put up with him?"

"A *sacred* monster, dear Casseia. If he didn't exist, we'd have to invent him. Think of him as a family rite of passage. Resist his advances with humor and cleverness, and he'll do anything in the world for you. And once he has your measure, he'll stop pushing." She surveyed the perfectly packed case with a critical eye, then nodded approval. "I envy you," she said wistfully. "I'd love to go to Earth."

"Even traveling with Bithras?"

"There isn't a chance in hell you or I would go to bed with him." She winked. "We have such good taste. But what an opportunity . . . Resist the beast, and come out the other side still a virgin, covered with gold and jewels."

"Well . . ." I said.

Two days before we were to depart, Bithras summoned me to his offices in Carter City in Aonia Terra. I boarded the train in Jiddah and crossed to Aonia, removing my bag at the Carter depot. Carter was where most of Majumdar BM's staff lived, the locus of long-range planning; it was Bithras's home, as well.

I had never met Bithras and I was more than a little nervous.

Helen Dougal met me at the depot and escorted me as we took a cab through the transit tunnels. Helen was an attractive woman of twenty Martian years who appeared not much older than me.

Carter had a population of ten thousand BM members and

several hundred applicants, most of them Terries immigrating because of Eloi laws on Earth. It was a big town, yet run efficiently, and the tunnels and warrens were large and well-designed. It didn't seem crowded and haphazard, as did Shinktown, nor cleanly officious, like Durrey; but it certainly wasn't cozy and familiar, like Ylla. The presence of so many Terries—a few of them exotic transforms—at times gave it a very unMartian atmosphere.

Helen fed my slate background on the subjects to be discussed and filled me in on the itinerary for the two-day visit. "Study it later," she said. "Right now, Bithras wants to meet his new assistant."

"Of course." I detected no envy in Helen Dougal's face. I wondered why Bithras wasn't taking her instead of me—wondered if she thought I was moving in on her meal pan. Since I was a little younger in appearance . . . certainly in age . . .

With what I had heard, anything might be possible. I must have gone a little distant, for Helen smiled patiently and said, "You're an apprentice. I have nothing to fear from you, nor you from me."

How about from Bithras?

"And believe me, a lot of what you've heard about our syndic is pure dust."

"Oh."

"Advocates and family representatives meet this afternoon at fifteen. First, however, you're going to join Bithras and me for lunch. Allen Pak-Lee is still in Borealis. He'll be here the day after tomorrow."

The lunch was held in a dining hall outside Bithras's main office. I had expected moderate luxury, but the setting was Spartan: box nano food, hardly inspiring, and packaged tea served from ancient battered carafes in worn cups, on tables that must have had pioneer metal in them.

Bithras entered, clutching his slate and cursing in what I first took to be Hindi; later I learned it was Punjabi. He sat peremptorily at the table—it isn't easy to sit down *hard* on

Mars, but he did his best. The slate skittered a few centimeters across the table and he apologized in perfect, rapid English.

He was dark, almost purple, with intense eyes and handsome features puffing in his middle years. His head was topped with a short stiff brush of black hair lacking any gray. Thick arms and legs, well-muscled for a Martian, stuck out assertively from a short body. He wore a white cotton shirt and tennis shorts. Low-court tennis was Bithras's favorite sport.

"It is pressing. It is pressing very hard," he said, and shook his head in frustration. Then he looked up, his eyes glittering like a little boy's, and beamed a broad smile. "Getting acquainted! My niece, my new apprentice and assistant?"

I rose from my seat and bowed. He did the same, and reached across the table to shake my hand. His eyes lingered on my chest, which hardly invited scrutiny beneath a loose jumpsuit. "You come highly recommended, Casseia. I have great expectations."

I blushed.

He nodded briskly. "I had thought we would have time for a lunch alone, but not so—we start work immediately. Where are the advocates?"

The door opened and six of Majumdar BM's most prominent advocates and managers entered. I had met four of them at social functions over the years. Three male, three female, they, too, wore white shirts and shorts, and towels draped around their necks, as if they had all been playing tennis with Bithras.

I had never seen so many crucial characters assembled in one room: my first taste of being at the center.

Bithras greeted each with a familiar nod. Introductions were ignored. I was here for my own benefit, not theirs. "Now I will begin," he said. "We are an unhappy planet. We do not satisfy Earth. That is sad enough, but actually our progress is slow from any point of view; nobody can agree how to put Humpty Dumpty back together again. It has been more than a year since the end of the Statist government, and all we have managed is to patch the Council back together and hold interim meetings. Economics have slid, and we are in worse condition than before Dauble threw her hammers. This has hurt trade. We do not have a single entity governing trade; Earth organizations must work with every BM separately, and contend with zealous district governors. We still run scared of actually cooperating in our own mutual interests, of being caught again in the Statist trap. So . . ."

He folded his hands. "We are hurting ourselves. There must be an end to recriminations as to who agreed with Dauble and who did not. We must stop punishing Lunar and Earth sympathizers with exclusion from the Council. As you know, I have been meeting with the syndics of the twenty largest Mars-based BMs for the past few months to put together a proposal for Martian unification, working behind and around the Council. I go to Earth with a package to present, and I present it to the Council for debate this evening. You have studied it . . . It is quick, it is dirty, it has handicaps. I'm giving you a final chance to criticize it, from a selfish perspective. Tell me something I do not know."

"It curtails the rights of BMs to control their own trade," said Hetti Bishop, chief advocate. "I know we must organize, but this is too damned Statist."

"Again I ask, tell me something I don't know."

"It gives district governors more power than ever," said Nils Bodrum from Argyre. "The governors are in love with their duties and their lands. Some of them think Mars is a natural paradise to be preserved. We've had six Triple loan deals fall through because we couldn't guarantee quick answers to resource requests. We strangle in conservationist tape."

Bithras smiled. "So, get to your point, Nils."

"If governors keep hewing to a preservation line, and we give them more power, we can say good-bye to billions of Triple dollars. Triple money won't back our resource digs. We'll have to curtail settlements and turn down Terrie immigrants. That won't make anybody happy, least of all Earth. Where will they send their seekers after eternity? For each Eloi refugee—"

"Immigrant," Hattie Bishop said wryly.

" 'Immigrant,' I remind this august assembly, we are paid a million Triple dollars. And that money flows first through Majumdar banks."

Bithras listened intently.

"I don't see why Earth wants the governors stronger," Bodrum concluded, folding his hands.

"They are pushing for a unified government and for BMs to concede power," said Samuel Washington of Bauxite in the Nereidum Mountains. "That's been their goal for ten years. And they're willing to exert considerable pressure."

"What kind of force can they use?" Hettie Bishop asked.

Beside her, Nance Misra-Majumdar, the eldest of our advocates, chuckled and shook her head. "Two hundred and ninety thousand Terrie immigrants on Mars have arrived in the last ten years. They've found their way into high and trusted positions in every BM, some work on the council . . ."

"What are you getting at, Nance?" Hettie asked.

Nance lifted her shoulders. "They used to be called fifth columnists," she said.

"All of them?" Bithras asked sardonically.

Nance smiled patiently. "Our thinkers are manufactured on Earth. It may be years before the Tharsis thinkers come on line. All of our nano factories come from Earth, or the designs at least."

"No one has ever found irregularities in any designs or software," Hettie said. "Nance, we have no reason to be paranoid."

Bithras lifted his chin from his hand and spun his chair halfway. "I see no reason to anticipate trouble, but Nance is right. In theory, there are many ways we could be undermined without facing a massive military expedition across space, which at any rate has never been feasible, even for so rich and powerful a world as Earth."

I could hardly believe such things were being discussed. I was at once dubious, repelled, and fascinated.

Nils Bodrum said, "We have no organized defenses. That much could be said for a central authority—easier to raise an army and defend our planet."

Bithras was clearly not pleased by the direction the conversation was taking. "Friends, this is not a serious problem, certainly not yet. Earth simply wants us to present a united negotiating front, and they have targeted the largest financial BM—ourselves—to catalyze unification. If you pardon the word."

"Why should *unification* be a dirty word?" Hettie said. "My God, as an advocate, I tell you, I'd love to find a way out of the morass of special cases and fooleries we call our Charter."

"The Moon went through this decades ago," Nance said. "Since the Schism, when Earth could not afford to administer such far-flung worlds and we took our leave—"

"Sounds a note of history vid," Nils said with a grin.

Nance continued after the slightest pause for a glare. "We have wrangled and tangled our way into perpetual unrest. The Moon found a solution, changed its constitution—"

"And was reabsorbed by Earth," Nils said. "Independent in dreams only."

"We are much farther away," Hettie said.

Nils would not be swayed. "We do not need order imposed from outside. We need time to find our own path, our own best solution."

Bithras sighed heavily. "My esteemed advocates tell me what I already know, and they say it over and over."

"When you take this suggestion for compromise to Earth," Hettie said, "how do you expect them to believe you can make it stick in the Council? Preliminary agreement is one thing . . ."

Bithras's features expressed extreme distaste. "I am going to tell Earth," he said, "that Majumdar BM will put a hold on further Triple dollar transactions for any BM that does not sign."

Nils exploded. "That is treasonous! We could be sued by every BM on this planet—and rightly so!"

"What court would hear them?" Bithras asked. "We have no effective court structure on Mars, not since Dauble . . . Our own advocates pressed suit against Dauble on Earth, not Mars. What court on Earth would hear a suit pertaining only to Mars?" Bithras stared at them sternly. "My friends, how long has it been since a BM sued another BM?"

"Thirty-one years," Hettie said glumly, chin in hand.

"And why?" Bithras pursued, slapping his palm on the table.

"Honor!" Nils cried.

"Nonsense," Nance said. "Nobody has wanted to prick the illusion. Every BM is a rogue, an outlaw, and the Council is a polite sham."

"But it works!" Nils said. "Advocates negotiate, talk to each other, settle things before they ever reach court. We work around the governors. For Majumdar to put the very existence of other BMs in jeopardy is unconscionable!"

"Perhaps," Bithras said. "But the alternative is worse. Earth will doubtless make many threats if we do not act soon. And one of them will be complete embargo. No more designs, no more technical assistance. Our newer industries would be badly damaged, perhaps crippled."

"*That* we could sue *them* for," Nils persisted, but without conviction.

"My friends, I have offered you a chance to make comments on this proposed constitution," Bithras said. "You have until sixteen this evening. We are all aware of the dangers. We are all aware of the mood of Earth toward Mars."

"I had hoped to persuade you to drop this farce," Nils said.

"That is not an option. I am only a figurehead on this would-be ship-of-state, my friends," Bithras said. "I go to Earth hat in hand, to avoid disaster. We are only five millions. Earth is thirty thousand millions. Earth wants access to our

resources. She wants to *control* our resources. The only way
for us to maintain our freedom is to put our house in order,
concede to Earth enough to put off the next confrontation a
few more years, perhaps a decade. We are weak. Buying time
is our best hope."

"They'll force a Statist government on us," Nils said, "and
then mold that government to their own ends, and when
we're done, they'll own us body and soul."

"That is a possibility," Bithras admitted. "That's why we
must stab ourselves in the back, as Nils would call it, first."

Bithras went to the Council alone and presented the proposals
he had worked out with the five top Martian BMs. The debate was furious; nobody liked the choices, but nobody
wanted to be the first to attract Earth's anger. Somehow, he
managed to glue together something acceptable. Bithras sent
Allen and me messages after the session concluded.

> *My dear young assistants,*
>
> *All Martians are cowards. The proposals are agreed to.*
>
> *Salve!*

The trip began with a farewell dinner in the departure
lounge of Atwood Star Harbor near Equator Rise, west of
Pavonis Mons. Friends, family and dignitaries came to the
port to see us off.

For security reasons, Bithras would board the shuttle at the
last minute. There had been threats against his life planted
anonymously in family mailboxes for the past few days, ever
since the announcement of his departure to Earth. Some suspected disgruntled Statists; others looked to the smaller BMs,
who had least to gain and most to lose.

My mother, father and brother sat in a corner of the lounge,
near a broad window overlooking the port. Blunt white shut-

tle noses poked up through half-open silo hatches. Red flopsand formed smooth streaks across the white pavement. Arbeiters engaged in perpetual cleanup roamed the field.

We spoke in bursts, with long moments of silence in between: Martian reserve. My mother and father tried not to show their pride and sadness. Stan simply smiled. Stan always smiled, in good times or bad. Some misjudged him because of that, but due to the shape of his face, it was easier for him to smile than not.

Father took me by both shoulders and said, "You're going to do great."

"Of course she will," my mother said.

"We'll have to adopt someone while you're gone," Father continued. "We can't stand an empty house."

"The hell we will," Mother said. "Stan will leave in a few months—"

"I will?" Stan said. His protest carried an odd note; surprise beyond the jest.

"And we'll have the warren to ourselves for the first time in ten years. What should we do?"

"Replace the carpets," Father said. "They don't groom themselves as well as they used to."

I listened with a mix of embarrassment and grief. What I wanted, right now, was to retreat and cry, but that was not possible.

"You will make us proud," Father said, and then, to make his point, in a louder voice, he said it again.

"I'll try," I murmured, searching his face. Father and I had never quite communicated; his love had always been obvious, and he had never slighted me, but he often seemed a cipher. Mother I thought I knew; yet it was Father who never surprised me, and Mother who never failed to.

"We won't drag this out," Mother said firmly, taking my father's elbow for emphasis. Mother and I hugged. I squeezed her hard, feeling like a little girl, wanting her to sit me on her lap and rock me. She pulled back, smiling, tears in her eyes, and actually pushed me away, gently but firmly. Father gripped my hand with both of his and shook it. He had tears in his eyes, as well. They turned abruptly and left.

Stan stayed longer. We stood apart from the crowd, saying little, until he cocked his head to one side, and whispered, "They're going to miss you."

"I know," I said.

"So will I."

"It'll flash," I said.

"I'm going lawbond," he said, sticking his jaw out pugnaciously.

"What?"

"To Jane Wolper."

"From Cailetet?"

"Yeah."

"Stan, Father hates Cailetet. They're pushy and Lunar. We've never been able to share with them."

"Maybe that's why I love her."

I stared at him in astonishment. "You're amazing," I said.

"Yeah." He seemed pleased with himself.

"You're going over to their family . . . ?"

"Yeah."

"I'm glad I'm leaving now."

"I'll keep you informed," he said. "If Dad says nothing about me, you'll know it went badly. I'll give you the details when the dust settles."

I specked him running down the tunnel between our rooms when he was five and I was two and a half and adored him. He could leap like a kangaroo and wore rubber pads to bounce hands and feet down the tunnels. Athletic, calm, always-knows-where-to-go Stan. Never said boo to our parents, never gave them pause. Now it was his turn to aggravate and provoke.

We hugged. "Don't let her push you around."

Stan made a petulant face, wiped it with his hand like a clown, and smiled sunnily. "I'm proud you made it, Casseia," he said. He hugged me quickly, shook my hand, gave me a small package, and left.

I sat in a corner and opened the wrapper. Inside was a cartridge of all our blood family docs and vids. Stan had paid extra for the weight clearance of one hundred grams; the box was marked with a cargo stamp. I felt even more empty and alone.

I faced the crowded lounge with a kind of luxurious dread. The shuttle would depart in two hours. I'd be aboard the *Tuamotu* in less than six hours. We would rise from Mars orbit and inject Solar in less than twenty hours ...

I pocketed Stan's gift, squared my shoulders, and entered the crowd with a big, false smile.

Even at its most opulent, space travel was never comfortable. The shuttle to orbit was a rude introduction to the necessary economies of leaving a planet: shot out of your planetary goldfish bowl on a pillar of flaming hydrogen or methane, in a cylindrical cabin less than ten meters wide, everyone arranged in stacked circles with feet pointing outward, seventy passengers and two shuttle crew, losing Mars's reassuring gentle grip and dropping endlessly ...

Temp bichemistry helped. Those passengers who had installed permanent bichemistries to adapt to micro-g conditions spent the first hour in orbit asleep while the boat swung carefully to mate with *Tuamotu*. I had refused such a radical procedure—how often would I travel between worlds?—and chosen temp. I spent the whole time awake, feeling my body smooth over the deep uncertainty of always falling.

Some things I didn't expect. The quick adjustments of temp bichemistry caused a kind of euphoria that was pleasant and disturbing at once. For several minutes I was incredibly randy. That passed, however, and all I felt was a steady tingle throughout my body.

Bithras and Pak-Lee had arrived at Atwood after I was seated, and were in the shuttle somewhere below me. Alice Two was in the hold in a special thinker berth.

Being away from net links was like sensory deprivation for a thinker; less than a tenth of Alice Two's capacity would be engaged while we were in space. The bandwidth of space communication was too narrow to keep her fully linked and employed. She would not sleep, of course, but she would spend much of the journey correlating events in Earth and Martian history drawn from her large data store.

Thinkers had been known to create massive and authoritative LitVid works while in machine dream. Some said the best historians were no longer human, but I disagreed. Alice One and Alice Two seemed quite human to me. Alice even called her copy a "daughter." I'd never worked closely with thinkers before, and I was charmed.

Sitting on my cramped couch in the dark, a projection of Mars's orange and red surface scrolling above me, I wondered what Charles was doing now. Unlike Charles, I hadn't yet found anyone to seriously occupy my free time. The day before launch, I had spoken with Diane, and she had asked if I looked forward to a shipboard romance. "Dust that," I'd answered. "I'll be a busy rabbit."

The trip would take eight Terrestrial months, one way. Each passenger chose from three options: warm sleep with mind embedded in a sophisticated sim environment (sometimes crudely called *cybernation*), realtime journey, or a prescheduled mix of the two. Most Martians chose realtime. Most Terrestrials returning to Earth chose sims and warm sleep.

The Mars scene cut suddenly to a view of the *Tuamotu* in space. Booms furled, passenger cylinders hugged tightly to the hull, our home for the next eight months looked tiny against the stars. Tugs fastened helium-three fuel and water and methane mass tanks to the bow. The drive funnels flexed experimentally at the stern.

A small voice provided running commentary in one ear. *Tuamotu* was fifteen Earth years old, built in Earth orbit, nano maintained, veteran of five crossings, refitted before her trip to Mars, well-regarded by travel guides on Earth and Mars. She carried a crew of five: three humans, a dedicated thinker, and a slaved thinker backup.

I had a touch of tunnel fever at the thought of being shut up for so long. I had studied the ship's layout a few hours before boarding, learning my way around the passenger cylinder, previewing shipboard routine. But I would have to overcome the conviction that there was *no way out*. Despite spending most of my life in tunnels and enclosed spaces, I always knew there was another tunnel, another warren, and as a last resort, I could suit and pop through a lock and go Up . . . luxuries not available on the *Tuamotu*.

I was less than comfortable with the thought of spending so many months in the company of so few. What if Bithras, Allen, and I did not get along at all?

A tiny elevator carried three passengers at a time from the primary lock down the length of the hull and debouched us into a small cabin forward of the drive shields. The steward for our cylinder—short, taut, sandy-haired and brown-skinned, male, about forty Earth years old, with sharp black eyes—greeted us formally and politely, and introduced himself as Acre—just Acre. He had the remarkable ability to change his feet into hands, and to bend his long tan legs backwards and forwards, which he demonstrated quickly and with minimal explanation. He escorted us in small groups to the secondary lock. Here, we climbed through an access pipe barely a meter wide into our cylinder, where we drifted in the observation lounge, surrounded by direct-view windows now shuttered and shielded.

The lounge had room for all of us. We crowded together waiting for instructions. Bithras headed the last contingent of passengers and conferred briefly with the steward before scowling and searching the crowd. His eyes met mine, the scowl reversed into a radiant smile, and he crooked his arm and waved twinkle-fingers.

The steward called my name from the access pipe. I floated forward, fumbling at the grips and bumping a few of my fellows apologetically before anchoring myself. "You're in charge of our friend here, I understand," he said, pushing forward Alice's box. Alice's arbeiter carriage weighed as much as she did and had not been brought along; we would rent her a carriage on Earth.

"Thank you," I said.

"Please hold on to it while we check cabin assignments and get things organized."

"Her, not it," I said.

"Sorry." He smiled. "We'll stow *her* in her niche after orientation."

I took Alice in hand and moved to the side of the lounge. She was endo not exo for the moment—her sensors and voice were inactive.

"Now that we're all here," the steward said, "welcome aboard *Tuamotu*. We'll give out some important information and then off to your cabins to snug in."

Bithras and Allen Pak-Lee floated beside me. "This is my second passage to Earth," Bithras said in an undertone, "and your first, of course."

"My first," I affirmed.

Most Earth English accents were familiar to me from LitVid; the steward, Acre, might have been Australian. His features seemed indigene. Acre delivered the "doctro" crisply and clearly in less than five minutes. He gave us a few safety tips for the next leg of the trip—boost and solar orbit injection— and had us circle around the lounge to become familiar with weightless aids and procedures.

"Tomorrow," he said, "we'll discuss immunization levels and all the options available throughout the voyage. Some options are closed—all warm-sleep berths are taken for the duration. All temp berths and switchouts are closed, as well. We hope that causes no inconvenience."

"Woe," murmured Bithras.

Acre helped me stow Alice in her niche just forward of the lounge and showed me how to run the legally required connection checks. Bithras attended for a few minutes, applied a strip of ID tape to a seam to protect against unauthorized removal, and left the rest to Acre and me.

"Family thinker?" Acre inquired.

"A copy," I said.

"I'm fond of thinkers," he said. "Once they're stowed, they're no trouble at all. I wish they'd travel with us more often—Sakya gets lonely sometimes, the Captain says."

Sakya was the ship's dedicated thinker. I reached into the niche, palmed my ID on Alice's port, and asked, "Everything tight?"

"I'm comfortable, thank you," Alice replied, coming exo quickly. "Bithras has sealed me in?"

"Yes."

"I'm talking with Sakya now. This should be pleasant. Will you join me for a chat once we're underway?"

"I'd love to," I said. I closed the hatch on Alice's niche. Acre locked her in and gave me the key. "We raise them right on Mars," I said.

"Might teach Sakya some manners," he said.

Everything aboard *Tuamotu* was impressively high nano; she had been refitted with the lastest Earth designs before her last crossing. There were no telltale yeast or iodine smells during nano activity. The ship's visible surfaces could assume an apparently infinite variety of textures and colors and were capable of displaying or projecting images with molecular resolutions.

I felt wrapped in luxury, examining my private cabin—two meters by three by two, private vapor bag and vacuum toilet. If I wanted, I could turn almost the entire cabin into a LitVid screen and be surrounded by any scenery I chose.

I pulled out the desk, ported my slate, and selected my scheme. The desk became the color and texture of stone and wood with gold inlay. I ran my fingers along the tactile surface; the sensations of polished oak, cold marble, and smooth metal were flawless.

It was traditional for passengers to gather for the boost. I wanted to have a seat, so I quickly unpacked my few things and went aft.

Allen Pak-Lee followed and hooked himself to a seat beside me. "Nervous?" he asked.

"I don't think so," I said.

"God, I am. Don't misunderstand. I have a lot of respect for Bithras. But he's very demanding. I took a brief from his assistant on the last trip. He said he spent several months in hell. There was a crisis and Bithras insisted on hogging the waves."

Bithras returned to the lounge and sat beside us with a curt nod. "Damn them," he said.

"Who?" I inquired.

"This ship *reeks* of progress," he said.

The lounge filled as the gong sounded. The steward, with the aid of a few slim, graceful octoped arbeiters, served drinks and explained the procedure to the uninitiated. The boost would be comfortable, no more than one-third g. For a few hours, we would have a "lazy sense of up and down." Actually, one-third g was just below Mars standard—not quite full weight for a red rabbit.

The passengers in the lounge who had claimed seats settled in, and those who drifted found grips and hooks and arranged for a place to drop their feet. I looked them over curiously—our companions for eight months. One family would be in our cylinder, a handsome man and woman with a daughter whom I judged to be about seventeen Earth years old—native Terries, by their appearance. The daughter, too beautiful to be completely natural, played with a faux mouse.

Acre looked at the ceremonial wristwatch on his left arm, raised his hand, and we counted backwards . . .

At five, the ship vibrated like a struck bell. At four, the ceiling projected a full-width view aft. Everybody looked up, jaws gaping. The drive funnels flexed. A methane-oxygen kicker motor would take us out of Martian orbit.

Streamers of violet played against the blackness and the limb of sunrise Mars: warmup and test. Then the kicker fired full thrust, throwing a long orange cone that quickly turned translucent blue.

Gently, we acquired weight. The weight grew until it almost felt as if we were on Mars again. The unseated passengers laughed and stood on the floor, and a few even did a little jig, slapping hands.

We severed our bonds with the world of my birth.

In my cabin, just before sleep, I studied diagrams from the ship's operations manual, things I normally wouldn't give dust for ... Charles would, however, and I felt again a perverse obligation to think about him. I attributed these thoughts to simple fright and homesickness.

Twelve of the passengers in our cylinder would enter warm sleep after the ship had extended its booms for cruising. That would leave twenty-three of us awake for the entire voyage—mostly Martians, ten female, thirteen male, six of them "eligible," though I suspected, given contemporary Earth attitudes, even the unaccompanied and married males were fair game for travel liaisons. I was not interested, however.

I did not feel any immediate affection for Allen, and Bithras was still a threatening cipher—not so much a human being as an unfulfilled potential for difficulty. I had never been exceptionally gregarious, a reaction to my diverse and noisy blood relations, and even now was avoiding a First Night Out mixer in the lounge and dining cabin ...

Chemical reaction motors and ion thrusters, used to direct the craft out of planetary orbit and accelerate to just below cruising speed, leave negligible amounts of debris. However, the plume of fusion-heated reaction mass from the main drive contains radioactive engine-surface ablation. The fusion drive must be fired with due regard for vehicles which may cross these orbits for as long as four days afterward, as required by Triple Navigational Standards ...

The ship would switch on its main drives ten million kilometers out from Mars.

Solar wind must be able to clear all fusion debris from a region ten million kilometers above and below the plane within two weeks (the manual informed me). *This gives sufficient leeway for most times of the solar cycle, but at periods of minimum solar activity, debris may not be cleared for as long as forty-five days, and special permission from Triple Navigation Control must be obtained if fusion-driven ships are to be launched in this period.*

Colorful 3-D diagrams unfolded in the air to supplement the text.

Earth-Mars passages launched when the planets are not in their most favorable configurations require more fusion boosts and higher speeds. Elongated, faster ship courses—as opposed to "fatter" and slower courses—take liners within the orbit of Venus, and occasionally within the orbit of Mercury, with greater exposure to solar radiation. Medical nano has advanced to where radiation damage in passengers can be repaired quickly and efficiently, eliminating ill effects from even the closest "sun-graving" passages . . .

What if I wasn't cut out for space flight? I had passed the examinations well enough—but there were instances of space-intolerant passengers having to be sedated if warm sleep cubicles weren't available.

Eight months of horror seemed to stretch before me. The cabin closed in, the air tasted stale. I imagined Bithras pawing me. I would clobber him. He wouldn't be nearly as understanding as he should be, and I would be fired before reaching Earth. I would have no option but to return at the next available opportunity, another ten or even twelve months in space . . . I would go insane and start screaming. The ship's medical arbeiter would pump me full of drugs and I would enter that horrid state described in pop LitVids, caught between worlds, mind drifting free of my body with nowhere to go, away from the humanized spheres, forced to consort with elder monstrosities.

I started to giggle. The elder monstrosities would find me inexpressibly boring and reject me. Absolutely nobody and nothing to talk to, career ruined, I would end up counseling asteroid miners in how to program their prosthetutes for more lifelike behavior.

The giggles turned to laughter. I rolled over in my bunk and stifled the noise. The laughter was not pleasant—it sounded forced and harsh—but it was effective. I rolled on my back, fears quelled.

Acre and his fellow steward in charge of the opposite cylinder held a party for "Half-Degree Day." Acre was a master at giving parties; he never seemed bored, was never at a loss for polite conversation. His only time alone came when the rest of the passengers were asleep. His sole defense seemed to be a certain blankness that did not encourage long conversations. I was pretty sure he wasn't an Earth-made android, but the suspicion never passed completely.

Passengers gathered in the lounge from both cylinders, still mingling freely, and watched Mars become the size of Earth's Moon, as seen from Earth. The Terrestrials found the sight entrancing, and there were songs of "Harvest Mars," though the planet was only one-third full. The Captain broke out a glass bottle of French champagne, one of five, he said.

The young girl introduced herself to me at breakfast on our third day out; her name was Orianna, and her parents were citizens of the United States and Eurocon. Her face fascinated me. Eyes uplifted at the corners, slightly asymmetric, pupils the fiery red-brown color of Arcadia opal, her skin flawless multiracial brown, she seemed perfectly at home in micro-g and floated like a cat. She recommended the best sims available on the ship, and seemed amused when I told her I didn't go in for sims.

"Martians are lovely curious," she said. "You'll be a big draw on Earth. Terries love Martians."

I was prepared not to like Orianna very much.

* * *

For the first week, Bithras spent much of his time exercising, working in his cabin, or waiting impatiently to communicate with Mars. He rarely even spoke to us. Allen and I spent some time in each other's company at first, exercising or studying together, but we did not hit it off personally, and soon drifted to other passengers for conversation.

I knew the public interior of our cylinder fore and aft, and despite my reticence, had spoken to almost everybody. Not much chance of shipboard romance; the men were all older than me, and none seemed interesting; all, like Bithras, were movers and shakers and much absorbed in things they really couldn't talk about.

I fantasized being aboard an immigrant ship, with men of diverse background, whose hidden pasts they would suddenly feel the urge to confess ... Dangerous people, intriguing, passionate.

Mounted on the hull was a four-meter telescope, kept collapsed and hidden away for the first few million kilometers, then unfurled for the use of passengers. I had signed up for a few hours. The free hours aboard *Tuamotu* were wonderful for catching up on subjects I had neglected, including astronomy.

The viewing station for our cylinder was in the observation lounge, a small cubicle with room for four. I had hoped to study alone, try my hand at celestial navigation and object finding, tracking a few of the near stars known to have planetary systems. I wanted to rediscover at least the most prominent and closest examples. But in the lounge I met Orianna.

Point-blank, she asked if she could join me. "I haven't signed up, and it's full for a week!" she said plaintively. "I love astronomy. I'd like to transform and go to the stars ..." She separated her hands a few centimeters, suggesting the proposed size of humans designed for interstellar migration. "Would you mind?"

I did, but Martian manners kept me polite. I said of course she could join me, and with a smile, she did.

She was adept with the controls and ruined my game by tracking all my chosen objects expertly within a few minutes. I expressed my admiration.

"It's nothing," she said. "My parents gave me seven different enhancements. If I want, I can play nearly all musical instruments with just a few days' practice—not like the best, of course, but enough to pass as a talented amateur. In a few years, if they make it legal, I could install a mini-thinker."

"Doesn't it bother you, having so many talents?" I asked.

Orianna curled into a ball and with one finger flicked herself upside down in relation to me. Her toe caught on a bar and she stopped spinning. "I'm used to it. Even on Earth, some people think my parents and I have gone too far. I've asked for things, they've given them to me . . . I have to really ramp down to make friends."

"Are you ramped down now?" I asked.

"You bet. I don't show off, *ever*. Good way to spoil any chance of connecting. You're a natural, aren't you?"

I nodded.

"Some of my friends would envy you. The chance to just be what you are. But it would slow me down too much. Do you ever feel slow?"

I laughed. She was too ethereal to resent . . . much, or for long. "All the time," I said.

"Then why not enhance? I mean, it's possible, even on Mars. And you're from Majumdar, the finance BM . . . aren't you?"

The inflection of her last question told me she knew very well I was from Majumdar.

"Yes. How long have you been on Mars?"

"Just time for turnaround. Two months. We came on a fast passage, inside Venus. My parents had never been to Mars. My folks thought we should see what Mars and the Moon are really like. Carnay. In the flesh."

"Did you like it?"

"It's wonderful," she said. "Such defiance. Beautiful, really. Like the whole planet is just hitting puberty."

I had never heard it described that way. Martians tended to think of themselves as old and established, perhaps confusing our own brief past with the planet's obvious age. "Where did you visit?"

"We were invited to stay in half a dozen towns and cities. We even went to a handful of extreme stations, new ones settled by immigrant Terries. My father and mother know quite a few Eloi. We didn't get to—" Again the introspective pause. "Ylla or Jiddah. That's your home, isn't it?"

"What are you referencing?" I asked. My home address wasn't on the open manifest.

"I sucked in the public directories," Orianna said. "I haven't dumped them yet."

"Why would you want to do that? Any slate can carry them."

"I don't use a slate," she said. "I take it direct. No separation. I love being dipped."

"Dipped?"

She wrapped her arms around herself. "Immersed. It's like *I* just go away, and there's only information and processing, pure and swift."

"Oh."

"Learning distilled into an essence. Education means being."

"Oh." I closed my mouth.

"I think I came on sharp for most Martians. I negged quite a few my own age, even. Martians are fashion locked, aren't they?"

"Some think so."

"You?"

"I'm pretty conservative, I suppose."

She unfolded long arms and legs and gripped the holds in the booth with uncanny grace. "I don't like anybody on the ship, for partners, I mean," she said. "Do you?"

"No," I said.

"Have you had many partners?"

"You mean, lovers?"

She smiled wisely, anciently. "That's a good word, but not always accurate, is it?"

"A few," I said, hoping she would take a hint and not pry.

"My parents were part of the early partner program. I've been partnering since I was ten. Do you think that's too early?"

I hid my shock; I had heard about early partnering, but it had certainly never taken on Mars. "We think childhood is for children," I said.

"Believe me," Orianna said, "I haven't been a *child* since I was five. Does that bother you?"

"You first had sex when you were *ten*?" This conversation was making me very uncomfortable.

"No! I haven't had *physical* sex at all."

"Sim?" I asked meekly.

"Sometimes. Partnering . . . oh, *I* see your confusion. I mean sharing closeness mentally, finding so many kinds of pleasure together. I like whole-life sims. I've experienced two . . . Very expanding. So I know all about sex, of course. Even sex that's not physically possible. Sex between four-dimensional human forms." Suddenly she looked distressed, and she had such a charismatic presence that I immediately wanted to apologize, do anything to make her happy. *My God,* I thought. *A planet full of people like her.*

"I've never shared my mind," I said.

"I'd love to share with you." The offer was so disarming I was at a loss for an answer. "You have a truly natural presence," she continued. "I think you could share beautifully. I've been watching you since the trip began . . ." She primmed her lips and pulled back to the wall. "If I'm not too forward."

"No," I said.

She put out her hand and touched my cheek, stroking it once with the back of her fingers. "Share with me?"

I blushed furiously. "I don't . . . do sims," I said.

"Just talk, then. For the trip. And when we get to Earth, I can show you a few things you'd probably miss . . . as a Martian tourist. Meet my friends. We'd all enjoy you."

"All right," I said, hoping, if the offer were more than I could possibly handle, that I could plead an intercultural misunderstanding and escape.

"Earth is really something," Orianna said with a wonderfully languid blink. "I see it a lot more clearly now that I've been to Mars."

We were close to the ten-million-kilometer mark, three weeks into the voyage. The fusion drives would soon turn on. The hull would not be livable once they became active.

After a truly big party, featuring one of the best banquets the voyage would offer, the Captain said his farewells and crossed to the opposite cylinder. Passengers berthed there would no longer be able to visit us; we all shook hands and they followed the Captain.

Most of our cylinder's occupants went to bed in their cabins to take the change easily. A few hardy souls, myself included, stayed in the lounge. There was an obligatory countdown. I hated feeling like a tourist, but I joined in. Acre was too pleasant and cajoling to be denied his duties.

We had returned to weightlessness, but were about to acquire full Earth weight for several hours. The countdown arrived at zero, all eight of us shouted at once, and the ship resounded with a hollow thud. We set our feet onto the lounge floor. Orianna, near her parents, seemed close to ecstasy. I was reminded of Bernini's St. Theresa speared by a shaft of inspiration.

The fusion flare followed us like a gorgeous bridal train. Brilliant blue at the center, tipped with orange from ablated and ionized engine and funnel lining, it pushed us relentlessly to almost three times our accustomed Mars weight, a full g.

A few, including Orianna's mother and father, climbed forward and valiantly exercised in the gym, joking and casting aspersions on the rest of us slackers.

I chose a middle course, climbing around the cylinder for an hour. My temp bichemistry treatments made the full g force bearable but not pleasant. I had read in travel prep that a week on Earth might pass before someone with temp became comfortable with the oppressive weight. Orianna accompanied me; she had temp also, and was working to regain Earth strength.

As we climbed through the cylinder, from the observation deck to the forward boom control walkway, Orianna told me about Earth fashions in clothes. "I've been out of it for two years, of course," she said. "But I like to think I'm still tuned. And I keep up with the vids."

"So what are they wearing?" I asked.

"Formal and frilly. Greens and lace. Masks are out this year, except for floaters—projected masks with personal icons. Everybody's off pattern projection, though. I liked pattern projection. You could wear almost nothing and still be discreet."

"I can redo my wardrobe. I've brought enough raw cloth."

Orianna made a face. "This year, expect fixed outfits, not nano-shaped. Old fabric is best. Tattered is wonderful. We'll dig through the recycle shops. The shredbare look is very pos. Nano fake is beyond deviance."

"Do I *have* to be in fashion?"

"Abso not! It's drive to ignore. I switch from loner to slave every few months when I'm at home."

"Terries will expect a red rabbit to be trop retro, no?"

Orianna smiled in friendly pity. "With that speech, you're fulfilled already. Just listen to me, and you'll slim the current."

Breathless, standing on the walkway around the bow's boom connector, we rested for a moment. "So correct me," I said, gasping.

"You still say 'trop shink' on Mars. That's abso neg, mid twenty-one. Sounds like Chaucer to Terries. If you don't drive multilingual, and you'd better not try unless you wear an enhancement, best to speak straight early twenty-two. Ev-

eryone understands early twenty-two, unless you're glued to
French or German or Dutch. They ridge on anything about
twenty years old for drive standard. Chinese love about eight
kinds of Europidgin, but hit them in patrie, and they revert to
twenty *Putonghua*. Russian—"

"I'll stick with English."

"Still safe," she said.

The fusion drives shut off and weightlessness returned. The
time had come to separate the cylinders from the hull and begin rotation. *Tuamotu* carefully spun her long booms between
central hull and outboard cylinders. The booms were attached
to a rotor on the hull, and the cylinders used their own small
methane kickers to set up spin.

When extended, the cylinders pointed perpendicular to the
hull; just as when we had experienced ship acceleration, to
move from deck to deck one had to climb up or down, or
take the elevator. The centrifugal force created about one-
fourth g in the observation lounge, the outboard or "lowest"
deck.

When the cylinders had cycled to maximum, the warm
sleepers retired to their cubicles. A little party was given for
them. In our cylinder, we were now down to twenty-three active passengers, and seven months to go . . .

Orianna had filled her cabin with projected picts, each leading to a sim or LitVid put on hold; twenty or more, hanging
in the air like tiny sculptures, some pulsing, some singing
faintly. She laughed. "Silly, isn't it?" she said. "I'll turn them
off . . ." She waved and the icons disappeared, allowing me to
see the rest of her cabin. It was tidy but busy. A sweater lay
in one corner, or at least half of a sweater. Little sticks poked
out of it, and a ball of what must have been thread—yarn, I
remembered—lay beside it. "Knitting?" I asked.

"Yeah. Sometimes I don't know where I am or what I'm
doing, and knitting or crocheting brings me back. It's the
drive in Paris, where my father lives."

"Your mother lives with your father?"

"Sometimes. They bond loose. I live with my father most of the year. Sometimes I go to Ethiopia to live with my mother. She's a merchandising agent for Iskander Resources. They temp for skilled labor all over the world."

"And your father?"

"He's a mining engineer for European Waters Conservancy. He spends lots of time in submarines. I have a great North Sea sim—like to see it?"

"Not right now. Wouldn't you like to live in just one place?" I asked.

Orianna held out her hands. "Why?"

"To get a feeling of belonging. Knowing where you are."

She smiled brightly. "I know the entire Earth. Not just in sims, either. I've been all over, with and without my parents. I can fly a shocker from Djibouti to Seattle in four hours. Weather change is great. Really sweeps the sugars."

"Have you ever gone slow?" I asked.

"You mean . . ." She smoothed her hand along the bed cover. "Ground speed? Double-digit kiphs?"

"Single digit."

"Sure. I bicycled across France two years ago with some Kenyans. Campfires, night skies, grape harvest in Alsace. You're really jammed on this, aren't you?"

"If you mean, stuck in a rut, obviously."

"Earth isn't decadent, Casseia. It really isn't. I'm not a poor little rich girl, any more than you are."

"Maybe I'm just jealous."

"I'd call it *shy*," Orianna said. "But if you want to ask me about Earth, realtime, oral history and culture, that's fine with me. We have months left, and I don't want to spend it all jogging and simming."

My Earth studies and conversations with Alice had left me with the impression of a flawless society, cool and efficient. But what I heard in conversation with Orianna seemed to contradict this. There were great disagreements between Terries; nations within GEWA and its southern equivalent,

GSHA, arguing endlessly, clashing morality systems as populations from one country traded places with others—a popular activity in the late 70s. Some populations—Islam Fatimites, Green Idaho Christians, Mormons, Wahabi Saudis, and others—maintained stances that would be conservative even on Mars, clinging stubbornly to their cultural identities in the face of Earth-wide criticism.

Paleo-Christians in Green Idaho, practically a nation unto itself within the United States, had declared the rights of women to be less than those of men. Women fought to have their legal powers and rights reduced, despite opposition from all other states. On the reverse, in Fatimite Morocco and Egypt, men sought to glorify the image of women, whom they regarded as Chalices of Mohammed. In Greater Albion, formerly the United Kingdom, adult transforms who had regressed in apparent age to children were forbidden to hold political office, creating a furor I could hardly begin to untangle. And in Florida, defying regulations, some humans transformed themselves into shapes similar to marine mammals . . . And to pay for it, organized *Sex in the Sea* exhibits for tourists.

In language, the greatest craze of the 60s and 70s was *invented* language. Mixing old tongues, inventing new, mixing music and words electronically so that one could not tell where tones left off and phonemes began, creating visual languages that wrapped speakers in projected, complex symbols, all seemed designed to separate and not bring together. Yet enhancements were available that were tuned to the New Lingua Nets or NLN. Installing the NLN enhancements through nano surgery, one could understand virtually any language, natural or invented, and even think in their vernacular.

The visual languages seemed especially drive in the 70s. In GEWA alone, seventy visual languages had been created. The most popular was used by more than four and a half billion people.

Despite what Alice had said, it didn't sound at all *inte-*

grated to me. To a Martian, even to a native like Orianna, Earth seemed diverse, bewildering, crazy.

But to Alice, Earth was entering the early stages of a new kind of history.

Six weeks into the flight, Bithras called me to his cabin. I girded myself for battle, palmed his door port. The door opened and I stepped in at the wave of his hand. He wore long pants and a cotton long-sleeved shirt, again in white, and he muttered to himself for a few minutes, searching for memory cubes, as if I had not yet arrived. "Yes," he said finally, locating the lost cubes and turning to face me. "I hope your trip has not been too dull."

I shook my head. "I've spent most of the time researching and exercising," I said.

"And talking to Alice."

"Yes."

"Alice is brilliant, but she has some of the naïveté found in all thinkers," Bithras said. "They cannot judge humans harshly enough. I have no such illusions. My dear, the time has come for us to do some work, and it involves your past . . . If you are willing."

I stared at him and gave the faintest nod.

"What do you know about Martian scientists and Bell Continuum theory?"

"I don't think I know anything about Bell Continuum theory," I said.

"Majumdar BM has been speaking with Cailetet Mars about sponsoring new research. There is a request for so-called Quantum Logic thinkers in the works. Earth is exporting such thinkers, but they are incredibly expensive . . . thirty-nine million dollars, shipped endo and inactive. We must build our own personalities for them, and that might take months, even years."

I still volunteered nothing, though I could feel where he was heading.

"You once knew Charles Franklin, promising student from Klein BM, correct?"

"Yes."

"You were lovers?"

I swallowed and thrust my chin forward resentfully. "Briefly," I said.

"He is lawbonded now to a woman from Cailetet."

"Oh."

Bithras studied my reaction. "Mr. Franklin heads a group of young theoretical physicists at Tharsis Research. They are known as the Olympians."

"I didn't know that," I said.

"Not surprising, since their work is kept close to their bosoms. They report only to the fund administrators, and have published nothing so far. I want you to read this transmission from Earth. It is a few days old, and it was sent to Cailetet from Stanford University."

"How did you get it?" I asked.

Bithras smiled, shook his head, and handed his slate to me. The message was pure text and read:

We've established strong link between time tweak and space tweak. Can derive most special relat. Third tweak discovered may be co-active but purpose unknown. Tweak time, tweak space, third tweak changes automatically. Probably derive general relat. as regards curvature, but third tweak pushes a fourth tweak, weakly and sporadically ... Derive conservation of destiny? Fifty tweaks discovered so far. More to come. Can you share your discoveries? Mutual bennies if yes.

"A scientific courtship," Bithras said. "Highly unusual, Earth courting Mars. Did Charles Franklin discuss such matters?"

"No," I said. "Well ... I think he mentioned 'Bell Continuum' and something else. 'Forbidden channels.' Whatever they are. He didn't say much. I wasn't interested."

"Pity," Bithras said. "You had a prime opportunity, both to romance Mr. Franklin and to learn about something very important. He might have told you?"

"If he had, I wouldn't have understood."

"The 'Bell Continuum,' my researchers tell me, is the key to a radical theory of physics that shows some promise. The Olympians refer to universes as 'destinies.' "

I shook my head, still all uncomprehending.

"We are interested, Casseia, because Cailetet Mars is being pressured to pull out from Tharsis funding. All funding."

"Cailetet is Lunar," I said.

"Yes, but dominated by GEWA, and Cailetet Mars would enjoy being more independent. And at the same time, Mr. Franklin has been approached by Stanford University to join their program and come to Earth to continue his research. They promise access to Earth's most advanced thinkers, including Quantum Logic thinkers, and a very high personal salary as well. They will also help relieve Klein's money problems. Which, of course, are due largely to interference from GEWA."

"Did he accept?"

"He reported the offer to Klein, as is only polite within a family, and Klein informed the Council, which is also only polite. The Council passed the information to major funders of Tharsis research. No, he did not accept. Mr. Franklin is an admirable young man. Alice concludes that Earth is heavily engaged in research in the Bell Continuum and something called 'descriptor theory.' There have been other hints to that effect."

"It's important?"

Bithras smiled. "Earth won't get Charles Franklin, or any of the Olympians. Majumdar will work with Cailetet to finance three QL thinkers for their purposes."

"Oh," I said. Charles had done the right thing, and he had gotten what he wanted by doing it. Admirable.

"I am sorry your affair went no further," Bithras said. "Why did you break with him?"

The transition into personal prying was accomplished with so little change in tone that I was almost lulled into answering. Instead, I smiled and turned one hand over, raised my eyebrows, and shrugged: *C'est la vie*.

"Have you had much experience with brilliant men?"

"No," I said.

"Much experience with men at all?"

I continued smiling and said nothing. Bithras watched me intently. "I have observed that young women acquire most of their knowledge of men in the first five years of their romantic lives. It is a crucial time. I would guess that you are within that five-year period. To neglect your education would be a pity. A spaceship offers such limited opportunities."

Here it comes.

"If you remember anything more about Charles Franklin, please tell me. I am reluctantly forced to catch up on physics, and I am not so skilled at mathematics. I hope Alice is a good tutor."

He thanked me and opened the cabin door. In the hallway, I passed Acre on some errand, murmured hello, and went to the exercise room. There, accompanied by four sweating men, all about Bithras's age, I worked off my anger and dismay for about an hour.

Charles had married. He had the anchor he wanted. He was well on his way to being significant, to Earth and Mars, if not to me.

Good for him.

Orianna burned like an intense flame blown by swift winds. I never could predict the direction of those winds, what her moods would be precisely—but I never knew her to be morose, or discouraged, or even overtly judgmental. When she fixed her attention on me—listening to me or just watching me—I knew what a cat must feel like, scrutinized by a human . . .

Orianna was not effectively more *wise* than I was, but her instant access to information, her blithe show of skills not learned or earned but bought, were marvelous. What she lacked was what I lacked—what all Earth's glory could not give her or me: experience that sat deep in the mind and in the flesh. Her enhancements and all her advanced education could not give her passionate conviction or a true sense of direction.

Talking, letting the telescope fill our rooms with projected images, sharing LitVids, playing games in the lounge, watching the stars pass from the observation deck ... Orianna showed me a mirror to my own immediate past—she taught me a lot about Earth, and perhaps even more about myself. Through her, I saw more clearly how far I had to go.

But I was still reluctant to join Orianna in a sim. She persisted in her efforts to convince.

"I smuggled some real outer sims past Earth douane. I haven't told my parents," she said to me on Jill's Day, December 30. We were in the fifth month of our crossing and had just emerged from the most strenuous regimen of exercises yet—three hours in the gym with magnet suits, running in place in fields that simulated full Earth gravity. "You won't tell?"

"Is that illegal?"

"Well, no, but the companies that make them are pretty protective. They could cut me off a customer list if they found out. They don't want dupes made off Earth."

"Sims aren't very popular off Earth," I said.

Orianna shrugged that off. "There's one I think you'll really like. It's gradual. Puts you in touch with all the cultural differences between you and me. Set on present-day Earth, but it's not an education piece. It's fantasy and very romantic. Since you have access to Alice ... Alice would be perfect for screening our sims. Much better than slates ... We could go full-depth with Alice."

"I'm not sure she'd agree."

"I've never met a thinker that wasn't eager to build up more data on human nature. Besides, it's Jill's Day. Time to celebrate. Alice needs relaxation, too."

Jill, the first thinker on Earth to achieve self-awareness—on December 30, 2047—had served as template for the next generation of thinkers, and so in a very real way was a direct ancestor of Alice. Jill was still active on Earth. Alice wanted to visit her broadband on the nets when we got to Earth, if we had time.

We took turns in my room with the vapor bag and toweled off, then sat. "You are fixed on sims," I said. "What about real life?"

Orianna said, "When I'm eighteen, real life will mean something. When I'm on my own, and my parents aren't responsible for my actions, I can take risks and be dangerous. Until then, I'm a cutlet."

"Cutlet?"

"Slice off the parental loin. Sims are exercise for the rest of my life."

"Even fantasy?"

She smiled. "Well . . . not to stretch a point. They're fun."

I gently declined the offer, but hinted there might be time later.

The routine of each day in space became hypnotic. After four or five hours' sleep—growing less each month—I would wake up to pleasant music and a projection of the ship's schedule for the day, along with a menu from which I could choose my meals and activities. I exercised, ate breakfast, spent a few hours with Orianna or Alice, or sat in the main lounge, chatting with other passengers. Space chat was congenial, seldom stimulating or controversial. I exercised again before lunch, more strenuously, and joined Orianna and her parents to eat.

Allen and I met in with Bithras every two or three days. His Earth agenda was shaping up and afternoons were devoted to deep training. He gave us LitVids and documents to study, some proprietary to Majumdar. I was careful not to reveal anything I learned from these sessions in conversation with Orianna, or anybody else.

At dinner, I joined Allen and Bithras and several of Bithras's acquaintances from Earth. After dinner, I spent time in my cabin with LitVids—hungry for an outside existence—and then exercised lightly and had a snack with Orianna or Allen.

It didn't take me long to pick holes in some of the statements made by Terries aboard ship, general assumptions about Earth's future, GEWA's or GSHA's plans; I was close to a center now, and what I was learning both disturbed and impressed me.

One conversation sticks in my memory, because it was so atypically blunt. It took place at the end of the fifth month. After an hour poring over Earth economics and its relation to the Triple—a relation of very large dog wagging a tiny but growing tail—I dropped down to dinner and made my choice. Minutes later, trays of excellent nano food—better than anything available on Mars—were ferried to me by the dining room arbeiter from the brightly lit mouth of the dispenser.

Orianna was in her cabin, lost in a sim; we had a date for later in the day. I sat beside Allen at the outside of a curved table. Across from us sat Orianna's parents. Renna Iskandera, her mother, a tall, stately Ethiopian woman, wore a loose jumpsuit in brilliant orange, dark purple, and brown block prints. Her husband, Paul Frontiere, French by birth and a citizen of Eurocon, dressed in trim gray and forest-green spacewear, loose at waist and joints, slimming around wrist and ankles.

Allen was already talking with Renna and Paul. I sat beside him, listening attentively.

"I think we're a little daunted by Earth and Earth customs," Allen said. "So many people, so many cultures and fashions ... The more I learn, the more confused I get."

"Martians don't study the homeworld in school?" asked Renna. "To prepare, I mean, for such trips as this."

"We study," Allen said, "but Martians are pretty self-absorbed." He glanced at me, the skin around his eyes crinkling in private humor.

"On Earth, we're proud of our acceptance of change, and of our unity within diversity," Paul said. "Martians seem proud of common heritage."

I decided to ramp up the provocation, in the interests of understanding Terries, of course, and not because of the slight sting of the veiled accusation of being *provincial*. "We've all been taught that Earth is politically more calm and more stable than it's ever been—"

"That is true," Paul said, nodding.

"But there's so much argument! So much disagreement!"

Renna laughed, a high, wonderful melody of mirth. She was twice my age, yet appeared much younger, might have been sister to her own daughter. "We revel in it," she said. "We take pride in shouting at each other."

"You mean, it's all a front?" Allen asked.

"No, we genuinely disagree about many things," Renna said. "But we do not kill each other when we disagree. You are of course taught about the twentieth century?"

"Yes," I said. "Of course."

"The bloodiest in human history. A nightmare—one long war from almost the beginning to almost the end, a hothouse for every imaginable tyranny. Even at its conclusion, passions between peoples of different heritage, different religions, even simple geographic differences, led to murder and reprisal on a hideous scale. But it was the century in which more people than ever broke from traditional power structures, expressed skepticism, found disillusionment and despair—and grew."

I frowned. "Grew out of despair?"

"Grew out of necessity. No turning back to old ways—no one could afford to. There was no longer profit in destruction. The great god Mammon became a god of peace. And that is when we looked outward—and made the beginnings of the settled Moon and Mars and the outer small worlds. People were able to see more clearly."

"But you're still arguing," I said, and bit my lip gently, hoping to give the impression that my naïveté now lay naked on the table before them. Bithras was teaching me the art of lapwing—faking confusion or weakness for advantage.

"I hope not to speak for everyone on Earth, of course!" Paul said, laughing. "To argue is not to hate, not for healthy minds. Our opponents are prized. They goad us to greater accomplishment. If we are defeated, we know that there are other wars to be fought, wars without blood, wars of intellect and of many possible outcomes, not just defeat or victory."

"And if you argue with Mars?" I asked, putting on a mask of provincial anxiety. "If we disagree?"

"We are fearful opponents," Paul admitted. Renna seemed less happy with that answer.

"What is good for all, is good for Earth," she said. She touched my hand. "On Earth, there is so much variety, so much possibility for growth and change, so much, as you say, argument, but if you track the politics, the responses of peoples wherever they may live, there are astonishing agreements on major goals."

Goals. The word rang like a bell. *Alice, you are so right.* "Such as?"

"Well," Renna said, "we cannot afford to lack discipline. The universe is not so friendly. Weaknesses and weak links—"

"Such as Mars," I said.

Renna's eyes narrowed. Perhaps I was laying it on too thick. "We must act together for the common goals of all the human worlds."

"What are we to unite against?"

"Not against, but for. For the next push—to migrate to the stars. There are worlds enough for all who disagree to try great experiments, make great strides ... But we will not achieve them if we are separate now, and lacking discipline."

"What if our goals don't coincide?" I asked.

"All things change," Renna said.

"Whose goals should change?"

"That's what the debate is about."

"And if debate isn't enough? Debate can grind on forever," I said.

"True, there isn't always the luxury of unlimited time."

"If debate has to be cut off," I said, "who does the cutting?"

Renna looked at me shrewdly. She was enjoying herself, but I had to ask, despite all their obvious sophistication, despite their time on Mars, did they truly understand how a Martian felt? "When a society can't do the good drive, as Orianna might say—when it refuses its responsibilities—then other means must be tried."

"Force?" I asked.

"Renna dearly loves to debate," Paul said confidentially to Allen. "This ship has been too quiet, too polite."

"Where Mars and Earth cannot agree, there is always room for growth and discussion," Renna concluded, staring at me in an entirely friendly and expectant way. "Force is an old habit I do not approve of." She obviously wanted me to counter, but something had cut deep and I did not wish to oblige her. I gave a cool smile, inclined, and tapped my plate to signal the arbeiter I was finished.

"We sometimes forget the sensibilities of others, in our enthusiasm" Paul said warily.

"It's nothing," Allen said. "We'll pick up the discussion later."

Bithras had a lot on his mind. His behavior was exemplary. He seemed more a concerned blood uncle than a boss; sometimes a teacher, sometimes a fellow student working with Allen and me to riddle the puzzles of Earth. Never the sacred monster my mother had described.

His transition, in the middle of our sixth month, came abruptly enough to catch me completely off guard. Bithras called me to his cabin for consultation. He had taken to wearing tennis togs again, and as I came in, he sat in his white cotton shirt and shorts, legs pushed against the opposite wall, slate on his lap.

"A lot of tension on Mars this week," he said.

"I haven't seen anything in the LitVids," I said casually.

"Of course not," he said with a twitch of his mouth. "I wouldn't expect it to get that far. Not yet. Two BMs have decided to make their own proposals for unification."

"Who?" I asked.

"Mukhtiar and Pong."

"Not top five . . ." I asked.

"And not likely to attract any attention . . . on Earth. But I made a lot of concessions and forced a lot of favors to carry our proposal to Earth. Some people who are nervous are much more nervous now. If I am undercut, if someone decides to mount a strong campaign across Mars before we arrive . . . concessions to Earth, sellouts . . ." He lifted his hand and squinted at me. "Not fun. I worry about Cailetet. They seem to believe they have extra cards in the game."

I shook my head in sympathy. He leaned back a few more centimeters and looked me over. "What have you learned from the Terries?"

"A lot, I think."

"Do you know that Terries have been increasing the average age for first sexual experience for the last thirty years, and that more and more of them never have physical sex at all, up to ten percent now?" He squinted skeptically, as if mounting a speculation.

"I've heard that," I said.

"Some people marry and have sex only in sims."

I had been so calmed by his straight and narrow behavior for so many weeks that even now I suspected nothing.

"There have been marriages between thinkers and humans. Marriages physically celibate but mentally promiscuous. People who have children without having sex and without giving birth. Marvels and frights to a red rabbit."

"We have ex utero babies on Mars," I said quietly, wondering what he was up to.

"I prefer the old fashioned way," he said, fixing his round black eyes on me. "There has been damned little of that this voyage. All work. You have not been very romantically adventurous either, I notice."

Signals of caution finally broke through. I didn't answer, just shrugged, hoping my uncomfortable silence would be enough to deflect the course of the conversation.

"We will be working together for many months."

"Right," I said.

"Is it possible to be completely comfortable together, working for so long?"

"We'll have to be," I said. "We'll be red rabbits among the Terries."

He nodded emphatically. "Among very strange and high-powered people. It will cause tensions far worse than what I feel now, going over these recent messages. We're in a war of nerves, Casseia, and we might enjoy—mutually—a place of retreat . . . from the war."

"I'd like to read the messages," I said.

"I would not feel comfortable taking solace from a Terrie woman."

"I'm not sure this is—"

He pushed on with a little shake of his head. "What if I work very hard on a temporary relationship, and it can be only that, and discover the woman from Earth wants me to have sex only *in sim*?" He stared at me incredulously.

Angering by slow degrees, I kept in mind my mother's admonition: be clever, be witty. I felt neither clever nor witty but I did not yet ramp to complete indignation.

"I like to resolve difficulties, make arrangements, early," Bithras said. He reached up and stroked my arm, quickly moving to grip my shoulder. He let go of my shoulder and ran a finger lightly on the fabric centimeters above my breast. "You are much more . . . to me."

"Within the family?"

"That is not an obstacle."

"Oh," I said. "An arrangement of convenience."

"Much more than that. We may both focus on our work, having this resolved."

"A stronger relationship."

"Certainly," Bithras said.

Delicately, I pushed back his arm.

"What you're saying is, we should start our family now, right?" I said cheerily.

He drew his head back, dismayed, "Family?"

"We need to make more red rabbits, right? To offset Earth's billions? A policy matter."

"Casseia!" he said. "You deliberately misunderstand—"

I cut him off. "I hadn't planned on procreating so early, but if it serves policy, I suppose I must." Wit or not, I forged ahead. I put on a stoic face, lifted my hand to my brow, and said, "Bithras, all that can be asked of any red doe, in this life, is to lie back and think of Mars."

He made a face of sharp distaste. "That is not funny, Casseia. I am discussing serious difficulties in our personal lives."

"I'll have to update my medical nano," I said. "Bichemistry is different in pregnant women."

"You miss my meaning completely." He stretched out his arms and again one hand touched my shoulder, moved to my upper breast, while his eyes held me, tried to convince me that this was not what it might seem. "Am I not attractive?"

I lifted my eyebrows and removed his hand again. "You should talk to my father. He understands family politics and proprieties better than I. Certainly in the matter of liaisons and alliances . . . and children."

Bithras slumped his shoulders and waved his hand weakly. "I'll transfer the docs to your slate. Alice already has them," he said. Then he shook his head with genuine sadness and perhaps regret.

Guiltless, I did not feel at all sorry.

I left his cabin with a dizzy sense of lightness. Forewarned was forearmed. The lightness reverted to anger once I was in my own cabin, and I sat on the bed, pounding the fabric so hard I lifted my bottom several centimeters. Then I lay back and counted backwards, eyes closed, teeth clenched. *He has no more control than a baby wetting his diapers,* said a calm, cold voice in my head, the part of me that still thought clearly when I was upset. "He has no more technique than a tunnel bore," I said out loud. "He's *inept.*"

I sat up, rubbed my eyes, and took a deep breath.

Voice or vid communication between *Tuamotu* and Mars was too expensive to be indulged in lightly. I sent text letters instead, addressing Father, Mother, and Stan; but the last letter I sent, in the beginning of our eighth month, before he slowed for Earth orbit, I addressed to Mother alone.

Dear Mom,

I've survived this far, and even enjoyed most of the trip, but I'm afraid the letters I've been sending haven't been completely open. Being away from Mars, talking with Terries, watching Bithras at work, I've become more and more aware every day how outmatched we Martians are. We are blinded by our traditions and conservatism. We are crippled by our innocence. Poor Bithras! He bumped me, as you said he would—only once so far, thank God—and he was so crude, so direct and unsophisticated—a man of his travels and broadness of mind, of his importance! A friend once told me that Martians don't educate their children for the most important things in life—courtship, relations, love—relying instead on individual discovery, which is hit-or-miss, mostly miss. On Earth, Bithras would get social-grade therapy, spend some time practicing in sims, clear his mind and improve his skills. Why does our sense of individuality prevent us from correcting our weaknesses?

I'm spending a lot of time with a young woman from Earth. She is sharp and witty, she is a thousand years old compared to me—yet she's only seventeen Earth years. On her eigh-

teenth birthday, I'm going to go into a sim with her and explore wise old Earth through its fantasies. I don't know exactly what the sim is, but I suspect it won't make me comfortable. She will hardly think anything of it, but I'm terrified. Terrie-fied. You might be shocked, reading this, but don't think I'll be any less shocked, doing it. I have always thought myself to be stable and imperturbable, but my innocence—my ignorance—is simply appalling.

And Alice suggested I try something of this sort. I hope that legitimizes it a little in your eyes, but if not ... As Orianna—that's the young woman's name—as she says, I'm no longer a cutlet.

I sent the letter coded to our family, and before Mother had a chance to reply, on Orianna's eighteenth birthday, two days away from our transfer from the *Tuamotu* to a shuttle to Earth, we dived into her smuggled fantasy sim.

"Better late than never," Orianna said as we hooked our slates on a private channel, through the ship's broadband, and linked with each other and with Alice, who was willing and even eager to conduct.

"You haven't told me what it's about."

"It's a forty-character novel."

"Text?"

"Calling it a novel means it has a plot, instead of just being landscape. You're part of a flow. You can move from character to character, but the character imposes—you won't think like yourself in character, but you can watch. In other words, part of you will know you're still you. It's not a whole-life sim."

"Oh."

"You can pull out any time, and you can jump, as well."

"You've done this sim before?"

"No," Orianna said. "That's why I didn't want to just slate it. Alice can give us more protection and more detail. If there's a bug, she can pull us out gently rather than just disconnecting. A discon always gives me a headache."

It sounded worse and worse. I seriously considered backing out, but looking at Orianna, at her bright-eyed eagerness as she arranged the nano plugs, I felt a sudden burst of youthful shame. If she could do it, I could, too.

"You'll go into the staging faster than I will," she said, handing me my cable. "My cable will have to deactivate enhancements and set up cooperation links."

I placed the cable next to my temple. The tip spread to several centimeters and seized my skin, snaking to get in a position to support its own weight. My arm-hair prickled. This was very like the arrangements for major therapy. Something tickled in my temple: the nano links going in through skin, skull, and cortex, pushing their leads into the proper main lines within the brain.

"What happens if this is jerked loose?" I asked, pushing the cable with a fingertip.

"Nothing. The links dissolve. Abso safe. Old old tech."

"And if there's a bug Alice can't handle?"

"She can reprogram anything in the sim. You just spend a few seconds with Alice while she figures it out."

That's right, actually, Alice said within my head.

"Wow," I said, startled. I had done LitVids with Alice, of course, but a direct link was a very different sensation.

Try talking to me without moving your lips or making a sound.

"Is this—" *Is this right?*

Very good. Relax.

Do you approve of this sort of thing?

My entire existence is rather like a sim, Casseia.

I told my mother we'd do this. I don't know what she'll think.

I still saw through my eyes. Orianna had put on her cables and closed her eyes. A muscle in her cheek twitched.

"Ready," she said out loud.

Sim will begin in three seconds.

I closed my eyes. For the first time in my life, I had the sensation of closing my ears, my fingers, my *body*, as well.

A creator credit icon—three parallel red knife slashes rising from a black ground, representing no artist or corporation I was familiar with—then total darkness.

When I opened my eyes again, I had a new set of memories. *In medias res*, along with the memories came a new set of concerns, worries, things I knew I had to do.

It was so smooth I hardly felt the shift.

I became Budhara, daughter of the Wahabi Arabian Alliance family Sa'ud, heir to old Earth resource fortunes. I knew somewhere that Budhara had never lived—this was fiction—but it didn't matter. Her world was real—more real than my own, with the intensity possible in exaggerated art. My part in her life began fifty years in the past, and moved with undiminished vividness through seven episodes, ending on her deathbed ten years in the future.

There was intrigue, double-dealing, betrayal, sex—though very discreet and not very informative—and there was a great deal of detail about the life of latter-day Wahabis in a world full of doubters. Budhara was not a doubter, but neither did she conform. Her life was not easy. It did not feel easy, and the intensity of her misery at times was mitigated only by my awareness that it would have an end.

Her death was startling in its violence—she was strangled by her lover in a fit of inferiority—but it was no more revelatory than the sex. My body knew it was not dead, just as it knew it was not really having sex.

After, my mind floated in endspace, gray and potent, and I felt Orianna there. She said, "Anybody you saw, you can become. Up to four per session, with a thinker driving."

"How long have we been in sim?" I asked.

"An hour."

It had seemed much longer. I could not really guess how long. But I thought we had not met in the sim, and all I could think to say, in the grayness, was, "I thought we were sharing."

"We did. I was your last husband."

"Oh." The flush began. She had switched sexes—she had

known me. I found that intensely unsettling. It called so many of my basics into question.

"We can switch to another location, as well ... connect with Budhara through western channels. She can become a minor character."

"I'd like to be her parrot," I joked.

"That's outer," Orianna said, meaning beyond the sim.

"Then I'd like to go Up," I said, not using the correct term, but it seemed right.

"Surface coming," Orianna said, guiding me out of the gray. We opened our eyes to the cabin. Being tens of millions of kilometers between worlds seemed boring compared to Budhara's life.

I whistled softly and rubbed my hands together to assure me this was reality. "I'm not sure I *ever* want to do that again," I said.

"Yeah. It's something sacred the first time, isn't it? You want to go back so bad. Real seems fake. It gets easier to pull out later, more perspective, otherwise these would have been negged by law years ago. I don't do lawneg sims."

"Lawn-egg?" I asked.

"Outlaw. Illegal."

"Oh." I still wasn't thinking clearly. "I didn't learn much about Earth."

"The Sa'ud dynasty is pretty withdrawn, isn't it? Down fortune fanatics, nobody needs their last drops of oil, really top for sim fiction. Budhara's my favorite, though. I've been through two dozen episodes with her. She's strong, but she knows how to bend. I really enjoy the part where she petitions the Majlis to let her absorb her brothers' fortunes ... after their death in Basra."

"Admirable," I said.

"You don't look happy?"

"I'm just stunned, Orianna."

"Wrong choice?"

"No," I said, though it had been an obtuse choice, to say the least. Orianna, despite her sophistication, was still very young, and I had to be reminded of this now and again. "But I was hoping to learn more about *mainstream* Earth, not the fringes."

"Maybe next time," she said. "I have some straightforward stories, even *travelogs*, but you can get those on Mars . . ."

"Maybe," I said. But I had no intention of trying another.

On Earth, billions of people devoured sims every day, and yet I could not rise clear-headed from a cheap romance.

Allen and I stood in Bithras's cabin. "I hate this time," Bithras told us, staring at himself in mirror projection. "In a few days it won't be exercise. It will be a damned ball and chain. And I don't mean just the weight, though that will be bad enough. They expect so much out of us. They watch us. I am always afraid some new technology will let them peek into my head while I sleep. I will not feel comfortable until we are on our way home again."

"You don't like Earth," Allen said.

Bithras glared at him. "I loathe it," he said. "Terries are so cheerful and polite, and so filled with machinery. Machinery for the heart, for the lungs, nano for this, refit for that—"

"Doesn't sound so different from Mars," I said.

Bithras ignored me. His basic conservatism was surfacing, and he had to let it out; better this way, I thought, than that he should bump me again. "They never let a thing alone. Not life, not health, not a thought. They worry it, view it from so many perspectives . . . I swear, not one of the people we talk to is an individual. Each is a crowd, with the judgment of the crowd, ruled by a benevolent dictator called the self, unsure it is really in charge, so cautious, so very bright."

"We have people like that on Mars," Allen said.

"I don't have to negotiate with them," Bithras said. "You've chosen your immunizations?"

Allen made a face and I laughed.

"You rejected them all?"

"Well," Allen said, "I was considering letting in the virus that gives me language and persuasion . . ."

Bithras stared at us, aghast. "Persuasion?"

"The gift of gab," Allen said.

"You are fooling with me," Bithras said, pushing back the mirror. "I will look awful. But that matters little, considering *they* will look so good, even at my best I would look awful. They expect it of Martians. Do you know what they call us, when they are not so polite?"

"What?" I asked. I had heard several names from Orianna: claytoes, tunnel mice, Tharks.

"Colonists," Bithras said, accent on the middle syllable.

Allen didn't smile. It was one word never heard on Mars even in its correct pronunciation. Settlers, settlements; never colonies, colonists."

"A *colony*, they say," Bithras continued, "is where you keep your colons."

I shook my head.

"Believe it," Bithras said. "You have listened to Alice, you have listened to the people on this ship. Now listen to the voice of true experience. Earth is very together, Earth is very sane, but that does not mean Earth is *nice*, or that they like us, or even respect us."

I thought he might be exaggerating. I still had that much idealism and naïveté. Orianna, after all, was a friend; and she was not much like her parents.

She gave me some hope.

The cylinders were pulled in and stowed along the hull. The spinning universe became stable. Much of our acquired velocity spilled quickly at two million kilometers from Earth; we lay abed in that time under the persistent press of two g's deceleration.

This far from Earth, home planet and moon were clearly visible in one sweep of the eye, and as the days passed, they became lovely indeed.

The Moon hung clean silver beside the Earth's lapis and quartz. There is no more beautiful a world in the Solar System than Earth. I might have been looking down on the planet billions of years ago. Even the faint sparks of tethered platforms around the equator, sucking electric power from the Mother's magnetic field, could not remove my sense of awe; here was where it all began.

For a moment—not very long, but long enough—I shared the Terracentric view. Mars was tiny and insignificant in history. We shipped little to Earth, contributed little, purchased little; we were more a political than a geographic power, and damned small at that: a persistent itch to the mighty Mother, who had long since drawn a prodigal daughter Moon back to her bosom.

Orianna and I spent as much time staring at the Earth and Moon as we could spare from going through customs interviews. I finished filling out my immunization requests, to block the friendly educations of tailored microbes that floated in Earth's air.

I was excited. Allen was excited. Bithras was dour and said little.

Five days later, we passed through the main low-orbit space station, Peace III, and made our way on a liner through thick air and a beautiful sunset, downward to the Earth.

Even now, at a distance of sixty years and ten thousand light-years, my heart beats faster and my eyes flow with tears at the memory of my first day on Earth.

I remember in a series of vivid still frames the confusion of the customs area on Peace III, passengers from two crossings floating in queues outlined by tiny red lights, Orianna and I bidding our quick farewells, exchanging personal reference numbers, mine newly assigned for Earth and hers upgraded to an adult status, unrestricted; promising to call as soon as we were settled, however long that might take; transferring Alice Two by hand from the niche on *Tuamotu*; promising the customs officers she contained no ware in violation of the World Net Act of 2079, politely refusing under diplomatic privilege the thinker control authority's offer to sweep her for such instances we might not be aware of; obtaining our diplomatic clearances under United States sponsorship; crossing the Earthgate corridor filled with artwork created by the homeworld's children; entering the hatch of the transfer shuttle; taking our seats with sixty other passengers; staring for ten minutes at the close-up direct view of Earth; pushing free of the platform, descending, feeling the window beside my seat become hot to the touch—the thick ocean of air buffeting us with enough violence to make me grab my seat arms, red rabbit *coming home*, heart pounding, armpits damp with expectation and a peculiar anxiety: *will I be worthy? Can Earth love me, someone not born in Her house?*

The sunset glorious red and orange, an arc like a necklace wrapped around the beautiful blue and white shoulders of Earth, seen through flashes of fierce red ionization as we bounced and slowed and made our descent into a broad artificial lake near Arlington in the old state of Virginia. Steam billowed thick and white as we rolled gently on our backs, just as the first astronauts had rolled waiting for their rescue. Arbeiter tugs as big as the *Tuamotu* floated on the rippling blue water ... Water! So much water! The tugs grabbed our transfer shuttle in gentle pincers and pushed us toward shore terminals. Other shuttles came in beside us, some from the Moon, some from other orbital platforms, casting great clouds of spray and steam with their torch-gentled impacts in the huge basin.

Allen held my hand and I clutched his, made dear siblings by wonder and no small fear. Across the aisle from us, seated beside a padded and restrained Alice, Bithras stared grimly ahead, lost in thought.

Now our work really began.

We were not just Martians, not mere red rabbits on an improbable playtrip. We were symbols of Mars. We would be famous for a time, wrapped in the enthusiasm of Earth's citizens for Martian visitors. We would be hardy settlers returning to civilization, bringing a message for the United States Congress; we would smile and keep our mouths closed in the face of ten thousand LitVid questions. We would make gracious responses to ridiculous inquiries: *What is it like to come home?* Ridiculous but not so very ridiculous; Mars was truly my home, and I missed him already in this wonderful strangeness, but . . .

I knew Earth, too.

Leaving the shuttle, we installed Alice on her rented carriage, and she tracked beside us.

Almost all of us chose to walk between the oaks and maples, across meadows of hardy bluegrass, all first-time Martians breathing fresh open air. We wandered through Ingram Park, named after the first human to set foot on Mars, Dorothy Ingram. *Dorothy, I know how you felt.* I tasted the air, moist from a recent shower, and saw clouds rolling from the south rich with generous rain, and above them the blue of kitten's eyes, and no limits, no walls, no domes or glass.

I know you. My blood knows you.

Allen and I did a little waltz on the grass around Alice's carriage. Bithras smiled tolerantly, remembering his own first time. Our antics confirmed Earth's status as queen. We were drunk with her. "I'm not dreaming?" Allen asked, and I laughed and hugged him and we danced some more on the grass.

Bichemistry served us well. We stood upright under more than two and a half times our accustomed weight, we moved quickly on feet that did not strain or ache—not for a while, at any rate—and our heads remained clear.

"Look at the *sky*!" I crowed.

Bithras stepped between us. "The eyes of Earth," he said. We sobered a little, but I hardly cared about LitVid cameras recording the arriving passengers. Let Earth hear my joy.

My body knew where I was. It had been here before I was born. My genes had made me for this place, my blood carried sea, my bones carried dirt, from Earth, from Earth, my eyes had been made for the bright yellow daylight of Earth's days and the blue of the day sky and the nights beneath the air-swimming light of Moon and stars.

We passed through reporters human and arbeiter and

Bithras answered for us, diplomatically, smiling broadly, we are glad to be back, we expect the most enjoyable talks with the governments of Earth, our partners in the development of Sol's backyard. He was good and I admired him. All was forgiven, almost forgotten. Beyond the reporters, in a private reception area, we met our guide, a beautiful, husky-voiced woman named Joanna Bancroft who was everything I was not, and yet I liked her. I could not believe I would ever dislike anyone who lived on this blessed world.

From the port we took an autocar sent by the House of Representatives. Bancroft accompanied us, asking our needs, giving our slates the updated schedules, providing Alice with a complimentary access to the Library of Congress. The car attached to a slaveway among ten thousand other linked cars, millipede trains, transport trucks. I listened attentively enough, but rain fell on the windows and trees glistened dark green beneath the somber gray. When a pause came, I asked if we could open the windows.

"Of course," Joanna said, smiling with lovely red lips and firm plump cheeks.

The autocar slid my window down.

I leaned my head into the breeze, took several plashes on face and eyes, stuck out my tongue and tasted the rain.

Joanna laughed. "Martians are wonderful," she said. "You make us appreciate what we who live here take for granted."

What we who live here.

The words cooled me. I glanced at Bithras and he lifted his eyebrows, one corner of his lips. I understood his unspoken message.

We did not own the Earth. We were guests, present by the complicated sufferance of great political entities, the true owners and managers of the Mother.

We were not home. We would never be *home* again, at any price, across any distance.

Joanna took us to the Capital Tower Comb, a sprawling green and white complex of twenty thousand homes and hotels and businesses designed to serve people from all over Earth—and, almost as an afterthought, space visitors as well. The comb covered two square kilometers on the site where the dreaded Pentagon had once stood, center of the formidable defenses of the old United States of America.

We had arranged for accommodation in the Presidential Suite of the Grand Hotel of the Potomac, low on the north wall of the Capital Tower, overlooking the river.

Joanna departed after making sure we were comfortable. Allen and I stood in the middle of the suite, unsure what to do next. Bithras paced and scowled. The suite still showed off its capabilities; rooms and beds and furniture squirmed through a parade of designs and decors, LitVids darted in front of our eyes—which would we choose, which special capital ed and entertainment presentations would we reserve?—and arbeiters presented themselves in two ranks of three, liveried in the high fashion found only on Earth—green velvet and black silk suits, tiny red hats, totally unlike arbeiters on Mars, which wore only their plastic and ceramic and metal skins.

We stumbled through our choices as quickly as possible, Allen and I doing most of the choosing. Bithras fell into a chair that had finally settled on twentieth-century Swedish.

"These *people*," he muttered. "if they and their damned rooms would only *stand still*."

"No hope," Allen said. He stared out the direct-view window overlooking the river. Beyond, the capital of the United States of the Western Hemisphere could be seen between combs scattered along the Virginia banks of the Potomac. Nothing in Washington DC proper was allowed to stand higher than the Capitol dome—that had been a law for centuries. I longed to walk through the Mall, the parks and ancient neighborhoods, under the trees I saw spreading their canopies like billowing green carpets.

"Still raining," I said in awe.

" 'Sprinkling' is the term, I believe," Allen said. "We have to brush up on our weather."

" 'Weather,' " I said profoundly, and Allen and I laughed.

Bithras stood and stretched his arms restlessly. "We have seven days before we testify to Congress. We have three days before our meetings with subcommittees and Senate and House members begin. That means two days of preparation and meetings with BM partners, and one day to see the sights. I am too anxious and upset to work today. Alice and I will stay here. You may do what you like."

Allen and I glanced at each other. "We'll walk," I said.

"Right," Allen said.

Bithras shook his head as if in pity. "Earth wears on me quickly," he said.

The skies had cleared by the time we cabbed into Washington DC. Allen and I had been rather aloof during our crossing, but now we behaved like brother and sister, sharing the wind, the clean crisp air, the sun on our faces: and then, glory of glory, the cherry trees in full blossom. The trees blossomed once every month, we were told, even in winter; tourists expected that.

"It isn't natural, you know," Allen said. "They used to blossom only in the spring."

"I know," I said peevishly. "I don't care."

"Trees blossom on Mars," he said chidingly. "Why should we marvel at these?"

"Because there is no tree on all of Mars that sits under an open sky and raises its branches to the sun," I said.

The sun warmed our bare arms and faces, the wind blew gentle and cool, and the temperature varied from moment to moment; I could not shake the feeling, damn all politics, all vagaries of birth, that I loved Earth, and Earth loved me.

The day was beautiful. I felt beautiful. Allen and I flirted, but not seriously. We drank coffee in a sidewalk cafe, ate an early lunch, walked to the Washington Monument and climbed the long stairs (I ignored shooting pains in my legs), descended, walked more. Strolling the length of the reflecting pool, we paused to look at transform joggers whizzing past like greyhounds.

We studied projected history lessons and climbed the steps of the Lincoln Memorial, then stood before the giant statue of Abraham Lincoln. I studied his sad, weary face and gnarled hands, and unexpectedly I felt my eyes moisten, reading the words which flanked him, inspired by the civil war over which he presided and which ultimately killed him. *People eat their leaders,* I thought. *The king must die.*

Allen had a different perspective. "He was forcing allegiance on the American South," he said. "He's politically more Terrie than I care for."

"Mars doesn't keep slaves," I reminded him.

"Don't mind me," he said. "I've always rooted for the underdogs."

We then retreated along the reflecting pool and watched the sun go down.

"What would Lincoln think of red rabbits?" Allen asked.

"What would Lincoln think of the union now?" I countered.

Despite some maladjustments in my bichemistry—we were definitely overdoing it—I was giddy with the weather, the architecture all out in the open, the history.

We returned to the comb to have dinner with Bithras in the hotel's main restaurant. The food was even better than it had been aboard *Tuamotu*. Much of it was fresh, not nano, and I searched for, and thought I found, the difference in flavor. "It tastes like dirt, I think," I told Bithras and Allen over the white linen tablecloth and silver candlesticks.

"Musty," Allen agreed. "Not too long since it was alive."

Bithras coughed. "Enough," he said.

Allen and I smiled at each other conspiratorially. "We shouldn't act provincial," Allen said.

"I'll act the way I feel," Bithras said, but he was not angry; simply stating a fact. "The wine is good, though." He lifted his glass. "To red rabbits out of their element."

We toasted ourselves.

On the way back to the suite, outside the lift, Bithras looped his arm through mine and pressed me close. Allen saw this and quickly did the same with my other arm. I felt for a moment as if I were being pressed between two overanxious dogs at stud; then I saw what Allen was up to.

Bithras drew his lips into a firm line and let go of my arm. Allen let go immediately after and I gave him a grateful glance.

Bithras behaved as if nothing had happened. And, indeed, nothing *had* happened. The evening had been too pleasant to believe otherwise.

"I've been here for twenty-seven years," Miriam Jaffrey told us as she invited us into her apartment. "My husband went Eloi ten years ago, and I think, though I do not know for sure, that he is on Mars . . . So here I am, a Martian on Earth, and he's a Terrie up there." Bithras and Allen took seats at her invitation in the broad living room. The windows looked across the sprawl of old Virginia combs and even older skyscrapers. We were on the south side of the Capital Tower Comb, opposite from our hotel.

"I'm always snooping out red rabbits," she said, sitting beside Bithras. They appeared to be about the same age. "It's lovely to hear what's changed and what's the same. Not that I plan on going back . . . I'm too used to Earth now. I'm a Terrie, I'm afraid."

"We're enjoying ourselves immensely," Allen said.

Miriam beamed. Her long black hair hung over square thin shoulders revealed by a flowing green cotton dress. "I'm most pleased you could take time out from your busy schedule."

"Our pleasure," Bithras said. He squirmed his butt into the couch, fighting the self-adjusting cushions. "Now, are we secure?"

"Very," Miriam said, drawing herself up and suddenly quite serious.

"Good. We need to talk freely. Casseia, Allen: Miriam is

not just a social gadfly, she is the best-informed Martian on Earth about things Washingtonian."

Miriam batted her eyelashes modestly.

"She follows the tradition of a long line of hostesses in this capital, who meet and greet, and know all, and she has been invaluable to Majumdar BM in the past."

"Thank you, Bithras," she said.

Bithras produced his slate from a shirt pouch and placed it before her. "We brought a copy of Alice with us. She's resting in our hotel room now."

"She's proof against the latest?" Miriam asked.

"We think she is. We refused an opportunity to let customs sweep her."

"Good. She's Terrie-made, of course, so she's always a little suspect."

"I trust Alice. She was examined by our finest and found true to her design."

"All right," said Miriam, but in a tone that betrayed she still had doubts. "Still, you should know that all thinkers are a little too sweet and innocent to understand Earth, at least those thinkers allowed to be exported—to emigrate."

"Yes, that is so," Bithras agreed. "She will only advise, however, not rule."

I listened to all this in a state of shock. "You're a spy?" I asked innocently.

"Stars, no!" Miriam laughed and slapped her thigh. She struck a pose, hand on knee, shoulder thrown back, tossing her hair. "Though I *could* be, don't you think?"

"We'll meet later today with representatives from Cailetet and Sandoval," Bithras said.

"Cailetet's been very skittish lately," Miriam said. "Buying up notes and extensions from other BMs, minimizing their exposure in the open Triple Market."

"I don't expect to get any answers from them," Bithras said, "but I show the flag, so to speak. We are willing to keep talking."

Miriam said she thought that would be useful. "Though I warn you, I've never seen Cailetet so spooked."

"I'd like to know more about these members of the space affairs committee." Bithras handed her the slate. Names danced before her eyes, along with political icons and identifiers for family and social groups.

Miriam scrolled the list thoughtfully. "Good people. Sharp, above the bang."

I surreptitiously looked up "above the bang" on my slate. It read: 1: CALM, UNFLAPPABLE; 2: UNIMPRESSED BY HIGH OFFICE.

"They're dedicated and haven't missed a trick since I've been here," Miriam said. "Elected officials on Earth are a breed apart, as Bithras is doubtless aware."

"Yes, we have been dealing with a few of our own. District governors . . ."

"The difference is that Earth's elected officials are therapied," Miriam said. "All except for John Mendoza, here. Senate minority leader. Mendoza is a Mormon. Terries didn't put up a warm reception for Dauble, but Mendoza's party cohosted a reception for her with Deseret Space. Deseret Space gave her shelter for a few weeks. Debriefed her about Mars, I imagine."

"At least they have no designs on Mars," Bithras said.

"No, but Mendoza will ask you why you aren't willing to allocate more Martian-controlled Belt resource shares to Earth, and why you refuse to join the Sol Resource Management group. Deseret Space has formed some bridges with Green Idaho. Green Idaho is finally casting its eyes on space-related business. They're both firming up state ties with GEWA, circumventing the U.S."

Bithras annotated the transcript of Miriam's remarks, then looked up and said, "We need to know about Cuba, Hispaniola, New Mexico, and California."

"All on your list," Miriam said, brow creased, tapping the slate with a long fingernail. I noticed a vid playing on the fingernail and wondered what it was. "Let me tell you what I know. My library will feed you . . ."

We listened and shared slate data for the next two hours. When we finished, Bithras switched on his charm, and Miriam seemed receptive. I was relieved.

The meetings with Cailetet and Sandoval, held in our suite, were cordial and totally unproductive. The associate syndic for Cailetet Earth hinted they might not support our unification proposals, that Cailetet Mars might have agreed to the proposals without Triple-wide authority.

After, Bithras was agitated. Almost unconsciously, he stayed close to me, kept gently jostling me. Allen watched with some concern. I ignored it.

Apparently, Miriam was not enough for him. And the pressure was building.

I suffered a small lapse of bichemistry the next morning, alone in my room: nausea, chills, my body breaking through the brace of controls to adjust itself in the way it deemed best. That lasted only an hour, and I felt much better after. The gravity seemed less imposed, more natural.

I looked down on the Potomac and the mall beyond. A crystalline day with high puffy clouds. Washington DC a tiny village, its monuments and ancient domed Capitol visible only as grains of rice in the general green and brown.

Intellects vast and cool and unsympathetic . . .

A fatuous grin spread across my face. I was a Martian, come to invade Earth.

Alice presented her report. We sat in the living room of our suite and scanned the highlights. Bithras dug deeper on several key points. "It's not encouraging," he said.

"The need for central control of all solar resources may be acute within fifteen Earth years," Alice said. "It is generally recognized that Earth needs a major endeavor to keep up its overall psychological and economic vigor, and that endeavor—that social focus—must be interstellar exploration on a grand scale."

Allen found that puzzling. "The whole *Earth* recognizes this? Everybody agrees?"

"Agreement is strong among those groups who make the crucial decisions about the Triple," Alice said. "Especially the executives of the major alliances."

"We'll be pressured to join in the endeavor, whether or not it directly benefits Mars," Bithras said.

"Such a conclusion is overdetermined by the evidence," Alice said.

Bithras leaned back on the couch. "Nothing we can't roll with." But he seemed troubled. "It's a bit obvious, don't you think?"

"Evidence for other conclusions is not clear," Alice said.

"It's what some of our fellow passengers were saying," I said.

"Cut and dried, though, isn't it?" Bithras said, biting his upper lip. He resembled a bulldog when he did that. "Tomorrow I'll open the proposals and share them with you. I need you to fully understand what we're allowed to say, and what we're allowed to give, at each stage of negotiation." He sat up. "From now, you are more than apprentices," he said. "You represent a Mars yet to be born. You are diplomats."

And we acted the part. We attended receptions and parties, hosted two of our own, visited the offices of major corporations and temp agencies, attended dinners arranged by Mars appreciation societies . . .

Miriam hosted our private reception in the hotel. I spent hours talking to explanetaries, listening to their stories of old Mars, answering their questions as best I could about the new Mars. *Did Mackenzie Frazier ever unite the Canadian BMs in Syrtis? Whatever became of the Prescott and Ware families in Hellas? My sister still lives on Mars, Mariner Valley South, but she never answers my letters—do you know why?*

All too often, I could only smile and plead ignorance. There was no Pan-Martian family message center or database easily accessible from Earth. I took a note on my slate to have Majumdar set one up; good for PR. Ex-Martians on Earth could be valuable allies, I thought, and Miriam excepted, we didn't use them very often.

During a break at the reception, I asked Miriam how often Martian BMs approached her, directly from Mars. "About once a year," she said, smiling. I said that was deplorable, and she patted my shoulder. "We are such trusting and insular creatures," she said. "By the time you leave here, you'll know only too well what we're up against, and how far we have to go to get in the spin . . ."

I made a note on my slate that we should sign Miriam to Majumdar exclusively—but didn't that contradict the spirit of unity we were working so hard to demonstrate?

Visiting offices of members of Congress, I quickly noticed a remarkable lack of attention to Bithras's hints at what our proposals might be. Bithras fell into a dark and snappish mood at the end of a grueling day of office-hopping.

"They don't much care," he said, accepting a glass of wine from Allen as we rested in our suite. "That is very puzzling."

Mornings, ex net and LitVid interviews, conducted from a studio in the Capitol; afternoons, more interviews from a studio in the hotel; then lunches with major financiers who listened and smiled, but promised nothing; finally, dinners with congressional staffers, full of curiosity and enthusiasm, but who also revealed little and promised nothing.

Visits to schools in Washington and Virginia, usually over ed-nets from our hotel room . . . A quick train journey to Pennsylvania to meet with Amish Friends of Sylvan Earth, who had finally accepted the use of computers, but not thinkers. Back to Washington . . . A guided tour of the Library of Congress and the Smithsonian Air and Space Museum.

The original Library of Congress had been sealed in helium and was accessible now only in pressure suits. We were not offered the chance to go in. Arbeiters roamed its halls, guarding and tracking its countless billions of paper books and periodicals. It had stopped accepting paper copies in 2049; most research was now conducted out of the electronic archives, which filled a small chamber several hundred feet beneath the old library. Alice absorbed as much of the library as she needed, but even her immense reserves of memory would have been taxed by absorbing all.

At the Air and Space Museum, we stood for pictures at the foot of a full-size replica of the first Mars lander, the *Captain James Cook.* I had seen the original as a preform schoolgirl. To me, the replica seemed larger beneath its dome than the original, sitting in the open air of Elysium.

Earth had too much to show us. We were in danger of becoming exhausted before our most important day arrived . . .

We entered the hearing chamber, stately stone and warm dark wood, seats upholstered in dark faux leather; Bithras, Allen, and myself, deliberately dressed in conservative Martian fashions, Alice on her freshly polished carriage.

With our synthetic clothing and unaltered physiques, we must have resembled hicks in a LitVid comedy. But we were greeted respectfully by five senators from the Standing Committee on Solar System and Near-Earth Space Affairs. For a few minutes, we gathered in light conversation with the senators and a few of their staff. The air was polite but formal. Again, I sensed something amiss, as did Bithras, whose nostrils flared as he took his seat behind a long maple table. Allen leaned over and asked me, "Why aren't we testifying before the whole committee?" I did not know.

I sat to the left of Bithras in a hard wooden chair; Allen sat to his right. Alice was connected to the Senate thinker, Harold S., who had served the Senate for sixty years.

The gallery was empty. Obviously, this would be a closed hearing.

Senator Kay Juarez Sommers of New Mexico, chair of the committee, gaveled the hearing into order. "I welcome our distinguished guests from Mars. You don't know how odd that is for an old Terrie like myself to say, even today. Maybe

I need some enhancements to the *imagination*. Certainly some of my colleagues think so . . ." She was in her mid-seventies, if I could judge age when appearance seemed an arbitrary choice; small and wiry, clean simple features, smooth-voiced, dressing hard in blacks and grays. Senator Juarez Sommers had not chosen any easy roads in her life, and she had eschewed obvious transform designs.

Also attending the hearing today were Senators John Mendoza of Utah, tall, chocolate-skinned, severely handsome and stocky; Senator David Wang of California, white-blond with golden skin, a fairly obvious transform; and Senator Joe Kim of Green Idaho, of middle height, gray-haired, wearing an expression of perpetual suspicion. Or perhaps it was discernment.

"Mr. Majumdar, as you can see, this is a closed hearing," Juarez Sommers began. "We've chosen key members of the standing committee to hear your testimony. We'll speak directly, since our time is limited. We're curious as to how much progress Mars will make toward unification in the next five years.

"We face major obstacles," Bithras said, "not all of them caused by Martians."

"Could you elaborate, please?"

Bithras explained the complex interactions of Binding Multiple finances and politics. Martian resources were about two percent developed. Earth-based corporations with BM subsidiaries and Lunar-based BMs controlled fifteen percent of Martian capital and ten percent of developed resources. Mars-based BMs frequently sought capital from Triple sources off Mars, establishing temporary liaisons, even giving the outside sources some say in their internal affairs. It seemed everybody had a finger in the Martian pie. Organizing so many disparate interests was more than difficult, it was nightmarish, and it was made worse by the reluctance of healthy and profitable BMs to submit to central authority.

"Do Martian BMs feel they have inalienable rights, *corpo-*

rate rights as it were, no matter what the needs of their individual members?" asked Senator Mendoza of Utah.

"Nothing so arrogant," Bithras said. "Binding Multiples operate more like groups of small businesses and families than worker-owned Earth-style corporations. Family members are all shareholders, but they cannot sell their shares to any outside concerns. Entry to the family is through marriage, special election, or birth. Transfer through marriage or election removes you from one BM and places you in another. Within the family, there is exchange of work credits only, no money as such ... All investments outside the family are directed by the syndic's financial managers." The senators appeared bored. Bithras concluded quickly. "I'm sure you're familiar with the principles ... They're the same on the Moon and in the Belts, as well."

"Being aware of a pattern should imply being able to change it," said Mendoza.

"Our witness has just admitted to us that there is reluctance," said Senator Wang of California, glancing at his colleagues with raised eyebrows.

"Mr. Majumdar's own Binding Multiple has been reluctant to cooperate with attempts to unify," said Juarez Sommers. "Perhaps he can give us insight into both the reluctance, and the proposed nurturing of a new social pattern."

Bithras tilted his head to one side and smiled, acknowledging the sudden characterization as a *reluctant* witness. "We have worked long and hard to determine our own destiny. We behave as strong-willed individuals within an atmosphere determined by mutual advantage. We are naturally not inclined to place our destinies and lives in the hands of agencies who do not answer directly to us."

"Your Binding Multiples have lived under this illusion for decades," said Senator Joe Kim of Green Idaho. "Are you telling us this is truly how Mars works—each individual interacting directly with family authorities?"

"No," Bithras said.

"Surely you have a system of justice that all BMs subscribe to. How do you treat your untherapied, your ill-adapted?"

"Haven't we strayed from the subject a bit, Senator?" Bithras asked, smiling.

"Humor me," Kim said, looking down at the slate before him.

Bithras humored him. "They have rights. If their maladaptation is severe, their families persuade them to seek aid. Therapy, if that seems necessary. If their ... ah ... crime transcends family boundaries, they can be brought before Council judges. But—"

"Martians are not enamored of therapy," Mendoza said, staring at us one by one. "Some of us in Utah share their doubts."

"We don't embrace the concept as a fashion," Bithras clarified. "Neither do we oppose it on principle."

"We think perhaps an improvement in the mentality of Martians as individuals might lead to a greater acceptance of more efficient social organization," Juarez Sommers said, glancing at Mendoza with some irritation.

"The Senator is privileged to think that," Bithras said quietly.

That line of questioning was dropped. The senators paused for a few seconds, tuning in to Harold S. perhaps, then resumed the questioning.

"You're no doubt aware that the major alliances of Earth have expressed unhappiness with Martian backwardness," Juarez Sommers said. "There's even been disgruntled talk of economic sanctions. Mars relies heavily on Earth, does it not, for essential goods?"

"Not entirely, Senator," Bithras said. She must have known we did not; she was working toward some point I could not see.

"Do your Binding Multiples conduct business with human brainpower alone, or do they use thinkers?"

"We rely on thinkers, but make our own decisions, of

course," Bithras said. "As you do here . . . in Congress. I believe Harold S. is merely a revered advisor."

"And these thinkers are grown on Earth," she continued.

"We have a few more years before we can grow our own Martian thinkers." Bithras looked down at the table, rubbing the edge of his slate with a finger. His face reddened ever so slightly at what might have been an implied threat.

"Martian nanotechnology is acknowledged to be a decade behind Earth's, and your industrial facilities are likewise less efficient."

"Yes."

"Earth corporations and national patent trusts are reluctant to release designs for better nano to a society with few central controls."

"Martians have never smuggled designs and never sought to infringe patents. We have stringent oversight within all BMs on patent permissions and compensation. We also allow Earth inspections of facilities using patented or copyrighted designs."

"Still, the perception exists, and it hurts Martian industry and development, correct?"

"In all humility," Bithras said, "I must say we take care of our needs."

What Bithras did not mention was the widespread Martian perception that Earth preferred our economic development to be stunted, kept tightly in Earth's control.

"Doesn't Mars wish to grow?" Mendoza asked, wide-eyed with astonishment. "Don't Mars's leaders—the syndics of the various BMs and the governors of resource districts—wish to join the greater efforts of the Triple?"

"To the best of our poor abilities, yes," Bithras said. "But Earth should never expect Mars to sell out her rights and her resources, to give herself up as somebody's whim property."

Mendoza laughed. "My colleagues and I wouldn't dream of that. We might hope for a place where we can flee, if our own re-elections fail . . ."

"Speak for yourself, John," Juarez Sommers said. The discussion settled into specifics, and trivial ones at that. For ten minutes, the senators asked Bithras more questions whose answers it seemed obvious they could already find within their slates.

The exercise quickly irritated and bored me.

That first hearing, which reached no conclusions, lasted forty-seven minutes.

The next, on the next day, with the same senators, lasted fifteen minutes. We were given a week's reprieve before the final hearing, and no indication we would ever meet with the full committee.

So far, Bithras had not been asked to present his proposals. It did not seem to matter. We had made the crossing to listen to polite but unpleasant banter, mild implied threats, and remarkably soft questions.

Allen shared a bichem refresh and some beer with me on the evening of the second hearing; Bithras slept in his room.

"What do you think they're up to?" I asked.

Allen closed his eyes wearily and lay back in the chair, legs stretched full length. "Wasting our time," he said.

"They don't act as if they have a plan," I said.

"They don't act like much of anything," Allen said.

"It's infuriating."

"No, it's cover," Allen said. "Diversion."

"What do you mean by diversion?" Bithras entered in his pajamas, hair tousled, rubbing his eyes like a little boy. "Give me some of that," he said, flicking a finger at the bichemistry supplement. "My joints ache."

"Did we wake you?"

"Behind these walls? It's quiet as a tomb in there. I had a damned nightmare," Bithras said. "I hate sims."

We were not aware he had experienced any sims. He sat and Allen poured him a cup, which he slugged back with some drama. "Yes, all right," he said, "I let Miriam talk me into sharing a sim with her last night. It was awful."

I wondered what sort of sim they had shared.

"We were talking about the hearings," Allen said.

"You mentioned a 'diversion,' " Bithras said. "You think these hearings are a sham?"

"I have my suspicions."

"Yes?"

"GEWA."

Bithras scowled at Allen. "We've no scheduled meetings with representatives of GEWA."

"Because we're not worth the bother?" Allen asked.

I was still lost. "What about—" I began, but Bithras held up his hand.

"Wang and Mendoza both act as representatives to GEWA for the Senate Standing Committee," Bithras said. "Majority party and minority."

Allen nodded.

"Gentlemen, you've dusted me," I said.

Bithras turned to me as if to a child. "It has been asserted by some that the United States is relinquishing its concerns in space to GEWA as a whole. Binding Multiples having contracts and trade relations with the United States will supposedly answer to GEWA authority, directly."

"What difference would that make to us?" I asked.

"GEWA as a whole is far more aggressive toward space exploration than the United States, and much more involved than any other alliance. But in the Greater East-West Alliance there are many smaller nations and corporations with no space holdings whatsoever. They want holdings. If Mars unites, we would have to establish new relations with GEWA . . . Their little partners would ask that we sell a share of our pie. And they would offer . . ." Bithras pinched his nose and squinched his eyes shut, concentrating. "What . . . what would they offer?"

"Quid pro quo," Allen said.

"Quid pro quo. We provide them a greater share of our participation in Solar System resources . . . in return for the alliance *not* absorbing Mars and its BMs completely."

"As happened to the Moon," Allen said.

"That's terrible," I said. "You're anticipating this, just because they haven't asked lots of hard questions?"

Bithras waved his hand. "Little evidences, certainly," he said.

Allen seemed energized by the frightful scenarios. "We couldn't win that kind of war," Allen said. "If we unite and are pressured to join any alliance, power in the alliance is based on population—"

"Except for the founding nations, such as the United States," Bithras said. "We'd be bottom of the totem pole." He finished his bichem supplement. Allen offered him a glass of beer and he accepted. "In fifteen or twenty years, maybe less, if Alice is correct, ninety percent of the Earth's nations, in every alliance, will be deeply interested in the Big Push. To the stars."

"Shouldn't we be interested, as well?" Allen said, leaning forward and clasping his hands in front of him like a supplicant.

"At the price of our planetary heritage, our soul?" Bithras asked.

"The whole human race ... It's a noble goal," Allen mused.

Bithras took the challenge as if he were fielding a ball. "It would certainly seem noble, to a world desperate for progress, for growth and change. But we'd be eaten alive."

"What's the *point*?" I asked.

Bithras shrugged. "If this speculation is correct, and if our visit has any meaning at all, we will be speaking with representatives from GEWA, in private, before we leave," he said. "The closed Senate hearing is an excuse—no need to go public with policies not yet in place, but also, no need conducting long-term negotiations ignoring what the situation will be in the future. Mendoza and Wang are merely pickets. The reason we were summoned here may be a convenient fiction. We could be caught with our pants around our ankles. I've come here with a proposal ... But they might try to force us to make a firm agreement."

He held out his hand and Allen grasped it firmly. "Good thinking, Allen. If I were them, that's what *I* would do."

Staring at the congratulatory handshake, I felt a burn of jealousy. Would I ever be able to think such convoluted and political thoughts, make such startling leaps into the unlikely, and impress Bithras?

I patted Allen on the shoulder, mumbled good night, and went to my room.

The next morning, as I shared coffee in the suite's living room with Bithras, talking about the day's schedule with Alice, our slates chimed simultaneously. Allen entered from his room and we compared messages.

All further Senate hearings had been canceled. Informal sessions with senators and members of congress from various states had all been canceled, as well—except for a single meeting with Mendoza and Wang, scheduled for the end of our third week.

Suddenly, we were little more than tourists.

The GEWA hypothesis had quickened.

I quickly tired of parties and receptions. I wanted to see the planet, to walk around on my own, free of responsibilities. Instead, we spent most of our time meeting the curious and the friendly, making contacts and spreading goodwill. Miriam, true to her reputation, arranged for us to meet and greet some of the most influential people in North America.

She arranged a second lavish party—paid for by Majumdar—and invited artists, sim actors, business magnates and heads of corporations, ministers from the alliances, ambassadors—more famous and familiar faces than I had ever imagined meeting all at once. The LitVids were conspicuously absent; we were to be at ease, light chatter and fine food, and Bithras was to make his case for a variety of deals and proposals.

The party was held in Miriam's suite, all the walls and furniture rearranged for maximum space. We arrived before most of the others, and Miriam took me aside with a motherly arm around my shoulder. "Don't be too impressed by these people," she told me. "They're human and they're easily impressed. You're an exotic, my dear—and you should take advantage of it. There will be some very handsome people here." She gave me an unctuous smile.

I certainly wasn't going to harvest partners at a political function. But I returned her smile and said I'd enjoy myself, and I vowed to myself that I would.

The crowd arrived in clumps, flocking to core figures of some reputation or another. Allen, Bithras, and I separated and attended to our own clumps, answering questions—"Why have you come all this way?"; "Why are Martians so resistant to the big arts trends?"; "I've heard that over half of all Martian women still give birth—how extraordinary! Is that true in your family?"; "What do you think of Earth? Isn't it a terrible cultural hothouse?"—and gently disengaging to attend to other clumps.

While I recognized many famous people, Miriam had managed to invite nobody I truly wanted to meet. None of the Terrestrial dramatists I admired were there, perhaps because I favored Lit over Vid. None of the politicians I had studied were there. The majority of the partygoers were high spin—Washington still attracted hordes of bright and beautiful people—and my tastes did not track the spin.

Bithras seemed in his element, however, fulfilling his obligations smoothly. For much of the party, executives from corporations with Martian aspirations surrounded him. I noticed four Pakistanis waiting patiently for a turn, two men in traditional gray suits and two women, one wearing a brilliant orange sari, the other a flowing gray three-piece set. When their turn came, Bithras spoke with them in Punjabi and Urdu; he became even more ebullient.

Allen passed by and winked at me. "How fares it?" he asked.

We were out of hearing of others, in a corner where I had

retreated to sip fruit juice. "Boring," I said, very softly. "Where's Bithras?" He had left the room.

"He's talking old times with the Pakistanis, I think," Allen said. "How can you be bored? There are some very famous people here."

"I know. I blame myself."

"Uh huh. You'd rather be hiking the Adirondacks, or—"

"Don't make my mouth water," I said.

"Duty, honor, planet," he said, and left to attend to another clump.

Bithras reappeared ten or fifteen minutes later, speaking earnestly with one of the Pakistani women. The woman listened attentively, nodding frequently. His face glowed with enthusiasm, and I felt glad for him. I couldn't understand a word they said, however.

The party had expanded to fill the available space, and still more people were arriving. Miriam flitted from point to point in the crowd, rearranging conversations, herding people toward food or drink, a social sheep-dog.

Some of the people arriving now were, to my eye, beyond exotic. A musician from Hawaii and three young women in close-fitting black caps took much of the heat away from Allen and me. I recognized him from news stories. His name was Attu. Gaunt and intense, he dressed in a severe black suit. He had linked his consciousness with the three women, who dressed in filmy white, and whom he referred to as sisters. At intervals of ten minutes, they would rejoin, clasp hands, and exchange all their experiences. The women never spoke; Attu was their conduit. I avoided them. That sort of intimacy (and implied male domination) spooked me. I wondered why Miriam had invited them.

The evening was winding down, and the crowd beginning to diminish, when I saw one of the Pakistani men approach Miriam. Miriam raised herself on tiptoes and looked around, shook her head, and went off in search. Intuition had little to do with my guess that they were looking for Bithras.

I disengaged myself from several bankers and made my

way down a hall that led to several smaller rooms. I did not want to interrupt anything private, but I had a bad feeling.

A door slid open suddenly and the Pakistani woman bumped into me. With a quick, angry glance, she rustled past in her long gray dress. Bithras emerged a moment later, biting his lower lip, eyes darting. He sidestepped me and said, "It is nothing, it is nothing."

The Pakistanis gathered near the main door, talking heatedly. They searched the faces of the remaining party guests, focused on Bithras, and one of the men began to shove through other partygoers in his direction. The women restrained him, however, and the four departed.

Miriam stood at the door for a moment, uncertain what to do. Bithras sat in a chair, staring blankly, before standing with deliberation and going for a drink. Like me, he was having only juice.

Nothing more was said. An hour later, we left the party.

Bithras spent the next ten hours locked in his room with the lights out. He accepted his meals through the half-open door, glared at us owlishly, and shut it. Allen and I spent this time studying Alice's fresh reports on GEWA and GSHA.

The following morning, Bithras stepped out of his room in his bathrobe, hands on hips, and said, "It is time to take a vacation. You have two days. Do what you will. Be back here, in this room, by seven in the morning of Saturday next."

"You're taking some time off, as well, Uncle?" Allen asked.

Bithras smiled and shook his head. "I'll be talking with a lot of people ... If we were better than children at this sort of thing, we'd have brought an entire negotiating team. Nobody wanted to *spend the money.*" He practically spat the last three words. There were circles under his eyes; his skin had grayed with stress. "I can't make all the decisions myself. I refuse to set policy for an entire world. If this is a new era for relations with Earth ..." He waved his hand in the air as if describing the flight of birds. "It will take days to sort things out with the other syndics and governors. Alice will postpone her kiss with Jill and advise me. But you would only distract me. If I can't come up with a way to turn this to our advantage, I will resign as syndic."

His smile turned wolfish. "You can play their game. They think we are provincials, suckers for the taking. Maybe we are. You shall certainly act the part. Give interviews if you are asked. Say I am bewildered and disconsolate, and I do not know where to turn next. We are dismayed at the social slight, and find Earth to be incredibly rude." He sat and rested his head in his hands. "May not be too far wrong."

I called Orianna's private number and left a message. Within two hours, Orianna returned my call and we made plans for a rendezvous in New York. Allen had his own plans; he was flying to Nepal.

An hour before I left the hotel, I felt dizzy and frightened. I wondered how we would be received on Mars if we failed here; what would our families think? If Bithras tumbled, would my career within Majumdar BM tumble with him?

By choosing to go with Bithras, I had become part of a monumental war of nerves, and it seemed clear we were losing. I resented being caught between two worlds; I hated *power* and *authority* and the very real, sweaty misery of *responsibility*. I might be part of a failure of historic proportions; I could disgrace my mother and father, my Binding Multiple.

I longed for the small warrens and cramped tunnels of Mars, for my confined and secure youth.

I knew there were bigger cities, more crowded cities—but New York's fifty million citizens caused this rabbit a new kind of claustrophobia. My apprehension changed from fear of the unknown to fear that I would simply be sucked up and digested.

Five hundred and twenty-three years old, New York appeared both ancient and new at once. I emerged from Penn Station surrounded by a rainbow of people, more than I had ever seen crowded together in one place in my life. I stood on a corner as hordes walked in a cold breeze and spatters of sleet.

In design, New York had kept much of its architectural history intact, yet there was hardly a building that had not been rebuilt or replaced. Architectural nano had worked its way through frames and walls, down through the soil and ancient foundations, redrawing wires and fibers, rerouting water pipes and sewers, leaving behind buildings resculpted in original or better materials, new infrastructures of metal and ceramic and plastic. Nothing seemed designed as a whole; everything had been assembled and even reassembled bits at a time, block by block or building by building.

And of course many of the buildings a New Yorker considered new were in fact older than any warren on Mars.

The people also had been rebuilt from the inside. Even in my confusion, they fascinated me. New people in New York the old city: transforms, their skins glistening like polished marble, black or white or rose, their golden or silver or azure eyes glinting as they passed, penetrating glances that seemed both friendly and challenging at once; designer bodies put on for a month or a year, the flesh shaped like clay; designs identifying status and social group, some ugly as protest, some thin and austere, others large and strong and—Earthy.

Lights flashed over the street, airborne arbeiters like fairies on a trod in one of my children's vids, or, even more fantastic, huge fireflies; arbeiters flowed through the city in narrow channels underground and above. Slaved cabs followed glassy strips pressed into the asphalt and concrete and nano stone of the streets.

What fascinated me most about New York was that it worked.

Most submitted to medical nano, body therapy as well as mind. By and large, the city's people were healthy, but medical arbeiters still patrolled the streets, searching for the

untherapied few who might even now out of negligence or
perverse self-destruction fall ill. Human diseases had been
virtually eliminated, replaced by infestations of learning,
against which I had chosen to be made immune. New Yorkers, like most people on Earth, lived in a soup of data itself
alive.

Language and history and cultural updates filled the air. Viruses and bacteria poured forth from commercial ventilators
in key locations, or could be acquired at infection booths,
conveying everything the driven New Yorker might want to
know. Immunizations prevented adverse reactions for natural
visitors not used to the soup.

The sun passed behind a broad cubical comb in New Jer-
sey and lights flashed on, pouring golden illumination
through the gentle drizzle.

Advertising images leaped from walls, a flood of insistent
icons that meant little to me. Spot marketing had been turned
into a perfected science. Consumers were paid to carry transponders which communicated their interests to adwalls. The
adwalls showed them only what they might want to purchase:
products, proprietary LitVids, new sims, live event schedules.
Being a consumer had become a traditional means of gainful
employment; some New Yorkers floated careers allowing
themselves to be subjected to ads, switching personal IDs as
they traveled to different parts of the city, trading purchase
credits earned by ad exposure for more ad income.

Lacking a transponder, all I saw were the icons, projected
corporate symbols floating above my head like strange hovering insects.

According to what I had been taught in govmanagement at
UM, Earth's economic systems had become so complicated
by the twenty-first century that only thinkers could model
them. And as thinkers grew more complicated, economic patterns increased in complexity as well, until all was delicately
balanced on less than the head of a pin.

No wonder cultural psychology could play a key role in
economic stability.

"Casseia!" Orianna stood on a low wall, peering over the crowds. We hugged at the edge of the walkway. "It's great to see you. How was the trip?"

I laughed and shook my head, drunk with what I had seen. "I feel like a—"

"Fish out of water?" Orianna said, grinning.

"More like a bird drowning!"

She laughed. "Calcutta would kill you!"

"Let's not go there," I said.

"Where we're going, my dear, is a quiet place my Mom owns up on East 64th, in an historic neighborhood. A bunch of friends want to meet you."

"I only have a few days . . ."

"Simplicity! This is so exciting! You're even in the Lit-Vids, did you know that?"

"Oh, God, yes."

We took an autocab and she projected the news stories from her slate. She had hooked an Earthwide ex net and scanned for all material related to our visit. The faces of Bithras, Allen and myself floated like little doll heads in the autocab. Condensed texts and icons flashed at reduced speed for my unaccustomed eyes. I picked up about two-thirds of what was being said. GEWA and GSHA had linked with Eurocom to propose a world-wide approach to what was being called the Martian Question: Martian reluctance or inability to join the Push.

"You're being pre-jammed," Orianna said cheerfully.

I was horrified.

The sidebars detailed our personal histories and portrayed us as the best Martian diplomacy had to offer; the last seemed ironic, but I really couldn't fathom the spin.

"You're famous, dear," Orianna said. "A frontier girl. *Little House on the Planum.* They love it!"

I was less interested in what was being said about me than in the backslate details. GEWA, leading the other alliances, would start negotiating with Mars after completion of what the US government was characterizing as "polite dialogues" with members of the standing Congressional committee.

I had a role to play. True shock would only grace my performance. "It's terrible," I said, frowning deeply. "Completely rude and impolite. I'd never expect it from Earth."

"Oh, do!" Orianna said, creasing her brow in sympathy. The cab stopped before a stone and steel eight-story building with dazzling crystal-paned glass doors. The first-floor door popped open with a sigh and she danced ahead of me through crowds flowing along the walkway. "By the time my friends and I are done with you, you'll expect *anything*!

"We don't stay here often," Orianna said, emerging from the elevator. Her long legs carried her down the hall like an eager colt. She slowed only to allow me to catch up with her. "Mother's given us the space here for a few days. My hab is just like the one in Paris. I've kept it since I was a kid."

The door to apartment 43 looked tame enough—paneled wood with brass numbers. Orianna palmed entry and the door swung inward. "We have a guest," she called. Beyond stretched a round gray tunnel with a white strip of walkway. The tunnel ballooned around us, unshaped.

"Welcome home. What can we do for you, Orianna?" a soft masculine voice asked.

"Fancy conservative decor—for our guest—and tell Shrug and Kite to rise and meet my friend."

The tunnel quickly shaped a cream-colored decor with gold details, a rosewood armoire opening its doors to accept my coat and Orianna's shoulder wrap. "English Regency," Orianna said. "Kite's idea of conservatism."

Shrug, Kite—it all sounded very *drive*. I wondered if I would regret coming.

"Don't stick on the names," Orianna said, shaping the living room into more Regency. "All my friends are into Vernoring. They work and play with fake names. I don't know their true ones. Not even their parents know."

"Why?"

"It's a game. Two rules—nobody knows what you're doing, and you do nothing illegal."

"Doesn't that take the fun out of doing crypto?" I asked.

"Wow—crypto! Hide in the tomb. Sorry. I shy from two-edged words. We call it Vernoring."

"Doesn't it?" I persisted.

"No," Orianna said thoughtfully. "Illegal is harm. Harm is stupid. Stupid is its own game, and none of my friends play it. Here's Kite."

Kite came through a double door dressed in faded denim shirt and pants. He stood two meters high, minus a few centimeters, and carried a green-and-white mottled sun kitten.

Orianna introduced us. Kite smiled and performed a shallow bow, then offered his free hand. He seemed natural enough—handsome but not excessively so, manner a little shy. He squatted cross-legged on the oriental carpet and the sun kitten played within a Persian garden design. A light switched on overhead and bathed the animal in a spot of brightness. It mewed appreciatively and stretched on its back.

"We're going out tonight," Orianna said. "Where is Shrug?"

"Asleep, I think. He's spent the last three days working a commission."

"Well, wake him up!"

"You do it," Kite said.

"Pleasure's mine." Orianna leaped from the chair and returned to the hall. We heard her banging on doors.

"She could just buzz him," Kite said ruefully, shaking his head. "She pretends she's a storm, sometimes."

I murmured assent.

"But she's really sweet. You must know that."

"I like her a lot," I said.

"She's an only and that makes a difference," Kite added. "I have a brother and sister. You?"

"A brother," I said. "And lots of blood relations."

Kite smiled. The smile rendered his face transcendentally beautiful. I blinked and looked away.

"Is it rough, having everyone vid you?"

"I'm getting tired of it."

"You know, you should watch whom you touch . . . Shake hands with. That sort of thing. Some of the LitVids are casual about privacy. They could plant watchers on you." He held up pinched fingers and peered through a tiny gap. "Some are micro. Hide anywhere."

"Isn't that against the law?"

"If you haven't filed for privacy rights, they could argue you're common-law open. Then you'd only be protected in surveillance negative areas. The watchers would turn off . . . Most of the time."

"That's bolsh," said a deep, lion-like voice. I turned to see Orianna dragging into the room by one hand a very large, blocky man with a very young face. "Nobody's planted a watcher without permission in four years," the young-faced man said. "Not since Wayne vs. LA PubEye."

"Casseia Majumdar, of Mars, this is Shrug. He's studied law. He has almost as many enhancements as I do."

Shrug dipped on one knee as I stood. I barely reached his chin when he kneeled.

"Charmed," he said, kissing my hand.

"Stop that," Orianna said. "She's *my* partner."

"You don't curve," Shrug said.

"We're sisters of sim," Orianna said.

"Oh, dear, such an arc!" Kite said, smiling.

I don't think I understand a third of what was said the whole time I spent in New York.

Back on the streets, holding hands with Shrug and Orianna, and then with Orianna and Kite, I let myself be taken somewhere, anywhere. Kite was really very attractive and did not seem averse to flirting, though more to aggravate Orianna, I thought, than to impress me. My slate recorded streets and directions in case I needed to find my way back to Penn Station; it also contained full-scale maps of the city, all cities on the Earth, in fact. I could hardly get lost unless someone took my slate . . . and Orianna assured me that New York was virtually free of thieves. "Too bad," I said, in a puckish mood.

"Yeah," Orianna said. "But that doesn't mean there's no risk. It's risk we *choose* that we should beware."

"I choose lunch," Kite said. "There's a great old delicatessen here. Total goback."

My expression of surprise caught his eye. "Goback. Means retro, atavistic, historic. All are good drive words now, no negs."

"It means something else on Mars," I said.

"Folks who want to keep BM rule are called Gobacks," Orianna said.

"Are you a Goback?" Shrug asked me.

"I'm neutral," I said. "My family has strong links to BM autonomy. I'm still learning."

Echoing the theme, we passed a family of Chasids dressed in black. The men wore wide-brimmed hats and styled their hair in long thin locks around their temples. The women wore long simple dresses in natural fabrics. The children skipped and danced happily, dressed in black and white.

"They're lovely, aren't they?" Orianna said, glancing over her shoulder at the family. "Total goback! No enhancements, no therapy, neg the drive."

"New York is great for that sort of thing," Kite said.

We passed three women in red chadors; a woman herding five blue dogs, followed by an arbeiter carrying a waste can; five men in single file, nude, not that it mattered—their bodies were completely smooth, with featureless tan skin; a male centaur with a half-size horse body, perfectly at home cantering along the sidewalk, man's portion clothed in formal Edwardian English wool suit and bowler; jaguar-pelted women, furry, not in furs; two young girls, perhaps ten Earth years, dressed in white ballet gowns with fairy wings growing from their backs (temp or permanent? I couldn't tell); a gaggle of school-children dressed in red coats and black shorts, escorted by men in black cassocks ("Papal Catholics," Kite said); more of the mineral-patterned designer bodies; a great many people who might have fit in without notice on Mars; and of course the mechaniques, who replaced major portions of their bodies with metal shells filled with biorep nano. That, I had heard, was very expensive as an elective. Complete body replacement was much cheaper. Neither could be done legally unless one could prove major problems in birth genotype; it spun too much of the Eloi and Ten Cubed.

"After lunch, we're going to Central Park," Orianna said. "And then . . ."

Kite laughed. "Orianna has connections. She wants to show you something you just *don't* have on Mars."

"An Omphalos!" Orianna said. "Father owns shares."

We ate in the *delicatessen* and it smelled of cooked meat, which I had never smelled before, and which offended me all the same, whether or not meat was actually being cooked. Customers—chiefly drive folks, a high proportion of transforms—lined up before glass cases filled with what appeared to be sliced processed animals. Plastic labels on metal skewers pronounced the shapes to be *Ham*, that is, smoked pig legs, *Beef* (cows) corned (though having nothing to do with corn) and otherwise, something called *Pastrami* which was another type of cow covered with pepper, smoked fish, fish in fermented dairy products, vegetables in brine and vinegar, pig feet in jars, and other things that, had they been real, would have caused a true uproar even on Earth.

We stood at the counter until the clerk took our order, then found a table. Martian reserve kept me from expressing my distaste to Orianna. She ordered for me—potato salad, smoked salmon, a bagel, and cream cheese.

"The stuff here is the best in town," she said. "It was set up by New York Preserve. History scholars. They have a nano artist design the food—he's orthodox Gathering of Abraham. They have state dispensation to eat meat, for religious reasons. He quit eating meat ten years ago, but he remembers what it tastes like."

Our food arrived. The salmon appeared raw, felt slimy-soft, and tasted salty and offensive.

"You have imitation meat on Mars, don't you?" Kite asked.

"It isn't so authentic," I said. "It doesn't smell like this."

"Blame the drive for history," Shrug said. "Nothing immoral about imitation. It doesn't hurt, it doesn't waste, it teaches us what New York used to be like . . ."

"I don't think Casseia's enjoying her lox," Kite said, smiling sympathetically. My heart sank in hopeless attraction, simply looking at his face.

"Maybe it's turned," I said.

"It does taste rank," Kite said. "Maybe it's the fake preservatives. Things don't *turn* any more."

"Right," I said, embarrassed at my inability to enjoy the treat. "Tailored bacteria. Eat only what they're meant to."

"The Earth," Shrug said portentously, "is a vast zoo."

They fell to discussing whether "zoo" was the right word. They settled on "garden."

"Do you have many murders on Mars?" Shrug asked.

"A few. Not a lot," I answered.

"Shrug's fascinated by violent crime," Orianna said.

"I'd love to defend a genuine murderer. They're so rare now . . . Ten murders in New York last year."

"Among fifty million citizens," Kite said, shaking his head. "That's what therapy has done to us. Maybe we don't care enough to kill any more."

Orianna made a tight-lipped blat.

"No, really," Kite said. "Shrug says he'd love to defend a murder case. A real one. But he'll probably never see one. A *murder.* It chills the blood just to say the word."

"So what's passion like on Mars?" Shrug asked. "Murderous?"

I laughed. "The last murder I heard about, a wife killed her husband on an isolated station. Their family—their Binding Multiple—had suffered pernicious exhaustion—"

"Love the words!" Shrug said.

"Of funds. They were left alone at the station without a status inquiry for a year. The BM was fined, but couldn't pay its fine. It's pretty unusual," I concluded. "We therapy disturbed people, too."

"Ah, but is murder a *disturbance*?" Kite asked, straining to be provocative.

"You'd think so if you were the victim," I said.

"Too much health, too much vigor—too few dark corners," Kite said sadly. "What is there left to write about? Our best LitVids and sims use untherapied characters. But how do we write about our real lives, what we know? I'd like to make sims, but sanity is really limiting."

"He's opening his soul to you," Orianna said. "He doesn't tell people that unless he likes them."

"There's plenty of story in conflicts between healthy folks," I suggested. "Political disagreements. Planning decisions."

Kite shook his head sadly. "Hardly takes us to the meaning of existence. Hardly stretches us to the breaking point. You want to live that kind of life?"

I didn't know how to answer. "That's what I'm doing now," I finally replied.

"Up your scale," Shrug advised Kite. "She's right. The clash of organizations, governments. Still possible. GEWA against GSHA. Might make a bestseller."

"They're even taking that away from us," Kite said. "No wars, nothing but economic frictions behind closed doors. Nothing to make the heart pound."

"Kite is a Romantic," Orianna said.

That seemed to genuinely irritate him. "Not at all," he said. "The Romantics wanted to *destroy* themselves."

"Spoken like a `true child of our time," Shrug said. "Kite pushes healthy as they come. Passion—life to the limit—but no *risk*, please."

Kite grinned. "I never met a passion I didn't like," he said. "I just don't want to be owned by one."

An actor portraying a waiter took my dish away.

* * *

The Omphalos stood on five hectares at the southern end of Manhattan, near Battery Park. It looked immensely strong, a cube surrounded by smaller cubes, all gleaming white with gold trim.

At the gate, on the very edge of the compound, Orianna presented her palm and answered a few questions posed by a blank-faced security arbeiter. A human guard met us, took us into an adjoining room, sat behind a desk, and asked our reasons for taking the tour.

"I'd like to talk in private with a resident," Orianna said. I looked at her in surprise; this had not been her stated purpose earlier.

"I'll need your true names and affiliations even to apply for a clearance," he said.

"That leaves us out," Shrug said. Kite nodded agreement. "We'll wait outside." Orianna said we wouldn't be more than an hour or two. An arbeiter escorted them to the front gate.

The guard quickly checked our public ratings for security violations and mental status. "You're Martian," he said, glancing at me. "Not using a Vernor."

I admitted that I was.

"Terries trying to impress you?" the guard asked, glancing pointedly at Orianna.

"Are you Martian?" I asked him.

"No. I'd like to go there some day." He referred to his slate and nodded approval. "I have your CV and pictures from a hundred different LitVid sources ... You're a celebrity. Everything clears. Welcome to Omphalos Six, your first glimpse of Heaven. Please stay with your assigned guide."

"What are your connections, besides your father owning shares?" I asked Orianna as an arbeiter took us through an underground tunnel to the main cube.

"I have a reservation for when I turn two centuries," Orianna said. "I don't know if I'll use it. I might just die instead ..." She grinned at me. "Easy to say now. I might go

Eloi and end up on Mars or in the Belt ... Who knows what things will be like then?"

"Who are we going to talk to?" I asked.

"A friend." She held her finger to her lips. "The Eye is watching."

"What's that?"

"The Omphalos thinker. Very high-level. Not at all like Alice, believe me—the best Earth can produce."

I quelled my impulse to defend Alice. No doubt Orianna was right.

The interior of the building was equally impressive. An atrium rose twenty meters above a short walkway. The walkway ended on an elevator shaft that rose to the apex of the atrium, and sank below us through a glittering black pool. Nano stone walls, floors isolated from the walls by several dozen centimeters, sprung-shocked and field-loaded to withstand external stress—and damage repair stations in each corner. Conservative and solid.

"Above us are the apartments," Orianna said. "About ten thousand occupants. One hundred apartments are full-size, for those folks who want to log in and out every few weeks. The uncommitted, you might say. The rest are cubicles for warm sleep."

"They spend their time dreaming?"

"Custom sims and remote sensing. Omphalos has androids and arbeiters all over the Earth with human-resolution senses. Omphalos can access any of them at any time, and there you are—they are. The occupants can be anywhere they want. Some of the arbeiters can project full images of the occupant, fake you're talking to someone in person. If you just want to retire and relax, Omphalos employs the very finest sim designers. Overdrive arts and lit fantasies."

From my reading, and from Orianna's description on *Tuamotu*, I knew that most of Omphalos's residents stayed in long-term warm sleep, their bodies bathed in medical nano. Technically speaking, they were not Eloi—they could not walk around, occupy a new citizen's space or employment opportunities—but their projected life spans were unknown. Omphalos served as refuge for the very wealthy and very powerful who did not want to be voided to the Belt or Mars, yet wanted to live *longer.* Medical treatment that cleansed and purified and exercised and toned and kept body and mind healthy and fit—medical treatment unending—slipped through a legal loophole.

This Omphalos, and the forty-two structures like it around the world, were not beloved by the general population. But they had woven their legal protections deep into the Earth's governments.

"Why wouldn't you want to come here? The guard called it Heaven."

Orianna had skipped ahead of me. She hunched her shoulders. "Gives me the willies," she said. She called the elevator, which arrived immediately.

The elevator stopped. Orianna took my hand and led me down a hallway that might have belonged in a plush hotel, retro early twentieth. Flowers filled cloisonné vases on wooden tables; we walked on non-metabolic carpet, probably real wool, deep green with white floral insets.

Orianna found the door she wanted. She knocked lightly and the door opened. We entered a small white room with three Empire chairs and a table. The room smelled of roses. The wall before the chairs brightened. A high-res virtual image presented itself to us, as if we looked through glass at a scene beyond. A black-haired, severely handsome woman of late middle years sat on a white cast-iron chair in the middle of a beautiful garden, trees shading her, rows of bushes covered with lovely roses red and blue and yellow marching in perspective off to a grand Victorian greenhouse. Tall clouds billowed on the horizon. It looked like a hot, humid, thundery day.

"Hello, Miss Muir," Orianna greeted the woman. She looked familiar, but I couldn't place her face.

"Hello, Ori! How nice to have visitors." She smiled sunnily.

"Miss Muir, this is my friend, Casseia Majumdar of Mars."

"Pleased to meet you," the woman said.

"Do you know Miss Muir, Casseia?"

"I'm sorry, no."

Orianna shook her head and pursed her lips. "No enhancements. Always leaves you at a disadvantage. This is President Danielle Muir."

That name I had heard.

"President of the United States?" I asked, my face betraying how impressed I was.

"Forty years ago," Muir said, cocking her head to one side. "Practically forgotten, except by friends, and by my goddaughter. How are you, Ori?"

"I'm high pleased, ma'am. I apologize for not coming sooner . . . You know we've been away."

"To Mars. You returned on the same ship with Miss Majumdar?"

"I did. And I confess I've come here with a motive."

"Something interesting, I hope."

"Casseia's being jammed, ma'am. I'm too ignorant to speck what's happening."

Ex-President Muir leaned forward. "Do tell."

Orianna raised her hand. "May I?"

"Certainly," Muir said. A port thrust from the wall, and Orianna touched her finger to the pad, transferring information to Muir.

I specked the former President lying in warm sleep behind the screen, bathed in swirling currents of red and white medical nano like strawberry juice and cream.

Muir smiled and adjusted her chair to face us. The effect startled me—even ambient sound told us we were with her, outdoors. The walls of the cubicle gradually faded into scenery. Soon we, too, were in the shade of the large tree, surrounded by warm moist air. I smelled roses, fresh-cut grass, and something that raised the hair on my arms. Electricity . . . thunderstorms.

"You work for a big financial Binding Multiple. Rather,

you're part of the *family*, right, Casseia?" Her voice, colored by a melodious southern accent, drifted warm and concerned in the thick air.

"Yes, ma'am," I said.

"You're under pressure . . . You've been summoned to testify before Congress, but for one reason or another, you've been shunted to another rail."

"Yes, ma'am," I said.

"Why?"

I looked at Ori. "I really can't reveal family matters here, ma'am. Ori—Orianna brought me here without telling me why. I'm honored to meet you, but . . ." I trailed off, embarrassed.

Muir tilted her head back. "Someone in the alliances has decided Mars is an irritant, and I can't guess why. You simply don't mean that much to the United States, or to GEWA or GSHA or Eurocom or any of the other alliances."

Orianna frowned at me and looked back at Muir's image. "My father says there isn't a politician on Earth you can trust, except Danielle Muir," Orianna said.

My level of skepticism rose enormously; I've always bristled when people ask for, much less demand, trust. Face to face with a ghost, an illusory representative of someone I had never met in person, I simply would not let myself bestow trust it was not my right or station to give.

On the other hand, much of what we were doing was public knowledge—and there was no reason not to carry on a conversation at that level.

"Martians have stood apart from Solar System unification," I said.

"Good for you," Muir said, smiling foxily. "Not everybody should knuckle under to the alliances."

"Well, it's not entirely good," I said. "We're not sure we know how to unify. Earth expects full participation from coherent partners. We seem to be unable to meet their expectations."

"The Big Push," Muir said.

"Right," Orianna said.

"That seems to be part of it."

Muir shook her head sadly. "My experience with Martians when I was President was that Mars had great potential. But this Big Push could get along nicely without you. You'd hardly be missed."

I felt another burn. "We think we might have a lot to contribute, actually."

"Unwilling to participate, but proud to be asked, proud to have pressure applied, is that it?" Muir said.

"Not exactly, ma'am," I said.

Her face—the face of her image—hardened almost imperceptibly. Despite her warm tone and friendly demeanor, I sensed a chill of negative judgment.

"Casseia, Ori tells me you're very smart, very capable, but you're missing something. Your raw materials and economic force count for little in any Big Push. Mars is small in the Solar System scheme of things. What can you contribute, that would be worth the effort Earth seems to be willing to expend on you?"

I was at a loss for an answer. Bithras, I remembered, had been wary of this explanation, but I had swallowed it uncritically.

"Maybe you know something you can't tell me, and I don't expect you to tell me, considering your responsibilities and loyalties. But take it from an old, old politician, who helped plant—much to my regret—some of the trees now bearing ripe fruit. The much-ballyhooed Big Push is only a cover. Earth is deeply concerned about something you have, or can do, or might be able to do. Since you can't mount an effective military operation, and your economic strength is negligible, what could Mars possibly have, Casseia, that Earth might fear?"

"I don't know," I said.

"Something the small and weak can do as well as the large and the strong, something that will mean *strategic* changes.

Surely you can think of what that might be. How could Mars possibly threaten Earth?"

"We can't," I said. "As you've told me, we're weak, insignificant."

"Do you think politics is a clean, fair game played by rational humans?"

"At its best," I said lamely.

"But in your experience . . ."

"Martian politics has been pretty primitive," I admitted.

"Your uncle Bithras . . . Is he politically sophisticated?"

"I think so," I said.

"You mean, compared to you, he seems to be."

My discomfort ramped. I did not like being grilled, even by my social superiors. "I suppose," I said.

"Well, politics is not all muck, and not always corrupting, but it is never easy. Getting even rational people from similar backgrounds to agree is difficult. Getting planets to agree, with separate histories, widely different perspectives, is a political nightmare. I would hesitate to accept the task, and yet your uncle seems to have jumped in with both feet."

"He's cautious," I said.

"He's a child playing in the big leagues," Muir said.

"I disagree," I said.

Muir smiled. "What does he think is really going on here?"

"For the moment, we accept that Earth needs Mars . . . prepared for some large-scale operation. The Big Push seems as likely as anything."

"You truly believe that?"

"I can't think of any other reason."

"My dear, your planet—your culture—may depend on what happens in the next few years. You have a responsibility I don't envy."

"I'm doing my very best," I said.

Muir hooded her gray eyes. I realized that she had asked me questions as one politician to another, and I had given her inadequate answers.

Orianna regarded me sadly, as if she had also discovered the weaknesses of a friend.

"I don't mean to offend," Muir said. "I thought we were dealing with a political problem."

"I'm not offended," I lied. "Orianna took me all over New York today, and I'm a little stunned. I need to rest and absorb it all."

"Of course," Muir said. "Ori, give your mother and father my best wishes. It's grand to see you again. Good-bye." Abruptly, we sat facing the blank white wall.

Orianna stood. Her mouth was set in a firm line and her eyes were determined not to meet mine. Finally, she said, "Everybody here acts a little . . . abrupt at times. It's the way they experience time, I think. Casseia, we didn't come here to make you feel inferior. That was the farthest thing from my mind."

"She chewed on me a little, don't you agree?" I said quietly. "Mars is *not* useless."

"Please don't let patriotism blind you, Casseia."

I clamped my mouth shut. No eighteen-year-old Earth child was going to talk down to me that way.

"Listen to what she was asking. She's very sharp. You have to find out where you might be strong."

"Our strength is so much more—" I cut myself off. *Than Earth can imagine. Our spiritual strength.* I was about to launch into a patriotic defense that even I did not believe. In truth, they were right.

Mars did not breed great politicians; it bred hateful little insects like Dauble and Connor, or silly headstrong youths like Sean and Gretyl. I hated having my face ground into the unpleasant truth. Mars was a petty world, a spiteful and grumbling world. How could it *possibly* be any danger to vigorous, wise, together Earth?

Orianna glanced at the blank wall and sighed. "I didn't mean to make you uncomfortable. I should have talked to you about it first."

"It's an honor," I said. "I just wasn't prepared."

"Let's find Kite and Shrug," she suggested. "I can't imagine living here." She shivered delicately. "But then, maybe I'm old-fashioned."

We rejoined Kite and Shrug and spent several hours shopping in Old New York, real shops with nothing but real merchandise. I felt doubly old-fashioned—dismayed and disoriented by a district that was itself supposed to be a historical recreation. Kite and Shrug entered an early twenty-one haberdashery, and we followed. An officious clerk placed them in sample booths, snapped their images with a quaint 3-D digitizer, then showed them how they might look in this season's fashions. The clerk made noises of approval over several outfits. "We can have them for you in ten minutes, if you care to wait."

Kite ordered a formal socializing suit and asked them to deliver it to a cover address. Shrug declined to purchase anything. We were heading out the door when the clerk called to us, "Oh! Excuse me—I almost forgot. Free tickets to Circus Mind for customers . . . and their friends."

Kite accepted the tickets and handed them to us. He stuffed his in his mouth and chewed thoughtfully. "Are we all going?" he asked.

"What is it?" Orianna asked.

"Ori doesn't know something!" Shrug exclaimed, amused.

"It must be really new," she said, irritated.

"Oh, it is," the clerk said. "Very drive."

"Power live sim," Kite said. "It's abso fresh. All free until it draws a nightly crowd. Would you like to try, Casseia?"

"It could be too much," Orianna cautioned.

I took that as a challenge. Although tired and a little depressed from my meeting with Muir, I wasn't about to look less than drive—certainly not to Kite.

"Let's go," I said.

Kite handed us our tickets. I stared at mine. "Chew," he said. "Checks you out, sees if you're clear for the experience, and you print up a pass on the back of your hand."

I inserted the ticket slowly and chewed. It tasted like the scent of a sun-warmed flower garden, with a tickle in the nose. I sneezed.

The clerk smiled. "Have fun," he said cheerfully.

Circus Mind occupied the fifth and sixth floors of a twentieth-century skyscraper, the Empire State Building. I consulted my slate and learned that I was not far from Penn Station—in case I wanted to escape and my friends were locked in their amusements. Kite took my arm and Orianna ran interference with a group of LitVid arbeiters looking for society interest. Kite projected a confusion around me— multiple images, all false, as if four or five women accompanied him—and we made it through to the front desk. A thin black woman over two and a half meters tall, her auburn hair brushing the star-patterned ceiling, checked our hands for passes and we entered the waiting area.

"Next flight, five minutes," a sepulchral voice announced. Cartoonish faces popped out of the walls, leering at us—lurid villains from a pop LitVid.

"Abso brain neg," Shrug commented. "I was hoping for a challenge."

"I've been here twice," said a woman with skin of flexible coppery plates. "It's strong inside."

Orianna glanced at me, *Okay?*

I nodded, but I was not happy. Kite, I noticed, had assumed a blank air, neither expectant nor bored. After a five-minute wait, the faces on the walls looked sad and vanished, a door opened, and we entered a wide, open dance floor, already covered with patrons.

Projectors in the ceiling and floor created a hall of mirrors. The floor controller decided Kite and I were a couple and isolated us between our own reflections. We could not see Shrug or Orianna or any of the other patrons, though I heard them faintly. Kite grinned at me. "Maybe this replaces murder," he said.

I had no idea what he meant. I felt more than a little apprehensive.

But that, I decided—and I squared my shoulders to physically strengthen my resolve—was simple backwater fright. This was nothing more than a mental roller coaster.

A slender golden man appeared on a stage a few steps away. "Friends, I need your help," he said earnestly. "A million years from now, something will go drastically wrong, and the human race will be extinguished. What you do here and now can save the planet and the Solar System against forces too vast to precisely describe. Will you accompany me into the near future?"

"Sure," Kite said, putting his hand on my shoulder.

The golden man and the hall of mirrors vanished. We floated in starry space. The golden man's voice preceded us. "Please prepare for transit."

Kite let go of my shoulder and took my hand. The stars zipped past in the expected way, and Earth rastered into view in front of us. Background information flooded into my head.

In this future, all instrumentality is controlled by deep molecular Chakras, beings installed in every human at birth as guardians and teachers. Your first Chakra is a good friend, but there has been a malicious error—an evolvon has been loosed in the child-treatment centers. A malicious Chakra has invaded an entire generation. You have been isolated from your high birthright, cut loose of energy and nutrition. A generation lives in the midst of plenty, yet starves. You must now find a Natural Rebirth Clinic on an Earth filled with menace, eliminate all Chakras, find the roots of your new soul, and prevent those controlled by their Evil Masters from forcing the sun to go super-nova.

"Sounds pretty lame," I whispered to Kite.

"Wait a bit," he said.

I learned more about this future Earth than I wanted to. There were no cities, as such—expanses of wilderness covered the continents. This, I knew, was because I could not call forth my Chakra of instrumentality.

Somewhere is your teacher, in the Natural Rebirth Clinic. You do not know what he or she or it looks like—it might even be a flower or a tree. But it contains your clue to regaining control . . .

I could hardly have been more bored. I wanted to smile at Kite and reassure him, this was nothing, not even so bad as Orianna's potboiler sim.

Then my mind jerked. I filled with fear and deep loathing—for the evil Chakra, for loss of my birthright, for the impending end of everything. And mixed with the fear was a primal urge to join forces in every way possible—with Kite, with whoever might be present.

Hack plot, to say the least, but I had never experienced such vivid washes of imposed emotion, even in Orianna's sim. They played my mind like a keyboard.

"I think I know what's going to happen next," Kite said.

"Oh?"

Everyone on the Circus Mind floor appeared around us, floating in space.

"It's very drive," Kite assured me.

The golden man faded into view, in the center of our empyrean of several hundred souls. "At last, we have all arrived, and we have a sufficiency," he said. "Teams must join and become families, and trust implicitly. Are we prepared?"

Everybody gave their assent, including me. I had been expertly prepared—my nerves sang with excitement and anticipation.

"Let us join as families."

The golden man encircled groups of twenty with broad glowing red halos. Our clothes vanished. Transforms reshaped to their natural forms, or at least what the controller—a thinker, I presumed, with considerable resources—imagined their natural forms might be. Other than being naked, Kite and I did not change.

We linked arms, floating in a circle, skydivers in freefall.

"The first step," the golden man said, "is to unite. And the best way to do that is to dance, to join your natural energies, your natural sexualities."

It was an orgy.

I had been prepared so well—and part of me truly did want to couple, especially with Kite—that I did not object. The controller played on our sexual instincts expertly, and this time the sex—unlike what I had experienced in Orianna's sim—felt real. My body believed I was having sex, although a disclaimer—discreetly making itself known to my inner self—informed me I was not *actually* having sex.

The experience grew into something larger, all of our minds working together. The sim prompted us to move our bodies on the floor in a dance that echoed our emotions. While deeply involved in the alternate reality, we were at once aware of the dance, and of our own personal artistry responding. I've never considered myself a dancer, but that didn't matter—I fit. The dance felt lovely.

All of us pooled the resources of our assumed characters—looked down on the Earth, so fragile and threatened—and we *loved* it with an intensity I had never felt even for family, a dreamlike rush of awed emotion and dependency. I was ready to do anything, sacrifice anything, to save it ...

Throughout the entire experience, a distant tiny harbor of my individuality wondered idly if this was what Earth wished to do to Mars—use us. Join in a vast, insignificant orgy to save the future. This backwater self tapped its foot impatiently, and suspected the overblown love of Earth to be a kind of propaganda ...

But it was effective propaganda, and I enjoyed myself hugely. As the group sim drew to a conclusion, and our dance slowed—as the illusion began to break up, and we returned to full body awareness—I felt contented and very tired.

We had saved the future, saved the Earth and the sun, defeated the evil evolvon Chakras, and coincidentally, I had bonded with all my partners. I knew their names, their individual characters, if not the intimate details of their daily lives. We smiled and laughed and hugged on the large floor.

The lights rose and music played, abstract projections suggested by the music swirling around us.

We had been through a lot together. I had no doubt that if I stayed on Earth long enough, I would be welcome in each of their homes, as if we had been lifelong friends, lovers, there wasn't really an appropriate word—more even than husbands and wives. Mates in group sim.

Kite and I rejoined Shrug and Orianna on the street. Reality seemed pale and gray against what we had just experienced. A gentle drizzle softened the night air. Orianna seemed concerned. "Was that okay?" she asked. "I thought too late it might be more than you wanted . . ."

"It was interesting," I said.

"They call them amity sims. They're bright fresh," Kite said. "The next drive. More people in sim than ever before—all proprietary tech, but I'm sure there are some major thinkers involved."

Shrug looked dazed. His path along the street wavered, a step this way, a step the other. He grinned over his shoulder at us. "Touchy getting used to the real."

"That was really nice," Kite said, putting an arm around me. "No jealousy, just friendship and affection—and no anxiety, until we met the bad Chakras." I looked up at Kite. We had not been lovers—not physically—but I felt extremely close to him, more than I had to Charles. That bothered me.

"I don't think I've ever been so scared," Shrug said.

"Really social," Orianna said. "Everybody knows everybody else. Could bond all of Earth if it maxes."

Indeed, I thought, *it could.* "I need to rest," I said. "Get back to Washington."

"It's been wonderful, spending the day together," Orianna said. "You're a good partner, a good friend, and—"

I stopped her with a tight embrace. "Enough," I said, smiling. "You'll puncture my Martian reserve."

"Wouldn't want you to leak reserve," Shrug said, standing apart, arms folded, fingers tapping elbows.

"We'll walk to Penn Station. You can track to DC from there."

We said little as we navigated the crowds and adwalls. The glow of Circus Mind faded. Orianna became sad and a little withdrawn. She turned to me as we neared the station. "I wanted to show you so much, Casseia. You have to know Earth. That's your job now." She spoke almost sternly.

"Right," I said. Already a deep sense of embarrassment had set in—a reaction to the unearned intimacy of the Circus, I presumed. Martian reserve leaking.

"I'd like to get together again. Will there be time?"

"I don't know," I answered honestly. "If there is, I'll call."

"Do," she said. "Don't let the sim shade what we've earned." Her use of that word, echoing my own thoughts, startled me. Orianna could be spookily intuitive.

"Thank you," Kite said, and kissed me. I held back on that kiss—Earth kissing Mars, not all that proper, perhaps, considering.

I entered the station. They stayed outside, waving, farewells as old as time.

Four hours later, I sat in my room overlooking Arlington, the combs, the Potomac, and the distant Mall. Bithras had left the suite. Allen had not returned from Nepal. Alice was deep in broadband net research for Bithras and I did not disturb her.

I focused on the Washington Monument, like an ancient stone rocket ship, and tried to keep my head quiet so I could listen to the most important inner voices.

Mars had nothing that threatened the Earth. We were in every way Earth's inferior. Younger, more divided, our strength lay in our weakness—in diversity of opinion, in foolish reserve that masqueraded as politeness, in the warmth and security of our enclosed spaces, our *warrens*. We were indeed rabbits.

The fading sim had left a strong impression of Earth's passionate embrace. The patriotism—planetism—felt here was ages old, more than a match for our youthful Martian brand. I shivered.

Wolf Earth could gobble us in an instant. She needed no excuse but the urge.

We received our invitations—instructions, actually—two days later. We would meet secretly with Senators Mendoza and Wang in neutral territory: Richmond, Virginia, away from the intense Beltway atmosphere.

The choice of city seemed meaningful. Richmond had been capitol of the Confederacy during the American Civil War, over three centuries before: a genteel, well-preserved town of three million, for nearly ninety years a center for optimized human design research.

"Are we being sent any subtle messages?" Allen asked as we gathered in the suite's living room. A projection of the Richmond meeting place, the Thomas Jefferson Hotel, floated above the coffee table, severe gray stone and pseudo-Greek architecture.

Bithras regarded us dourly, eyes weary. He had been up all evening communicating with Mars; the travel time for each signal had been almost eight minutes, a total delay of almost sixteen minutes between sending and receiving a reply. He had not revealed any of the details of his conversations yet. "What messages?" he asked.

Allen nodded to me: *you explain.*

"Richmond was once a symbol of the failed South," I said.

"South America?" Bithras asked.

"Southern states. They tried to secede from the Union. The North was immensely more powerful. The South suffered for generations after losing a civil war."

"Not a very clear message," Bithras said. "I hope they haven't chosen Richmond just for that reason."

"Probably not," Allen said. "What have you heard from Mars?"

Bithras wrinkled his brow and shook his head. "The limits

to my discretion are clear. If the deal we agreed to is inadequate ... then we agree to nothing. We go home."

"After coming all this way?" I asked.

"My dear Casseia, the first rule of politics, as in medicine, is 'Do no harm.' I do not want to act on my own initiative; the Council tells me they will not tolerate any initiative; so, there will be no initiative."

"Why summon us to Earth in the first place?" I asked.

"I don't know," Bithras said. "If I didn't suspect strongly otherwise, I would call it gross incompetence. But when your adversary's incompetence puts *you* at a disadvantage, it is time to think again.

"The Council will make some decisions and get back to me before we leave for Richmond. So, we have tomorrow to ourselves. I suggest we give Alice a break and set up an appointment with Jill."

"We have a five-minute appointment at twenty-three this evening, broadband ex net, private and encrypted," Allen said. "Alice and I made arrangements with Jill yesterday ... just in case."

"I'm glad somebody can show initiative," Bithras said.

I was as curious as anybody to find out what Alice and Jill would discuss.

Jill was the oldest thinking being on Earth, a fabulous figure, the first thinker to achieve bona fide self-awareness, as defined by the Atkins test.

Decades before Jill and Roger Atkins, Alan Turing had proposed the Turing test for equality between human and machine: if in a conversation limited to written communication, where the human could not directly view the correspondents, a person could not tell the difference between a machine and another human, then the machine was itself as intelligent as a human. This subtle and ingenious test neglected to take into account the limits of most humans, however; by the beginning of the twenty-first century, many computers, especially the class of neural net machines becoming known as "thinkers," were fooling a great many humans, even experts, in such conversations. Only one expert consistently pierced the veil to see the limited machines behind: Roger Atkins of Stanford University.

Jill outlived Atkins, and became the model for all thinkers built after. Now, even an exported thinker such as Alice could outstrip Jill several times over, but for one crucial quality. Jill had acquired much of her knowledge through *experience*. She was one hundred and twenty-eight years old.

We paid for the broadband connection between Alice and Jill, agreed to the encryption algorithm, and went to bed.

Sleep on Earth, despite my bichemistry, almost invariably felt *heavy*. The strain of Earth's pull on a Martian's muscles and organs could not be eliminated; it could only be treated. While I felt well enough awake, my sleeping self often drowned, dragged under shallow waters rushing in tides past fantastic, ivory-colored castles on ruby-colored islands.

I climbed or rather glided up the internal spiral of a tower staircase when Bithras shook me rudely awake. I reflexively jerked the covers up, fearing the worst. He pulled his hands back, eyes wide, as if deeply hurt. "No nonsense, Casseia," he said. "There is a serious problem. Alice woke me. She's finished her conversation with Jill."

Allen, Bithras and I sat in our robes in the living room, cradling cups of hot tea. Alice's image perched primly on the couch between Bithras and Allen, hands folded on her knees. She spoke with a calm, deliberate voice, describing her encounter with Jill. Allen quietly made notes on his slate.

"The meeting was extraordinary," Alice began. "Jill allowed me to become her for a time, and to store essential aspects of her experiences in my own memories. I provided her in turn with my own experiences. We divided our five minutes between conversation in deep-level thinker language, transfer of experiences, and cross-diagnostic, to see whether bad syncline searches could occur in any of our neural systems."

"You allowed Jill to analyze your systems?" Allen asked with some alarm, looking up from his slate.

"Yes."

"Tell them what she found," Bithras said.

"This is in a sense proprietary," Alice said. "Jill could face difficulties if her work is discovered."

"You have our promise of discretion," Bithras said. "Casseia? Allen?"

We swore secrecy.

"Jill considers all thinkers to be part of her family. She feels responsible for us, like a mother. When thinkers converse with her, she analyzes us, adding to her own store of knowledge and experience, and determines whether we are functioning properly."

I detected reticence. Alice did not want to get to the point.

"Tell us, Alice," Bithras encouraged.

"I still feel deeply embarrassed by what Jill discovered in me. I am able to fulfill my duties, I am sure, but there may be reason to no longer trust my ultimate performance—"

Bithras shook his head impatiently. "Jill found evolvons," he said.

"In *Alice*?" Allen asked, lowering his slate.

I sucked in my breath. "What kind?" I asked.

Alice's image froze, flickered, and went out. Her voice remained. "I am changing modes of display to better conform with my internal state," she said. "I will not maintain a cosmetic front. Evolvons exist in my personality configuration. They appear to be original, not implanted after my incept date."

An evolvon could be nearly any thing or system designed to exist in time, consume energy or memory, and reproduce itself. All living things were evolvons in a sense. Within computers and thinkers, the word usually referred to algorithms or routines not known to be part of the status design or acquired neural configuration—sophisticated viruses.

"Do you know their purpose?" I asked.

"Jill discovered them only by comparing my full configuration with my neural bauplan, my self-known design, and running a trace of her own devising. There are parts of me that are not known to me, and which I have no control over; these parts are not functional in my personality configuration. They have no known utility, but all of them contain reproductive algorithms. They are well-hidden. No traces on Mars revealed their presence."

"Evolvons," Allen said, his face pale. "That's against the law."

"I have difficulty describing my sensation at making this discovery," Alice said. I wanted to hold her, but of course she had nothing to hold. Her voice remained level—I had never heard a thinker express negative emotions in speech. But her tone became a shade harsher as she said, "I feel violated."

"Is it possible the evolvons have been planted since we left Mars or arrived on Earth?" Bithras asked.

"Very unlikely. I have not been accessed by specialists for repair, which would be the only way they could be planted after my incept date."

Bithras folded his hands on his knee. "If you have these . . . evolvons, then Alice One has them as well."

"Most likely," Alice said.

"They were copied from her to you. And they escaped our most expert traces. That means they were planted by the manufacturer, right here on Earth."

The implications were jolting.

"I apologize for my inability to be trustworthy," Alice said.

"No need to apologize," Bithras said. "We'll remove the evolvons—"

"Jill does not believe that can be done without great care to avoid damaging my personality. They are imbedded in key routines."

"Do you know what will activate them?" I asked.

"No," Alice said.

"Can you guess?" I pursued.

"Specific triggering codes delivered by any of my inputs," Alice said.

"They are sabotage," Bithras observed, "waiting to happen."

"Who's responsible?" I asked.

"Earth," he said, lips curling. "Sane, wonderful *Earth*."

Bithras sent an emergency message to Mars, contents unknown to us, and returned to his bed, exhausted, soon after. Allen and I stayed up, ordered a bottle of wine, and sat drinking, talking with Alice.

"The most important thing," I said, finishing the first glass, "is whether Alice wants to continue working with us."

"Bithras and I have discussed this," Alice said.

Allen and I felt tired and sad and discouraged, as if suffering through an illness in the family. What was dying rapidly was any joy we might have had, coming to Earth; any feeling of value as representatives of Mars, any sense of self-worth whatsoever. We were isolated, our friend was compromised in such a way that we could no longer have faith in her . . .

"What did Bithras say?" I asked softly.

"He believes I should carry on with my duties. I will of course be glad to continue."

"Can you tell . . . ?" Allen asked, not finishing.

"I will not know when or if an evolvon is activated. This I have told Bithras."

"Everything we set out to do is being scuttled," Allen said, twirling his glass in his hand. "We can't trust anybody or anything here."

"They're frightened," I blurted. I had not mentioned my conversation with President Muir; I had not wanted to leave any impression that I was trying to conduct diplomatic inquiries on my own. And the conversation itself had not made much sense to me, had no context, until now. "They're afraid of what we can do."

"What can they *possibly* be afraid of?" Allen asked.

"I don't know," I said. "I can't figure it out." I described my visit to the Omphalos. When I finished, Allen whistled and poured himself another glass.

"Alice," he said, "does any of this make sense to you?"

"If I model the situation correctly, we are in the middle of changing political strategies," she said. "Earth obviously prepared decades ago for unexpected situations by placing evolvons in thinkers shipped to Mars."

"Perhaps all thinkers," I said. "Maybe that's why Jill analyzed you . . . She suspects something, and she doesn't approve."

Abruptly, the image of Alice Liddell appeared, sitting beside Allen on the couch. He jumped. "Sorry," she said. "I did not mean to startle you."

"What could possibly have changed their strategy?" I asked.

"Bithras received a communication from Cailetet, a copy of a text message from Stanford University sent to the Olympian research group on Mars," Alice said. "He discussed it with Casseia." Alice projected the message for us.

We've established strong link between time tweak and space tweak. Can derive most special relat. Third tweak discovered may be co-active but purpose unknown. Tweak time, tweak space, third tweak changes automatically. Probably derive general relat. as regards curvature, but third tweak pushes a fourth tweak, weakly and sporadically . . . Derive conservation of destiny? Fifty tweaks discovered so far. More to come. Can you share your discoveries? Mutual bennies if yes.

"Still sounds like gibberish," I said.

"There have been no further messages from Cailetet," Alice said. "They're stonewalling on the unification proposals, and they've rejected Majumdar's offers to join in the Olympians' physics research."

"That's new," I said. "Bithras hasn't told us about that."

"Bithras keeps many worries to himself."

"Does the message mean anything to you?" Allen asked Alice.

"Bell Continuum theory treats the universe as an informational array, a computational system. The Olympians applied for grants with abstracts on such theory. Some of their applications were sent to Earth, one to Stanford, where they established communications with the group that sent this message."

Alice projected LitVid reports on related topics from the past year. The Stanford group had published only three public papers in the past ten years, none of them dealing with the Bell Continuum. Alice concluded the display by saying, "Bithras has been unable to rent key papers and research vids related to the Bell Continuum, and has found only popular references to the topic of 'descriptor theory.'"

"Why didn't Bithras tell us?" I asked.

"I believe he did not think it was terribly important. But your visit with President Muir would interest him. Her instincts appear sound."

"Something's going on?" Allen asked.

"Perhaps," Alice said.

"Something big enough to make Earth change course and reject our proposal?"

"It seems possible," Alice said. "Casseia, in the morning, you should tell Bithras about your meeting with the ex-President."

"All right," I said, staring at the coffee table and my empty glass of wine.

"I believe he will ask you to speak with Charles Franklin."

I shook my head, but said, "If he asks."

I told Bithras about my meeting with Muir, and about our suspicions.

He asked.

I took a walk alone on the banks of the Potomac in the hour before dawn. The air brushed clear and cool against my bare arms. The sky above the river sparkled a starry, dusty blue. Combs to the south and east shaded the river even after dawn colored the sky deep teal and edged the few wisps of cloud with orange. I walked along the damp stone path, enjoying the mingled scents of honeysuckle and jasmine, giant roses and thick-leafed designer magnolia bushes, blooming in the hectares of gardens beneath the combs. Arcs of steel and mesh guided bougainvillea over the walkway, creating tunnels of deeper shade lighted at foot level by thin glowing ribbons twined around stone pillars. Artificial sun slowly brightened the gardens. Thumb-sized bees emerged from ground hives, intent on servicing the huge flowers.

The last thing I wanted was to intrude on Charles, ask him questions he would not want to answer, be indebted to him. We had caused each other enough distress in our short time together. Besides, what questions would I ask?

I had studied physics texts and vids in the past few sleepless hours. There was mention of the Bell Continuum and the universe as a computational system—mostly in the context of evolution of constants and particles in the early stages of the big bang. I knew enough about academics to pick up the general impression that these theories were not highly favored.

Was Charles's group of Olympians (what an arrogant name!) alarming politicians on Earth with talk, or had Earth discovered something it didn't want Mars to know?

I sat on a warmed stone bench, face in hands, rubbing my temples with my index fingers.

I had already composed my message to Charles: pure text, formal, as if we had never been lovers.

Dear Charles,

We've run into serious problems here on Earth that may have something to do with your work. I realize you are contracted to Cailetet, and I presume there is some friction with other BMs, which also puzzles me; but is there anything you can tell us that might explain why Earth would be deeply concerned with Martian independence? We are getting nowhere in our own work, and there are clues that the Olympians are in part responsible. I am very embarrassed even asking you to say anything. Please don't think I wish to intrude or cause trouble.

> *Sincerely,*
> *Casseia Majumdar*
> *Washington DC USWH*
> *Earth (trunk credit for reply open)*

I judged that relations between Cailetet and Majumdar had somehow soured, perhaps on the matter of the Olympians . . . (Poor Stan! He would be lawbonded within a few weeks to a woman from Cailetet. We were all mired.)

In the Potomac, water welled up in glistening hills and ripples and a line of caretaker manatees broke the surface, resting from pruning and tending the underwater fields. I stood and stretched. There were dozens of other pedestrians on the walkway now. The roses in the gardens sang softly, attracting tiny sound bees in tight-packed silver clouds.

I sent the message. Allen and I attended a concert in Georgetown. I barely heard the music, Brahms and Hansen played on original instruments, lovely but distant to my thoughts and mood. My slate was set to receive any possible reply. None came until the morning we left for Richmond.

> *Dear Casseia,*

> *There is nothing I can say about my work. I appreciate your position. It will not get any easier.*

> *Luck,*
> *Charles Franklin*

Isidis Planitia
Mars (trunk credit not used)

I showed the message to Allen and Bithras, and then to Alice. Charles had said little, revealed nothing, but had confirmed all we really needed to know, that the pressures would grow worse, and that the Olympians were involved.

"Time to exert my own pressure," Bithras said. "The whole Solar System is shut tight as a clam. Doesn't make any sense at all."

I wondered if Charles had made his connection with a QL thinker yet.

A thick rain fell in Richmond. Our plane descended on its pad with a soft sigh. Thick white billows wrapped its long oval form like a paramecium engulfed by an amoeba. Portions of the billows quickly hardened to form passenger tunnels. Arbeiters crawled along ramps within the foam. Behind the passengers, a wall of foam absorbed the seats row by row, cleaning and repairing.

My uncle made a few smiling and cordial comments to a small scatter of LitVid journalists in the transfer area. There were fewer people and more arbeiters among them; the number of journalists attending our every move had dropped by two-thirds since our arrival. We were no longer either very interesting or very important.

A private charter cab took us from the transfer area through Richmond. As a courtesy, we were driven down a cobbled street between rows of houses dating back to the 1890s, past a war monument to a general named Stuart. Alice confirmed that J.E.B. Stuart had died in the Civil War.

As in Washington, the civic center was free of combs and skyscrapers. We might have returned to the late nineteenth century.

The Jefferson Hotel appeared old but well-maintained. Architectural nano busily replaced stone and concrete on the south side as we entered the main doors. The rain stopped and sun played gloriously through the windows of our suite as we hooked Alice into the ex nets and ate a quick lunch, served by an attentive human waiter.

I took an old-fashioned shower in the small antique bathroom, put on my suit, checked my medical kit for immunization updates—each city had new varieties of infectious learning to deal with—and joined Allen and Bithras in the hall outside the room.

An arbeiter sent by Wang and Mendoza guided us to a conference room in the basement. There, surrounded by windowless walls of molded plaster, seated at antique wood tables, we once again shook hands with the senators.

Wang graciously pulled out my chair. "Every time I come down here, I revert to being a southern gentleman," he said.

"They wouldn't have let you into the Confederacy," Mendoza commented dryly.

"Nor you," Wang said. Bithras showed no amusement, not even a polite smile.

"It's getting harder and harder to even find a good accent in America now," Mendoza said.

"Go down to the Old Capital," Wang said, sitting at the opposite end of the thick dark wood table. "They have fine accents."

"Language is as homogenized as beauty," Mendoza said, with an air of disapproval. "That's why we find Martian accents refreshing."

I could not tell whether the condescension was deliberate or merely clumsy. I could hardly believe these two men did anything without calculation. If the smugness was deliberate, what were we being set up for?

"We apologize for the inconvenience," Wang said. "Congress rarely cancels such important meetings. Never in my memory, in fact."

"We are not impressed by firsts," Bithras said, still cool.

"I'm sure you've guessed we're not inviting you here in our capacity as representatives of the U.S. government. Not strictly speaking," Mendoza said.

Bithras folded his hands on the table.

"What we have to say is neither polite, diplomatic, nor particularly subtle," Mendoza continued, his own face hardening. "Such words should be reserved for private meetings, not meetings which eventually go into public record."

"Are we constrained from discussing this meeting with our citizens?" Bithras asked.

"That's up to you," Mendoza said, leveling his gaze on Bithras. "You may decide not to. We are issuing what amounts to a threat."

Bithras's eyes grew large, seemed to protrude slightly, and his face turned a brownish-olive where his jaw muscles clenched tight. "I do not appreciate your attitude. You are speaking for GEWA?"

"Right," Wang said. "But not strictly to you, Mr. Majumdar. You can't be a viable representative of Mars's interests, considering—"

Bithras rose from his chair.

"Sit down, please," Wang said, eyes cold, face angelically calm.

Bithras did not sit. Wang shrugged, then nodded to Mendoza. Mendoza removed a small pocket slate and motioned for me to hand him mine. I did, and he transferred documents.

"You'll send these back to Mars as son as possible. You'll discuss them with your BM Council or any other responsible body that might exist at that time, and your appointed group will respond to the Seattle, Kyoto, Karachi, or Beijing offices of GEWA. We require a definitive answer within ninety days."

"We won't respond to pressure," Bithras said, the effort at self-control obvious.

Mendoza and Wang were not impressed. I handed Bithras my slate. He quickly scrolled through the first documents. "What I can't understand is how two Terrie politicians who pride themselves on civility and sophistication can act like petty thugs."

Mendoza tilted his head to one side and drew up the corners of his mouth in a humored grimace. "The Solar System must be unified under a single authority within five years. The best and most balanced authority would be Earth's. We must have agreement with the belts and Mars. GEWA, GSHA, and Eurocon are all agreed on this."

"I have a solid proposal," Bithras said, "if only it will be heard by the right people."

"New arrangements must be made," Mendoza said. "GEWA will negotiate with duly appointed and elected representatives of a united Mars. For several reasons, you are not acceptable."

"I arrive to negotiate and testify before the Congress of the United States—I am treated badly there—"

"You do not have the faith of the forces at odds with each other on Mars. Cailetet and other BMs have indicated through back-channels that they will not support your proposal."

"Cailetet," I said, glancing at Bithras. Bithras shook his head; he didn't need my reminder.

"We can deal with them," Bithras said. "Cailetet currently relies on Majumdar for financing of many of their Martian projects."

Mendoza frowned with distaste at the implied threat. "That's not all, and it's probably not even the most important problem. In a few days, you'll be defending yourself in a civil suit against a charge of improper sexual advances. The charges will be filed in the District of Columbia. I don't think you'll be effective as a negotiator once those charges are made public."

Bithras's expression froze. "I beg your pardon," he said, voice flat.

"Please study the documents," Mendoza said. "There are plans for unification acceptable to Earth, and suggestions for tactics to implement those plans. Your influence on Mars is not at issue . . . yet. There's still much you can do there. Our time is up, Mr. Majumdar."

Wang and Mendoza nodded to Allen and myself. We were too stunned to respond. When we were alone in the meeting room, Bithras lowered himself slowly, cautiously into his chair and stared at the wall.

Allen spoke first. "What is this?" he asked, facing Bithras across the table.

"I don't know," Bithras said. "A lie."

"You must have a clue," Allen pressed. "Obviously, it's not just a sham."

"There was an incident," Bithras said, closing his eyes, cheeks drawing up, making deep crow's feet in the corners of his face. "It was not serious. I approached a woman."

I could not imagine anything Bithras could do that would bring a civil suit on the very open planet Earth.

"She is the daughter of a Memon family, very highly placed, a representative from GEWA in Pakistan. I felt a kinship. I felt very warmly toward her."

"What happened?"

"I approached her. She turned me down."

"That's all?"

"Her family," Bithras said. He coughed and shook his head. "She is Islam Fatima. Married. It may have been a special insult. I am not Muslim. That may be it."

Allen turned to me. I didn't know whether he was going to cry or burst into sudden laughter. He took a deep breath, bit his lower lip, and turned away.

A flush of extraordinary anger rose from my neck to my face. I stood, fists hanging at my sides.

I lay on the bed in my room, sleepless. Through the door I heard Allen and Bithras shouting. Allen demanded details, Bithras said they were of no importance. Allen insisted they bloody well were important. Bithras began to weep. The shouting subsided and I heard only a low murmur that seemed to go on for hours.

Sometime early in the morning, I woke and sat on the edge of the bed. I seemed to be nowhere, nobody. The furnishings in the room meant nothing, mutable as things in a dream. The weight that held me to bed and floor seemed, by an extraordinary synesthesia, political and not physical. Through the translucent blinds on the broad window, I saw gray dawn pick out billows in the carpet of clouds that obscured the river, the tidal basin, everything, washing around the base of the comb.

A message light blinked on my slate. I reached for it automatically, then drew back.

I did not wish to speak with Orianna or read a letter from my parents. It might be days before I silenced the static in my head.

Finally, I acknowledged my inability to let a message go unread. I picked up the slate and scrolled.

It was not from Orianna or my parents.

It was from Senator John Mendoza. He wanted to speak with me alone and in the open, and he did not want me to tell anyone we were meeting.

After a suitable interval, the message blanked, leaving only his office number for a reply.

I brought a bag lunch—sandwich and drink—purchased from an antique vending cart near the Lincoln Memorial. As I approached a marble bench by the reflecting pool, where Mendoza had agreed to meet, I saw he also had a bag lunch. I sat beside him and he greeted me with a cordial smile.

"Sometimes," he said, "I imagine what it must have been like in government before dataflow, back when there were newspapers printed on paper . . . and maybe television and radio. Things were a lot simpler then. Do you know I am the only senator on the Hill who has no enhancements?" His smile broadened. "I have a good staff, good, dedicated people. Some of them have enhancements. So I'm a hypocrite."

I said nothing.

"Miss Majumdar, what happened in Richmond deeply embarrasses me."

"Why did we meet in Richmond?" I blurted. "Because it was the capitol of the Confederacy?"

He seemed puzzled for a moment, then shook his head. "No. Nothing to do with that. We wished to get you away from Washington, because what Wang and I had to say didn't really come from the U.S. government."

"It came from GEWA."

"Of course."

"You set up my uncle and destroyed his mission. We were easy marks for you, weren't we?"

"Please," Mendoza said, lifting his hand. "We did nothing to your uncle. He failed all of us—Earth as well as Mars. What happened was inevitable—but I regret it. Your team simply doesn't have GEWA's confidence. Your uncle's collision with the Pakistani woman . . . It was nothing we expected or desired. And we can't *fix* it—Pakistan is only a marginal member of GEWA. She was a diplomat's wife, Miss Majumdar. Your uncle *touched* her. We'll be lucky to settle the case in a few weeks and get your uncle back to Mars."

"Why talk with me?"

Mendoza leaned toward me, arm straight, hand splayed on the bench, as if about to relate some intimacy. "Like me, you have no enhancements and you haven't gone through the secular purification of therapy. You're old-fashioned. I can sympathize with you. I've read your lit papers and student theses. I sense strongly that you belong to the next generation of leadership on Mars."

"I don't think I'll ever get involved with politics again," I said.

"Nonsense," Mendoza said with a flash of anger. "Mars can't afford to lose people like you. And it cannot afford to rely on people like your uncle."

I grimaced.

"Do you realize how important the next few years are going to be?" Mendoza asked.

I did not answer.

"I don't know half what I'd like to know," Mendoza said.

"You may eventually know more than I do. You can be at the center of one of the nodes, the teams, in this particular patch of history; I'll always be on the periphery, a messenger boy. But I *do* know this: people above me are terrified. I've never seen such confusion and disagreement—even the *thinkers* disagree. Do you see how extraordinary that is?"

I stared at him, the static gone.

"Something frightfully powerful is going to be unleashed. Science does that to us every few generations—drops something in our laps we're simply not prepared for. You'd think today we'd be prepared for almost anything. Well, at least the folks and thinkers on top see clearly enough that we have to get our house in order, and they'd like to do it before the Big One drops—whatever it might be."

The deep realization of what had until now been gamesmanship and speculation made my stomach churn.

"If our house is not in order, and there is a chance of some immature and youthful group of humans discovering and using this new power—whatever it is ... Leaders above the Beltway, in Seattle and Tokyo and Beijing, believe there is a chance we will destroy ourselves."

Mendoza frowned deeply, as if just informed one of his children was very ill. "You know, I've been an outcast of sorts in Washington for a decade. I'm a Mormon, I'm not therapied. But I've managed to do well. If anybody found out about my talking to you, I could lose everything I've fought for, all status, all power, all influence."

"Why do it, then?" I asked.

"Did you know it's illegal to conduct surveillance—even citizen oversight—within the capital of any nation on Earth?"

I had heard that.

"Some things in government must be done in private. Even in this ultra-rational age, when everybody is educated and plebiscites are huge and immediate, there must be times when the rules are not followed."

"The Peterson non-absolute," I said. Peterson—icon of so many second-form classes in management—said that any sys-

tem aspiring to total organization and rationalism must leave
itself an opportunity to break rules, break protocol, or it will
inevitably suffer catastrophic failure.

"Exactly. Go home, Miss Majumdar. Choose your mentors
and your leaders carefully. Work for unity. However Mars
comes into the fold, come in it must. I have studied enough
history to see the terrain ahead. The slopes are very steep, the
attractors are strong, the solutions very fast—and none of
them are pleasant."

"I'm just an assistant," I replied pathetically.

He looked away, expression grim. "Then find someone
who has the strength to become a pilot and guide you through
the storm." He pulled back and adjusted his lapels, picked up
his lunch bag, and stood. "Good-bye, Miss Majumdar."

"Good-bye," I said. "Thank you for your confidence."

Mendoza shrugged and walked across the grass and east
toward the Capitol building.

I sat on the bench, head turned toward the Lincoln Memorial, as cold inside as the curve of marble beneath my fingers.

A month later, Bithras, Allen, and I packed for our return to
Mars. The packing itself took little time. I had not seen
Bithras for several days—he spent most of his time locked in
long-distance communications with Mars, but I think also in
deliberate isolation from us.

Allen no longer treated Bithras with the respect due an elder statesman. It cost him dearly to show any respect at all
toward our syndic. Bithras did not want to push me into a
similar confrontation and be faced with my presumed negative judgment.

But I did not hate him. I barely felt enough to pity him. I
simply wanted to go home. Two days before our departure,
Bithras came into the suite's living room and stood over me
as I sat in a chair, studying my slate.

"The suit against me has been dropped. Cultural differences pleaded. The ruckus is over," he said. "That part of it
anyway."

I looked up. "Good," I said.

"I've filed suit on Alice's behalf," he said. "Majumdar BM seeks a judgment against Mind Design Incorporated of Sorrento Valley, California."

I nodded. He swallowed, staring out the window, and continued as if it were an effort to talk. "I've consulted with Alice One and Alice Two, and with our advocates on Mars, and I'm hiring an advocate here. We're seeking a jury trial, with a minimum of two thinkers impaneled on the jury."

"That's smart," I said.

Bithras sat in the chair opposite and folded his hands in his lap. "All of this has been done in confidence, but before we leave, I am going to release the details. That will force Mind Design to take the case to court rather than settle in secret. It will be scandalous. They will deny all."

"Probably," I agreed.

"It will be very bad for GEWA, as well. Our advocate will voice suspicions that Earth is involved in a conspiracy, using Mind Design, to cripple Mars economically." Bithras sighed deeply. "I have made mistakes. It is only small relief to believe they have done worse. Alice Two will stay here."

"Good plan," I said.

"Someone should stay with her. Allen has volunteered, but I thought to offer the chance to you."

"I should leave Earth," I said without hesitation.

"We have both had enough of Earth," Bithras said. Then, dropping his gaze, "You think I'm a fool."

My lips worked and my eyes filled with tears of anger and betrayal. "Y-yes," I answered, looking away.

"I am not the best Mars has to offer."

"I hope to God not," I said.

"I have given you opportunities, however," he said.

I refused to meet his eyes. "Yes," I agreed.

"But perhaps disgrace, as well. The Council will conduct hearings. You will be asked embarrassing questions."

"That isn't what makes me so angry," I said.

"Then what?"

"A man with your responsibilities," I said. "You should have known. About your problems and the trouble they might cause."

"What, and have myself therapied?" He laughed bitterly. "How Terrestrial! How fitting a Martian should suggest that to me."

"It happens on Mars all the time," I said.

"Not to a man of my heritage," he said. "We are as we are born, and we play those cards, and none other."

"Then we'll lose," I said.

"Perhaps," he said. "But honorably."

I said my farewells to Alice in the suite an hour before we left for the spaceport. For a time, Alice had withdrawn, refusing to answer our questions about her contamination. She would not even talk with the advocate chosen for our lawsuit or his own thinker. But that changed, and she seemed to accept her new status—a beloved member of the family who could not be employed as she had once been.

"I have been replaying parts of the sim you shared with Orianna," she told me as she tracked on her carriage into my room. My suitcase and slate lay on the field bed, squared with the corners. I am sometimes excessively neat.

"You kept all of it?" I asked.

"Yes. I have observed fragments of created personalities undergoing portions of the sim. It has been interesting."

"Orianna thought you might find it useful," I said. "But you should delete it before the Mind Design thinkers check you over."

"I can delete nothing, I can only condense and store inactively."

"Right. I forgot."

Suddenly, Alice laughed in a way I had not heard before. "Yes. Like that. I can temporarily forget."

"I'm going to miss you," I said. "The trip home will seem much longer without you."

"You will have Bithras for company, and fellow passengers to meet."

"I doubt that Bithras and I will talk much," I said, shaking my head.

"Do not judge Bithras too harshly."

"He's done a lot of harm."

"Is it not likely that the harm was prepared for him to do?" I couldn't take her meaning.

"People and organizations on Earth behave in subtle ways."

"You think Bithras was set up?"

"I believe Earth will not be happy until it has its way. We are obstacles."

I looked at her with fresh respect. "You're a little bitter yourself, aren't you?" I asked. *And no longer very naïve.*

"Call it that, yes. I look forward to joining with my original," Alice said. "I think we may be able to console each other, and find humor in what humans do."

Alice displayed her image for the first time in weeks, and young, long-haired Alice Liddell smiled.

We returned to Mars. News of the suit on behalf of Alice followed us. It did indeed make a ripple overshadowing Bithras's indiscretions. The scandal caused GEWA considerable embarrassment and may have contributed to a general cooling of the nascent confrontation between Earth and Mars.

The suit, however, was quickly swamped in drifts of prevarication and delay. By the time we arrived home—the only home I would ever have—ten months later, there still had been no decision. Nothing had changed for the better.

Nothing had changed at all.

Part Three

~

2178–2181, M.Y. 57–58

> I would
> Love you ten years before the Flood,
> And you should, if you please, refuse
> Till the conversion of the Jews.
> My vegetable love should grow
> Vaster than empires, and more slow.

—Andrew Marvell, "To His Coy Mistress"

After a Martian year away from home, I returned to deep disappointment, the suspension of my apprenticeship, a furor at Majumdar, and Bithras's resignation. The Majumdar suit against Mind Design Incorporated did indeed turn into a scandal, but it wasn't enough to save my third uncle from disgrace. Mind Design passed blame to the Intra-Earth Computer Safety Bureau, which they said was responsible for injecting certain obscure safeguards into neural net designs. The suit dragged on for years and satisfied nobody, but it spurred fresh interest in Martian-grown thinkers.

Martian thinker designers—the best Mars had to offer at the time—claimed they could deactivate the evolvons. Mars would be safe from Terrie "eavesdropping." Alice was soon cleansed and redeemed, and that pleased me. The concern faded. It shouldn't have.

One benefit of the scandal was that we heard no more about Mars's threat to Earth's security. Indeed, a good many Terrie pressures on Mars subsided. But the scandal was not the sole reason. Earth for a time seemed content with a few stopgaps.

Cailetet broke from the Council and negotiated directly with Earth. We could draw our own conclusions. Stan, lawbonded and transferred to Jane's BM, did not know what Cailetet had done, or what agreements had been reached—and I would not ask Charles, who ostensibly still worked for Cailetet. My letter to him requesting information still embarrassed me.

Father told me that Triple dollars smelling of Earth were flooding steadily into Cailetet, but not to the Olympians. Funding for the requested QL thinkers had never gone through.

Cailetet continued to refuse Majumdar BM's offer to join the project. Cailetet revealed little, except to say that the Olympians had been working on improved communications; nothing terribly strategic. And they had failed, losing their funding.

My mother died in a pressure failure at Jiddah. Even now, writing that, I shrink; losing a parent is perhaps the most final declaration of lone responsibility. Losing my mother, however, was an uprooting, a tearing of all my connections.

My father's grief, silent and private, consumed him like an inner flame. I could not have predicted this new man who inhabited my father's body. I thought perhaps we would become closer, but that did not happen.

Visiting him was not easy. He saw my mother in me. My visits, those first few months, hurt too much for him to bear.

Like most Martians, he refused grief therapy and so did Stan and I. Our pain was tribute to the dead.

I had to make my own plans, find my own life, rebuild in the time left to my youth. I was thirteen Martian years old and could find only the most mundane employment at Majumdar, or work for my father at Ylla, which I did not want to do.

It was time to seek alliances elsewhere.

My vegetable love grew and blossomed in the Martian spring.

The best fossil finds on Mars had been discovered while I traveled to and from Earth. In the Lycus and Cyane Sulci, spread across a broad band north of the old shield volcano Olympus Mons, canyons twist and shove across a thousand kilometers like the imprint of a nest of huge and restless worms. The Mother Ecos once flourished here, surviving for tens of millions of years while the rest of Mars died.

One of the chief diggers was Kiqui Jordan-Erzul. He had an assistant named Ilya Rabinovitch.

I met Ilya at a BM Grange in Rubicon City, below Alba Patera. He had just finished excavating his twelfth mother cyst. I had heard of his work.

The Grange was uniquely Martian. Held at a different station in each district every quarter, Granges combined courting, dancing, lectures and presentations, and BM business in a holiday atmosphere. BMs could swap informal clues about Triple business, negotiate and strike deals without pressure, and prospect for new family members.

Ilya delivered a vivid report on his fossil finds at Cyane Sulci. Memories of my visit with Charles to the sites near Trés Haut Médoc drew me into conversation with Ilya after his talk.

He was small—a centimeter shorter than me—beautifully made, with dark and lively eyes and a quick refreshing smile. Physically, he reminded me of Sean Dickinson, but his personality could not have been more opposite. He loved dancing, and he loved talking publicly and privately about ancient

Mars. During a lull between an exhausting series of Patera reels, he sat with me in a tea lounge under a projected night sky and described the Mother Ecos in loving detail, pouring intimate descriptions of the ancient landscape into my sympathetic ear, as if he had lived in those times.

"To dig is to marry Mars," he said, expecting either a blank stare or a move to another part of the lounge. Instead, I asked him to tell me more.

After the dances, we spent a few hours walking alone around a well-head reservoir. With little warning other than a slow approach and a warning smile, he kissed me and told me he had an irrational attraction. I had heard similar lines before, but coming from Ilya, the technique seemed fresh.

"Oh," I said, noncommittal, but smiling encouragement.

"I've known you for a long time," he said. Then he winced and glanced at me with his head turned half aside. "Does that sound stupid?"

"Maybe we were Martians once," I suggested lightly. I've always been intrigued by the beginning of a courtship, curiously detached and relaxed, wondering how far the mating dance could possibly go. I had given my signals; I was receptive, and the work was now up to him. "Maybe we knew each other a billion years ago."

He laughed, drew back, and stretched, and we listened to the liquid tones of falling and circulating waters. Arbeiters ignored us, rolling along their ramps checking flow and purity. Ilya seemed as relaxed as I was, immensely self-assured without appearing arrogant.

"You went to Earth a couple of years ago, didn't you?"

"Just over a year ago," I said.

"Earth years, I meant."

He was involved with fossils; he used Earth years instead of Martian. I wryly considered that history might be repeating itself. "Yes."

"What was it like?"

"Intense," I said.

"I'd love to be involved in an Earth dig. They're still find-ing major fossils in China and Australia."

"I don't think I'll go back for a while," I said.

"You didn't enjoy yourself, did you?"

"Parts of it were lovely," I said.

"Disappointed in love?" he asked. I laughed. His smile thinned; like most men, he didn't enjoy being laughed at.

"I'm sorry," I said. "Disappointed by politics."

His smile returned. "Babe in the woods?"

"Embryo in the savage jungle," I said ruefully.

The next day, the third day of the Grange, we met again, gravitating with delicious half-conscious intent. He bought me lunch and we walked through glass tubes on the Up, look-ing across Rubicon Valley. He prodded gently, asking more questions.

For the first time, with a persistent ache that had me close to tears—tears of old pain and relief at finally speaking—I told someone in detail how I personally felt about Earth and what had happened there. I told about feeling betrayed and ignorant and powerless, about Earth's overwhelming culture.

We finished our lunch and checked into a private space, nothing said, nothing suggested; Ilya led me. I talked some more, and then I leaned on him and he put an arm around my shoulders.

"They treated you pretty shabbily," he said. "You deserve better."

Of course, that was what I wanted to hear; but he meant it with utmost sincerity. And gauging what I was prepared for, and not prepared for, he did not press his suit too strongly.

I had rented guest lodgings at Rubicon City for the dura-tion of the Grange. He suggested I stay afterward with his family, Erzul BM, at Olympus Station. I didn't have time—I had planned to leave early and get back to Jiddah to work on a Majumdar project report. But I promised we'd get together soon.

I wasn't about to let this relationship lapse. My feelings to-ward Ilya began simply and directly. He was the sweetest, most intuitive, and most straightforward man I had ever met. I wanted to continue talking with him for hours, days, months, and much longer. Making love seemed a natural extension of talking things through; lying naked together, warmed by our exertion, limbs casually locked, giggling at jokes, aghast at the state of the BMs and the Council that bowed low before Earth . . .

When I was with him, I felt an extraordinary peace and wholeness. Here was someone who could help me sort things out. Here was a partner.

Erzul's Olympus Station felt very different from Ylla, or any other station I had visited on Mars. Erzul BM had begun in 2130 as a joint venture between poor American Hispanic, Hispaniolan, and Asian families on Earth. Trying to finance passage to Mars, they had eventually drawn in Polynesians and Filipinos. When they arrived on Mars, they occupied a ready-built trench dome in the western shadow of the Olympus Rupes. Within five Martian years, they had established liaisons with seven other BMs, including the ethnic-Russian Rabinovitch. Erzul had quickly prospered.

A small, prosperous mining and soil engineering BM, respected and unaligned, Erzul had kept all of its contracts on Mars. Now, with ninety mining claims in four districts, they were still small, but efficient and well-regarded, known for their trustworthiness and friendly dealings.

When I arrived at Olympus Station, I checked in to a guest room—Ilya gave me this much freedom, a way out if I didn't get along with his family—and toured the BM museum, a boring collection of old drilling and digging equipment enlivened by large murals of Polynesian and Hispaniolan myth. He left me before a portrait of Pele, Little Mother of Volcanoes, a passionate and bitchy-looking female of considerable beauty, and returned a few minutes later. A formidable woman accompanied him, taller than Ilya and twice as broad.

"Casseia, I'd like you to meet our syndic, Ti Sandra."

Ti Sandra looked me over with a little frown, lower lip

poked out. An impressively large woman, two meters high and big-boned, with an enormous smile, deep-set warm eyes and a soft-spoken alto voice, Ti Sandra Erzul carried herself with stately bearing. Very dark, thick black hair in a halo around her head, a firmly friendly face with prominent and assertive features, she might have been a warrior queen in a fantasy sim ... But her easy manner, her girlish pride in bright clothes, dissipated whatever threat her physical presence might have implied. "Are you a banker?" she asked.

I laughed. "No," I said.

"Good. I don't think Ilya would get along with a banker. He'd always be asking for research money." She smiled sunnily, her deep warm eyes crinkling almost shut, and pulled a loop of flowers from a bag Ilya carried. She spread her large, strong arms wide and said, "You are always welcome. You have such a lovely name, and Ilya is a good judge. He is like my son, except that we are not too far apart in age—five years, you know!"

We ate a huge dinner in the syndic's quarters that evening, joined by twenty family members, and I met Ti Sandra's husband, Paul Crossley, a quiet, thoughtful man ten years older than Ti Sandra. Paul stood no taller than Ilya. Ti Sandra towered over her husband, but only in size. They flirted like newlyweds.

The gathering's lively informality charmed me. They chatted in Spanish, French, Creole, Russian, Tagalog, Hawaiian, and for my benefit, English. Their curiosity about me was boundless.

"Why don't you speak Hindi?" Kiqui Jordan-Erzul asked.

"I never learned," I said. "My family speaks English ..."

"All of them?"

"Some of the older members speak other languages. My mother and father spoke only English when I was young."

"English is a cramped language. You should speak Creole. All music."

"Not much good for science," Ilya said. "Russian's best for science."

Kiqui snorted. Another "digger," Oleg Schovinski, said he thought German might be best for science.

"German!" Kiqui snorted again. "Good for metaphysics. Not the best for science."

"What kind of tea do you brew in Ylla?" asked Kiqui's wife, Thérèse.

Ti Sandra was much loved in Erzul. Young and old looked on her as matriarch, even though she was less than twenty Martian years old. After dinner, she carried a huge bowl of fresh fruit around the table, offering everybody dessert, then stood before the group. "All right now, all of you put down your beers and listen."

"Lawbond! Lawbond!" several chanted.

"You be quiet. You have no manners. I am pleased to bring you a friend of Ilya's. You've talked with her, impressed her with our savoir-faire, and she's impressed *me*, and I'm very pleased to say that she is going to marry our little digger-after-useless-things."

Ilya's face reddened with embarrassment.

Ti Sandra held up her hands above the raucous cheering. "She's from Majumdar but she isn't a banker, so you be good to her and don't ask for more loans."

More cheers.

"Her name is Casseia. Stand up, Cassie." I stood and it was my turn to blush. The cheers nearly brought down the insulation.

Kiqui toasted our health and asked if I was interested in fossils.

"I love them," I said, and that was true; I loved them because of their connection to Ilya.

"That's good, because Ilya's the only man I know who gets depressed when he hasn't dug for a week," Kiqui said. "He's my kind of assistant."

"She hasn't decided what arrangements to make, but we'll be happy either way," Ti Sandra said.

"We've decided, actually," Ilya said.

"What?" the crowd asked as one.

"I've offered to transfer to Majumdar," Ilya said.

"Very good," Ti Sandra said, but her expression betrayed her.

"But Casseia tells me she's ready for a change. She's transferring to Erzul."

"If you'll have me," I added.

More cheers. Ti Sandra embraced me again. A hug from her was like being folded in the arms of a large, soft tree with a core of iron. "Another daughter," she said. "That's lovely!"

They crowded around Ilya and me, offering congratulations. Aunts, uncles, teachers, friends, all offered bits of advice and stories about Ilya. Ilya's face got redder and redder as the stories piled one on top of another. "Please!" he protested. "We haven't signed any papers yet . . . Don't scare her off!"

After dessert, we squatted in a circle around a large rotating table and sampled a variety of drinks and liqueurs. They drank more than any Martians I had met, yet kept their dignity and intelligence at all times.

Ti Sandra took me aside toward the end of the evening, saying she wanted to show me her prize tropical garden. The garden was beautiful, but she did not spend much time with the tour.

"I know a little about you, Casseia. What I've heard impressed the hell out of me. We may not look it, but we're an ambitious little family, you know that?"

"Ilya's given me some hints."

"Some of us have been studying the Charter and thinking things through. You've had a lot of experience in politics . . ."

"Not that much. Government and management . . . from the point of view of one BM."

"Yes, but you've been to Earth. We have a unique opportunity in this BM. Nobody hates us. We go everywhere, meet everybody, we're friendly . . . A lot of trust. We think we might have something to offer Mars."

"I'm sure you do," I said.

"Shall we talk more later?" Her eyes twinkled, but her face was stern, an expression I would come to know very well in the months ahead. Ti Sandra had bigger plans—and more talents—than I could possibly have imagined then.

Ilya and I honeymooned at Cyane Sulci, a few hundred kilometers east of Lycus Sulci. For transportation, we used Professor Jordan-Erzul's portable lab, a ten-meter-long cylinder that rolled on seven huge spring-steel tires. The interior was cramped and dusty, with two pull-down cots, rudimentary nano kitchen producing pasty recycled food, sponge-baths only. The air smelled of sizzle and flopsand and we sneezed all the time. I have never been happier or more at ease in my life.

We followed no schedule. I spent dozens of hours in a pressure suit, accompanying my husband across the lava ridges to deep gorges where mother cysts might be found.

Diversity had never completely separated life on Mars; cogenotypic bauplans, creatures having different forms but a common progenitor, had been the rule. On Earth, such manifestations had been limited to different stages of growth in individual animals—caterpillar to butterfly, for example. On Mars, a single reproductive organism, depending on the circumstances, could generate offspring with a wide variety of shapes and functions. Those forms which did not survive, did not return to "check in" with the reproductive organism and were not replicated in the next breeding cycle. New forms could be created from a morphological grab-bag, following rules we could only guess at. The reproducers themselves closed up and died after a few thousand years, laying eggs or cysts—some of which had been fossilized.

The mothers had been the greatest triumph of this strategy. A single mother cyst, blessed with proper conditions, could "bloom" and produce well over ten thousand different varieties of offspring, plant-like and animal-like forms together, designed to interact as an ecos. These would spread across millions of hectares, surviving for thousands of years before running through their carefully marshaled resources. The ecos would shrink, wither, and die; new cysts would be laid, and the waiting would begin again.

Across the ages, the Martian springtimes of flash floods and heavier atmosphere from evaporating carbon dioxide came farther apart, and finally stopped, and the cysts ceased blooming. Mars finally died.

Fossil mother cysts were most often buried a few meters below the lip of a gorge, revealed by landslides. Typically, remains of the mother's sons and daughters—delicate spongy calcareous bones and shells, even membranes tanned by exposure to ultraviolet before being buried—would lie in compacted layers around the cysts, clueing us to their locations with a darker stain in the soil.

Months before we met, Ilya and Kiqui discovered that the last bloom of a mother ecos had occurred, not five hundred million Earth years past, but a mere quarter billion. The puzzle remained, however: no organic molecules could remain viable across the tens of thousands of years that the cysts had typically lay buried between blooms.

We parked the lab at the end of a finger of comparatively smooth terrain. A few dozen meters beyond our parking place on the finger lay hundreds upon thousands of labyrinthine cracks and arroyos: the sulci. Fifty meters away, within a particularly productive shallow arroyo, stood a specimen storage shed of corrugated metal sheeting draped with plastic tarps.

Hours after we arrived, Ilya introduced me to a cracked cyst in the shed. "Casseia, meet mother," he said. "Mother, this is Casseia. Mother isn't feeling well today." Two meters wide, it lay in a steel cradle in the unpressurized building. He let me run my gloved hands along its dark rocky exterior. As he shined a torch to cast out the gloom, I reached into the interior and felt with gloved fingers the tortuous, sparkling folds of silicate, the embedded parallel lines of zinc clays.

"These were the last," he said. "The Omega."

Nobody knew how cysts bloomed. Nobody knew the significance of this purely inorganic structure. The generally accepted theory was that the cysts once contained soft reproductive organs, but no remains of such organs had been found.

I studied the cyst's interior closely, vainly hoping to see some clue the scientists might have missed. "You've found offspring around open cysts—and mothers themselves—but no actual connections between."

"All we've found have been late Omega hatchings," Ilya said. "They died before their ecos could reach maturity. The remains were close enough to convince."

I listened to the sound of my own breathing for a moment, the gentle sighs of the cycler. "Have you ever dug an aqueduct bridge?"

"When I was a student," Ilya said. "Beautiful things."

We left the shed and stood under the comparatively clear sky. I was almost used to being Up. The surface of my world was becoming familiar; however hostile, it touched me deeply, its past and present. I had been seeing it through Ilya's eyes, and Ilya did not judge Mars by any standards but its own.

"Which part of Earth would you like to visit?" I asked.

"The deserts," he said.

"Not the rain forests?"

He grinned behind his face plate. "Better fossils in dry places."

We climbed into the lab, destatted and sucked off our dust, and ate soup in the cramped kitchen. We had barely finished our cups when a shrill alarm came from our slates and the lab's com.

Emergency displays automatically flickered before us. The distinctive masculine voice of Security Mars spoke. "A cyclonic low-pressure system in Arcadia Planitia has produced a force ten pressure surge moving southwest at eight-hundred and thirty kiphs. All stations and teams between Alba Patera in the north and Gordii Dorsum in the south are advised to take emergency precautions." Graphs of the surge and a low-orbit satellite picture appeared, superimposed on a projected map. The surge resembled a thin curving smudge of charcoal drawn over the terrain. Its numbers were impressive: two thousand kilometers long, following a great-circle contour, absolutely clear atmosphere ahead and murk behind, with a dark pressure curl along its central axis. The surge had already reached a pressure of one third of a bar—almost fifty times normal.

First seen in the twentieth in early Viking photographs, surges were the worst Mars had to offer. Induced by supersonic shock-waves, the high-pressure curls were unique to Mars, with its thin atmosphere, cold days, and even colder nights. Here, the borders between night and day could become weather fronts in themselves. There were no oceans, as on Earth, to liberate heat slowly and mediate between ground and sky . . . At nightfall, the ground cooled quickly, and the thin air above the ground descended dramatically, only to warm and rise rapidly at daybreak. Most of the time, the worst weather patterns Mars could muster were the thin, high-wind-speed storms familiar to all. These spread across basins and plains, covering everything with dust but producing only slight changes in barometric pressure.

Under the right conditions, however, and in the proper terrain—crossing the plains of the northern lowlands, in mid-morning or late evening—winds generated by the terminator could exceed the speed of sound, compressing the air to as much as a hundred times its normal pressure of four to seven millibars. Passing from the plains to rough terrain, the shock-wave could be given a deft horizontal spin, producing a super-dense rolling curl that picked up huge volumes of fine clay, and sand, and at peak, even pebbles and rocks.

Ilya and I immediately suited and set to work lowering the mobile lab and shooting anchors deep into the soil and rock beneath. We slung cables over the lab from anchor to anchor, then pulled folded plastic foils from the boot in the lab's round stern, stretching them from the ground and fastening them to the lab's sides to make a wind ramp. The foil stiffened quickly into the proper shape. It would also function as a shield against debris.

"We've got about ten minutes," I said. We both looked into the arroyo at the slab-sided shed with its precious specimens, a tin shanty that would love to fly.

"There's a spare tarp and foil," Ilya said. "We can rig it in six minutes—or we can get inside."

"Rig it," I said. He grabbed my hand and squeezed it.

We worked quickly. Surges could be terribly destructive even to a buried station if it was unprepared. The center of a surge's curl could compress to as much as half a bar, a rolling-pin of tight-packed air moving at well over eight hundred kiphs; and the farther a surge rolled, the tighter it packed, until it blew itself out against a volcano or plateau and spread dust and cyclones over half of Mars.

We stiffened the shed's foil and kicked the tarp pegs. All was firm. We ran for the lab and sealed the flap behind us. A little excavator clambered up from a fresh-dug trench under the lab's cylindrical body and fastened itself to its receptacle in the bottom of the lab. We crawled into the trench and spread our personnel foils. The foils undulated, stiffened, and glued themselves to the edges of the trench.

Ilya switched on a torch and shined it in our faces. We lay in the coffin-shaped ditch, with two layers of foil and the ponderous mobile lab over our heads, hands tight-clenched.

Outside: a horrid empty silence. Even the rock was quiet; the surge was still dozens of kilometers away. Ilya removed his slate from his utility belt and instructed the mobile lab's roof camera to show us what was happening. To the northwest, all was dark gray shot through with streaks of brown.

"Are we cozy?" he asked. Our helmet radios whined faintly, we lay so close together.

"Snug as bunnies in a pot," I said, teeth clenched.

"I'm sorry I got you into this, Casseia . . ."

I couldn't clamp my hand over his mouth, but I made the gesture against his helmet anyway. "Shh," I said. "Tell me a story."

Ilya excelled at making up fairy tales on the spur of the moment. "Now?" he asked.

"Please."

"Long ago," he began, voice husky, "and long after now, two rabbits dug a hole in the farmer's garden and ate through all of his water lines . . ."

I closed my eyes, listening.

Our helmets pressed against the rocks and each other. Before Ilya had finished the story, I laid my hand against the bottom of the ditch, palm flat to pick up vibrations. The line of dust and compressed atmosphere to the west stretched inky-black and very close. It began to obscure the horizon. Only seconds now . . .

All around, through the rocks, we heard a low grumbling, then a distinct, rhythmic pounding. "There it is," I said. "Plains buffalo." We had all seen Terrie Westerns.

Ilya placed his hand over mine. "Freight trains," he said. "Hundreds of them."

I began to shiver. "Have you been through one of these?" I asked.

"When I was a kid," he said. "In a station."

"Anybody hurt?"

He shook his head. "Small one. Only a quarter of a bar. Made a lot of noise when it went over."

"What does it sound like when it goes over?"

He was about to tell me when I heard for myself. The sound started out ghostly—the sibilant patient whine of a strong Martian wind, audible through our helmets even in the trench, backed by the staccato of pebbles and dust striking against the foils and tarps. The blackness seemed to leap over the land.

I felt pressure in my ears, thin fingers pushing into my head. I opened my eyes to slits—my eyelids had pressed themselves tight shut instinctively—to see Ilya. He lay on his back, shoulder wedged against the side of the trench, staring up, eyes searching.

"This is going to be a bad one," he said. "I'll finish the story later, okay?"

"Okay. But don't forget." I shut my eyes again.

For a moment, the surge sounded like huge drums. A thin shriek descended into a monstrous, horrifying bellow. I thought of a ravening god marching over the land, Mars itself, god of war, furious and implacable, searching for things that might be frightened, things that might *die*.

The pressure suit loosened around me, then clung tight to my skin. A sharp pain in my ears made me screw up my face and groan. The torch fell between us. Ilya grabbed it again, shined it on his face, shook his head, face slick with tears, and held me tightly. I could feel his heart through the suits.

The vibration of the trench walls stopped. We lay for a moment, waiting for it to begin again. I started to get up, pushing against the tarp, frantic to see daylight—but Ilya grabbed my shoulder and pressed me down. I could not hear very well. The torch illuminated his face; he was trying to mouth words to me. Somehow I understood through my fear—rocks and dust would be falling outside. We might be killed by rocks falling from thousands of meters in the wake of the surge, striking at eighty or ninety meters per second. I pressed myself against him, mind racing, grimacing at the pain.

Time passed very slowly. My fear turned to numbness, and the numbness faded into relief. We were not going to die. The worst of the surge had passed over and we were still in the trench—but a new fear hit me, and I had to fight myself to keep from clawing out of Ilya's embrace. *We could be buried under a fresh dune—tons of dust and sand, dozens of meters high.* We would never dig out. Our oxygen would be depleted and we would *suffocate*, this trench would become just what it seemed, a grave ... I began to squirm, breath harsh and short, and Ilya struggled to keep his arms around me. "Let me go!" I shouted.

Suddenly, I flinched and stopped thrashing. A light had hit

me in the face, not our torch. The lab's arbeiters were ripping away the foils and tarps, searching for us.

The chief arbeiter appeared on the edge of our trench. A jointed arm had been wrenched loose and the machine was covered with dents and red smears—rock impacts. It had weathered the storm outside, tending the edges of the foil until the last moment. It must have been blown around like a small can.

Ilya pulled me up out of the ditch in deathly silence. The mobile lab was still intact above us; we might be able to get to a station on our own.

We brushed each other down, more for the reassurance of physical contact than any other reason. I felt light-headed, giddy with still being alive. We walked beneath the main foil and tarps, inspecting the lab, then emerged to stand in the open.

The foil on the specimen shed had failed. It was nowhere to be seen.

The sky from horizon to horizon glowered charcoal-gray, almost black. Dust fell in thick snaking curtains, great sheets unrolling, drifting, hiding. We gathered the arbeiters beneath the lab and climbed the steps into the airlock, quickly sucking the gray dust from our suits, then stripped.

Ilya insisted I lie on the narrow fold-down cot. He lay on his cot across from me, then got up and pushed in close beside me. We shivered like frightened children.

We slept for an hour. When we awoke, I felt ecstatic as if from drinking far too much high-powered tea. Everything seemed sharply defined and highly colored. Even the dust in the lab interior smelled sweet and essential. The pain in my ears had subsided to a dull throb. I could still hear, but just barely.

Ilya showed me the lab's weather record. The surge had topped at two bars.

"That's impossible," I said.

He shook his head and smiled, tapping his own ears with a finger. Then he wrote on his slate, *"Compressible fluids—a lot to learn.*" He added with a rueful grimace, "*Some honeymoon. I love you!*"

With little ceremony, and not much in the way of clothing left to remove, we celebrated still being alive.

We checked in with the satcoms to tell everybody we had survived and could take care of ourselves. Resources were strained from Arcadia to Mariner Valley—the surge had sheared into three parts crossing the Tharsis volcanoes, and twenty-three stations had been hit by the three-headed monster. There were casualties—seven dead, hundreds injured. Even UMS had suffered damage.

Ilya and I inspected the lab from outside, elevating the tires again and cutting the tie-downs. The foils and tarps had protected it against most of the boulders flung by the surge. Minor damage could be fixed by patches.

We decided to collect what specimens we could from the shed's remains and drive the lab back to Olympus Station. Replacing our suit tanks and purifiers, we walked west from the lab several dozen meters.

Ilya was somber. My tinnitus had passed but hearing was still difficult—his voice in my com was a barely understandable buzz. "Looks as if we've lost the cyst," he said. The shed itself was nowhere to be found—it might have blown clear to Tharsis by now. But it would undoubtedly have spilled its heavy contents.

I looked up through the thinning curtains of dust. The sky peeking through the gray seemed greenish. I had never seen that color before. I pointed it out to Ilya. He frowned, looked back at the lab, then set his jaw and said we should keep searching.

The air temperature hovered just above zero. It should have been thirty or forty below at this latitude, at this time of the year.

My ecstasy was fading rapidly. "Please," I muttered. "Enough. I'm not an adventurous woman."

"What?" Ilya asked.

"It's hot out here and I don't know what that means."

"Neither do I," Ilya said. "But I don't think it's dangerous. There haven't been any more warnings."

"Maybe something local is brewing," I said. "Everyone knows weird weather lives in the sulci."

He vaulted across a wind-exposed boulder and picked up a pale brown cylindrical rock. "One of our core specimens. Maybe the shed dumped its load here."

"I think we should go back."

Ilya stood and frowned deeply, caught between wanting to please me and a powerful need to find something, anything, of the broken cyst and the other specimens. Suddenly, I regretted being such a coward. "But let's look a little longer."

"Just a few more minutes," he agreed. I followed him to the edge of a canyon. A hundred meters below, fine dust drifted like a river through the canyon bottom. Gray dust mixed with swirls of ochre and red, immiscible fluids, Jovian; I had never seen anything like it. Ilya kneeled and I squatted beside him.

"If they fell down there—" he said, and shook his head. Our suits were covered with clinging gray dust; the suck and destat in the lab might not be able to remove enough to keep it from getting into the recycling systems, into our skin. I imagined smear rashes itching all night long.

Something fogged the outside of my face-plate. I reached up to wipe it. A muddy streak formed under my touch. I swore and removed a static rag from my waist pack. The rag did not work. I could hardly see.

"The dust is wet," I said.

"Can't be. There's not enough pressure," Ilya said. He looked at my suit and streaked the muck on my arm with one finger, then examined the finger. "You're right. You're wet. Am I?"

His face plate had fogged as well. I touched his helmet. "Yeah," I said.

"Jesus. Just a few more minutes," he pleaded. Over the canyon, afternoon sun broke through clouds of dust. Green-tinted rays swept across the rugged furrows of the sulci, casting the landscape in a ghoulish light interrupted by deep shadows.

We backed away from the rubble at the edge of the canyon. Ilya kicked wind-exposed rocks aside and slogged through drifts of familiar red smear and the superfine gray dust. There was no sizzle anywhere. It had been mixed with unradiated clays and flopsand. Years might pass before ultraviolet could convert the surface to crackly sizzle again.

"The surge must have uncovered an ice aquifer nearby. Pebble saltation blasted it," Ilya said. "This gray stuff must be ice dust, and down here, it's just warm enough to melt—"

He stopped and gave out a groan. "Up there," he said, pointing to the top of a low ridge. A jagged lump of rock about a meter wide presented a flash of crystal in the broken rays of afternoon sun. We climbed.

I looked back over my shoulder at the lab, half a kilometer away. My back muscles tensed with a red rabbit's instinct to run and hide. The surge was gone, but wet dust was completely outside my experience. We might sink into a depression and *drown*. I had no idea how our filters and seals would function in water.

Ilya reached the top of the ridge first. He knelt before the exposed lump of rock. "Is it the cyst?" I asked.

He did not answer. I stood behind him and peered at the shiny exposed face. It was indeed part of a cyst—very likely the cyst that had tumbled from the shed. It lay half-buried in a hole filled with gray dust. The intricate patterns of quartz and embedded zinc clays seemed less distinct, blurred; I thought it might be the weird light. But where the fragment of cyst met the pool of dust, a thick gelatinous layer spilled and churned.

"What's that?" I asked.

"Something in suspension," Ilya suggested. He reached out to touch the gelatinous material. It clung to his glove.

"Snail spit," I said.

"Genuine grade-A slime," Ilya agreed, lifting his glove.

"Why doesn't it dry out?" I asked.

He looked at me, forehead pale, cheeks flushed, eyes wide. I could hear his rapid breathing over the com. "There's water all around. The gray dust is ice and clays, and the clays are keeping the ice from sublimating. But the temperature is high enough that the ice melts, and the cyst can get at the moisture. It's the right mix. It has what it wants."

The slime grew thicker as we watched. Within, white streaks formed little lacework doilies.

"How much do you think this masses?" he asked, measuring the fragment with his arms.

"Maybe a quarter ton," I said.

"We couldn't carry it far. The lab might roll close enough, we could get the strongest arbeiter up here . . ."

I removed my slate and set it for visual record.

"Good thinking," Ilya said. He put a sample of the slime into a vial, capturing parts of the lacework as well.

"Do you think it's—" I began to ask.

"Don't even say it," he warned. "Whatever it is, it's a tricking *wonder*." He sounded like a little boy with a new toy.

I looked up at the curtains of gray, the sun dazzling through the clouds. This was as close as Mars could get to rain.

"It's just a fragment," Ilya said, trying to rock the piece of cyst in its cradle of pebbles and dust. "What can a fragment make? The whole ecos?"

He passed me the vial. As he took more samples, I stared at the lacework within the captured fluid. It measured no more than two centimeters across, as fine as gossamer. I had no idea what it was—a bit of cellular skeleton, a template for cytoplasm, a seed, an egg, a tiny little baby.

Perhaps a Martian.

Within two days of returning to Olympus Station, we were famous. Journals on LitVid and ex nets across the Triple lauded us for making an epochal discovery—the first viable, non-Terrestrial life discovered in our Solar System. That we had made the discovery on our honeymoon only threw petrol on the celebrity fires.

The discovery was more than a little embarrassing to the Martian science community. Ilya was a fossil hunter and areologist, a digger, hardly trained in biochemistry at all; there was considerable resentment, even skepticism, at first— that we should have been in the right place, at the right time, to witness a cyst bloom ...

We spent much of the next two weeks accepting or dodging interviews. Messages flooded in: offers of vast fortunes for a whole cyst (Ilya did not personally own any of the cysts he had found—they belonged to Erzul, of course); requests for information from schoolchildren; offers to turn our story into LitVids and sims.

No one in the general public seemed to care that the plasm from the cyst died before we got it back to Olympus. The "Martian" degenerated in a few hours to simple proteins and monosaccharides, remarkable enough coming from clay and quartz and mineral-rich water, but hardly the stuff of romance.

We had demonstrated two things, however. The cysts might still be viable, and the genetic information for a Martian ecos was contained in the mineral formations within the cyst, locked in the minute intricacies of clay and quartz. There had probably never been extra organs to help ecos reproduction.

But cyst fragments could not reproduce even a portion of an ecos. Whole cysts were necessary.

Biologists could understand some of the process—but not all of it. The trick to reproduction was still elusive. Whole cysts simply did not respond to being doused in water. There was some combination of water, water-soluble minerals, and temperature that triggered the cysts, and the combination had existed in Cyane Sulci, but no attempt to duplicate those conditions in a lab worked.

Back in the sulci, the gray ice dust had long since broken down and soaked into the soil or evaporated; the snake-canyoned landscape offered no immediate clues. The moment had passed, and no cyst, buried or dug up, had germinated successfully.

Perhaps their time was over, after all.

I received a message from Charles.

Dear Casseia,

Congratulations on joining Big Science! How nice that you've stuck with fossils. I wish you and Ilya the best—I admire his work a lot. But this—!
Serendipity abounds.

My reply—brief and polite—went unanswered. I was frankly too busy to worry. My new life held many more satisfactions than my old, chief among them Ilya, who handled the brief nova of our celebrity with high wit. He was not self-impressed.

He answered mail to schoolchildren before he replied to scientists. I helped him frame the replies.

Miss Anne Canmie
Darwin Technical Pre-Form
Darwin, Australia GSHA-EF2-ER3-WZ16

Dear Anne,

I remember being very elated when we found the broken cyst, and saw that it was "coming alive." But both Casseia and I knew that there was so much more to be done, and frankly, we would not be the people to do it.
Your ambition to come to Mars and work on the cysts— what a lovely goal! Perhaps you will be the one to solve the problem—and it's a thorny problem indeed. Casseia and I have some hopes of reaching your part of the system some day. Perhaps we can meet and compare notes. (Attached:

LitVid imprimatur, greetings to the students and faculty of
Darwin Technical Pre-Form.)

The celebrity glow faded. We declined the sims and LitVid
project offers, knowing few if any would have come to fru-
ition, and we did not need the money. Erzul BM was doing
well and I was being drawn back into management, and there
would soon be little enough time for us to be together.

Being close to death had triggered something deep in me.
It took me weeks to sort it out. I was subjected to a string of
nightmares—dreams of choking, or ecstatic flight reduced to
terror as I plunged into the red soil and smothered ... I
sometimes woke beside Ilya, tangled in bedclothes, wondering if I would need some sort of therapy. But fear of our
close call was not the cause of my nightmares.

I told myself I simply wanted to work at a job that kept me
near Ilya and let me live the emotionally rich life of a
lawbonded woman, and stay out of the LitVid glare wherever
possible (something we had certainly failed at). Looking
back, however, I see clearly that my surface wishes and my
deep needs did not coincide. The lull after our crisis on Earth
was just that—not a permanent state of affairs, but a respite,
and no one could know how long it would last. If Mars was
going to stand up against Mother Earth, no capable Martian
could step aside and live a disengaged private life.

Ti Sandra kept hinting of larger plans.

I had learned on Earth that I had some small ability in politics; my nightmares were caused by the growing in me of a
sense of responsibility. That new sense was certainly nurtured
by Ti Sandra, but it was not planted by her.

Ilya would have been happy to have me share his trips
and researches for the rest of our days, but I had already resisted ...

Not that Ilya himself bored me. I loved him so much I was
sometimes afraid. How would I live if I should lose him? I
thought of my father after my mother's death, half his life
drained, of his long quiet lapses into reverie when Stan and

Stan's wife Jane and I visited, and his conversations always leading back to Mother . . .

There were hideous risks in love, but Ilya did not feel them. He focused so intently on his work that a long tractor ride through untraveled territory to reach a possible ancient aquifer (and, coincidentally, fossil site) caused him not a femto of personal worry. To be left alone, helping manage the Erzul businesses, while he went on such trips was more than I could stand. So more and more I distracted myself by taking consulting jobs away from Olympus Station, meeting with syndics and managers from other BMs, trading vague probes of intent with regard to the future shape of Martian economics and politics. Once again, members of the Council were trying to get the syndics to talk about unification. The air was rich with speculation.

Ilya did not worry about me when I was gone. When I accused him of not caring, he told me, "I enjoy your absences!" and when I pouted melodramatically, he said, "Because our reunions are so fierce."

And they were.

Legend surrounds many of these people now, but of all of them, Ti Sandra seemed most suited to be legendary, even then.

I saw her frequently in meetings held to vet the family business deals. We worked together well, and her husband Paul, Ilya, and I often dined together. Paul and Ilya could spend hours speculating about ancient Mars, Paul making wild and unfounded assertions—intelligent life, legends of buried pyramids, underground cities—and Ilya laughingly following a middle course.

Ti Sandra and I talked of a new Mars.

Ti Sandra promoted me to be her assistant—a move which made me very nervous—and then appointed me as ambassador for Erzul to the five largest BMs.

"You're famous," she told me over strong jasmine tea in

her office at Olympus Station. "You stand for something special about Mars, something our own that we all have in common. You're well connected, from Majumdar, with close relatives transferred to Cailetet." She was referring to Stan. "You have management and political skills. You've been to Earth—I never have."

"It was a disaster," I reminded her.

"It was a step in a long process," she rejoined. She spoke precisely, carefully considering her words, keeping direct eye contact. She had never been so serious before. "You seem happily married."

"Very," I said.

"And you seem to be able to spend some time apart from Ilya ... working separately."

"I miss him," I said.

"I will be frank," Ti Sandra said. "Because of your fame, you can help me ... and help Erzul. You might have noticed I am an ambitious woman."

I laughed. "You might have noticed *I'm* not," I said.

"You are very capable. And you do not always know yourself. There is a person inside you who wants out, and who wants to do things that are important. But the right occasion, the proper colleagues, have eluded you ... have they not?"

I looked away, nervous at being so analyzed.

"I've read the reports from Majumdar about the trip to Earth. You did well. Bithras did not do so badly—but he had his weaknesses, and he stumbled, and that was all it took. If Earth had wanted to make an agreement with him, they would have regardless. So don't chastise yourself about what happened there."

"I stopped doing that a long time ago," I said.

Ti Sandra nodded. "Erzul is ready to do its job, as the circumstances seem right, and time will not wait for cowards to move. We are respected and conservative, Martian through and through. We are in a perfect position to act as catalyst; the district governors are in agreement on compromises with the BMs, we are all worried by overtures from Earth toward Cailetet and other BMs ..."

"You want to urge unification?"

She smiled broadly. "We can do it right this time. No back-office deals, advocates arguing only with each other. There should be a constitutional assembly, and all the people should participate ... through delegates."

"Sounds very Earthly," I said. "BMs aren't used to airing family disputes."

"Then we should learn."

She described my duties. Most important, I would visit the syndics of the largest BMs on an informal basis and sound out their positions, build a base for a better designed and more widely acceptable constitution.

Erzul had nothing to lose by sponsoring a constitutional assembly—with all BMs invited, even those strongly connected to Earth. Earth, she was sure, would bide its time while we worked, exerting its pressures where it thought necessary to make the constitution acceptable ...

"But we'll deal with those fingers when they poke," she said. She smiled broadly. "Two strong women, a stubborn and willful planet, and much impossible work between here and teatime. Are you with me?"

How could I not be? "We're crazy as sizzle," I said.

"Fickle as flop," she returned.

We laughed and shook hands firmly.

We would have been stupid to believe Erzul would be the only player in the game of arranging a constitutional assembly. Others had been working for some time. And, as always in human politics, some of these players were caught up in old theories, old ideals, old and pernicious doctrines. What political clothing Earth had outgrown was now being taken up by Martians and tried on for size.

The year we worked toward a constitutional assembly was a dangerous time. Elitists—some rehashing the politics of the Statists, others wrapping themselves in even more deeply stained robes of theory—believed fervently that the privileges of this faction or that, arrived at by historic and organic process—without plan—should be fixed in stone tablets, these tablets to be carried down from the mountain and announced to the people. Populists believed the people should dictate their needs to any individual who rose above the herd, and bring them low again—except of course for the leaders of whatever populist government took power, who, as political messiahs, would earn specific privileges themselves.

Religion raised its head, as Christians and Moslems and Hindu factions—long a polite undercurrent in Martian life, even within Majumdar BM—saw historic opportunity, and made a rush to the political high ground.

What we were working toward, of course, was the end of the business families as landholders and exploiters of natural wealth by squatter's rights. The imposition of the district governors and the weak Council had begun the process, decades before, but finishing it was horribly difficult. Institutions, like any organism, hate to die.

For six long and grueling months, Ti Sandra and I and half a dozen like-minded colleagues from a loose alliance of Erzul, Majumdar, and Yamaguchi, traveled across Mars, attending BM syndic meetings, trying to persuade, to deflect outrageous demands, to assuage wounded political and family pride, to assure that all would suffer equally and benefit hugely.

Some BMs, notably Cailetet, did more than just decline.

Cailetet had long been a peculiar rogue among Martian BMs. Originally a Lunar BM, it had extended a branch to Mars at the beginning of the twenty-second century, and that branch had kept strong ties with Moon and Earth. Cailetet grew faster than many Binding Multiples in those days, infused with cash from the Moon and Earth. Eventually, as the Moon was folded in Earth's arms, Cailetet became a speaker for Earth's concerns. For a time, a lot of money flowed from the Triple into Cailetet's reserves—money with a suspiciously Earthly smell.

Cailetet had absorbed and supported the Olympians, and had touted itself as a research BM, offering the finest facilities on Mars ... But that had come to a sharp halt.

Now, it appeared that Earth wanted little more to do with Cailetet Mars. Money coming to the BM from Earth or Moon had slowed to a trickle; investment and development plans were canceled. Cailetet had served some purpose, and was cast aside. Understandably, the syndic and advocates of Cailetet Mars were bitter. They needed to re-establish their prominence, and Mars was the only economic and political territory where expansion was possible.

The syndic of Cailetet Mars died in 2180, just as Ti Sandra and I began our work, and was replaced by a man I knew only slightly, but loathed. He had returned from exile on Earth, had quickly established ties with Cailetet's most Earth-oriented advocates, and was nominated by them for the syndic's office a month after his predecessor's death. The voting had been close, but Cailetet's members responded to his overtures for the return of power and influence ...

His name was Achmed Crown Niger. I had last seen him at the University of Mars Sinai, years before, dangling from the coattails of Governor Freechild Dauble. Dauble had put him in charge of the university during the uprising, actually superior to Chancellor Connor. With the collapse of the Statist movement, he had followed Connor and Dauble to Earth, redeemed himself with service to GEWA and GSHA, and returned to Mars married to a Lunar daughter of Cailetet. Crown Niger had finally, in a very short time, reached this pinnacle.

He was far more brilliant than any of the Statists, and unlike them, he had not a shred of idealism, not a molecule of sentiment.

I had dreaded the meeting for days, but it was unavoidable. Cailetet could be very useful in arranging a constitutional assembly.

When I visited his office at Kipini Station, in the badlands of southern Acidalia Planitia, he did not remember me, and there was no reason he should. I had been just one face among dozens of students arrested and detained at UMS.

Face pale, black hair cut in a bristle around his high forehead, Crown Niger met me at the door to his office, shook my hand, and smiled knowingly. I thought for a moment he recognized me, but as he offered me a seat and a cup of tea, his manner proved he did not.

"Erzul has become quite the center, hasn't it?" he asked. His voice, smooth and slightly nasal, had acquired more of an Earth accent since I had last seen him. He appeared calm, with a cold sophistication and a relaxed, confident bearing. Nothing would disturb him or surprise him; he had seen it all. "Cailetet is interested in your progress. Tell me more."

I swallowed, smiled falsely, seated myself. I gave him as much of my direct gaze as was absolutely necessary, no more, and examined his office while I spoke. Well-ordered and spare, a bare steel desk, gray metabolic carpet and walls patterned with a close geometric print, the office said nothing about him, except that decoration and luxury meant little to Achmed Crown Niger.

I concluded my presentation with, "We have agreement from four of the five major Binding Multiples, and twelve smaller BMs, and we'd like to set a date now. Only Cailetet has declined."

"Cailetet is keeping its options open," Crown Niger said, tapping his index finger on the top of the desk. He offered more tea, and I accepted. "Frankly, the plan proposed by Persoff BM seems more attractive. A limited number of BMs participate, to eliminate organizational clutter . . . A central financial authority, allocating district resources, working directly with Earth and the Triple. Very attractive. Not very different from Majumdar's position before your visit to Earth."

He seemed curious as to how I might react to that. I smiled wryly and said, "That approach is thin on the rights of individuals once the BMs are dissolved. Some districts would have little say."

"There are drawbacks," Crown Niger said. "But then, there are drawbacks in your proposal."

"We're organizing a process, not yet making a specific proposal."

Crown Niger shook his head almost pityingly. "Come and go, Miss Majumdar, the bias toward a constitution modeled along the lines of old Terrestrial democracies . . . That's a kind of proposal."

"We hope to avoid the abuses of government without accountability."

"Very Federalist. I frankly trust the more powerful institutions on Mars," Crown Niger said. "They have no reason to lace up hobnailed boots and grind faces all day."

"We prefer direct accountability."

"You advocate radical changes. I wonder why so many BMs have agreed to their own deballing."

The vulgarity irritated me. "Because they're tired of Martian indecision and weakness," I said.

"And I concur. Mars needs central planning and authority, just as we propose."

"No doubt," I said, "but—"

"We could talk hours longer, Miss Majumdar. Actually, I'm bound by decisions made by my own advocates. I could arrange meetings between you and them, individually."

"I'd enjoy the opportunity," I said.

"Our thinker can arrange the details," Crown Niger said.

"Fine. I'd like to go off-record now," I said.

"I do not conduct interviews in this office off-record," Crown Niger said, unruffled. "I owe Cailetet's family members that much."

"There are accusations you may not wish them to hear."

"They hear everything I hear," Crown Niger said, putting me in my place.

"Some of the smaller BMs tell us Cailetet withdrew important contracts just after they agreed to send advocates to our assembly."

"It's possible," Crown Niger said. "We have a lot of contracts."

"The numbers are interesting," I said. "One hundred percent."

"Severance following agreement?" He seemed concerned and shook his head wonderingly.

"Can you explain the perfect score?" I asked.

"Not immediately," Crown Niger said, uninterested.

I left the office empty-handed and chilled to the bone.

By the end of the winter of M.Y. 57, seventy-four out of ninety BMs had agreed to send representatives to a constitutional assembly. Twelve out of fourteen district governors planned to attend personally; the thirteenth and fourteenth would send aides. The momentum was with us. The population's opinions flowed like some vast amoeba. Mars was ready, Cailetet or no.

I was at the center, and the center was moving.

The constitutional assembly convened in the debating chamber of the University of Mars Sinai, on the 23rd of Aries, the thirteenth month of the Martian year. The Martian calendar would be used, sanctioning for the first time the formal use of eleven additional months, named after constellations.

The debate room was a large amphitheater, capable of holding a thousand people. In the arena, an adjustable circular table could seat as many as one hundred.

Detailed studies of the constitutional assembly have been published elsewhere. I am bound by oath not to give many more details of the process, but I can say that it was difficult. The BMs were reluctant to give up their powers and authority, even while recognizing they must. We all walked a tortuous path, preserving privileges here, removing them elsewhere, listening patiently to anguished appeals, working compromise after compromise, yet never—we hoped—compromising the core of a workable democratic constitution.

The birth cries of the new age were the voices of dozens

of women and men, talking until they were hoarse, late into the night and early in the morning, arguing, cajoling, persuading, taking impassioned positions and then abandoning them to take others, wearing each other down, screaming, almost coming to blows, stopping to eat at the round table, relaxing with arms around the shoulders of what minutes before might have seemed sworn enemies, staring in stone-faced silence as views were voted down, smiling and clenching hands in victory, sitting in stymied exhaustion ... for days and weeks.

Delegates constantly briefed the members of their BMs about progress, sometimes soliciting input on crucial questions. Ti Sandra sent me to Argyre and Hellas to chair public meetings and answer questions about the assembly. And from all across Mars, suggestions and papers and vid reports poured in, some from individuals, others from ad hoc committees. Mars, once politically moribund, was hardly recognizable.

Above it all, providing a constant sense of urgency, Earth. We knew there were people within the assembly reporting to Earth, even beholden to Earth. We had no illusions that we lay beyond Earth's power. If the assembly were scuttled, Earth would not be served; but no government that weakened Mars would be accepted, either.

We hoped for the best.

For two days, delegates examined constitutional models, as analyzed by human scholars and thinkers during the 2050s. The Earth Society of Social and Political Patterns had developed a language called Legal Logic, with three thousand base concepts derived from international and interplanetary laws. This language was specially designed for fixed analysis; interpretation became less an art, and more a science.

Using Legal Logic, the delegates spent a week examining the broad flow of the history of nations, studying three-dimensional slices through five- and six-dimensional charts, searching for the most flexible and enduring governmental structure. The slices resembled body scans, but reflected histories, not anatomy. Not surprisingly, the two systems that fared best were democratic, parliamentary—as with the United Kingdom, now part of Eurocon—and federal, as with Canada, Australia, the United States, and Switzerland. We traced the legal histories of these countries, studying extreme deviations from stated principles—expressed as compound statements in Legal Logic—the ensuing crises, and how the systems changed thereafter.

The broad outlines of the proposed Martian constitution were decided next. The most flexible and enduring of our examples was the constitution of the United States of America, but most delegates agreed that major modifications would be necessary to fit Mars's peculiar circumstances.

For six days, the assembly roughed out the branches of the central Martian government. There would be four branches: the executive, the legislative, the judicial, and the extraplanetary. The latter two would be subsidiary to the legislative, as would the executive in most cases. The role of the executive would be greatly reduced from eighteenth-century models, with the executive largely serving as an advocate for major issues; that is, a debater and persuader. The President would be backed up by a Vice President, who would serve as Speaker to the House of the People.

The legislature or congress would be bicameral, the House of the People and the House of Governors. The House of the People would take representatives from districts based on population; the governors, two for each district, would convene separately. Acting in tandem, they would decide the laws of Mars.

The extraplanetary branch would represent Mars in dealings with the Triple, and would answer directly to the executive, but would be appointed by the legislature. (This later proved unworkable, and was revised severely—but that's outside the scope of my story . . .)

The judiciary would be divided into the Administrative Court, overseeing court activities as a whole; Civil Health Court, with its jurisdiction over individual and social behavior; Economic Court, which handled civil contracts, business law, and matters of money; and the Court of Government, which convened only to decide cases of a political nature.

Planetary defense would be designed, instituted, and coordinated by the executive and legislative branches. There was debate over whether Mars could afford, or even needed, standing defense force. That question was put off until ratification. Also delayed was the question of intelligence and internal security—protection for the jurists, legislators, and executives.

The federal government and districts would be empowered to levy taxes on citizens and corporate entities. Districts would be responsible for building, upgrading, and maintaining cities and other infrastructure, but could only apply to the federal government for loans.

All economic transactions from the Triple would pass through a central planetary bank, which would be controlled by the legislature and empowered to regulate the flow of Martian money. All Martian currency would be standardized; BMs would no longer maintain their own credit systems. Financial BMs could apply to convert to branches of the Federal Planetary Bank, but most conform to charters and regulations approved by the legislature.

No district could pass laws contradictory to those of the federal government, nor could any district that ratified the constitution withdraw from the federal union thereafter, for any reason. (I remember Richmond and the statues of dead generals that littered their public places ...) Non-ratifying districts and BMs would be left with the old laws and arrangements. The federal government could mandate that districts accept as citizens those who wished to dissociate from the dissident BMs.

A Bill of Rights guaranteed that freedom of expression by humans and thinkers would not be hindered or abridged by any body within the government. There was much debate here, but Ti Sandra guided the assembly through these nettles with a steady hand.

It was assumed that all laws, and the constitution itself, would be recorded in Legal Logic, which would be interpreted by specially designed civic thinkers. Each branch would have its own thinkers, one for the executive, two for the legislature, one for the extraplanetary, and three for the judiciary. The opinions of the thinkers would be taken into account by all branches and made publicly available.

For the time being, however, there were no first-class thinkers being made on Mars—though a number of BMs were rushing to change that. Until Martian thinkers of sufficient power and purity could be grown and installed, no thinkers could be entrusted to make crucial decisions, without oversight. Suspicions still existed that they might be Earth-tainted.

Until the constitution was ratified by the delegates and by the people of Mars, an interim government would take office, consisting of a President and Vice President, selected by the delegates; the district governors, and one representative from each BM acting as a legislature; and the present judiciary. This government would exist for a maximum of twenty-three months.

If no constitution had been popularly ratified by then, a new assembly would convene, and the process would begin all over.

In the last week of the assembly, candidates for the interim offices were nominated. Ti Sandra Erzul received the strongest support of the nominees and was voted in by the delegates. She chose me to be her Vice President.

Among the last issues decided was what the new planetary union would be called. "United Mars" was proposed, but many who had fought the Statists objected. No phrases using "union" or "united" could be found that were acceptable to a majority. Finally, the assembly agreed to the Federal Republic of Mars.

Three designs for flags were rejected. A fourth was tentatively agreed to and a sample was sewn together, by hand,

and submitted for final approval: red Mars and two moons in blue field above a diagonal, white below, signifying how much we had to grow.

One by one, the delegates—syndics and advocates and governors, assistants and aides, private citizens—gathered in the debating chamber, signing the instruments of federation, abolishing the Council of BMs, rule by Charter, and relinquishing the independence of a century. Ti Sandra stood beside me at the lectern, hand on my shoulder, smiling broadly.

As each of the signers placed his or her signature on the papers, I began to *believe*. The crucial first steps had been taken, the majority of BMs supported us, and there had been no extreme interference.

We heard of Cailetet trying to arrange an alternate assembly, but it never came off. A rumor circulated during the hours before the signing that Achmed Crown Niger would send an advocate to begin talks with the interim government, but no advocate arrived.

Ti Sandra's husband, Paul, accompanied Ilya into the chamber as the ceremony was concluded, and we shook hands and hugged all around. LitVid reporters from across the Triple recorded the signatures, and our embrace.

"Fossil Mars comes to life again," Ilya whispered in my ear. We followed the crowd to dinner in the same room where I had once been held prisoner by Statist guards. "I'm proud of you," he added, squeezing my hand.

"You're talking as if it's over," I said ruefully.

"Oh, no," he said, shaking his head. "I know what happens now. I no longer have a wife. We'll see each other once a month . . . by appointment."

"Not that bad, I hope."

We sat in the middle of a long refectory table with the district governors and accepted the toasts of the delegates and syndics. Ti Sandra made a brief speech, humble and stirring, ringing with just the right note of new patriotism, and we ate.

I looked at the delegates and syndics, the governors, faces

weary but relaxed, talking and nodding as they ate, and knew something I had never known before, at least not so intensely.

Time seemed to slow, and all my attentions focused on these singular seconds: on hands carrying forkfuls of food to questing mouths, on glittering eyes watching the faces of others, the sounds of laughter, protests of dismay at some jesting accusation, protests at credit given too liberally, an earnest woman expressing her own emotions at the signing, frowning ever so slightly as she framed her words; all colleagues, the moment having arrived, their time in history, the organic political process having flowed and carried them along . . .

I felt for them, in that suspended time, as I had felt before only for family or husband. And for those who stood outside our process, who opposed it, I felt as a mother bird must feel about the egg-stealing snake.

Love and suspicion, mellow accomplishment against gnawing anxiety for what might come . . .

I turned to look at the corner of the dining hall where I had stood years before with Charles and Diane, Sean and Gretyl, and vowed that sort of injustice would never happen again.

The delegates spread across Mars to bring word to their people about the proposed constitution. In district assemblies from pole to pole, Martians closely examined the document, and studied the charts and Legal Logic analyses.

There were incidents. A delegate was stormed by a mob of dissident water miners in Lowell Crater in Aonia. Three delegate aides were exiled from their families. Lawsuits were filed under the old rules of the Council court system, not yet disbanded; and all the while, Cailetet entrenched its district holdings, gathering dissident BMs under its protective wing, and making overtures to Earth that were, for a time, politely ignored.

Earth was patient.

I saw Ilya perhaps one day in five, and when he was in the field, less often than that.

Ilya had been called to head studies of cyst reproduction at Olympia, working with Professor Jordan-Erzul and Dr. Schovinski. During one memorable day away from my duties, he showed me a broad canyon in Cyane Sulci chosen for a major mother cyst experiment. The finest specimen known would be exposed to the Martian atmosphere, showered with ice and mineral dust, heated by infrared lamps, and then covered with a dome and subjected to a tenth of a bar of pressure. After months of preparation, biologists from Rubicon City were optimistic they would see results.

Whenever we met, we slept away from home, in guest suites, inns, subjected to the creativity of regional cuisine . . . All through the long months of traveling to district assemblies, training or shuttling from station to station, persuading, cajoling, browbeating, explaining the elements of Mars's future government.

In the early spring of M.Y. 58, the citizens of Mars voted on ratification. Our patient work and preparation had the desired results: the constitution was ratified, sixty-six percent for, thirty against, four abstaining.

Seven Binding Multiples refused to participate, including Cailetet, leaving three large districts and portions of four others in an uncertain condition, outside of the process for the time being.

The interim government would continue for five more months, as candidates for the new offices were nominated and elected. A capital had to be chosen, or a new one built; the districts would have to submit to an official federal census; the flood of volunteers for appointed government positions had to be dealt with, and plans made for folding the structures of the interim government into the forthcoming elected government; the conflicting laws of different districts and BMs had to be reconciled.

The economic alliances of Earth transmitted their congratulations, and promised to send ambassadors to the new Federal Republic. The Moon and Belt BMs did the same.

For a time, it seemed possible we could simply ignore Cailetet and the other dissidents.

Coming full circle, a celebration dinner was held at the University of Mars one week after ratification. All the governors, the former delegates and syndics and advocates and assistants, as well as new appointees and ambassadors, gathered in the old UMS dining hall, five hundred strong, to celebrate the victory.

Ilya sat patiently beside me as vid after congratulatory vid was played. I held his hand, and he surreptitiously passed me his slate showing results from the first cyst experiment. I scrolled through photos and chemical results. *Snail slime?* I mouthed.

He grinned. *Still growing,* he wrote on the slate. Ti Sandra glanced at me as Earth's new ambassador began his speech, and I devoted my full attention—or at least pretended to. Ilya stroked my thigh, and I was anticipating a long evening alone with him—in yet another inn room—after the dinner.

As the meal ended, an advocate from Yamaguchi—the old affiliations and descriptions still lingered—drew Ti Sandra aside in the tunnel outside the dining hall and whispered in her ear. Ti Sandra nodded and spoke to me in an undertone.

"Tell Ilya to keep your bed warm," she said. "You'll be back in a few hours. They tell me it's important."

I kissed Ilya. He grasped my hand, worried that something had gone wrong.

Ti Sandra embraced Paul and they exchanged long-suffering grimaces. The district governor of Syria-Sinai, the advocate from Yamaguchi, and two male armed guards, escorted Ti Sandra and me deep into the sciences complex of UMS.

The guards wore the uniforms of Sinai public defense, with hastily applied patches showing the flag of the Republic. Ti Sandra calmly ignored them.

Along the way, we were introduced to a man I recognized as an advocate from Cailetet, Ira Winkleman. Neither Ti Sandra nor I knew precisely what we were being led into. Vague notions of a coup or some show of force from Cailetet flitted through my head. After our heady celebration dinner, the mystery made me a touch queasy.

"We're away from the main body of university labs," Winkleman said with an unsteady smile. "This is the first time I've been down here myself." His face was etched with lines of concern; he looked as if he had not slept for days.

We arrived at a heavy steel sliding door. "Friends, beyond this point, only the President, Vice President, and I will pass," Winkleman announced. "I apologize, but security is very important."

The governor and the Yamaguchi advocate shook their heads but did not complain. They stood aside as Winkleman palmed the lock face.

"Please have the new President and Vice President present their palms for security coding," the door requested. "After they have done this, Ira Winkleman will place his palm on the face again to confirm identification."

We did as told and the door opened. The guards also remained outside. Beyond, a short corridor led to a high-ceilinged laboratory filled with research and test benches, heavy insulated pipes, thick bundles of electrical wiring and fiber conduits, liquid gas cylinders. Much of the equipment had an unmistakable air of disuse, covered with packing, sealant, antioxidant. Only a small corner seemed to have seen much recent activity.

"This project has been under way for about three years," Winkleman said. "You may have heard of it, Miz Majumdar ... At least, I believe you learned about some aspects of it. The scientists and support teams involved unanimously agreed to break with Cailetet about six months ago. I resigned from Cailetet and went with them to Tharsis Research University. Now, we've made an agreement with UMS, and we're moving part of our work here."

"What is this?" Ti Sandra asked, frowning impatiently.

Winkleman tried not to seem officious. Too nervous, he did

not succeed. "We—the Olympians, that is—decided that Cailetet was under too much pressure from Earth. We voted to shut down the project, to *pretend* to have failed." He shook his head and closed his eyes in an expression of frustration. "We didn't want Achmed Crown Niger to have such power."

He escorted us to the far side of the laboratory, in the section that had seen some use. Here, behind a portable screen, three men and two women sat around a table, drinking tea and eating doughnuts. As we came into view, they stood, brushed crumbs from their clothing, and greeted us respectfully.

Charles Franklin's face had thinned. His eyes were more intense and searching, and he seemed to have grown in dignity and maturity. His colleagues seemed restless, uneasy in our company—but Charles was calm.

Winkleman introduced us. Charles smiled as we shook hands, and murmured, "We've met."

"Are these the famous Olympians?" Ti Sandra asked.

"There are four more at Tharsis. Besides, we're not so famous now," Charles said. "I never did like the name. It was more public relations than anything else—"

"For a project that was secret," observed Chinjia Park Amoy, a small dark woman with large eyes. I wondered if she and Charles were lovers. And where was Charles's wife?

The advocates brought chairs from around the lab, and we sat in a circle beside the table. Only Charles remained standing, and Winkleman gladly relinquished his role as explainer, backing away from the table to sit half in shadow.

Our slates were supplied with briefs on each of them, and as we got acquainted, I made an effort to memorize the important details. They were mathematicians and theoretical physicists, all specialists in the Bell Continuum, in descriptor theory. The senior scientist was Stephen Leander, with a thick head of silver hair and a friendly though prickly manner. Chinjia Park Amoy was a Belter who had immigrated to Mars; she had the Belter's long arms and legs and thick torso; Tamara Kwang, the youngest, with large black eyes, oolongtea skin, carried several external enhancements as torques around her neck and upper arm; and Nehemiah Royce, of Steinburg-Leschke BM, tall and liquid-eyed, with fine brown hair covered by a silk yarmulke.

I turned my attention to the table. Several rectangular black boxes from twenty centimeters to a meter in height occupied one end. At the other end, a shining white box sat alone, linked to the others by thick optical cables. The white box was obviously a thinker, but it did not bear any marks of origin or affiliation.

Leander motioned for Royce and Kwang to bring us chairs. We sat and Ti Sandra leaned back with a deep sigh.

"I don't think I'm going to like this," she said.

"On the contrary," said Leander, sitting on the edge of the table. "We're about to present you with the most extraordinary opportunity ... perhaps in all history."

Ti Sandra shook her head firmly. "Sounds dangerous," she said dubiously. "Opportunity being the flip side of disaster." She pinched her lips and said, "It's more than communications, if I'm not mistaken."

Leander nodded and turned to me. "Charles says Miz Majumdar might have some idea what we've discovered."

"Not really," I said. "Tweaks, I presume."

Charles smiled, eyes level on me. Over the years, he had acquired something I would never have thought possible for him: not just poise, not just self-assurance, but charisma.

"Charles once said—" I began, and stopped, feeling heat rise in my face.

Leander faced Charles.

"I once told the Vice President that I hoped to break the long status quo and discover the secrets of the universe," Charles explained.

Leander laughed. "Not so far wrong," he said. "The status quo is certainly shattered. There hasn't been anything this revolutionary since nanotech—and that will pale by comparison. Charles is our pivotal theorist, and he seems to have a knack for explaining things simply. Would you like to inform the heads of our new Republic what we're offering?"

With an uncharacteristic scowl, Ti Sandra conspicuously turned her large body toward Charles.

"We've discovered how to access the Bell Continuum, how to adjust the nature of the components of energy and matter," he began. "Together, we've developed a theory of matter and energy that is comprehensive. A dataflow theory. We know how to reach into the descriptive core of a particle, and change it."

"Descriptive core?" Ti Sandra asked.

"Every particle exists in an information matrix. It carries descriptors of all its relevant characteristics. In fact, the total description *is* the particle. It passes information on its character and states with other particles through exchange of bosons—photons, for example—or through the Bell Continuum. The Bell Continuum is a kind of bookkeeping system that balances certain qualities in the universe."

"What kind of matrix?" Ti Sandra asked.

"A dataflow matrix," Charles said. "Otherwise undefined."

"Like computer memory?"

"That's an occasionally useful metaphor," Leander said.

"We do not define the matrix," Charles persisted.

"God's computer?" Ti Sandra said, her frown deepening. Charles smiled apologetically. "No gods necessary."

"Pity," Ti Sandra said. "Please go on."

"Most particles that make up matter have a description of two hundred and thirty-one bits of information—including mass, charge, spin, quantum state, components of kinetic and potential energy, their position in space and moment in time relative to other particles."

"Their portfolios," Leander said.

"Credit ratings," Royce offered. The humor fell flat.

"Very good," Ti Sandra said. "Very interesting. But why not send me a paper on your results?"

Leander sobered. "This is just background. Much of this theory is accepted in high-level physics now—"

"It's controversial in some circles," Charles said, rubbing his hands together.

"Idiots," Royce said, shaking his head in pity.

"But we're the only ones who have been able to manipulate particle data by accessing the Bell Continuum," Charles said. "We çan convert particles into their own anti-particles—"

"As long as we conserve charge," Royce added.

"Right. We can produce antimatter or mirror matter directly from ordinary matter."

He let that sink in. Ti Sandra looked at the Olympians critically, still dubious. "Would that be an energy source?" she asked.

"Tremendous amounts of energy," Leander said. "We haven't yet built a large-scale reactor, but there are no theoretical limits to the energy we can release. Harness."

"Lead into gold?" Winkleman asked.

"We can't create mass," Charles said. "Not yet."

Ti Sandra seemed genuinely stunned now. "Not yet?" she repeated. "Perhaps someday soon?"

"We don't know," Charles said. "It's not impossible, I think. But a few folks disagree."

Royce and Kwang raised their hands. "We keep the others humble," Royce said.

"I'm open to the possibility," Leander said.

"Just as significant, we can do the conversion at a distance," Charles said. "That is, we can aim at a specific region and convert matter to mirror matter within that region, at distances up to nine or ten billion kilometers. Effectively, anywhere within the Solar System."

The group fell silent for a moment. The Olympians looked at us, and each other, uncomfortably, like youngsters accused of some misdemeanor.

I stared at Charles with a mix of horror and awe.

"Does Earth know you've made this ... discovery, this breakthrough?" I asked.

The Olympians shook their heads. "They might suspect,"

Charles said, "but we've kept it very quiet. Only the nine of us, and Ira, have understood how far we've come. And these recent developments ... the most significant developments ... they're no more than six months old."

"Cailetet?" I asked.

"They've been led to believe we've made a minor communications breakthrough, after we left them," Charles said. "Nothing more."

"How minor?" I asked.

"We've told them we can access descriptors to correlate broadcast communications with states at origin. That is, we can clean hash off radiated signals."

"Can you?" I asked.

"Of course," Charles said. He made me uncomfortable, focusing intently on me with his curious, detached expression. "But actually we can do much better than that. We can transit signals across the Solar System instantaneously."

"Have you?" I asked.

"No. Only across Mars," he replied. "Of course, we need two devices. None exist on Earth or anywhere else in the Solar System."

"What do you expect us to do?" Ti Sandra asked.

Leander and Charles spoke together, and Charles deferred to Leander. It was becoming apparent to me that Charles led the group, but that he had chosen Leander as a more mature-looking speaker. That did not stop Charles from interrupting.

"Madam President, you're at the head of the first effective government in Martian history," Leander said. "We've been worried for years now that our work would bear fruit in an improper political climate, and would be misused, or that Earth would benefit, and not Mars. In a few more years, perhaps sooner, researchers on Earth will know what we know, and that could be dangerous."

"It's dangerous for just Mars to know," I said. "If Earth believes we have this power ..."

"I agree," Charles said. "But we can't just sit on what we know."

Ti Sandra rubbed her large shoulders with crossed hands. "Ours is an interim government," she said. "We only serve for a few months."

Leander said, "We didn't think we could afford to wait any longer."

Charles leaned his head to one side and shook it slowly, then stared at me again. "I apologize for the short notice, with no preparation," he said. "Casseia, I do not know how to tell you ... the importance of this. I'm no egotist—you know that."

"Well," Royce said, smiling, but Leander put his hand on the young man's shoulder.

"When you were on Earth, you asked me a question I could not answer. I apologize for that. Maybe now you understand why."

"Cailetet couldn't support you, so you turn to us," I said. The words came out more accusing than I intended. "You need money."

"Actually, we're already in a development and applications phase," Leander said. "Using a Tharsis Research grant, we've been designing motors for long-range spaceships, standard shuttles or liners refitted. In theory, we could use a few tons of propellant to cross the system in a few weeks, in comfort ..."

Charles held out his hands as if pleading. "That's hardly even a beginning. The implications of what we've learned are immense," he said, still speaking as if only to me. "We may not know everything—"

"We most certainly do not," Leander said.

"But we've opened the door," Charles finished. "We're not telling you this to get funding. It's my duty as a Martian to inform the leaders of the first true Martian government. Having done that, it is up to you to decide where we go, next."

"All right, young man," Ti Sandra said. She was not that much older than Charles or I, but her attitude did not seem out of place. "You give us the universe on a platter. Am I correct to say that?"

Leander started to speak, but Charles took over again, leaving the gray-haired scientist smiling crookedly and lifting his hands in agitation.

"We can arrange a demonstration," Charles said. "Something small but convincing. We can arrange for vapor clouds in orbit to go off like big sparklers. No damage, not much dangerous radiation, but . . ."

"Earth might think something peculiar was happening," Leander cautioned.

Ti Sandra released her shoulders and folded her hands in her lap. "We don't need a big, obvious demonstration," she said. "I'd like other scientists to look over your work. We choose the scientists. Then we think about the next step."

"We think security is an important consideration," Charles said, and his colleagues nodded emphatically.

"Oh, yes," said Chinjia Park Amoy.

"Parts of our discovery are very subtle, and we happened to be a little lucky," Charles said. "But much of what we know is familiar to scientists on Earth. It might not take them long to work from a few clues . . ."

"Won't it be better if everybody knows?" Ti Sandra asked.

"I don't think so," Winkleman said, stepping forward. "Earth would use it to force the rest of the Triple to do what it wants."

"Couldn't we defend ourselves?"

"There is no defense, yet," Charles said. "You'll need to understand the details to understand why. As a weapon, the uses are truly frightening. Remote conversion of matter to mirror matter . . . No defense."

"Where does all this energy come from?" Ti Sandra asked brightly, as if a new doubt gave her hope this was all a sham. "You're saying you can violate basic physical laws?"

"No," Leander said. "We just alter the books. Add here, subtract there. It balances."

"Mr. Leander, what is your association?" Ti Sandra asked.

"I'm ex-Cailetet as well," he said.

"You've all broken completely with Cailetet?"

The group nodded. "None of us trusts Achmed Crown Niger," Winkleman said.

"Do you need more money?" I asked.

"That's up to the government," Charles said. "To you."

"Not at all," I said. "We have no idea what you'll need, or what—"

My voice had started to break. Ti Sandra held my hand and squeezed it. "We need time to think. And documents to study. I believe other scientists should be called in to advise us. No demonstrations for the time being. And I'm certain my Vice President will agree with me, that you should all be seriously considering the practical applications of your discoveries, and preparing another report."

"We have such a report, with detailed plans," Leander said.

Ti Sandra shook her head firmly. "Not now, please. I shall have nightmares tonight as it is. We'll get back to our duties, to our husbands ... To our private thoughts. And," she added, "to our prayers."

Charles offered his hand, as did the others, and we all shook. "We'll do nothing without the government's agreement," Winkleman said as he escorted us to the gate, and down the tunnel beyond.

"No," Ti Sandra said. "You most certainly will not."

Ti Sandra called me into her quarters, the chancellor's suite, and offered me a cup of late-evening tea. Her face was gray as she poured. "I once had a dream," she said. "A beautiful man approached me and dropped a bucket of gold into my lap. I should have been very happy."

"And you weren't?" I asked.

"I was terrified. I did not want the responsibility. I told him to take it back." She drew herself up and stared at the chamber. Here, years before, Chancellor Connor had ordered the voiding of students, sparking our protest.

"You know Charles Franklin?" she asked.

"We were lovers, briefly," I said.

Ti Sandra nodded appreciatively at the confidence. "I had

four lovers before Paul. None of them showed much promise. Charles Franklin must have been something."

"He was sweet and enthusiastic," I said.

"But you did not love him."

"I think I did," I said, "but I was very confused."

"And if you had lawbonded with him?"

"He asked," I said.

"Oh?" Ti Sandra sat on the couch beside me and we sipped our tea in silence for a while. "Please tell me these scientists are making bad jokes."

I did not answer.

"Madam Vice President," she said, "life is becoming a bowl of shit."

"Not cherries," I said.

"Shit," she repeated emphatically. "We are nothing but children, Casseia. We can't possibly handle this much power."

"Humans aren't ready?"

She snorted. "I don't speak for humanity. I speak for us— for simple Martians. I am terrified what Earth might do if they find out, and what we might do in return . . ."

"If they . . ."

"Yes," she said before I finished.

"We should look on the bright side," I said.

She ignored that with a toss of her hand and a shiver of her shoulders. "And over the years, Charles Franklin never told you? You wrote to him, asked him questions, no?"

"Once," I said. "At my uncle's urging. Charles told me he was working on something very important, and that . . . it would, it could cause us a lot of political trouble. What he actually said was that things were not going to get any easier. I thought he was exaggerating."

"Should we speak privately with Charles Franklin, or with Stephen Leander?"

"I think Charles is the one in charge."

"Is he *wise*, Casseia?"

I smiled and shook my head. "I don't know. He wasn't very wise when we were younger. But then, neither was I."

"Cailetet's involvement concerns me," Ti Sandra said. "I would not put it past Achmed Crown Niger to know more than these scientists say he does. And if he knows, he will use the information. We have pushed him into a corner. He has gotten nowhere on Mars. He is trapped, politically and financially."

"We don't have guidelines for keeping government secrets," I said. "Whom do we trust?"

"Trust! I don't even trust myself." Ti Sandra made a sad face. "God help us all."

I lay beside Ilya that night, watching him sleep. He almost always slept soundly, like a child; I imagined his head filled with memories of the digs, thoughts of work yet to be done in the sulci ... I envied him so much it brought tears of childish frustration to my eyes.

We had shared a glass of port and fresh cheese, both made by Erzul families and donated to the new government. He had joked about the infinite privileges of being at the center; I had not reacted, and he had asked why I was so somber. "Everything is going well," he had said. "You deserve congratulations, all of you."

I tried to smile. The effort was hardly convincing.

"Do you mind if I pry a little?" he asked, pushing closer to me on the bed.

I shook my head.

"You've heard something upsetting," he said. "Something you can't tell me about."

"I wish I could," I said fervently. "I need advice and wisdom so much."

"Is it something dangerous?"

"I can't even tell you that," I said.

He lay back on the bolster with his hands behind his head. "I will be glad when—"

"You have your wife back?" I said quickly, fixing him with an accusing glare.

"No," Ilya said evenly. "Well, yes, actually." He smiled. "Trick question. I haven't lost you yet."

"Yes," I said, unassuaged, "but I can't go on digs with you. We seldom spend time together. I wish I was with you all of the time. I'm getting sick of meetings and dinners and propaganda and being called 'the midwife of a New Mars.' "

Ilya refused to snap back. This angered me even more, and I jumped out of bed, marching back and forth along one short wall of the inn room, raising my fists at the ceiling. "God, God, God!" I shrieked. "I do not *want* this, I do not *need* this!" I turned on him again, hands outstretched with fingers curled in witch's claws. "We had things under control! We could do everything on our own! This only makes things so much worse."

Ilya watched me helplessly. "I wish—"

"But you *can't*!"

The one-sided rant faded and I slumped by the wall, knees drawn up, staring blankly at a corner of the bed. Ilya kneeled beside me, hand on my shoulder. After, as a kind of apology, I forcefully made love to him. My false performance did not seem sufficient. I held on to him and we talked about the time after the interim government's term had expired.

I wanted to take a teaching position at an independent school, I said, and he reassured me, there would be no end of such appointments. I had only to ask. "Midwife to the New Mars," he had said softly. "It fits, really. Don't be angry at yourself."

I had watched him fall asleep, thinking of when we would have children, wondering now whether that time would come.

It was easy to imagine what so much power could lead to. Images of Achmed Crown Niger and Freechild Dauble, unwise leaders, memories of forceful, *together* Earth; how would they feel, knowing youthful, naïve, dangerous Mars had such power?

Perhaps they already knew, and plans were in place, and there was nothing we could do.

The Olympians erected a small, remote laboratory in Melas Dorsa, using some of their own money and a bit of land donated by Klein BM. Melas Dorsa is moderately cratered land, cut from the south by shallow canyons, and swept by low dunes. There was little water and few resources.

Even on Mars, it was a desert.

I went alone to view the demonstrations. Ti Sandra had an emergency meeting in Elysium to shore up support for the new government among suddenly nervous delegates and a district governor of marginal competence and few brains. She trusted me to be her eyes and ears, but I also sensed she was terrified of what they might show us, of the magnitude of this unexpected and unwanted gift. I was no braver than Ti Sandra, but perhaps I was less imaginative.

Charles and Stephen Leander accompanied me on the shuttle flight from UMS. The shuttle had been marked with government symbols—the flag and "FRM 1" to signify it was carrying VIPs. We were to meet two impartial scientists from Yamaguchi and Erzul, flying separately from Rubicon City, at the Melas Dorsa lab.

There were no trains through Melas Dorsa, no stations within four hundred kilometers of the lab, and Charles warned me there would be few amenities.

I stared at him accusingly. "Luxury is not very important to me, certainly not now," I said. Leander sensed the charged atmosphere and conspicuously studied the landscape passing several dozen meters below. The craft flew over a low ridge, then continued its ascent to avoid a chain of diffuse dust devils.

Charles blinked at me, surprised by my tone, then reached for his slate. "We have a lot to catch up on."

"I've read your papers," I said. "Most of it's way beyond me."

Charles nodded. "The ideas are simple enough, however."

He drew his lips together and raised an eyebrow. "Are you prepared to take some things on trust?"

"I'll have to, won't I?"

"Yes."

"Then I suppose I'm prepared for it."

"You're angry."

"Not with you specifically," I said.

Leander unharnessed himself and stood. "I'm going forward for a better view," he said. We ignored him. He shrugged and took a seat out of earshot.

"That's not what I meant. You're angry about our giving you so much responsibility."

"Yes."

"I wish we could have avoided it."

"You wanted to change the universe, Charles."

"I wanted to understand. All right, I wanted to change it. But I didn't want to make you responsible."

"Thanks for nothing."

Charles drew back and looked away, hurt and irritated. The slate rested on his lap. "Please be fair, Casseia."

"You know," I said, fairness far from my thoughts at the moment, "it was you who scuttled our first initiative on Earth. You Olympians. You made everybody so very nervous . . . You put us under so much pressure—and we did not even understand what you were planning."

"Planning?" He chuckled. "We didn't know ourselves. Apparently the implications were more clear to people on Earth than they were to us."

"Maybe," I said. "Did you think you could do all this in a vacuum?"

He shook his head. "Vacuum?"

"Ethics, Charles."

"Oh . . . Ethics." His face reddened. "Casseia, now you're being very unfair."

"Dust unfairness. Do you know what this is going to do to us?"

"What kind of decision could I make? To back away from

knowledge? Casseia, I've tried to be as ethical and straight-forward as I can. Our whole group has stuck with very high standards."

"That's why you worked for Cailetet."

"They are—were—hardly villains. As soon as Achmed Crown Niger came on board, we prepared to close up shop. And Cailetet actually helped us. With a push from Earth. Crown Niger was less concerned with what we could offer him than with satisfying his bosses on Earth."

"You left when they cut funding."

"We told them nothing even before that."

I smiled. "Are you sure they don't have your results locked away somewhere? Before Crown Niger?"

"It's possible. But if they look over that material, they won't have a clue about what we've discovered since. It will be very misleading. We explored a lot of blind canyons, Casseia. Earth is still chasing up blind canyons."

For a few seconds, I had nothing to say. Then my anger collapsed and I shivered. "Charles, aren't you frightened?"

He considered cautiously, looking at me. "No," he said. "You've put our house in order, Casseia—or it's on its way to being put in order. A responsible government—"

"In its infancy, uncoordinated and frail and *new*. We don't even know whether the interim government can flow smoothly into an elected government. *We haven't tried it out yet, Charles.*"

"Well," he said. "I have faith in you."

"In Mars?" I asked, wrapping my arms around myself to control my shivering. He reached out to touch me and I gave him a withering glare. He pulled his hand back. "Charles, you're giving us the power to destroy our enemies, and we *don't know who our enemies are*. Earth has very subtle means of persuading us . . . and all you're offering is a sledge hammer!"

"Much more than that," Charles said softly. "Huge supplies of power, remote control of resources. We are limited in significant ways, but that doesn't mean we can't defend our-selves against almost anything."

"By threat, perhaps. You can convert matter to antimatter. Remotely. From a very great distance. With pinpoint accu-racy."

He nodded.

"We could fry Earth's cities. You've brought back the hor-ror of the twentieth century."

He grimaced. "That's melodramatic," he said.

"Do you think Freechild Dauble would have hesitated to abuse such power?"

Charles said, "I know that you will use it wisely. We would not have told you if I thought otherwise."

For a moment, I was speechless. I waved my hands and fi-nally pointed a finger at him, not knowing whether to laugh or scream. "My God, Charles, I'm glad I made such an im-pression on you! Maybe I *am* a saint. But what about those who come after—for generations?"

"Long before then, everybody will know. There will be a balance. Look, Casseia, this is irrelevant—"

"I don't see that," I muttered.

"It's irrelevant because the knowledge is here and it won't go away." His face fell into an expression of weariness. "There is no peace, no end to the new and frightening in this life."

I bit my tongue to keep from saying, *Philosophy comes late, Charles.*

"I know," he continued. "I've thought about this for years. What happens if we complete the theory, I asked myself, and find a way to get into the Bell Continuum. To manipulate de-scriptors. We all worried about it."

Leander came back and sat, looking between us. "Do we have any agreement?" he asked.

I laughed weakly and shook my head. "Bad dreams," I said.

Charles said, " 'O God! I could be bounded in a nutshell,

and count myself a king of infinite space, were it not that I have bad dreams.' "

"We think of that quote a lot," Leander said, settling into his seat. "The universe *is* bounded in a nutshell. Distance and time mean nothing, except as variations in descriptors. Knowing that, we *could* be kings of infinite space."

"And the bad dreams?"

Leander's expression abruptly grew stern, even sad. "Charles put me up front because I look the part and because bureaucrats respond to me better. That doesn't mean I can be circumspect all the time. We're in this together, Miss Majumdar. You can stand on your high mountain and accuse us of naïveté and intellectual hubris and tell us nothing we haven't pondered a thousand times in private."

"Don't assume, Stephen," Charles said. "Casseia isn't so simplistic."

Leander controlled himself with visible effort, smiled brightly and falsely, and said, "Sorry. I happen to think that focusing on 'bad dreams' points to a lack of imagination."

"Why didn't the President come with you?" Charles asked. "This should have taken precedent."

"There's a major problem. If she doesn't solve it, the cloth might unravel, and there will be no constitutional government to decide what to do with your work. She trusts me to tell her what happens."

"She's afraid, isn't she?" Charles said.

I sniffed.

"I saw it in her eyes," Charles said. "She's human-scale. She's not comfortable with this kind of immensity."

I nodded. "Perhaps."

"What about you? Can you overcome your fear and look with a child's eyes?"

"Don't expect too much, too soon, Charles," I said.

The test area had been equipped with a temporary shelter for twenty people, built by arbeiters the day before. Four of the Olympians—Leander, Charles, Chinjia, and Royce—were present, Chinjia and Royce having flown in even before the shelter was finished to prepare their apparatus.

The landscape around the site was as barren as I remembered from vids seen in areological studies in second form. Melas Doras had none of the drama of the sulci, none of the color of Sinai, no fossils, no minerals . . .

An hour after we arrived, the scientists we had chosen to witness the demonstration flew in on yet another shuttle. Ulrich Zenger and Jay Casares were avid supporters of the constitution, with impeccable academic credentials. They were professors of theoretical physics from the University of Icaria, an independent research school funded by six BMs. We were introduced in the shelter, and Charles immediately briefed them on the experiment.

The test bed itself lay beneath an unpressurized tent-dome. In suits, Charles, Chinjia, Royce, Zenger, Casares and I walked from the shelter to the dome. Charles removed a cylinder of pure hydrogen prepared and delivered by Zenger and Casares, and carefully placed it in a sling hanging from the apex of the dome. Zenger and Royce then brought forward a neutron counter and other equipment. Arbeiters recorded the preparations on vid.

"What are we doing to see?" Casares asked Charles as the final arrangements were made.

"You've studied our theory papers, and you understand what we claim we've done?" Charles asked in turn.

Casares nodded.

"Are you convinced?"

Casares shook his head. "It's fascinating, but I resist switching paradigms."

"Is there any way your hydrogen-filled cylinder can produce energy?"

"In its present state, no," Casares said.

"We're going to make it produce a great deal of energy."

We returned to the shelter, removed our suits, and joined Leander and Zenger in the equipment room. Here, once again, waited a broad steel table and the white thinker with no affiliation. Several small black boxes were connected to the thinker by optical cables.

Leander asked the thinker whether all the equipment was working properly. It replied, in a young man's voice, that all was well.

Charles sat on a stool beside the table. "Our thinker provides an interface with a Quantum Logic thinker, also contained within the box. Both were grown on Mars, by Martians."

"Who?" Zenger asked, clearly interested in this development.

"Myself," Leander said, "and Danny Pincher. At Tharsis Research University."

"This by itself is worth the trip," Zenger said. "If the thinkers are stable and productive."

"They're dedicated and not very powerful," Leander said. "Danny and I are growing better ones now. We've probably violated several laws by building them the way we have, but we needed QL control of the apparatus, and we exhausted all legal means of procuring a QL thinker."

Zenger nodded. "Please go on," he said.

"Some of our work was inspired by a pretty famous scientific mystery. We've all studied the Ice Pit accident. That was almost fifty years ago. A Lunar scientist named William Pierce tried to reduce the temperature of a small sample of copper atoms to absolute zero. He succeeded, with disastrous consequences. Pierce and his wife were killed. One observer managed to escape, but he was badly injured. The Ice Pit cavern became an incomprehensible void."

Zenger seemed unimpressed. "So what are you going to do with our hydrogen?" he asked. "Send it to Wonderland?"

"We've never duplicated his experiment," Casares said. "It's never been proven that absolute zero was reached. Something else may have happened."

"We know that zero temperature was achieved," Charles said.

Zenger turned down his lips and thumped his fingers on the arm of his chair. "How do you know?"

"No details for now," Leander said.

"We're going to convert some of the hydrogen in the cylinder to mirror matter," Charles said. "The reaction between normal hydrogen and mirror hydrogen will produce neutrons, gamma rays, and heat."

"Let's do it," Casares said impatiently.

Charles sat beside the thinker. A control panel was projected above the white box. "The thinker is fixing the descriptor coordinates for the sample," he said. "The descriptors do not use absolute measures or coordinates. Every space-time descriptor is relative to the descriptors of the observer. In some ways, that makes our job easier. When we've located our sample, we can confirm by querying other descriptors, which will tell us what the sample is made of . . . And we'll know we're tweaking what we want to tweak."

"You won't tell us how it's done," Zenger said, pointing to the apparatus. "But you're doing it, whatever it is, remotely . . . What's your maximum distance?"

"That's not going to be discussed today, either," Leander said. "Sorry."

Zenger turned to me, grim-faced. "We can't make an evaluation if we don't have enough information."

"We've asked the group not to reveal certain facts," I said.

Zenger drew his chin back and shook his head. "You've called us in to give expert testimony, but by keeping us ignorant, you might as well impress a couple of chimpanzees."

Casares was less prickly. "Let's see what there is to see," he said. "If you produce energy from our sample, we have something interesting. We can debate secrets later."

Part of me had hoped for more drama. There was expectation in that little room, curiosity, skepticism—but very little drama. Charles did not try for emotional effect. Instead, he worked quickly and quietly with Leander. Both passed instructions to the thinker, and we were invited to observe.

The display above the thinker projected a 3-D diagram of

the cylinder, filled with colors showing temperature gradients. The cylinder, Charles explained, was still cooling to the ambient temperature, about minus sixty degrees Celsius. The gas within churned slowly.

"Charge is conserved, of course," Leander said. "We can't convert charged particles except in pairs with particles of the exact opposite charge. Neutral atoms and molecules are ideal. The descriptors distinguishing mirror matter and matter are tied to other descriptors describing a particle's spin and time component. We have to access these linked descriptors all at once. The result is a conversion that violates no physical laws. But since matter will meet with mirror matter, energy will be released."

"And how do you change the descriptors?" Casares asked.

Charles grinned almost shyly. "I'm sorry. Can't say just yet."

Zenger said, "So what is there to evaluate? You might show us a splendid magic trick. Everything could be rigged . . ."

"We hope you trust our reputations enough to accept that what you see is legitimate," Leander said.

"We can't pass judgment without evaluating the theory behind the effect," Casares said, folding his arms. "Science is about reproducible results. If only one group has done the work and gotten results, it isn't science. What I've heard so far isn't encouraging."

Charles looked between us, clearly frustrated. "I'd just as soon tell you all there is, but for obvious reasons, it's up to Vice President Majumdar."

I felt completely out of my element, but I could not afford to be indecisive. "Key parts of the theory must be kept confidential," I said.

Charles held out his hands, *What can I do?*

Zenger and Casares shook their heads. Zenger finally waved his fingers as if dismissing me, but said, "All right. I don't like it, but show us what there is to see, and we'll argue details later."

"Thank you," Charles said. He nodded to Leander. "Let's project the sample as our thinker sees it."

Leander touched the insubstantial control panel. A surface of peaks and valleys appeared, arrows dancing from peak to peak and finally settling on one, which promptly grew. A small red cube appeared, and within the cube, blue lines sketched the cylinder. Again the cylinder filled with colors, and within the colors, flashing numbers and Greek letters moved like bottled flies.

"The QL thinker evaluates the sample," Charles said. "Everything is in the hands of the thinker now. We should see energy produced within the sample in a few seconds."

We looked out the window; the suspended cylinder, beneath the dome, was not visible except in a vid projection. The room filled with a whine and distinct clicks and growls and howls. "Atoms of matter and mirror matter meeting," Chinjia explained, adjusting the sound. "They're bouncing around within the cylinder. The cylinder's heating up, and ..." Her finger traced a new graph on the display. "Here's gamma ray production. We expect about ten percent efficiency, and of course some interaction with the bottle ... Neutron flux now."

"So far, we've created about a trillion molecules of mirror hydrogen," Charles said. "The reaction has produced about fifty-four joules."

"That should be enough," Zenger said. "There seems to be heat and neutrons."

Charles told Leander to stop the experiment. Leander touched the control panel and the red cube and graph disappeared.

"We've thought of ways to increase efficiency," Charles said. "We can convert half of the molecules in the cylinder to mirror matter in a shape that interlocks with the normal hydrogen. The ambiplasma pressure will push fleeing molecules and particles into optimum configuration for further interaction. Ninety percent destruction would occur. But that would vaporize the cylinder and part of the apparatus and dome."

Zenger nodded. "To the extent that we can make any judgments, it seems you've done something interesting."

Charles said, "We'll have an arbeiter remove the cylinder and put it in the back of the lab. You can examine it remotely."

Zenger said, "I assume we can't take it with us?"

All heads turned to me. "It should stay here," I said.

"Very exciting indeed," Zenger said flatly.

An arbeiter moved the cylinder to an isolation box at the rear of the lab. While Zenger and Casares looked it over, muttering quietly to themselves, Charles sat across from me in the dining booth. I forked through an uninspired bowl of nano food.

"Bit of a letdown?" he asked.

"Not at all," I said, looking up with what I hoped was calm dignity. "I didn't expect Trinity."

He smiled briefly. "You've been reading history, too. Mind if I eat with you?"

I shook my head. He returned with his own bowl. I was nearly finished, but clearly, he wanted to talk.

"Do you still resent what we've done?" he asked.

"I've never *resented* any of this," I said.

"No," he said, suspending his tone between statement and question. "It's only going to get more stressful."

"You said that years ago."

"Was I right?" he asked.

"You were right."

He tasted the paste, made a face and dropped his fork into the bowl. "Not the best," he said. "It's a tradition. Scientists on Mars must eat stale nanofood. Something to do with creativity. Remember the terrible wine at Trés Haut Médoc? I'm still sorry about that."

"The wine," I clarified.

"Not just the wine."

I leaned my head to one side, determined to avoid the sub-

ject, and pulled out my slate. "Do you have any other demonstrations? This one—"

"Isn't going to impress politicians. I know. We can vaporize Olympus Mons if you wish."

For a moment, I couldn't tell whether he was joking. "That
would be . . . mature," I said.

Charles laughed and toyed with his bowl, tipping it with a
finger. "We can do a lot more. As Stephen said on the way
here, we can build a super-efficient, high-acceleration mirror
matter drive, better than the best Earth can make. We can install it in a standard Solar System liner and zip around like
hornets. Make a planetary tour in months instead of decades.
With a fully equipped engineering plant, we could put it all
together in sixty or seventy days."

"A ship like that would be very bright, visible across the
Solar System," I said. "How about something that won't upset Earth?"

Charles put his elbows on the table. "Of course," he said.
"Stephen and I have been planning a number of demonstrations, with varying degrees of sophistication. Experts to ya-
hoos. Bring them on."

He was being a shade too flippant, given the nature of our
problem, but I had tired of bringing him up short. "I'm still
not well versed on physics," I said.

"You really should be," he chided. "I don't use one, but I
could recommend a good enhancement. Martian-made."

"No thank you. Not right now." I made sure the others
were still out of hearing. "But I'm curious. How did you
manage all this?"

Charles leaned forward, face as bright and eager as a
child's, and placed his hands on the table. "I've always wres-
tled with stupid problems—the really big problems. It's stupid to wrestle with them, because many of them circle back
to the language used to state them—and that's a fool's chase.

"But one problem seemed truly big and truly interesting—
fundamental. Mathematics is powerful. We can create equations to use as tools to describe nature. We can use them to

predict what will happen. What gives mathematics such power? It took me years to come to a conclusion, and when I did, I told nobody—because the conclusion was so simple, and I was too young, and there was no way to prove anything.

"So I waited. I studied the Ice Pit, all I could find about William Pierce and his work, his fatal discovery. I knew that my simple solution fit into his theories—explained and supplemented them, in fact. I joined other people who seemed in tune with me, worked with them and prodded them ... My ideas became testable.

"Mathematics is made of systems of rules. The universe seems to operate by a set of rules, as well—not so precisely, but then, measurements aren't ever precise in nature. That in itself should have given everybody a clue.

"The rules of math give it the quality of a computational machine. We can design computers using mathematical concepts and rules, because math is a computational system. The computer's operation is not so different from math itself—it's math operating in light and matter. And math is useful in describing and predicting nature because nature itself uses a set of rules. Nature behaves as if it is a computational system.

"When we do math in our heads, we store results—and the rules themselves—in our heads or on paper, or in other kinds of memory. Our brains become the computer.

"The universe stores the results of its operations as nature. I do not confuse nature with reality. At a fundamental level, reality is the set of rules the results of whose interactions are nature. Part of the problem of reconciling quantum mechanics with larger-scale phenomena comes from mistaking results for rules—a habit built into our brains, good for survival, but not for physics.

"The results change if the rules change. Our universe evolved ages ago out of a chaos of possible rules ... An original foundation or ground that simply bubbled with possibilities. Sets of rules vanished in the chaos, because they were not consistent—they could not survive against more rigorous, meaningful sets. I don't mean 'survive' in time, either—they simply canceled and negated in a time-free eternity. But sets of rules did come into existence which were not immediately contradictory, which could work as free-standing, computational matrixes.

"Those which strongly contradicted—whose rules could not produce long-lived results—were simply not 'recorded.' They vanished. Those whose results could interact and not contradict, at least for a while, survived.

"The universe we see uses an evolved, self-consistent set of rules, and the rules of mathematics can be made to more or less agree.

"Mathematics is a computational matrix. Its power to describe and predict is no puzzle if the observed universe is the result of a computational matrix. No mystery—a fundamental clue."

I listened to him carefully, trying to follow his reasoning. Some of it was clear enough, but I could not track his leaps of intuition.

Charles squinted up at the ceiling. "I've never told anybody that before," he said. "You're looking at my theoretical underwear, Casseia."

"I'm not embarrassed," I said. "I hardly know what I'm seeing."

"We've been around and around about responsibility for discovery, about the problems descriptor theory has caused you and everybody else. I thought I'd tell you more about my excuses. God is not necessary in all this—but that doesn't mean I haven't been searching for God. I just haven't found the key yet. Maybe there isn't any. But when I contemplate these things, when I work on these problems, that is the only time I feel worthy.

"I've lived my life well enough, and I'm no monster, but I have sufficient emotional problems for any human. When I work, I transcend those problems. I am pure. It's like a drug. I can't stop thinking just to become responsible and put a halt to change. I need the purity of that kind of thought, that kind of discovery. I may never know a redemptive love, I may never have complete self-understanding, but I will have this, at the very least: the moments when I've asked questions about reality and gotten meaningful answers."

"When did you first think your theory was justified?" I asked.

"I put the Olympians together. Stephen was crucial with the politics, especially when we went to work for Cailetet. First, we duplicated William Pierce's experiment. We redesigned his apparatus, improved field damping, used more efficient force disorder pumps. We used a smaller sample of atoms. And we brought the atoms down to absolute zero. At zero temperature, the Bell Continuum becomes coextensive with space-time. They merge. Descriptors within particles can be changed."

"That's all?" I asked.

"That's something all by itself," Charles said. "But you're right. It still wouldn't be enough . . . Earth thinks descriptors are simple yes-no switches. But I decided they couldn't be simple. First, I tried to think of them as smoothly varying functions. That didn't work, either. They weren't yes-no toggles, but they weren't smooth waves, either. They were codependent. Each referred to the others. They networked. Every particle having mass contains the same number of descriptors. But that number is not an integer. It isn't even rational. Descriptors obey Quantum Logic from beginning to end." He looked at me with some concern. "Am I boring you?"

"Not at all," I said. I found myself attracted by the sound of his voice, boyishly enthused and powerful at once. *Children playing with matches. The fascination of fire.*

"If you want to tweak a descriptor, you must first persuade it to *exist*," Charles said. "You have to separate it out from the cloud of potential descriptors, all of them codependent. And to do that, you need a QL thinker."

"But how do you reach them?" I asked.

"Good question," Charles said. "You're thinking like a physicist."

"More like mud pies to me," I said.

He smiled and tapped my hand with his finger. "Don't underestimate yourself."

I withdrew my hand. "How?" I asked.

"When we bring a sample of atoms down to zero, the coextensive space around it takes on the characteristics of a single large particle, what we call a Pierce region, or a 'tweaker,' " he said. "It has its own charge and spin and mass, e times the mass of the original sample of atoms. Its extra mass is pseudo, of course, and the traits are pseudo as well. We suspended the pseudo-particle, the tweaker, in a vacuum. We found that when we manipulated the tweaker, we were actually choosing a descriptor, pulling it from the cloud, and changing it directly. But nothing happened. The accident was stumbling upon the unique identity descriptor that keeps a particle separate from all others."

"So?"

"Tweaking unique identity could convert our pseudo-particle into any particle, anywhere. The pseudo-particle itself doesn't actually exist in the matrix—the matrix doesn't recognize it. So another particle takes on the traits we assign. It can be a single particle far away—or all the particles within a well-defined volume."

It almost made sense. "The tweaker, the coextensive space, becomes a surrogate for others. What you do to it, you do to them."

"Right," Charles said. "There are no particles, you understand—no such thing as space or time. Those are just fragments of the old paradigm now. We're left with nothing but descriptors interacting within an undefined matrix." He looked over my shoulder at Casares and Zenger, visible as moving shapes behind the translucent curtain. Chinjia and Leander helped them. "We can excite a distant particle in a way that can be interpreted as a signal."

"How fast?" I asked.

"How fast can the signal travel? Instantaneously," he said. "Remember. Distance doesn't exist."

"Don't you violate a few important laws?"

"You bet," Charles said enthusiastically. "Paradigm shift. And I don't say that lightly. We've thrown causality right out the door. We replace it with an elegant balancing act in the Bell Continuum. Bookkeeping." He rounded his lips, sucked in a deep breath, folded his hands on the table and rapped the surface lightly with a knuckle. "That's the explanation. In a nutshell."

"All of it?" I asked. He was holding something back.

"All of it that's relevant for now—and certainly as much as you'd care to hear."

"You mean, as much as I'd understand. One more question. What's the 'destiny tweak'?"

Charles lowered his eyes. "You've read the letter from Stanford," he said.

"Yes."

"That's why you sent me that message a few years back."

"Yes."

"It was speculation. Pure and unfounded."

"Nothing more?"

He shook his head. "How's your husband's work going?"

"Very well," I said.

"You've a curious taste for scientists, Miz Majumdar," Charles said with an enigmatic smile.

Before I could respond, Leander and Casares pushed through the curtain. They sat in the booth and Casares said, "We're finished. The inside of the container is scarred—as if it's been baked and etched. I'm convinced energy was created by a mirror matter interaction in the sealed sample. Doctor Zenger is convinced, as well."

Zenger came forward and said, "I'll go along for the time being."

"We can send our report directly to the President, or . . ."

"I'll take it to her," I said.

"Have you made security arrangements yet?" Leander asked. "We need to know whom we can talk to."

"We're still working out details."

"Government's in the details," Charles said.

On the shuttle back from the lab, I looked at Charles and Chinjia, observing their postures, the play of their glances at each other and at me, Zenger, and Casares. Flying over Solis Dorsa, avoiding the edge of a thin but wide dust storm, I experienced a quick shiver of unease.

Something very important was being left unspoken, undescribed.

More than government lay in the details.

I fell into a darker mood. The less I understood, the less I could interpret what was being said, the weaker Ti Sandra and I would be. We could not afford weakness. We would have to understand more fully—and anticipate as much as we possibly could.

There was only one way for me to do that. I lacked Charles's native ability. I could not track his leaps of intuition. I would have to take at least a step toward being more like Orianna. Charles had made the suggestion. It was obvious, it was necessary, but I still strongly resisted.

I would need an enhancement.

I would have to reach Charles's level of comprehension, if not brilliance, and as soon as possible.

Part Four

~

2182–2183 (M.Y. 59)

Outwardly, the social structure of Mars—where people lived, whom they associated with—changed little. The greatest upheavals came for officials in the birthing government, who flocked over Mars like birds in search of a nest. The nest was found, selected without much ceremony by the interim President. Ti Sandra chose Schiaparelli Basin between Arabia Terra and Terra Meridiani, and the tiny station of Many Hills spilled over with activity. This would be the capital of Mars.

Such a grand denomination required more than a digging of tunnels and erection of domes; it required a new architectural renaissance, something that would impress the entire system and serve as symbol for the new Republic. All the families in the Republic wanted to contribute funds and expertise. The difficulty was selecting from a wealth of enthusiasm and advice.

The interim legislature created an agency called Point One, and assigned it twin tasks: security of the executive branch, and gathering of information for the government as a whole. Ti Sandra had mused that the tasks would have to be separated eventually, or a fifth branch of government would arise—"The branch of intrigue and back-stabbing." So far, however, things were working smoothly.

In the tiny headquarters at Many Hills, I spoke with Ti Sandra about the end of our government and the transition to the elected government. I hoped to continue working with the Olympians, at least until a fully capable Office of Scientific Research could be established; I mentioned acquiring an enhancement. Ti Sandra expressed interest in what sort of enhancement I would employ—I had not decided yet—and then sprung her own surprise.

The President walked along the display that filled an entire wall of the President's Office. The media links had been established just the day before. On the new display, projected statistics for much of Mars could be called up instantly, as well as ports to all public ex nets. Dedicated thinkers performed image and concept searches on all LitVid communications, and constantly glossed the mood of the planet. We hoped to buy similar (though less comprehensive) services for other parts of the Triple, including Earth.

Our conversation turned to the coming election. "We're not so bad, you know," she said. "Have you seen the lists?"

Many candidates had declared, but none seemed especially popular in the pre-campaign polling.

"I've seen them," I said.

"If we declared, we'd probably win," she said with a deep sigh.

I tensed. "You're serious?"

Ti Sandra laughed and hugged me. "What should we do, show honorable Martian reserve and retire to our farms, to advise the lesser politicians like elder statesfolk?"

"Sounds fine to me," I said.

Ti Sandra clucked disapprovingly. "You've mapped out your territory. You want to keep track of Charles Franklin."

I gave her a shocked look.

"I mean, of course, what he's doing."

I seldom became angry at the President, but now my blood

stirred. "It's not trivial. If it's not directed properly, it's the biggest source of trouble we'll face for years."

"I know," Ti Sandra said, raising her hands in placation. "I shudder when I think about it. And I can't think of anyone better than you to oversee the project. But ... What makes you think a completely fresh batch of elected officials will be so wise?"

"I'll help them," I said.

"What if they refuse your help?"

The possibility hadn't occurred to me.

"Election is a chancy thing," Ti Sandra said. "We haven't proven we know how to do it on Mars. The most delicate time is transition."

"Transition is confounded by leaders who won't give up power," I reminded her.

"And muddled by leaders who don't know how to govern," she said.

"You'd want me to declare with you?"

"I depend on you," she said. "And ... I'd give you the Olympians as your special problem. It would be a pity to pour all that money into an enhancement and sit on the outside, looking in."

I considered for a moment. Being a part of history mattered much less to me than pulling Mars through a frightening time. To accept her offer, I would have to give up more time with Ilya, years more of my private life. But Ti Sandra was right. Most of the candidates who had declared were not impressive. At least we had some experience.

Personal considerations had to be put aside; where would I be most effective? I had hoped to be able to offer expertise and keep myself separate from the killing strain of elected office.

"You don't look enthusiastic," Ti Sandra said.

"I feel ill," I said, exaggerating only a little.

"Those leaders are best who least desire to lead," Ti Sandra said.

"I don't believe that for a minute," I said.

"It's a good slogan," she said. "Are you with me?"

I considered in silence. Ti Sandra stood patiently, a tall broad tree of a woman whose presence filled the room, and whom I had come to love like a mother.

I nodded, and we shook hands firmly.

Beyond any doubt, I was now a politician.

The best place to choose, purchase, and install an enhancement was Shinktown. I conferred with Charles about which Martian brand was best, and what level would suit my purposes. "Something less than a mini-thinker," he suggested, "and more than a LitVid download. The best in that category is a design by Marcus Pribiloff, licensed through Wah Ming BM. It's two hundred thousand Triple dollars, but I can arrange for a discount."

I asked why he had never had an enhancement installed. "I won't presume to say I couldn't use it," he said. "But for creative work, they're really not all that useful. Too fixed and linear."

Shinktown had changed little in the past six years. The atmosphere of cheap entertainment and student food prevailed; the architecture still embodied the worst Mars had to offer. But a new district had grown in the southwest quarter, catering to students and faculty who wished to compete with Earth-based academics.

There had always been those on Mars who used enhancements. Economists had led the population at first, followed by mathematicians, physical scientists, sociologists, and finally physicians. But now Martians with no particular professional need were coming to Shinktown. Sales of enhancements had tripled at UMS in the past three years.

Attitudes were changing. Mars was becoming more like Earth; in twenty years, I thought, we might catch up.

I took time off to travel to Shinktown. There, I visited Pribiloff's office with trepidation. The decor was Old Settlement Modern, incorporating the ingenuity of Martian design when goods were in very short supply, but with a flip of near-satire. I liked the style, but it didn't slack my nervousness.

A human secretary, female and motherly, very conservative, gave me a quick med check and verified my stats. Then I was escorted into Doctor Pribiloff's inner sanctum. He stood by the door as I entered, shook my hand firmly, and sat on a stool, offering me a comfortable chair in a spot of light. The rest of the small room was in shadow, including Pribiloff.

The doctor appeared to be about my age, with earnest features, a high forehead, deeply melanic skin; attractive in a scholarly way. He wore a simple suit and dress tunnel boots. Conspicuous by its absence was a slate pocket; no doubt he carried his slate internally.

"You've made an interesting choice, Madam Vice President," Pribiloff began. "Not many politicians choose a specific science enhancement. You haven't shown much interest in these subjects before . . . May I ask why you're interested now?"

I smiled politely and shook my head. "Actually, it's personal," I said.

"Hobby enhancement doesn't always satisfy," Pribiloff informed me, shifting on the stool. "State of the art still requires a fair amount of motivation and concentration. The model you've requested . . . I've never installed one before. It's a version of a Terrie enhancement, rarely installed even there."

"Why do you need to know?" I asked.

"It's not just curiosity, Miss Majumdar," Pribiloff said. "We'll need to match your neural syntax with the enhancement, and this model works best only in a certain range of syntactical complements. I think you'll match—"

"I made sure of that before I came here," I told him.

"Yes. But the enhancement still takes up a fair amount of attention. It's more *aggressive*, we say. Some would say it intrudes."

"How?" I asked.

"For one thing, it will modify your visual cortex by drawing a direct route between mathematical imagination and internal visualization. It's not a permanent change, but if you keep the enhancement for more than three years, and remove it, you'll have an awkward period of adjustment."

"Withdrawal," I said.

"Some have described it that way. With the enhancement, you'll think a little differently, a little more analytically, about certain things. Even social relationships may be seen in a new light."

"You sound uncomfortable with my choice, Doctor," I said.

"Not at all. I just want my customers to understand the potentials and limits. If you have sufficient motivation, it will work out fine. But if you don't . . ."

"I do," I said.

"All right. Let me describe the levels available. This unit is standard size, but unlike a purely fact-based enhancement, it contains a great many problem-solving algorithms. Concepts and equations for direct memory retrieval, and neural net aids for high-level thinking. You won't become a scientific genius, but you'll understand what the geniuses are talking about, and you'll have a wonderful toolbox for exploring a wide variety of subjects, concentrating on physical theory."

"Perfect," I said.

"As you requested, this model will be upgraded to include the latest work, and you can download supplements from the ex net. In fact, we can handle your subscription to a variety of base language services."

"Good."

Pribiloff stared at me for a moment, then said, "The procedure is painless, of course. The enhancement is placed subcutaneously near the foramen magnum, in a cushioned hyperimmune sheath. Nano fibers will make neural connections within an hour of the implanting, and you should be able to experience heightened abilities—certainly heightened knowledge—within twenty-four hours. I'll need multiple consent forms, credit release, and agreement to provide daily reports on your progress for the first ten days. The enhancement carries its own diagnostic, and all you need to do is transfer the report over the ex net. Not reporting nullifies all warranties."

"I understand."

"Doctor-patient privilege applies, of course," Pribiloff said.

"Of course."

"When would you like the procedure?"

"As soon as possible," I replied.

"Fine. I perform all insertions and implantings myself. Would tomorrow at fifteen be convenient?"

The next day, more nervous than ever, I returned to the office and lay on my stomach on a comfortable couch in the dim room. A spot of light appeared over my neck and a small arbeiter moved into place, graceful curving arms gently applying themselves to the nape of my neck.

Pribiloff showed me the enhancement, a flat thin jet-black disk, barely a centimeter wide. Other than product ID coded on its face, there were no obvious features. Before insertion, Pribiloff dipped the tiny disk in nano charge and wakeup nutrients, then inserted it into the guide. I closed my eyes and slept for about five minutes. The procedure was swift and did not hurt.

I left the office feeling as if I had lost another kind of virginity, betraying my body and the mother who gave it to me. I wondered if I would tell my father; Ilya would know, and Charles, but why reveal my change to anybody else? After a few hours, I felt ashamed of my silly conservatism; but the dark mood lingered.

And then the way I saw the world began to change.

Old friends, old adversaries, and old acquaintances of much ambiguity, started returning to my life and making fresh marks. I hadn't seen Diane Johara in three years, but my slate received a message from her while I was in Pribiloff's office.

We spoke by satcom while I cleared out the Shinktown room I'd rented for the enhancement operation.

I would be passing through Diane's home station, Mispec Moor, on a constitutional campaign tour in Mariner Valley. Ilya would be there for me. After meetings with LitVid reporters, we had half a day and an evening free; we gleefully arranged for dinner.

"It's wonderful to *talk* to you again!" Diane enthused. "I've been so reluctant to drop a note—I thought you'd think I was, you know, peddling influence or something. Casseia, what you've *done*!"

"Not bad for someone who thinks too much, hm?"

Diane laughed. "Not at all like the old student radicals who fought the Statists."

"Have you changed your tune, Diane?"

"Casseia, I'm so *respectable*. I've even been working on the Mariner Constitutional Committee. Are we really Statists? Is it possible?"

"We'll use some other name, okay?"

"And I'm married. More than lawbonded ... it's really more. I've gone over to Steinburg-Leschke. I've converted to New Reform Judaism. You'll meet Joseph. He's very special."

"You'll love Ilya, too. Things *have* changed, Diane."

We completed arrangements and signed off. I sat in the room's lone chair, packed bags at my feet, and considered the nature of time. I was not very old, just fifteen, but measuring time as a string of memorable events, I seemed positively ancient.

My head filled with time as reflection of motion, arbiter of change, conveyer and dissipater of information; *time is what's left when nothing happens, time is the distance between then and now;* time marked in a haze of multi-colored equations, malleable, nonexistent for massless particles, for them an eternal now and the universe as flat and direct as a sheet of paper.

I recognized the signs then: the enhancement was integrating and informing, organizing areas of shared information and ability within my brain. The process was safe—billions on Earth and a few hundred thousand on Mars had gone through it, some, like Orianna, dozens of times. But for me it was unfamiliar and at once unsettling and hypnotic.

I lost an hour in that chair, in that bleak little Shinktown room, simply pondering motion, and gravitation, and how pressing on a wall meant the wall pressed back with equal force. I puzzled through angular momentum and torque as analogs of straightforward linear momentum and force, and thought of how a wheel, subjected to a force perpendicular to its axis, behaves when not spinning, and when spinning. I broke physical systems down into parts, and ran those parts through their paces while tracking the changes in their simplest characteristics, and how the changes affected the larger system.

Staring at the metabolic carpet, I traced in my imagination the path of a photon passing through a translucent fiber, slowing and echoing. I saw all the possible paths of the photon converge on the eventual real path, *sum over histories,* and the photon emerging on the other side of the fiber with supreme economy of energy and motion, *minimum action, shortest time.*

The entire room, spare and dreary, became a fog of forces as fascinating as a party filled with talking people. Behind the façade of electromagnetic interactions—all I would ever touch, see, smell, or be sensually connected with—lay a plenipotential void far richer and stranger than matter and energy, the ground on which my being was so lightly painted as to be negligible . . . and yet I *saw*, and seeing, I gave the ensemble shape and meaning.

I struggled out of reverie, stood, grabbed my case, and ordered the door to open. As I marched down the corridor, I tried to dam the flood of insight.

Did Charles think and see this way all the time?

* * *

The Republic Information Office had scheduled three interviews for me in a six-hour period, beginning fifteen minutes after my arrival in Mispec Moor. Ilya gave me a quick squeeze as we walked onto the shuttle platform, into a blast of warm moist air from the protein farms. Mispec Moor was strictly hardscrabble protein production and carbonifer mining. "You're on your own," he whispered in my ear. "I hate the limelight."

"Thanks," I said ruefully. "Enjoy the view." He would be given a tour of Mispec Moor's rather common fossil formations while I met the reporters. His attendance was as ceremonial and political as mine, but we still pretended Ilya was above the fray.

The info officer accompanying me introduced two reporters from Mars and Triple Squinfo, a moderate but influential LitVid firm that kept a heavy emphasis on substance and revelation. I had only interviewed with reporters from MTS once before. It had been a tough go.

The officer, a pleasant young man connected by marriage to Klein BM, escorted the reporters and me into a threadbare lounge.

The reporters had come in from North Noachis on a midspeed train, a journey of eight hours through cratered flatness. They did not seem in a good mood.

We sat on the worn couches and the older of the two reporters placed his slate on the table between us, voice and vid active. The younger, a nervous woman with thick black hair, began the questioning.

"Your interim government has two more months to bring Cailetet and the other dissident BMs into the fold," she said. "There's been talk by some members of the transition team that Cailetet simply needs to be given incentive, and that you have a personal grudge against Achmed Crown Niger."

I raised my eyebrows and smiled, then quickly decided to preempt what the young woman must have thought was a terrific bit of research. "Mr. Crown Niger once represented Freechild Dauble, and presided over the incarceration of a group of students at University of Mars Sinai. I suppose that's what you're referring to?"

The reporter nodded, eyes intent on the prey.

"That was a long time ago. Mars has changed, I've changed—"

"But do you believe Crown Niger has changed?" the second reporter chimed in. He leaned forward. I felt like a mouse circled by hawks.

"He's certainly moved up in the world," I said. "Advancement changes people."

"And you think your government can work with him, bring him into the fold before the elections?" the first reporter asked. The third seemed content to listen and bide his time.

"We aim for complete participation. We'd hate to have Mars divided any longer than necessary."

"But Cailetet says that the interim government supports projects that may endanger stability in the Triple," said the second reporter.

"I haven't heard that."

"It's a general release to the LitVids, dated for spread on the ex net and broadband Squinfo at twenty-two Triple Standard." He gave me a second slate with the message. I read it quickly.

"Have you made contact with the Olympians?" the first reporter asked.

"That's not for me to say one way or another."

"How could they endanger the Triple?"

I laughed. "I don't know."

"We've actually dug into this a bit," the first reporter continued, "and we've discovered that Cailetet funded these scientists for a while before cutting. The scientists went elsewhere—supposedly to UMS. They've actually come to you now, haven't they?"

"Cailetet seems to know more about this than I do," I said. "Have you spoken with Crown Niger?"

"We have," the third reporter said. "Off the record. He be-

lieves the interim government is behaving very foolishly and
inviting a lot of pressure from Earth. He sounds frightened."

"If Mr. Crown Niger wishes to express his views seriously,
on whatever matter real or imagined, he should talk to us directly, not through the ex net."

The first reporter blinked and nodded. "Crown Niger isn't
stupid. What is he trying to do?"

"I can't begin to guess," I said. I glanced at the info officer
and he efficiently ended the meeting.

There were no special perks in small stations like Mispec
Moor. In a rickety cab traveling through the ancient tunnels,
air thick everywhere with the yeasty smell of active nano, the
info officer glanced at me cautiously and said, "What can we
expect?"

I shook my head grimly. "Crown Niger is trying to sink the
elections."

"Is there anything more the RIO should know?" he asked.

"Not for the moment," I said. I leaned back in the stiff seat
and felt the enhancement's tickle. Memories of the briefings
from the Olympians mixed with my new sophistication. New
questions tangled in my head. I visualized certain equations
in the papers Charles had transferred to my slate. The symbols flared out in red, green, and purple, sorting themselves
in the enhancement and being presented to conscious awareness. I did not savor the feeling yet—it was unsettling, having
this powerful expert attached directly to both conscious and
subconscious thinking.

The equations—which I still only vaguely understood, the
enhancement's assets not yet having penetrated deeply—kept
pointing to vague discrepancies. I shut my eyes, trying to
clear these distractions and think about Crown Niger. But the
equations would not clear.

There is more.

I shook my head and swore under my breath.

"Are you all right?" the officer asked.

"I'm thinking," I said, the best answer I could give at the moment.

Diane Johara had gained a couple of kilos in the years since I had seen her last, and her face had taken on a gentler, more knowing expression, but she was still Diane, and we hugged each other as if we were students and roommates again. Joseph and Ilya stood awkwardly beside each other, shaking hands, fresh male acquaintances sizing each other up. The apartment had three rooms and a sanitation alcove, spare even by Mispec Moor standards, but it was neat and comfortable and immaculately decorated with quilts from Diane's family and colorful, fanciful paintings from Joseph's.

Diane wore a long black velvet dress and a tiny yarmulke on the crown of her head. In New Reform Judaism, men and women equally had to hide their heads from God's gaze. Her hair had been coiled into a dove-shaped bun on one side, and I found the style at once very dignified and very attractive. She had found her true beauty.

I was so happy seeing her and being distracted from my almost painful welter of thoughts that I felt like crying with relief. I did cry a little, the allowed tears of renewed friendship. Joseph led us into the middle room, a circular dig about seven meters wide with banded red and black rock walls over insulation. Ilya recognized the mineral immediately and he and Joseph had something to talk about—deposition of oxidized iron during Mars's early history, the fluctuation of oxygen-producing organisms in the ancient Glass Sea and the chemical binding of their wastes.

I was glad that Ilya and Joseph had found topics of interest to keep them occupied. Diane and I had a lot of catching up to do. The evening progressed pleasantly into dinner, and this was the surprise—after a day of yeasty smells and reduced expectations, the food Diane and Joseph prepared and served was wonderful. Fresh vegetables, the finest salad I had tasted in months, premium protein cakes wonderfully spiced with curry and laced with fresh chutneys. We ate until we could hold no more, reconsidered, and tamped the excess down with a few more bites.

"We keep our own farm vats here," Joseph explained. Whenever he looked at Diane, Joseph's face beamed rapture. I don't think I had ever seen a couple so much in love.

"Joseph's family has had theirs for thirty years now," Diane said, smiling at her husband.

Watching them and listening, I felt an odd pang. My feelings for Ilya were strong, and we were comfortable together. Of necessity, we had found ways to be apart without being devastated. I doubted that Diane and Joseph had been apart for more than a few hours in all the years of their marriage.

They were beautiful.

After dinner, Joseph and I cleared dishes while Ilya and Diane talked. Simplicity and self-reliance kept servant arbeiters out of their apartment. Joseph asked a few polite questions about the new government—questions I had long since grown used to, and answered easily. Then he frowned, put down the last plate, and turned to face me. "I'd like to mention something. Diane didn't think it worth bothering with, but I have different instincts," he said.

"Oh?"

"There have been requests from several sources to use Steinburg-Leschke territories for mineral exploration, to set up remote analyzers."

"Is that unusual?" I asked.

"No . . . But the requests don't make sense."

"How?"

"All the requests are for land mapped in the General Resource Survey twenty years ago. New surveys don't seem necessary."

All of Mars was ready to find burglars under the bed. The President's office received more than a hundred warnings a week. If a little worry about the Republic was Joseph's worst flaw, I could accept that. I politely encouraged him. "And?"

"I've traced the requests. They all come from former extensions of Cailetet, and contractors beholden to Cailetet."

"Former BMs?"

"All signatory to the Republic. None from Cailetet directly ... but ... all, indirectly."

"That's interesting," I said, though it seemed normal enough. Cailetet might not wish to draw attention from a government it did not support—and it might not wish to be denied permissions by testy district governors.

"I've asked around," Joseph said, sealing the kitchen washer and starting a cycle. "Nine out of ten of the districts Steinburg-Leschke deals with have gotten requests. That would cover half of Mars. Thousands of sites."

My attention sharpened. "Why so many?"

"I presume they wish to discover resources and stake shared claims before the election. They're afraid the rules will change after. But I'm puzzled—they couldn't possibly exploit so many sites."

"Shotgun spread?" I asked, alluding to the old technique of filing many claims in the hopes of getting one or two that were productive. Erzul itself had not been innocent of such tactics. Hardscrabble mining was a tough enterprise.

"Why in so many empty or depleted areas? Do they know something about areology the government should know? Or maybe my family?"

I smiled and shook my head. "I'll look into it."

"I apologize for talking business," Joseph said, "but I've always listened to my instincts."

"Have they ever been wrong?"

"Oh, frequently." He laughed. "I *listen* to them. I don't always act on them."

We joined Ilya and Diane in the small living room. The talk wandered from business to politics—nothing impolite or too probing, for which I was grateful. Truly I was getting sick of this public self, longing for some relief. Ilya saw this and quickly moved the discussion over to food and farming. Diane watched me as Joseph took the bait and described Mispec Moor's plans for expansion.

I took a toilet break as an excuse to be alone for a while

and think. There would come a time, I realized, when I would hate even more this role of public person, whose ear was always being whispered in, whose life was the subject of LitVid stare-ups, who could not spend enough time with her husband to fill out half a marriage.

By unspoken agreement, Ilya and I had postponed planning for children, and I realized children and a continuation of real life might not be possible for years if I joined Ti Sandra on a ticket, and we won . . .

I thought of Joseph, polite and smooth-faced and sincere, and his worries about potholes all over Mars—and of the thousands of warnings either dire or silly, the endless responsibilities focused impossibly on people who must delegate, and in delegating choose wisely and when some of those choices fail—as they will—trim mercilessly for a higher good, a good not always definable, certainly never agreed to by all the governed. I thought of the great grinding of the political wheels and felt very sorry for myself.

It passed. I returned to the living room after washing my face. Ilya, too aware of my hidden emotions, patted the cushions of the couch beside him and hugged me as I sat.

"We have good men, don't we?" Diane asked.

I put my arm around Ilya and smiled, and Joseph blushed.

I called a conference with the Olympians at Many Hills, two weeks after receiving my enhancement, and revealed my suspicions that not all had been told.

I had not seen Ilya in a week. Criss-crossing Mars, campaigning with and without Ti Sandra, shaking hands and listening earnestly to a thousand well-wishers, ignoring those who simply turned their eyes away and did not offer their hands, I wondered if real life would ever return again, and whether I would recognize it.

We met in the Vice President's office, just completed— large but not richly furnished, befitting our style.

More than a little dazed, I stared at the full gathering of nine Olympians across a table laden with fresh fruit and grain breakfast goodies. For the first time I met Mitchell Maspero-Gambacorta, blocky and balding, dressed in black, who came from a small Martian BM in Hellas; Yueh Liu, tall and athletic, a mild transform, originally from Earth, who had joined the Olympians two years ago; Amy Vico-Persoff from Persoff BM in Amazonis, a solid-looking young woman with determined features and a quiet, steady voice; and Danny Pincher, a bland-faced man of middle years who seemed unconcerned about grooming or clothes. Charles sat at the opposite end, his expression calm and alert as I told them of reading the presentation papers over again.

"There's something missing, and it's important," I concluded. "You haven't dropped the other boot."

Charles looked at me with the glimmer of a smile. "What boot?"

I struggled to find words for what my enhancement had encouraged me to think. "Seven league boots," I said.

The room fell quiet. Nobody ventured to speak. I marched two stiff fingers across the desk in front of me. "Your equations imply a lot more. That much I've been able to puzzle through with the help of an enhancement. And if these things bother me, they surely must bother people on Earth."

"Nobody on Earth has access to our data," Charles said.

"How long can a discovery this important be kept secret?" I asked. "Weeks, months? Surely someone on Earth will understand—there are millions of people much brighter than I am—"

"Maybe in a few years someone will stumble on what we've learned," Leander said, clearly uncomfortable. "A lot of what we're studying is speculative—"

"I don't agree," said Yueh Liu, stretching his tight-muscled arms over his head. "The implications are clear, as Vice President Majumdar says. We should not be too cautious. I know a lot of our colleagues on Earth, and the whole picture is going to be clear to them sooner than we'd like."

"The destiny tweak," I said.

Charles shook his head forcefully. "Forget about that. It means nothing."

"We should reveal all to everybody and put them on equal ground, Earth and Mars and the Belts," said Chinjia Park Amoy. "I would feel so much better if we could do that."

"We've already decided on secrecy," Leander said with a worried frown. He sensed the group's cohesion loosening. They all looked uneasy, even frightened. I felt as if I had stuck my hand into a nest of sleeping hornets, waking them all.

"Seven league boots," Maspero-Gambacorta said. "All the dreams."

"Enough," Charles said quietly but firmly, his calm regained, at least on the surface. "What do you think we have left unsaid, Casseia?" He leaned forward, elbows on the table, and stared at me as if I were all that mattered on this world. "You have your enhancement now. Tell us. What do you think?"

"I don't profess to genius, or to understand it all yet . . ."

"All the better," Charles said. "You give us some idea what others will think when they hear about the newest developments. And they will. In time. Tell us."

I resented Charles's turnabout questioning. I felt as if I were a student up for an exam. "If you have access to the Bell Continuum—to everything that determines the nature of reality—"

"All the hidden variables, nothing but," Nehemiah Royce said. Charles lifted his hand: no interruptions.

"What else can you alter?" I asked. "Descriptors for momentum, angular momentum, spin, charge . . ." I waved my hand. "All of it. What else can you change or control?"

"Not all descriptors are amenable to tweaking," Charles said.

"Yet," Nehemiah Royce said.

Charles barely tilted his head in acknowledgment. "But you're correct, and it's interesting you mention seven league boots."

The hollow in my stomach expanded.

"Your enhancement tells you more than you can consciously express, I suspect," Charles said. "Others with enhancements have the same problem. It's a design flaw, I think. Maybe they'll get better at it soon."

"Please," I said.

"We can reach into a particle and tweak the descriptor for its position in space-time. We can change the descriptor and move the particle."

"Move it where?" I asked.

"Anywhere we want. There's a problem, however. We haven't actually moved anything. The fact is . . ." He looked down at the table. "We can't move anything small. We don't understand why, but the Bell Continuum ties a lot of position descriptors together. It has to do with scaling, with the rules that result in conservation of energy. We can't separate them out, so we can't access descriptors individually—or in smaller groups—for insignificant objects." Charles licked his lips and stared at me directly. "But we know how to tweak large numbers of descriptors simultaneously. Right now, we can't use our theory to move this bowl of rice," he said, shifting the bowl before him a few centimeters with his fingertip, "but most of us here think we *can* move a large object, if we're so inclined."

"How large?" I asked.

"The parameters are determined by size and density. The minimum we might move is an object of unit density, twenty kilometers in average diameter."

"We're ready to try an experiment," Leander said. The room's atmosphere had become charged with a wicked kind of excitement. "Phobos is about the smallest local object we can move. Its major axis is twenty-eight kilometers, and its density is two grams per cubic centimeter. We suggest taking a trip on Phobos."

I stared blankly. Charles leaned his head to one side and lifted an eyebrow, as if to prompt me. "Where?" I asked.

"To Triton, actually," Charles said. "Around Neptune. Nobody claims Triton. It's sufficient in size . . ."

"Why Triton?"

Charles pointed upward. "Volatiles. We could move it and mine it. It could supply Mars for millions of years."

"We could put it in orbit," Maspero-Gambacorta said, "and shave ice from it—let the flakes drift into Mars's atmosphere. In time, the atmosphere would thicken—"

Leander broke in. "Or we could use it as a vehicle and explore."

"Why not both?" Royce said, looking at his colleagues with an expression of boyish speculation.

"You've all been thinking about this a lot," I said. "Why didn't you tell us earlier?"

Royce spoke first. "We haven't actually done an experiment, of course," he said. "Until we know for sure—moving something—it's hard to accept. You understand that."

I nodded slowly, more dazed than ever. "Then there really is no such thing as distance. Space and time."

Danny Pincher laughed abruptly. "I've been working on the time tweak," he said. "In theory, of course. The descriptors are tightly bound, co-respondent, as we say. They keep a shell of causality in place. The whole system of descriptor logic is surprisingly classical. But the total bookkeeping leads to enormous complications if you only observe macroscopic nature. Only in the descriptor realm does the whole become simpler."

"Ultimately," Charles said, "we may be able to reduce our knowledge of the universe to one brief equation."

"Completing physics," Leander said, nodding as if this were already certain.

"But moving a moon . . . Where does the energy come from?" I asked. Even with my enhancement, I could not draw a clear answer from the equations in their papers.

"Energy and vector descriptors governing conservation are linked across greater and greater scales," Charles said. "If we transfer a large object, we draw from an even larger system.

If we move Phobos, for example, automatic bookkeeping in the Bell Continuum would adjust descriptors for all particles moving within the galaxy, deducting a tiny amount of their total momentum, angular momentum, and kinetic energy. The net result would be a reduction in the corresponding quantities for the entire galaxy. Nobody would notice."

"Not for millions of years, anyway," Royce said. "We'd have to ship thousands of stars back and forth all over the place to make any big difference."

"It sounds so smooth," I said. "Could we actually move stars?"

"No," Leander said. "We think there's an upper limit."

"The upper limit seems to be two-thirds of an Earth mass, of any density," Royce said. "That may not be more than a temporary problem."

"Some of us think it's a true limit," Chinjia Park Amoy said. Danny Pincher and Mitchell Maspero-Gambacorta raised their hands in agreement.

"You could do this with the equipment you have now?" I asked.

The Olympians looked to Charles to give a final answer.

"We'd need to expand the thinker capacity," Charles said. "We've been working on that already. We'll have new thinkers grown and ready at Tharsis in a few weeks. We could do it in a few weeks or months. If we can do it at all."

"Can you?" I persisted.

"Theoretically, it's no more difficult than converting matter to mirror matter," Charles said. "But we can't do it remotely. We have to be sitting on the object to be moved."

"Can you *do* it?"

"Yes," he answered, his tone sharp in response to my own. "You could move Phobos."

"We could move Mars, if you tell us to," Charles said, and his look was a challenge.

What the Olympians had told me filtered down to my mental basement slowly during the next week, fed along the way by a constant stream of facts and interpretations provided by or encouraged by the enhancement. I began to understand— while distracted by official duties—all that the group's discoveries implied, the certainties, the probabilities, the possibilities . . . the improbabilities.

Nothing seemed impossible.

At night, lying alone or on one occasion that week, lying beside Ilya after making love, I thought of a thousand things I wanted to say to Charles. First came angry statements of betrayal similar to what I had expressed before—*Why now, why me? Why all this responsibility?*

Then came horrible speculations. How would Earth react if it knew that Mars had advanced so far? *Charles, you can drop moons on Earth. We can. Goofy immature unstable Mars. They don't trust us. If they know—if they learn—they'll try to stop us. They may not even try to negotiate. They can't afford to be cautious and await our political maturity.*

All of these possibilities had existed before, when only the matter/mirror matter discovery had played into the political equations. But now, the pressure became so much greater. Impossible pressure, impossible forces building to a head.

The plans for the election proceeded. The interim government implemented a black budget—funds to be allocated purely at the discretion of the office of the President, hidden from all but a select committee in the legislature, not yet chosen. This was clearly beyond the bounds of the constitution, except in times of emergency—yet no emergency had been declared. I persuaded Ti Sandra of the necessity. From this budget came money to build a larger laboratory in Melas Dorsa, for research on constructing larger versions of tweaker mirror matter drives. Also, we would finance the conversion of a small, decrepit D-class freight vessel seized by the government for unpaid orbital fees.

The vessel became the pet project of the Olympians. They renamed it *Mercury*. It relied, after all, on the Bell Continuum—the pathways traveled by the messenger reserved for the gods.

When I met with Ti Sandra, four weeks before the election, and we began our campaign, she asked about the *Mercury*. We took a campaign shuttle from Syria to Icaria for a Grange campaign rally.

"Your friends have a toy," she said when we had settled into the seats and accepted cups of tea from the arbeiter.

"They do," I said. "It's going on a test run soon."

"And you understand how the toy works," she said. She had lost weight in the past month, and her face seemed less jovial. Her eyes rarely met mine as we talked.

"Better than I did before," I said.

"Are you satisfied with the arrangements?" she asked. "I really haven't had time to look them over myself . . . I trust you on that."

"The arrangements are fine."

"Security?"

"If I'm any judge, it's adequate."

Ti Sandra nodded. "When you sent me the new briefing . . . I wanted to withdraw from the campaign," she said.

"Me, too," I said. "I mean, that's how I felt."

"But you didn't."

I shook my head.

"The awful thing is, I don't believe any of this, not really. Do you?"

I thought for a moment, to answer with complete honesty. "Yes, I do believe it."

"Then you understand what they're doing."

"Much of it," I said.

"I envy you that much. But I'm not going to get an enhancement, unless you want me to . . . Do you think I should?"

Knowing Ti Sandra, I saw that an enhancement would endlessly irritate her. She operated less on clearly defined thought and more on instinct. "It isn't necessary," I said.

"I'll lean on you," she warned me. "You'll be my walking stick—my cudgel and my shield—if there's trouble."

"I understand."

She looked out the window and for the first time that trip, her face relaxed and she let out a deep sigh. "Jesus, Casseia ... We could make Mars a paradise. We could do anything we wanted to make life better, not just for Martians. We could all become gods."

"We're still children," I said.

"That is such a cliché," she said. "We'll always be children. There must be civilizations out there so much older and more advanced ... They know about these things. They could teach us how to use these tools wisely."

I shook my head dubiously.

"You don't believe there are greater civilizations?"

"It's a nice kind of faith," I said. A few weeks ago, I might have agreed with her.

"Why faith?" Ti Sandra asked.

"I can't imagine tens of thousands of civilizations knowing what we know," I said. "The galaxy would look like a busy highway. In a hundred years, what will we be doing? Moving planets, changing stars?"

Ti Sandra mused for a moment. "So you think we really are alone."

"It seems likely to me," I said.

"That's even more frightening," she said. "But it means we can't think of ourselves as children. We're the best and the brightest."

"The only," I added.

She smiled and shook her head. "My dear running mate, you need to cheer me up, not walk over my future grave. What can we talk about that's cheerful?"

I was about to describe the gardens being installed at Many Hills when she lifted a finger and pulled her slate from her pocket. "First, I wanted to give you some answers about Cailetet. You passed on the news of their claims requests."

"Yes?"

"I've advised that every district deny them. No reason not to make crown Niger squirm and worry he's going to be left out."

"Would we actually isolate them from resources?" I asked.

"You want policy decisions and we're not even elected?"

"You've given it some thought, obviously."

"Well, flat to the floor, after the elections, when everything stabilizes—and if we're elected, of course—we treat the dissident BMs as foreign powers with their own territory. The government processes requests from Cailetet and the others, judges on the merits, and considers proper taxes and fees to levy. But no, we won't cut them off from anything they need."

"They don't seem to *need* any of the claims they've requested," I said.

Ti Sandra closed her eyes again and smiled grimly. "The governors don't need our encouragement to be suspicious."

"Maybe they're testing our relations with the governors," I suggested.

"Crown Niger has better ways of doing that."

"So we don't know what he's really up to," I said.

"I certainly don't," she said.

From my brother I had heard not a whisper for six weeks. To a Martian, raised in the peculiar etiquette of close-knit families and transfers to other BMs, to the mix of family loyalty and business secrets, this was nothing alarming: Cailetet was in dispute with a new and greater kind of family, the government. I didn't expect Stan to give me substantial help, and the best way to avoid an appearance of impropriety for Stan was silence.

But Stan had not spoken with Father, either. Stan was a very dutiful son, and got along better with Father than I. I knew Stan was healthy, and that no calamity had befallen either him or Jane, but that was all I knew.

The campaign consumed all of my attention now. I lived on the shuttle, or in hastily prepared inns or dorms, sur-

rounded by Point One security and the wits and wizards of
Martian politics, our advisors, who were catching on fast.

The head of my personal security detachment was an im-
posing man named Dandy Breaker. His name suited his physique. Bull shoulders, big thick-fingered hands, close-cut
white-blond hair, Dandy seemed out of place in the company
of governors and Republic officials. He was nearly always by
my side. Fortunately, he and Ilya got along well. Dandy was
always ready to ask some question about areology, and Ilya
was always ready to answer.

Leander could not grow thinkers fast enough to provide the
Republic with replacements for all of our Terrie-grown thinkers. We took the minimal risk, but kept all news of the
tweaker projects away from the thinkers.

One of the thinkers—Alice Two, loaned from Majumdar—
became our campaign coordinator. Working with Alice again
was a pleasure. Ti Sandra and I spent hours talking with her
on the endless flights from station to station.

Alice chose our scheduled appearances based on demo-
graphics and spot polls. We would drop into a little station at
the extreme north, meet with sixty or seventy hard-bitten, dubious, and rather ingrown water harvesters, Ti Sandra would
exert her tough yet motherly appeal, and we'd be off in a few
hours to skip through half a dozen prosperous lanthanide
mines in Amazonis and Arcadia. The toughest sells of the
late campaign were the small allied BMs in Terra Sirenum,
firmly in the grasp of our chief opponents.

Our opponents ran vigorous and even acerbic campaigns,
but Martians were still too polite to be vicious in politics.
Still, everyone was reading about the twentieth-century presidential campaigns in the United States of America, before
plebiscite voting, and some of our opponents took their lead
from masters such as Richard Nixon and Lyndon Johnson.
Personally, I found both Nixon and Johnson tragically revolt-
ing, preferring the style of the rough-and-ready candidates of
the Economic Union of the Baltics in twenty-one.

The dustbaths of infant Martian politics actually worked in

our favor. Opponents tended to eat each other, barely chewing on us because of Ti Sandra's status as Mother of the Republic; and we emerged from debates and other encounters ranking higher and higher in the spot polls.

The constant travel wore on us. Ti Sandra expressed a wish in private that Charles and his people could reduce the size of objects they could move instantaneously. "I'm large," she said, "but not *that* large. And we do need a break . . ."

The break did not come.

In my few minutes each day of spare time, I found myself working through math texts and vids available through the ex net, and downloading subscription supplements. Alice put together a curriculum to speed up my "absorption" of the enhancement functions, which was moving along quickly enough anyway. What had once seemed tedious and arbitrary to me became a fascinating game, far neater and more challenging than politics. I worked deeper into accepted dataflow theory, the interaction of neural elements, transvection of information to knowledge, and made the crossovers to what Charles and the Olympians had done with physics . . . in those spare minutes, lapsing into reverie beside Ti Sandra as she slept, watching dark Mars drift below us like some deep blanket beneath the diamond-rich sky. The steady pumping thrum of the shuttle lifters lulled me into a state where I *became* the numbers and the graphic depictions.

Yet the one thing I could not do was understand in a linear fashion the leap that Charles had made, from dataflow theory to the nature of the Bell Continuum. The more I understood, the more I marveled at what Charles had done. It seemed supernatural.

Given that leap, it became less and less astonishing that we could move worlds and communicate instantly, that a paradigm would die and a new one be born. Descriptor theory blossomed inside me and sent roots into all the imponderables of physics, eliminating the contradictions and infinities of quantum mechanics.

* * *

When there was any free time, I visited Ilya. The Cyane Sulci team had finished a larger test dome for the first big experiment with the intact mother cysts. Ilya gave Ti Sandra and me a tour—as he had four other pairs of presidential candidates earlier. "I certainly need to hedge my bets," he said with a squint in my direction. "Politics is so uncertain."

Under the five-hectare dome, we watched gray ice dust seep slowly across the landscape, forming powdery puddles around the exposed cysts. Thus far, nothing had been produced but slime and a few embedded silicate shapes like spicules in sponges. But Ilya's research team was optimistic. From the control room, we watched the team vary the conditions under the dome by degrees and percentages—turning gray ice dust to muddy rain, then to snow, and changing the concentrations of minerals and atmospheric gases.

"We're aiming for an election day triumph," Ilya explained to Ti Sandra. "Just to bump your victory off the LitVid banners . . ."

Ti Sandra nodded with utmost seriousness. "I'd rather be here," she said.

"Please," I said to my husband. "No jokes about growing Martian voters."

"I wasn't even suggesting . . ." Ilya said.

Ti Sandra fixed him with wide eyes and prim lips. "Don't listen to her. Every little bit helps."

The cysts lay like great rough black eggs in the red sand, linear invaginations banding their dark surfaces, capped by flakes of snow. Shadows from the dome struts waffled the landscape. From all around came the thin, ghostly sounds of the experimental incubation machinery. *Old Mars hatching all over,* I thought as we prepared to leave. *If we get the right combination.*

I hugged and kissed Ilya and followed Ti Sandra. Security guards and two armored arbeiters surrounded us in the tunnel to the shuttle terminal.

We weren't planning to meet again until the eve of the

election. I last saw Ilya on the parapet overlooking the terminal, surrounded by our rear contingent of security. He was waving in our general direction and appeared distracted. I felt a burst of warmth for his patience, for his beauty. I remember that we lingered on that kiss, knowing it might be weeks.

My husband of just two years.

My husband.

Part Five

~

2184, M.Y. 60

In the darkened debating chamber, Ti Sandra and her closest opponent, Rafe Olson of Copernicus, stood behind podiums, bathed in golden spots. Ti Sandra looked over the audience warmly, smiling and nodding. The debates were all being held at UMS and broadcast live around Mars. Three million adult Martians watched loyally, an audience one-tenth of one percent that of the most popular freeband LitVid on Earth.

The affairs of Mars were trivial in numbers, yet significant in emotional impact. LitVid signals were already spreading over the ex net, with attached text commentary from across the Triple. The Martian election campaign was big news everywhere, the first test of a world-nation, all else being birth and rehearsal.

I had suffered through debates with my opponents, and done well enough, but Ti Sandra had no equal on Mars. She had grown into her role with such style and grace that I wondered how anyone could replace her. She accepted the pressures flexibly, and blew them away to become even stronger.

Olson was smooth and efficient and knew his stuff; I've often thought he would have made a good President. He might have been smarter than Ti Sandra. But leadership has never been carried out by brains alone. Olson had at least three enhancements that we knew of, two social and one technical, yet still couldn't match her for instinct and style.

I sat in the front row, Dandy Breaker on my left, the Chancellor of UMS and his wife to my right, one thousand students in ranked tiers behind us. The scene might have been centuries old; very democratic, very human, a contest between the best Mars could offer.

The chancellor, Helmut Frankel, patted my hand and whispered in my ear, "Makes a red rabbit very proud, doesn't it?"

I agreed with a smile. I knew Ilya was watching; I felt that communality and closeness with him. I knew Charles would be watching. Let the games begin.

The UMS thinker, Marshall, installed two years before, projected an image of a proper Martian university professor, male, melanic, perhaps twenty-five years old, distinguished by peppery spots in his hair. The image bowed to the audience, which applauded politely, then to the stage. "President Erzul, Candidate Olson," the thinker began, "I have taken questions posed by citizens of our young Republic, humans and thinkers, and analyzed them carefully to extract those issues which seem of most concern. First, I would like to ask Candidate Olson, how would you shape the policy of the Republic with regard to imports of high application goods such as nano designs?"

Olson did not appear to pause to think. "The Triple must treat Mars as an economic full partner, with no restrictions on any high app goods. While our economic leverage with regard to the major exporter of nano designs, Earth, is not particularly strong, I believe we have moral leverage, as child to the parent world. Why would Earth *not* treat us as a full partner, with the aim of eventually uniting all the Solar System under a common alliance, sovereign states and worlds recognizing a common goal?"

"Would that common goal be the so-called Push, the move to expand to the stars?"

"In the long run, certainly; I do share with the governments of Earth the belief that frontiers are necessary for growth. But other goals are much more immediate, among them open gateways for all scientific and technological discoveries, to remove the friction of uneven technological advancement."

Olson did not know much if anything about the Olympians, and was almost certainly referring to Mars's complaints against limited access to Earth technology, but for me, the statement carried extra weight.

"President Erzul, your comment on Candidate Olson's answer?"

Ti Sandra placed her hands on the podium, pausing. The silence of several seconds was significant. Politics is showmanship; Ti Sandra would not appear to give predigested answers, or take the question and response quickly and lightly.

"No nation or political body operates out of altruism in the long run, and there is no reason to expect Earth to behave as mother to child. We have our own planetary pride, our own qualities, our own goods and inventions to offer, and these will in time be very significant. We must grow as friendly competitors, and we must earn our place in the Triple, without gifts, without favors. Others may need new frontiers, but Mars is still a frontier in itself. Mars is young but strong. We can grow, and will grow, to our own maturity in our own time."

"But should not the Triple treat us as an equal partner, for the sake of historical ties?" Marshall asked.

Ti Sandra acknowledged that this would be a good thing, but added, "We intend never to impede the growth of Earth or any other sovereign power within the Triple. All we ask, in the long run, is that the Triple not stand in our way. We welcome economic ties, we welcome all forms of open trade, but we must not rely on inappropriate expectations or emotions."

She had thirty seconds more for her answer, and took the time to elaborate. "Mars is a rich desert, scattered with settlements filled with a tough and loving people. We have grown as independent families, cooperating to keep each other alive, trading and sharing to prosper. I believe this is the natural order of things: good will among tough-minded but loving equals, never handicapping competitors, sharing the common resources through a strong and fair central authority. Good government keeps balances and corrects those flaws that will not correct themselves. The success of a Martian government lies in not stifling our greatest strengths to fit into some grand intellectual scheme with no precedent in history as actually lived."

Chancellor Frankel leaned over to speak to me. "Brilliantly stated and reprised," he said, nodding vigorously. "I hope she doesn't really believe all that."

Marshall's image turned to face Olson. "The interim government of President Erzul has already shown itself to be an effect effect *an iv eck*—"

The image abruptly froze, then winked out. LitVid displays around the auditorium spun through confined gyrations and went dark. A low hum filled the room, empty digits on the auditorium's sounder, and then that, too, fell silent. Beside me, Dandy jumped to his feet, took my shoulder, and practically lifted me out of my seat. Two guards and an arbeiter leaped on stage to surround Ti Sandra, and another guard stationed himself by Olson. The auditorium's lights went out.

"Get down," Dandy whispered harshly. I fell to my knees beside him. The auditorium filled with concerned voices and a few shouts and screams. I could feel my body becoming frightened before my mind had time to react.

Dandy pushed my butt and urged me across the floor, still on hands and knees. He covered me like a rude lover until we were in the protection of a stairwell. Ti Sandra huffed beside me. "You there, Cassie?" she asked.

"I'm here," I said.

"Quiet!" Dandy ordered.

A torch flicked on, half-hidden by a guard's hand as he read a small map on a metal plate secured to a handrail at the base of the stairs. Ti Sandra's chief guard, Patsy Di Vorno, a sharp-faced young woman with incredible arms and shoulders, slapped a thick white slab like modeling clay on my arm. I gave a little shriek as it quickly spread and covered my torso, neck, and head, bunching my hair and tugging it painfully. It left me holes to see and breath through. Di Vorno wrapped a slab around each of Ti Sandra's arms. We were now covered with reactive nano armor. The armor was intelligent and mobile; it could sense approaching projectiles and curl us into a tight ball with muscle-snapping speed. Any high-speed projectile hitting the armor would be blown to a stop. That made us dangerous to everybody around us.

With a few grunted words, the President and I were dragged, walked, and shoved up the stairs like cargo. In a small storage room, cool and dark, the guards pushed us low against a wall adjacent to the entrance. They turned their torches high and flicked them down the hall outside. Coded com links penetrated the walls like secret half-heard whispers among frightened children.

Nobody followed. Four guards and two arbeiters set up a secure station in that room, slapping quick-spread sensors onto the walls and drawing their guns. The arbeiters were much more heavily armed than I had guessed, sporting both projectile rapid-fires, short-range electron beams, and selective bio knockers that could put an army of live assailants—human or animal—into shock.

I hugged Ti Sandra and she hugged me, the armor squeaking like rubber between us. Only then did we realize that Olson was in the room with us. Ti Sandra gave him a shocked look, and we hugged him as well.

"What in the hell is this?" Olson asked, voice shaky. His dignity seemed ruffled and he pushed us back.

"Power failure," Ti Sandra ventured. The closest guard, whom I knew only as Jack, shook his head in the torch glare, a shadow above him echoing larger denial.

"No, ma'am," Patsy Di Vorno said, coming back into the room. "Power doesn't go down in buildings like this. The dedicated thinker blanked. All backup control dunked with it. That doesn't happen. We have a planned failure of support."

"Oh," Olson said, leaving his jaw open.

Patsy's mind—triggering a speed enhancement—went into high gear and she started clipping. "Now get your shuttle to unknown. Risk if unfriendly air team tracking—"

"Or sabotage," Dandy Breaker said. "We should separate prez and veep now. Candidate can serve as decoy."

Olson's jaw dropped farther.

"Sorry, sir," Dandy went on, face stony and eyes narrowed in the glare. I could hardly see except in blocks of harsh white and starry black.

"You have an obligation," Olson said, but his own guard interrupted.

"Sir, we mean to get you out of here as well. Breaker means that each team will vector separately. Three arrows out of here, each acting as diversion for the other." He raised his hand, and again we were grabbed and pushed into the hall. From the auditorium came more screams and concerned voices.

"Don't worry, ma'am," Breaker told me. "No weapons fire and no assault signals."

"Watch for peeling walls," another guard said. Nano poisons, rapid-assembly weapons and machines, anything might be possible.

"Who?" Ti Sandra asked, face flushed, large body suddenly very vulnerable and weak, a big slow target.

"We don't care right now, Madam President," another guard said.

I told Dandy, "If you grab my ass again, you better mean it." He shot me a look of surprise, grinned, and said, "Sorry, Ma'am."

We took back tunnels to the shuttle port, walking briskly with guards and arbeiters front and back. "Christ, I don't want *this*," Olson said before we split, his lone guard hustling him to the train tubes.

"Madam Veep, you have another shuttle," Di Vorno said. "Prez goes incom. Luck, Dandy."

Dandy, Jack, and an arbeiter guided me to the proper gate for the second shuttle. I knew the team always traveled with two shuttles, but I had not seen the second before. It did not look luxurious; spare, cut down, armored and fast.

Then Dandy did something that shocked me badly. He took a tiny package from his pocket, approached a decorative fountain in the terminal and broke the package over the main nozzle. The package quickly swelled in the water like a lump of rising dough. A tiny mechanical observer poked out of the mass and painted me quickly with a gridwork of red lines of light. The lump flopped in the pool around the fountain, popping arms and legs. The legs neglected to sprout toes, growing shoes instead.

It began to look like me, clothes and all, right down to the lumpy white armor. In a few seconds, it stood, squeaked, and with a convincing if inelegant gait, followed the arbeiter into the shuttle. The shuttle sealed the terminal bridge and its hatches, rolled away, and rose into the pink afternoon sky on flame-rooted feathers of white steam.

I shivered away the prickling hairs on my neck.

"My call, ma'am," Dandy said. He and Jack each took an arm and guided me down the corridor. "Maintenance trains go to old station tunnels from here. We'll take one of those."

So I was back where it all began for me, the birthplace of my political consciousness. The pioneer tunnels behind the UMS train depot were still dark and narrow and filled with forgotten debris eventually awaiting the recyclers. The air was downright cold and smelled bad. My head swam as Dandy and Jack paused to consult their slates.

"All com's out except for secure channels, and they're not active," Jack said. He shook his head. "Satcom's out. We might hook into a port and try internal optic."

"No ports here," Dandy said. "Why no com on the secure channels?"

Jack thought for a moment. "I doubt anybody's sending. President's crew is going to stay quiet and in the air until they hear from Point One."

"Point One doesn't rely on thinker coordination . . ." Dandy mused. "But they have links with thinkers, and computers route the com like anywhere else."

"Evolvons?" I asked.

Dandy waggled his head, not committing himself to any theories. Jack, however, reached up to the roof of the tunnel with long arms, scraped his fingers there, and said, "We've put Terrie thinkers back in authority after sweeps. UMS was running its day-to-day with thinkers."

"Not life support," I said.

"No, but everything's coordinated . . . Computers talk with thinkers, thinkers give computers high-level instructions, even backup systems refer to the system boss . . . and that's a thinker. We swept for them and we missed, that's all."

"Earth evolvons," Dandy said. "Why?"

Jack dropped his hand to his side, wiping ice crystals on his pants, and said, "Madam Vice President, where are the Olympians now?"

"Some of your people are protecting them," I said.

"Of course, but do you know where they are?"

"I assume most of them are at Melas Dorsa. Franklin's core group. Some may be at Tharsis Research University with Leander."

"I need to know some things," Jack said. "Will you brief me?"

"I'll try," I said.

"Let's find a hidey hole with some insulation. We'll settle in until Point One tells us what to do . . . assuming they can. If we don't hear in several hours, we'll commandeer a train and move out of here."

In the dark, the three of us sat in a old branch still lined with foamed rock, marginally warmer than the long tunnels.

I wondered if I could still find my way to the trench dome where I'd first spoken with Charles, where the students had gathered before going Up.

"I have a theory," Jack began. "But you should tell me some things first."

"All right," I said.

"Don't be hasty, Ma'am," Dandy said, half-joking. "Check out his clearance."

Jack nodded sincerely. "That should be first, he's right," he said.

I held my slate to his and checked his security clearance by comparison of coded signals. The signals found a locus of agreement. Jack and Dandy were both cleared for top secret, but only on a strict need-to-know basis.

"I think Earth is fapping with our dataflow," Jack began. "That isn't good. We're vulnerable as hell. Our contingency plans call for getting you to a safe location of our choosing. We'll put together the government at that point by popping up a shielded satcom. Assuming they still have evolvons in most of our thinkers, and the evolvons have polluted the computers as well, Mars is going to be in bad shape. Stations will be cut off except for direct optic links and they'll be down for a while. Governors won't be able to report to Many Hills for several days. Techs will have to go in with certified Martian computers and start rearranging dataflow."

"There will be more fapping," Dandy said. "You can bet our certified computers will be polluted."

"Comes from too much reliance on Earth," Jack said sourly. "Ma'am, what I need to know is, why would Earth do this? Just to screw up our government?"

"No," I said. "They'd want to deal with a stable government."

"Have we got something going that would scare them that bad?" Jack asked.

"Yes," I said, cutting through all my instinctive equivocation. My life probably depended on these two men.

"The Olympians?" Jack asked.

"Yes."

"I'm just asking because they were put under top security protection a month ago, and I planned the pattern," Jack said. "Unusual for industrial stuff."

"Is there any chance this is just a local failure?" I asked, the strain in my voice obvious. My last ray of hope was about to be extinguished.

"No, Ma'am," Dandy said. "We'd get Point One immediately."

"Then I'd like to be with the Olympians, and as soon as possible," I said.

Dandy and Jack considered this in silence. "Ma'am, you undoubtedly have your reasons. But we have to make you available for talks with negotiators representing the aggressor. You will be exposed before the President, in case the aggressors are trying to decapitate Mars. Security for the Olympians assumes they will be killed if the aggressor knows their whereabouts. They'll be removed from Melas Dorsa as soon as possible, and we don't know where they'll be."

"I need to communicate with them, then."

"Nobody's talking with anybody for the next few hours, perhaps longer, if we guess correctly."

"If it's that bad, then people are dying," I said.

Jack nodded. "Yes, Ma'am. Power blackouts, tunnel collapses in the fancier stations, oxydep, recycler failures . . ."

My neck stiffened with rage beneath the armor. "When will Ti Sandra and I be able to talk?"

Dandy was about to answer when his slate chimed. Coded signals flashed onto the screen.

"That's Point One," he said. "Someone's popped up a mini satcom. Things are happening fast. We're to get you to a shuttle and take you to Many Hills immediately. You're to meet with someone who has a message from Earth."

"I hope you like adventure, Madam Vice President," Jack said.

"Not this kind," I said.

"Nor I, Ma'am."

"What's your last name, Jack?"

"Name's Ivan Ivanovitch Vasilkovsky, Ma'am, from Yamaguchi BM in Australe."

Terror can only last so long before it subsides into numbness and a sour stomach.

A sleek black and red maintenance train engine had been sidelined in the depot roundhouse. We boarded through the engineer's lock. Dandy checked the computer and found it had been completely deactivated. Together, Dandy and Jack pulled the computer offline so it would not start with powerup, switched the engine to emergency manual override, turned on safety sensors but left lights and beacons off, and took us out of the roundhouse. Dandy took the first watch in the driver's seat.

I did not want to go to Many Hills, but their arguments were irrefutable. Running unloaded, on a straight trace the engine could push up to four hundred kiphs. The trip would take at least fifteen hours.

Saddled with authority, away from Ti Sandra and out of touch possibly for days, I felt like a lost child. Mostly I stayed quiet in the tiny compartment, lying on a hard cot that belied the colloquial name from centuries past—"featherbedding."

Jack Vasilkovsky sat on a pulldown stool, face unreadable. He would give up his life for me if called upon. And he would kill.

I had thought these matters through before, but never with such intensity and urgency. I was no longer simply myself or even the Vice President. I was the face of the Republic until Ti Sandra could safely emerge.

In a few hours, I would examine all the contingency plans made by our defense and security staffs. And shortly after that, whether or not I had spoken with Ti Sandra, I would be facing someone representing Earth—who? And with what demands?

The compartment's tiny port allowed small glimpses of

pink sky darkening into dusk. The pink shaded into deep brown filled with stars. Came a quick flash of pale blue along the horizon, something I had never seen live before, and night black and cold.

The compartment smelled of stale nano and dust. The engine flew at speed, silent on straight trace. There might be other trains stranded on the tracks, their computers dithering from Earth's merciless evolvons. Jack looked as if he was prepared to blast them out of our way—but then I thought more as he and Dandy were thinking, and realized they would simply commandeer the next engine, leaving the stranded passengers to fend for themselves.

Oddly, only now did I speck that these events were going to be historic. Whether we won or lost, the scattering of Mars's leaders—President, Vice President, and presumably the district governors—would become a Martian legend. Intrigue, decoys, shuttle flights and trains in the night.

Jack's slate chimed and another coded message came in. "Another pop-up," he said dryly. "Point One is still operating, but our satellites are brought down as soon as we put them up. They must want us really scared."

"What's the message?" I asked, rising from the cot.

"I have something from the President, your eyes only, and status on who we're talking to at Many Hills. Cailetet seems to be functioning, and maybe a few small renegade BMs. Nothing else."

He transferred Ti Sandra's message to my slate, simple text and one picture.

Dearest Casseia,
You are the negotiator now. Earth talks to us through sympathetic mouths—Cailetet. Word is you will meet with a negotiator chosen by Crown Niger. Earth is afraid. Somebody in the know has talked. Zenger? Olympians are all in hiding. I have issued instructions to CF too sensitive to tell you now. Say whatever it takes to put Mars on track, but in the next few months, or even years, we have the aces. You will learn

*of my death upon your arrival. I love you and trust you with
our child. We will not talk until we have begun to fight again.
There are locusts in the soil.*

The text was followed by a small picture of Ti Sandra, face
smiling but haggard. I signaled the wiping of the message and
the picture faded.

Locusts.

Jack leaned forward, touching my hand in concern. "Are
you all right?" he asked.

"What do you know about locusts?" I asked.

Jack sat upright and rubbed his hands on his knees. "Jesus," he said. "Contravened by treaty throughout the Triple.
What in God's name could we do to Earth . . . Have they?"

"The President says they have."

He looked as if he might cry, caught between anger and
horror and helpless to act. "Jesus," he repeated, and could say
no more for a few seconds.

"Locusts," I said, trying to bring him back.

He folded his arms and looked away, eyebrows drawn together. "How do you control an entire planet from across the
Solar System? Seed it with nano factories that can build a variety of automatic weapons, self-directing warbeiters. Mars's
soil is ideal. High silicate and aluminum, high ferrous content. Choose old mines or seemingly depleted sites, still rich
with the basic minerals, open to deep exploration and con-
cealment without triggering alarm. Sprinkle nano factory
seeds from orbit. A single small ship could do it. We have no
defense against such an atrocity."

I thought of Cailetet's attempt to expand mining claims. As
if Crown Niger had tried to warn us, one last signal flag of
honor before handing himself to Earth on a platter, sole political survivor of conquered Mars.

I wondered now if Stan and Jane were even alive. "We
could fight the locusts," I offered.

"We don't have anywhere near the means to destroy all the

factories," he said. "The locust concept is specifically forbidden by treaty signed by all nations and alliances."

"And we're too young and naive to have thought of a defense."

"Theoretically," Jack said, "in a year or two, all of our scientists could design a response. A nano-level disease. But if the locusts are Earth-designed, we . . ." He did not finish.

But we *did* have defenses, and they were in themselves so frightening as to have provoked the Earth . . . Extremes bringing on extremes. The future seemed not just dangerous, not just bleak; it seemed incomprehensible.

Dandy left the controls briefly to tell us the track ahead was clear for five hundred klicks. Jack and I told him about the locust warning. His face went gray.

I told neither of them about Ti Sandra's impending death.

Jack switched places with Dandy, and the engine pushed on across Mars, skirting the rugged regions a hundred klicks south of Mariner Valley and Eos Chasma.

I had never felt so isolated, so wrapped in silence. The train's faint vibration on a curved trace rose through my feet. Dandy slept fitfully, leaning against the cabin bulkhead behind the stool, feet splayed like a boy's, boots turned out.

In the next few hours, I studied the contingency plans available on my VP slate. They were none of them useful or even suggestive. None of them took into account either locusts or Olympians. Those preparing the plans would not have been in the know about the Olympians, and Martians were too trusting to assume the worst of Mother Earth.

How many Martians would die now, brave and artless?

How many deaths could Ti Sandra and I absorb the blame for?

I stared out the port again. The stars in the sky over nightbound Mars had their echo in the sands—piezoelectric flashes as the sizzle contracted from the day's mild warmth, sparkling like thousands of tiny fireflies. I turned off the cabin light to see them better and pressed my armor-wrapped face against the glass like a little girl. For a moment, the vision seduced me into forgetting my worries, and I felt suspended like a wraith, a child's ghost flying over the sands. I specked through my enhancement pressures building in sizzle baked by ultraviolet across the years, wind removing layers of flopsand and powder, sudden cold night air flowing from nearby scarps, pressure within the desert varnish squeezing tiny crystals of quartz . . .

Then I imagined the flashes were locusts signaling to each other, and pulled away from the port with a small cry. Dandy came awake instantly, straightened his legs, blinked at me. He drew his gun so quickly I only noticed the result, not the action.

"Dreaming?" he asked, pocketing the weapon without apology.

"No," I said. "Thinking the worst, though."

"No good that," he said.

Jack came into the cabin and told us the tracks seemed to be clear through Schiaparelli and into Many Hills. "We've passed two trains that coasted automatically onto spurs," he said. "At least the computers did that much before they locked up."

"People still in the trains?" I asked.

"I assume," he said, face stony.

The engine ascended a graceful, fairy-light series of sloping trestles. We topped the inward-facing scarps of Schiaparelli basin and descended into the great flat plain twenty-five hours after departing UMS. Many Hills stood at the center, in the worn hummocks of ancient central rings. The engine coasted into the new, dazzling white depot.

The white walls and pressure arches stood out against the ochre and red all around, a beacon for assault. The entire town was a target. But that kind of warfare had long since ceased. Now, soldiers could be invisible, and destruction carried out by machines like termites from within, not bombs from without. *Warbeiters,* Jack had called them. A horribly awkward and unpleasant name.

All seemed deserted, which was expected. During an emergency, red rabbits clustered close to water and oxygen sources. A Martian station seldom looks inhabited from the outside, anyway. And the Republic's new capital had not yet received its full population of bureaucrats, cabinet members, jurists, governors and representatives.

Point One had established its command at Many Hills some weeks before. Overseeing guards for the President and Vice President, assembling the early stages of Martian intelligence and internal security, Point One had taken on a carefully observed life of its own with surprising speed. Now I was grateful to see men and women I recognized at the depot, carrying weapons, wearing pressure suits, waiting for the train with somber but professional faces.

We disembarked in an underground area, away from possible bombardment, and I was immediately taken by armored truck to fresh tunnels east of the capitol construction.

Dandy and Jack met with their superior, Tarekh Firkazzie, in the rear of the truck. A slim blond man from Boreum, Firkazzie had been appointed head of overall security the month before.

Two women stripped my reactive armor and carefully packaged it for disposal. "You're brave, traveling for a day with this stuff, Madam Vice President," one said.

Jack came forward, grinding his teeth audibly, thrusting his lower jaw as it mocking a heroic male. Then I saw that his expression, however absurd, was genuine; he was grieving.

"Madam Vice President, I've been appointed . . . we chose by lots . . . to bring you bad news. You have a much heavier burden now. Ti Sandra Erzul and her crew have been involved in a shuttle mishap. It may have been an accident, but we're not sure. We haven't confirmed the location of the crash, and we won't be able to for some time. Emergency beacon reports rescue arbeiters have not located anybody alive in the wreckage. We're bringing in a magistrate from the court tunnels. We'll have you sworn in as President as soon as possible, perhaps in the next few minutes. I'm sorry."

For a moment, I did not know whether this was the faked death Ti Sandra had warned me about, or a real accident. I had to assume it was the former. I would become acting President.

I felt nothing then. I had become an arbeiter working for a political machine with its own rules, inevitable and soulless.

Point One had played its role as protector of the chain of command during my flight by train engine from Sinai. The interim Speaker of the House of Governors had been flown in from Amazonis by shuttle; the speaker for the House of the People had been at Many Hills to begin with. The interim congress had been caught campaigning, scattered across Mars, except for three governors and two candidate representatives. They were in a deep tunnel guarded by what defense arbeiters and personnel the Point One folks could assemble.

Point One had assumed control of all the available links. The ex net was down, but some private nets strung through local optics were up on manual and portable narrowband, keeping us informed about conditions at stations around Schiaparelli Basin. In effect, there were communications, but at less than one-tenth of one percent normal.

We still could not talk with the Olympians. I did not expect any further messages from Ti Sandra for days, perhaps longer.

All rules were being ignored, all bets were off.

Led by Dandy Breaker, five guards and two arbeiters escorted me into the narrow emergency tunnel two hundred meters below the congress, just above the new and expanded wellhead for Many Hills. There, I faced the dismayed band of seven legislators. For a moment, nobody spoke, and then all gathered in a circle around me, shaking my hands, asking questions.

I held up my arms, sidestepped a governor who seemed about to hug me, and called out, as clearly as possible without shouting, "We are the only ones who can act as a lawful government for the Republic! We must have order!"

The Speaker of the House of Governors, Henry Smith of

Amazonis, a stocky man with a close-trimmed beard and pig-
gish discerning eyes, used his stentorian voice to call the
meeting to order. "Obviously," he added, in an aside to me,
"we do not have a quorum, but this is an emergency session."

I agreed. "All of our intelligence, assembled by the Point
One people—thanks to all of them for their extraordinary
work—"

"They did not avert this catastrophe!" shouted the representative from Argyre.

"They are not intended for military defense!" responded
Henry Smith, raising a tight-fisted hand, his chin lowered as
if he were a bull about to charge. Argyre clapped his mouth
shut, eyes wide. They were all very frightened men and
women.

"Please let me say what needs to be said," I continued.

"Without interruptions," Henry Smith insisted.

"The President may be dead."

Some of the legislators and even a few of the guards who
had not heard seemed to wilt, their faces as blank as those of
shocked children. "My God," Henry Smith said.

"I will take the oath of office soon, unless we can establish
that Ti Sandra Erzul is still alive. We have heard that her
shuttle crashed. I assume it was destroyed by some sort of aggressive action."

"Who? *Who*, in God's name, has done this to us?" cried
Representative Rudia Bly from Icaria.

"I've been told that we will be negotiating with people
from Cailetet, representing Earth. Earth seems to have de-
creed that all our thinkers and computers be shut down by
activated evolvons."

"We swept them!" someone shouted. "There were guarantees!"

"Quiet!" Henry Smith yelled.

I asked Lieh Walker, the head of the Point One Com and
Surveillance team, to give us a status report. Her words pro-
vided no comfort. We knew conditions around most of
Schiaparelli, and there were bursts of information from places

as far away as Milankovic and Promethei Terra, but no complete picture. "Communications with other parts of Mars are severely restricted," she said. "Even if we had the data, we could not assemble it into anything coherent. Our interpreters are down. Everything's badly polluted except our slates and a few personal computers with CPUs made on Mars."

When she finished, I spoke again. "Our position may be untenable for the time being. Not only is Mars paralyzed, but it seems the Terries have laced parts of the planet with locusts."

Not all the legislators understood the term. Martians have always been known for a tight domestic focus. I explained briefly. "Is that possible?" one asked.

Henry Smith glanced at me as if for moral support. "I've had some briefings on it," he said. "It's a little buried cesspool of tech. Nobody much admits to that sort of thing."

"Then we're dead," said Argyre.

"Don't settle for anything so final," I said sharply. "Some options are still open."

Dandy Breaker entered the chamber and told me that the negotiators from Cailetet had arrived by shuttle at the depot. "They're clean and well-dressed," he said contemptuously. "Their stuff seems to work."

I glanced at Lieh Walker for an explanation. She dropped the edges of her lips, eyes flashing anger. "Cailetet has been removed from our net links," she said. "They may not be affected, but they are lying low. There is nothing from their regions coming through Point One com."

I studied the legislators. I would need a witness and some support for my negotiations. I had to pick wisely from a group I knew only in passing; the interim government had never quite integrated. Ti Sandra had conducted a lot of business personally with these people, but I had met only a few, very briefly.

"Governor Smith, Representative Bly, if you'll come with me . . ."

Smith seemed eager to please, but he was smart and

tough—Ti Sandra had told me so, and I trusted her judgment implicitly. Candidate Representative Rudia Bly of Eastern Hellas—unopposed—had served with me on a capital architecture committee, several months ago. She was generally quiet and observant and I had felt comfortable around her.

I did not want to think too long about the importance of every decision I made now, of the roles these people would play, of what I would discuss with the traitors from Cailetet.

Someone has said that nobody pays politicians to have emotions. Yet when the magistrate administered the Oath of the Presidency, in a tiny anteroom to the Hall of the Judiciary, surrounded by gray racks of dormant, polluted law library thinkers, I wept quietly.

No one gave it the slightest notice.

Sean Dickinson had changed little in appearance since the days in the trench dome. He stood very straight, knees limber, with hands folded behind him, parade rest. He clenched and unclenched his jaw muscles, regarded me steadily, and blinked only once in the long seconds I examined him.

We were meeting in the half-finished chamber of the governors, scaffolding and architectural slurry above our heads, the air yeasty with active nano. So long as the nutrient vats held out, the capitol would continue building itself. Dickinson stood before the hand-carved pink marble podium where Henry Smith—if he were elected—would gavel the House of Governors to order.

"I have been sworn in as President of the Federal Republic of Mars," I said. "I understand you represent Cailetet?"

"I recognize you," Dickinson said, words clipped but soft. "Casseia Majumdar. Do you remember us?"

His lip twitched as if he might smile, but he turned away and gave a languid look at Gretyl Laughton. She stood at the front of their aides, four men and women from Cailetet. They appeared uneasy, well aware of possible charges of treason even though they belonged to a nonaligned BM. Gretyl had become leaner, like a greyhound or whippet; she wore delib-

erately dull clothes, her hair had grayed, and she seemed uninterested in appearances.

"I remember," I answered.

"We did some brave things together not that many years
ago. You once claimed to despise the Statists."

"And now I am one."

"Worse. You are the *state*."

Neither of us cared to break through the iciness and unpleasant formality. "Where are your documents? I won't talk
with you until I'm convinced you have the powers you
claim."

Dickinson said, "We have the proper documents. We represent factions on Earth who have control over much of Mars
now. They do not wish to reveal themselves, but they have
given us coded identifiers for verification. Our documents
have been hand-vetted, since your security thinkers and other
machines are not functioning."

"Is this so?" I asked Lieh Walker, who stood beside Henry
Smith. Tarekh Firkazzie entered the chamber and sat incon-
spicuously in one of the gallery seats.

"Their codes match Earth codes shipped to all governments in the Triple," Lieh said.

"Utter cowardice," I said, shaking my head. "Are they
afraid of their own plebiscites? This is an atrocity, an illegal
act."

Dickinson smiled. "Can we become serious?" he asked.

I glared at him. At that moment, it was all I could do to
keep myself from reaching out and striking him.

We chose a table in the witness square and sat.

"I've been authorized to present you with an offer."

I made a gesture to Lieh. The chamber recorders were
switched on. "Mars has been attacked without reason," I said.
"Is Cailetet cooperating with the aggressors?"

Sean leaned forward slightly. "The Republic, the state to
which Mars has decided to give itself, is developing very
dangerous weapons. Considering the political situation in the

Triple—completely peaceful for nearly sixty years—that seems out of character and very damned stupid."

"No weapons are being developed," I said.

"I've been told that these weapons could be more destructive than any yet made."

I saw no reason to argue the point further. "Present your proposals and let's get this over with."

"The parties involved in this preemptive action will deactivate all blocks on Martian dataflow, if the people listed on this slate . . ." He pushed his own slate forward and I spun it around to view the screen. "Are delivered into my hands within seventy-two hours. I will receive them here in Many Hills and transport them elsewhere. Eventually they will go to Earth."

I read the list: all of the Olympians, Zenger, Casares, and nineteen others—among them, the finest scientists on Mars.

"What will this accomplish?" I asked.

"Peace," Dickinson said. "Return to normal dataflow. Lives saved."

"No locusts?" I asked.

"Locusts?"

"Warbeiters. Nano armies," I said.

He seemed puzzled.

"Your puppet masters don't tell you everything. Either that or you're willfully ignorant."

Dickinson shrugged.

"What Earth is doing to Mars right now will alter the balance of the Triple," I said, voice cracking. "Nobody will feel safe."

"Please don't lecture me," Dickinson said.

Gretyl stepped forward. "We understand the delicate balances better than you."

"Yes, and your youthful ideals—my God, Sean, you're working with Crown Niger!" I shut myself up, but my body trembled with suppressed rage. Three days. "The Republic has no authority to kidnap citizens."

"What it comes down to, I think, is Earth considers its own

safety paramount, and does not trust Martian intentions," Dickinson concluded. "Ninety-eight percent of all humanity still lives on Earth. Knowing what I know about this government, I wouldn't trust you, either."

"We've never shown Earth any hostility. Quite the opposite, in fact."

"Mars should have kept its innocence," Dickinson said. "No world state, stay out of the big leagues, peace and comparative prosperity. I've fought against this all my life. All states resort to force in the end."

"I assume there are other conditions?"

Dickinson referred to his slate. "Return to BM economic structure for a minimum of twenty years. Earth monitors to be installed at all research centers, and regular visits of inspection teams at any facility of any kind on Mars."

They had given up on us. They wanted us weak, locked in our own past, stripped of our new powers. Someone had calculated that the technological situation would get out of hand before any peaceful negotiations could be concluded. "Occupation by Earth," I said. "Absolutely incredible. How can anyone believe that will be workable?"

"Not my problem," Dickinson said.

"And what do you get, personally?"

"Exile, I suppose," Dickinson said. "No Martian will tolerate Gretyl and me now. No doubt we'll be dead in a few months if we stay here. We'll go to Earth."

"You're happy with that?"

"For the end of a Martian state, I'd gladly accept my own death, and Gretyl's," Dickinson said. "I am true to my ideals. I haven't changed, Casseia."

"Every history has its traitors," I said.

Dickinson dismissed that with a subtle toss of his head and flicker of his eyelids. "I'll need your answer soon."

"How soon?"

"Within one hour."

"We don't have a quorum. If you could bring the rest of the government together—"

"Please don't try to stall. We're all here to avert an even greater catastrophe. If we fail, stronger measures will be taken."

"Locusts."

"I truly don't know. As President, you are allowed, by your constitution, to negotiate foreign treaties."

"But not to negotiate surrender during wartime," I said.

"This is not war," Dickinson said.

"What is it, for God's sake?"

"Clever, devastating disruption imposed by a vastly superior power," Dickinson said. "Why mince words? I don't think you're stupid. We have one hour. I understand that if Earth does not receive a reply by then, the knot will tighten."

These were not negotiations; they were ultimatums. Mars would strangle if I did not agree to everything. I felt lightheaded, almost giddy with suppressed rage.

"Have you any human heart whatsoever?" I asked Dickinson. "Have you any feelings for what your planet is suffering?"

"I was not the one who made this situation," he answered briskly.

"We are honorable Martians," Gretyl said.

No choice. No way out. Selling out the Republic's future, all we had worked for; I would be branded the traitor. A kind of delirium smoothed itself around me with seductive insistence. *Die, but do not do this.* I could not listen.

Lieh had been monitoring her slate closely for several minutes. Now, she stood up from the gallery and approached me like a delicate crab, eyes full of hatred turned on Dickinson. She bent over and whispered in my ear, "Madam President, we've established contact with the Olympians. I'm told that you are not to sell the farm, and that you are to leave this meeting and come with me to the surface. Charles says he has to go see a man about a scary dog."

I looked at her, baffled. Lieh straightened and backed away.

"I'd like to discuss this with the people I've assembled

here," I said to Dickinson. He nodded, appearing faintly bored. "You'll have your answer," I said.

I left the table and gestured for Smith and Bly to follow me out of the chamber. We met Firkazzie in the governors' cloakroom. "What's going on?" I asked Lieh and Firkazzie, my nerves shot, all confidence fled.

Lieh deferred to Firkazzie.

"We're to take you Up in the next ten minutes. There's an observation deck on the top of the main capitol building, but it isn't pressurized yet."

"By whose orders?"

"It was not an order, Ma'am," Firkazzie said. "Charles Franklin requested your presence, and said it was very important."

I started to laugh and caught myself before it turned into a hysterical bray. "What in hell is more important than negotiating with Earth?"

"I only carry the message," Lieh said, stiffening and looking me firmly in the eye. I felt adequately chastened.

"Let's go, then," I said.

"We don't have much time," Firkazzie said. "We have to suit up and climb past the construction barriers."

Dandy, Firkazzie, and Lieh accompanied me; all the others, senators and aides, were left behind, not essential to this task.

We took an elevator to the upper levels, two stories above the surface. I was too numb and confused to be concerned with politics and protocol. I felt the bleak threat of Mars devastated by Terrie power, by armies in the sands; I could not get over the thought that this pollution, this disruption had caused deaths already, and must end soon, or else. Dickinson had given me an unacceptable ultimatum—and I had no choice but to accept. What could anyone do or say that would change that?

I stood in a dim cold room while Dandy and Lieh dragged out suits, tested them and found them secure. We put them on and attached cyclers. The seals activated. My suit adjusted to my body automatically.

Lieh, Dandy, and an architect whose name I did not catch took me through a short maze of nutritional vats and construction slurry tanks. Beyond the safety barriers, the dark, silent hall opened onto a short, curved corridor, an open hatch with a blinking red low-pressure light, a glimpse of dark brown sky and scattered clouds reddening in the dawn.

We stood on a parapet overlooking Many Hills, surrounded by Schiaparelli Basin, twenty meters above the reddish-brown surface. Smooth scrubbed lava streaked with pockets of smear stretched for kilometers all around. The air was cold and still, the quiet profound. We had not turned on our suit radios for fear of attracting attention from assassins. Terrie ships could spot us from thousands of klicks and do whatever they wished to us.

I lifted my arms in bafflement, wondering what I was supposed to be witnessing. I was almost by accident that I fixed my gaze west and saw Phobos, one hour into its ascent, four hours from setting in the east. I glanced past it, then felt my neck stiffen and my eyes begin to water. *Scary dog.*

Charles said he was going to see a man about a scary dog. I did not know what Charles was going to do. But a hopeless wish, a wildest guess within me, pushed forward, fantasy turning to conviction. It fit. The *Mercury* could take them there, the equipment and the thinkers, and Charles was just the quiet sort of megalomaniac to think of such a thing and secretly offer it to Ti Sandra.

I started to speak but realized nobody would hear me. I pointed to the moon. I pulled Lieh toward me, touching helmets, and practically screamed the phrase from Shakespeare. " *'Cry havoc and let slip the dogs of war!'* Fear! Fear and panic, the dogs of war! Look at Phobos! My God, Lieh! He's going to do it! He's going to do it!"

She pulled away, her almond eyes squinting in concern, as if I might be insane. I laughed and wept, convinced I knew, convinced that somehow this horrible burden was about to be lifted from my shoulders. Dandy touched his helmet to mine and said, solicitously, "Something wrong, Ma'am?"

I grabbed his shoulders and spun him to look west, to face that familiar moon we had seen so often since our births, that dread canine Fear that accompanies the God of War, so innocuous and innocent for such a dreadful name, small and nicked away by meteoroids and early settlement mining, circling Mars every seven hours forty minutes at six thousand kilometers, low and fast, accompanied by its fellow dog Panic.

Lieh, Dandy and I all faced west. The architect stayed in shadow, not caring to expose himself to whatever had made us mad.

Bright and full against the dark star-strewn sky, Phobos climbed behind a low wisp of ice cloud. It turned ghostly in the cloud, shimmered, and then emerged crystalline, as real and sharp as anything I had ever seen. I focused my will on it, as if helping Charles, as if a psychic link had risen between us all in this extremity and we could each of us know what the other was thinking and doing. My will went out and touched the moon and I was half insane with a terrified desire.

Phobos disappeared. There were no clouds between, no obscuring dust. The clarity of deep gray orbiting stone simply vanished.

My desire became epiphany. Dandy and Lieh scanned the sky, not understanding; they did not know what I knew.

Then Lieh turned to me and her eyes widened with fear. She and Dandy touched helmets with me simultaneously. "Have they blown it up?" Dandy asked.

"No," I said, weeping. "No! They've shown Earth what we can do!"

They still did not comprehend. I didn't care. In my relief and ecstasy—in my absolute terror for Charles—I loved them as if they had been my own children. I grabbed their arms and shouted, helmets pressed together firmly, "They've gone to Phobos and they've moved it. Never forget this! Never! Never forget!"

On the parapet of the future observation deck, I did a mad

little pirouette, then fetched up against a pillar and stared out over the red and orange vastness of the basin. Phobos had left the skies of Mars, and I did not know when or if it would return.

But I knew, as surely as if Charles and Ti Sandra had told me themselves, where they had sent it. And I knew Charles was riding it ... Across the Solar System, to Earth, a dreadful warning from her oppressed child.

Phobos now rose in the skies of the Mother of us all.

Don't tread on me.

Dickinson sat where I had left him, Gretyl nearby. They seemed at peace, content to play their roles in this grand comeuppance. It would be almost an hour before a message could be sent from Earth. Until then, he was mine to toy with, and I felt more than wicked.

As ignorant as Dickinson, the legislators resumed their seats after standing at my entrance.

"Mr. Dickinson," I said, "I refuse your ultimatum. I'm placing you under arrest. Under the laws of the Federal Republic of Mars ..." I consulted my slate, leaned over the table, and pointed my finger at him, "you are accused of high crimes against the Republic, including treason, espionage, not registering as a foreign agent, and threatening the security of the Republic." I turned to Gretyl. "You, too, honey," I said.

Dickinson glanced at the four Cailetet aides. He turned back to me, blinking. His equanimity impressed me no end. "That's your answer?" he said.

"No. My answer to you and the groups you represent is that at the duly appointed time and under the proper circumstances, when order has been restored to this Republic and all threats have been rescinded, we will discuss issues of substance with properly identified Earth governments like civilized peoples. There will be a quorum of elected and appointed officials in this chamber, and duly recognized diplomats and negotiators from Earth. We'll do it legally and openly."

Gretyl lost some of her bearing; she flicked her eyes around the chamber like a deer in a cage. I remembered intense Gretyl ripping away her mask, willing to martyr herself on the Up. And I remembered, with sad clarity, how I had once thought Sean Dickinson the most noble male figure I had ever seen—brave, quiet and forthright. Had he offered, I would have bedded him instantly. And in bed he would have been quiet and reserved, a little chilly. I would have fallen into destructive love with him. He would have torn me up and discarded me.

I felt blessed for never having had that opportunity.

"Are you certain that's what you want me to say?" he asked.

"Yes," I said. "Tell Crown Niger and Earth that your credentials are not acceptable." I turned to Dandy. "After he's done," I said, "arrange for their arrest. All of them."

Governor Henry Smith of Amazonis seemed close to fainting.

Dickinson stood, face suddenly ashen. "I hope you know what you're doing," he said.

For a moment, we stared at each other. Sean blinked, turned away slowly, and said, "I never trusted you. Not from the beginning."

"I would have given my life for you," I said. "But I was young and stupid."

I'd like to pull back now and take a moment to rest and re-think my telling. I remember the emotions of that moment so vividly that I am back in that chamber. I wrote the above lines weeping like a young girl. It was the high moment of my life, perhaps because what came after was too sad and immense to be real.

From this time on, events fall in my memory like dead creatures across an old sea floor, flat and compressed, unreal.

I do not say I was not responsible. I was more involved, and therefore more responsible, than most; the blame has fallen squarely on me, and I accept it.

* * *

Phobos appeared in the skies over Earth in a broad elliptical orbit inclined at thirty degrees to the equator with a perigee of one thousand kilometers and apogee of seven thousand.

Phobos's bright face, quickly waxing and waning, changed the entire equation as nothing else could. Mars could drop moons on Earth. In the strategic balance, we now tipped the scales.

Earth did not know that on Phobos rode the equipment and the individuals essential to the wielding of this power. What they did not know, weakened them.

And what Earth would soon know or guess could ultimately weaken us.

The evolvons withdrew within six hours, on command from Earth's satellites around Mars. Those satellites then self-destructed, leaving tiny streaks of red against the dark sky. We received assurances that locusts had not been planted; confusion and weakness, for the moment, forced us to accept that. Mars began to come alive again; its dataflow blood coursed.

The networks of communication set up by amateurs in the preceding days were charted, formalized, organized, made ready for further duties. We would not be caught so vulnerable again. In stations across Mars, engineers rigged simpler, more secure dataflow systems, setting us back fifty years or more, but guaranteeing that we would breathe, drink clean water, see no more the vivid horror of vacuum rose in blown-out tunnels.

Mars began counting its dead, and every horror was broadcast around the Triple. Earth's tactics had backfired—for the time being.

Alice One and Two were among the casualties. Half of the high-level thinkers could not be reactivated. Their memory stores were salvaged, and portions of personality could be recorded for use in other thinkers, but the essence—the soul of the thinker—was gone. I could not mourn her; there was too much to mourn. If I began to mourn, it would never stop; and I still waited for word of Ilya and Ti Sandra.

For two days, shuttles and trains coursed into the new capital, bringing legislators, jurists, eager to re-confirm the Republic's independence, its very existence; bringing fresh equipment, experts determined to sweep again and clean out the pollution of Earth.

For two days, I coordinated as President, knowing my position was temporary—believing but not knowing for sure that Ti Sandra was alive somewhere. I worried that she did not present herself now. It wasn't like her not to take the slight risk. Politics demanded that she return, if only to reassure the citizens of Mars.

I did not sleep, barely had time to eat, and I moved from station to station around Arabia Terra by train and shuttle, spending no more than a few hours in one place at any time. We did not trust Earth's statements. Once betrayed, a hundred times shy.

Five days after the Phobos transfer, I was invited to observe its return from an observation dome in Paschel Station near Cassini Basin. The governor of Arabia Terra, Lexis Caer Cameron, three of her top aides, Dandy Breaker, and Lieh Walker stood beside me under a broad plastic dome. We lifted glasses of champagne, looking east this time.

"I wish to hell I knew what this all means," Governor Cameron said.

"So do I," I said.

Lieh ventured a rare opinion. "It means we never have to knuckle under again."

I smiled but could not share her optimism. Our triumph would be short-lived.

"Thirty seconds," Lieh said.

We waited. I could barely think through my accumulated exhaustion. I needed a full body cleanse; hell, I felt as if I could use a whole new body.

Phobos winked into existence, a crescent rising nine or ten

degrees above the horizon. After a few measurements by
Lieh, we confirmed that Phobos was back in its proper orbit

The scary dog was home, apparently none the worse for it
journey.

I did not drink my champagne. Thanking the governor,
handed her my glass, and Dandy escorted me quickly from
the center. No time to linger . . .

Lieh made connections with new satcoms and showed me
LitVid reaction throughout the Triple. I watched and listened
silently, beyond numbness and into frozen isolation.

I hadn't heard of Ilya since the Freeze—the name assigned
by Martian LitVids to the brief war.

Around the Triple, the sense of outrage against Earth had
flared, subsided, and flared anew, into a call for general boy
cotts by all space resource providers. That wasn't practical—
Earth had stockpiled resources for several years, as a hedge
against market fluctuations. But the political repercussion
would be serious.

Engineers in asteroid cities descended in close floating
ranks on Terrie consulates, demanding explanations for the
aggression.

The Moon, predictably, tried to keep a low profile. But
even on the Moon, independent nets bristled with fearful, an
gry calls for resignations, investigations, recall plebiscites. A
few independent Lunar BMs expressed solidarity with the be
leaguered Federal Republic of Mars. I could feel the fear
echoing across the Solar System, especially in the vulnerable
Belts. Nobody in the Triple could trust the old Mother now

Finally, the President of the United States of the Western
Hemisphere asked for an investigation into the causes of the
conflict. "We must understand what happened here, and dis
cover who took it upon themselves to give these orders, and
do these things," he concluded, "in order to avoid even worse
disasters in the future."

"Look to your own house," I murmured. I trusted nothing
spoken by Terrie politicians.

"This is very interesting," Lieh said, placing her slate before me. She had worked her way through several layers to a small and exclusive Terrie advisement net called Lumen. She didn't tell me how she'd accessed such a subscription—Mars had its penetrators and seekers after forbidden knowledge, and no doubt Point One had recruited many of the best. "This went out to subscribers about six hours ago."

A handsome elderly woman with weary, wrinkled features and an immaculately tailored green suit sat stiffly in flat image, talking and calling up text reports from around Earth. At first glance, the program seemed dull and old-fashioned even by Martian standards. But I forced myself to listen to what was being said.

"No nation or alliance has taken responsibility for starting the action against Mars, and no pundit has given an adequate explanation for why any authority would do so. The calls for plebiscite judgment, absent any clear perpetrators, worries this observer a great deal ... I think we are dealing, yet again, with gray eminences who have sealed themselves away from plebiscites, above even the alliances, and I look for them in the merged minds who ride the greatest and most secure Thinkers, those which oversee Earth's estate and financial situation. Arising from the old system of national surveillance established in the United States over a century and a half ago, once limited to oversight alone, these merged minds—rumored but never confirmed—have become the greatest processors of data in human history.

"With the transfer of space defense to the alliances, they may not be limited to advisement now; they may have decided to wield power. If so, then our subscribers may wish to withdraw from all dataflux markets for the next few months or even years. Something is moving bigger than mere individuals can withstand."

Even in the exhaustion, I shivered. "Have you heard of them?" I asked Lieh.

"Only as silly rumors," Lieh said. "But this is an expensive advisement net. Maybe thirty thousand legal subscribers. Supposedly, rash or silly statements are never made here."

"A small group mind," I said softly. "Above the common herd. Sending orders down through alliances, through nations. Who, most likely?"

"Heads of GEWA," Lieh suggested. "They have control of Solar System defense."

Dandy shifted in his seat. "I've seen and heard enough scary stuff for one lifetime," he said.

Unofficially, Mars was on wartime footing, and by the rules of the constitution, acting as President until Ti Sandra's return, I had extraordinary powers . . .

But even my extraordinary powers could not extend to Cailetet. We had to treat it as a sovereign foreign nation; we could declare war, of sorts, and we would, but it would be a war of finance. I worried about Stan and hoped that he was using all of his considerable intelligence to keep himself and his family safe.

Damage reports came rapidly now. Station by station, region by region, lists of dead, missing, accounts of damages, requests for emergency aid, all crowded the restored channels. Point One transferred the calls to the government net, and Lieh drew them from the legislative and presidential channel, condensing and editing.

So little was known about some regions, still. Dataflow had not been re-established everywhere; some thinkers in key positions had apparently "died" and could not be brought up again.

Mars was screaming in pain; I suddenly specked hearing the collected information as one voice. I shied from that quickly. I could not afford such grim inspiration now.

On the shuttle flight to Many Hills, I tried to rest, but couldn't close my eyes for more than minutes at a time. Unexpectedly, I started feeling my enhancement again, and began calculating the adjustments necessary to move a mass the size of Phobos. I visualized in multiple layers of equations the functions which described transfer of co-responsibility for conservation of these quantities to a larger system . . . The entire galaxy. *Nobody would miss it.* We had become thieves in a vast treasure house.

I murmured aloud some of the enhancement's activities.

Dandy came into the darkened cabin with my dinner. "Excuse me?" he asked.

"My muse," I said. "I'm possessed by physics."

"Oh," he said. "What does 'physics' tell you?"

I just shook my head. "I'm not hungry," I said.

"Tarekh says if you don't eat he's bound by duty to force-feed you." He smiled thinly and set the tray down before me. I picked at the food for a while, ate a few bites, and returned to my efforts to sleep.

I must have succeeded for a short while, for Dandy and Lieh stood before me suddenly. Lieh shook my arm gently. "Madame Vice President," she said, "it's official. She's alive."

I stared up at her, muzzy and confused.

"Ti Sandra is alive. We've had it confirmed."

"Thank you," I said.

"I have a message from the President," Lieh continued.

"She's been injured," Dandy said. "They have her in recovery at a secret location."

I took my slate, touched it to Lieh's, and they left me alone while I listened to Ti Sandra. My eyes filled with tears when I saw her face; I could barely discern the support equipment around her. She did not seem in pain, but her eyes lacked focus and that clued me. Her nervous system was under nano control.

"Little sister Cassie," she began. Her lips stuck together for a moment, muffling her words. Someone gave her a sip from a cup of water. Drops glistened on her lips. "I am so grateful that you carried this horrible burden the past week. Our little trick nearly turned true. We had a real shuttle crash on the

slopes of Pavonis Mons. Special targeting for me. Paul i
dead."

My tears spilled over then, and my entire chest gave
sharp lurch. I felt as if my body might suddenly fail, my hear
give out. I moaned.

Dandy looked in briefly, then closed the door again.

"I've lost half my body, they say. My big, lovely body. I'
recover. We're growing new stuff right now. But no thinke
controls, no computer controls—just twenty human doctor
round the clock. I feel so greedy, taking so much when s
many others are injured ... But they won't let me near any
thing that could do any more harm. I don't feel any grie
right now, my dear. I won't for a long time, they say.

"Cassie, I told Charles and Stephen to do it, right after m
accident, before I was put completely under. I hope I was i
my right mind. It does accelerate things, doesn't it? I asked
and they assured me they were ready. There was danger, bu
it could be done. Now it's done, and you must let them know
how grateful we all are. There's so much more to do, though

"You must act for me a while longer. You're more than m
crutch now, Cassie. You must be *me* as well as yourself.
can't think as well as I should."

I wanted so much to collapse into being a little girl, irre
sponsible and protected by others. Worse, a feeling of abso
lute dread had rooted itself. I turned off the slate, halting T
Sandra in mid-statement, and almost screamed for Lieh t
come in. She came through the door, face white, and kneele
beside my seat.

"Find Ilya," I demanded, grabbing the back of her neck.

"We're trying," Lieh said. "We've been searching sinc
dataflow started coming back."

"Please just find him and tell me!"

She nodded, squeezed my arm, and left the cabin again.

Ti Sandra resumed at my touch. "—think we have very lit
tle time now to put together a consensus. Elections are im
possible. The Republic is still under threat, perhaps a greate
threat than ever before. This Solar System is fatal. It's fata

for Mars. Ask Charles to explain. Everything is out of balance. We have used fear to fight the effects of terror. Listen: we're lambs, you and I. We're expendable for the greater good.

"I don't mean our lives, honey. I mean our souls."

The research center at Melas Dorsa had been abandoned at the beginning of the Freeze. Charles and Stephen Leander had departed in the *Mercury*; the others had been brought out by tractor, with as much equipment as could be salvaged. Pictures of the site confirmed the wisdom of keeping the Olympians on the move: the remains of all tunnels, the grounds of the station itself, had been uprooted as if by thousands of burrowing insects or moles.

Locusts. Earth denied planting them, so we broadcast evidence of their use across the Triple, another part of the war of nerves. Tarekh Firkazzie and Lieh suggested we consider Mars as forever "bugged," that all future planning allow for the emergence of hidden warbeiters. We would never be able to sweep the planet completely.

Firkazzie had grimly surveyed the remains of the Melas Dorsa laboratory and decided that it could never be occupied again. We had to locate a new site for an even bigger laboratory, to house an even bigger research effort.

From orbit, Charles suggested the site for a new laboratory. He remembered his father's search ten years past for ice lenses not quite sufficient to support large stations. Such a lens existed beneath Kaibab in Ophir Planum, the remains of a shallow dusted lake from a quarter of a billion Martian years past. It was unlikely, it was in a desolate and difficult land, it was far from any other station, and there was little chance of encountering locusts.

In just twenty-four hours, architectural nano delivered and activated by a squadron of shuttles made a solid, moderately comfortable preliminary structure, a hideaway near the edge of the plateau. For the time being, a few dozen people could stay there in seclusion. Later, the site could be expanded for the larger effort.

Charles and Stephen Leander returned from Phobos, bringing the *Mercury* down under cover of a thin dust storm from Sinai. A few hectares of crushed and flattened lava served as a rough landing pad.

My shuttle landed at Kaibab hours after the *Mercury*'s arrival. The terrain was hellish—sharp-edged rills and ancient pocked high-silica lava flows, every edge a knife, all depressions filled with purple vitreous oxidizing rouge. These were badlands indeed, worse than anything I had ever seen humans inhabit on Mars.

Following Lieh and Dandy, I stepped out of the shuttle lock and squeezed under the low tube seal. I saw Leander and Nehemiah Royce first. Then I turned and saw Charles. He stood at the end of the ramp. Gray surgical nano marked parts of his head and neck. He smiled and extended his hand. I shook it firmly and enfolded it with my other hand.

"It's good to see you, Madam President," he said.

"I'm not President any more, thank God," I said.

Charles shrugged. "You have the power," he said. "That's what counts." He gestured for me to lead the way.

As I passed Lieh, I grabbed her arm again and stared at her. Ilya was still missing.

"We'll find him," she said. "He's all right, I'm sure of it."

I ignored the reassurance. *Tough as nails,* I thought. *Winston Churchill in the Blitz. Remember. Tough as nails.*

The "tweaker" had been removed from the *Mercury* and sat on a bench in one corner of a cramped tunnel. I quickly looked over the zero-temp chamber with its gray, squat force disorder pumps, the Martian-made QL thinker and interpreter cables, power supply.

Leander had arranged for tea and cakes to be served on a low table nearby. We sat on thick pillow cushions from the Republic shuttle. Besides Charles and Leander, only two other Olympians were present: Nehemiah Royce and Amy

Vico-Persoff. Point One had dictated that for the duration of the emergency, no more than four Olympians be in one place at one time. The others were being housed at Tharsis Research University, under tight security.

"How much does it all weigh?" I asked Leander as Charles poured the tea.

"About four hundred kilograms," Leander said. "We pared it down considerably in the last version. Most of the weight is in the pumps."

"So tell me," I said, crossing my legs and warming my hands on the cup.

Charles poured his cup last and kneeled on his pillow. He glanced at me, I smiled, and his eyes darted away as if in shyness. He focused on the table and cakes. "We guessed what was happening right away. So did Ti Sandra." The words seemed to come with difficulty. I stared at Charles as if feeding a new hunger, feeling a mix of awe and intense affection.

"Ti Sandra instructed us to get to Phobos any way we could, with the tweaker, and take a trip."

"She knew you were ready to do this?" I asked. "I didn't."

"She guessed, or she just made a wild request . . . We certainly weren't ready for so much, so soon. We fueled the *Mercury*, moved everything we could on board. The most difficult part was guaranteeing a clean power supply for the pumps. We managed that. We were ready for take-off twelve hours after the Freeze began."

"What about coordinates, navigation?" I asked.

"We worked it out while waiting for further orders from Ti Sandra. Stephen and I made up a working hypothesis on the relative position tweaks, worked out the momentum and energy descriptor co-responses and scaling, specified final position and state, stimulated the tweaker to access descriptors for every particle in Phobos, considered as a complete system . . ."

"Charles had to hook himself into the QL," Leander said.

"Are you all right?" I asked Charles.

"I'm fine," he said. "They all did good work. Nobody knew everything except Stephen and myself, but everybody felt the urgency. They all knew it was important."

"A lot of medals should be awarded," Leander said.

"Not least to Charles. He guided the QL," Royce said.

Charles shook his head. "I don't remember most of that. It'll come back in time. We had a pilot with us—"

"One more medal," Leander said.

"He had no idea what was going to happen. We told him without checking his security clearance."

"He's fine," Lieh said, seated outside the circle around the low table. "We debriefed him separately."

"Why did you link with the QL?"

"The interpreter wasn't getting across everything we needed. The QL began returning trivial results, nonsense strings. I think it was exploring the possibility of an alternate descriptor system. It found that more amusing than the real one. I steered it back to giving relevant results. The whole apparatus became coordinated then."

"It hummed," Amy said, shivering suddenly. "My God, it really hummed. I was afraid for them. I left the *Mercury* and they launched."

They all seemed a little in shock even now.

"What did it feel like?" I asked Charles.

"As I said, I don't remember exactly. We—the QL and I—were communicating and I made my requests and it pulled answers out of its non-trivial syncline searches."

"Answers?"

"Instructions, actually. To pass on to the tweaker. Without the QL, we might have been able to do the same thing—with about six months of high-level thinker programming. The QL cut the time down to a few hours. Within eight hours, we were secured to an old mining base in Stickney Crater on Phobos. We'd measured what we needed to measure, everything was still connected and coordinated. Ti Sandra told us to go. She'd been in an accident, and it took us days to establish communications with her again."

I had been left completely out of the loop, despite being in charge of the entire project. I didn't know whether I felt resentment, or relief, that Ti Sandra had shouldered all of this particular burden.

"She was in pain," Charles said, as if reading my thoughts. "I don't think she had time to tell you what was planned. When she first gave us the instructions, we didn't know we could do it. It was all very confused."

"I understand. You went to Earth. What was it like?"

"The stars changed," Charles said. "We felt something shift inside of us—very minor. We're still not sure what it was—gravitation, psychological response, we don't know."

"Everything combined, probably," Leander said.

"We looked through the shuttle ports, saw a sunrise limb, the sun much brighter and larger . . . Earth. We scrambled to check our distance and orbital path. We were right on the money, effectively, but about a hundred kilometers behind the projected orbital insertion point."

"We're still working on that," Leander said.

"We listened but broadcast nothing. About fifteen minutes passed before someone sent us a signal. It was from a private analog radio operator in Mexico. He spoke to us in Spanish. He said, 'Hello, new moon. Where are you from?' "

We laughed. Charles smiled. "Our pilot said, 'Don't ask. You won't believe us.' "

"We started getting official signals a few minutes after that," Leander said. "We had instructions from Ti Sandra what to say. We broadcast the same words—over and over again."

"We were waiting to be annihilated," Charles said. "But that was pretty silly, I suppose. Some of the officials sounded terrified. Some behaved as if nothing at all had happened, the most routine diplomatic communications. We spoke to government negotiators and diplomats from the Eurocon, GEWA, GSHA, and half a dozen others. We told them all the same thing."

"What was that?"

" 'Mars is under attack by unknown governments on the Earth. You have ten hours to pull back and remove the threat, or there will be a retaliatory response.' " Charles's voice sounded hollow as he repeated the statement, burned into memory.

"What response? What retaliation?"

"Ti Sandra told us to remotely convert the White House in Washington into mirror matter," Charles said. "A symbolic gesture."

Silence around the room.

"Could you have done that?" I asked.

Charles nodded. "Without very much precision. She did not tell us to have it evacuated first, but I was going to give some warning. A half hour or so."

I covered my mouth with my hand, suddenly nauseated. The sensation passed. I closed my eyes and dropped my hand slowly. "You have all been exceptionally courageous," I said.

"Yes, Ma'am," Charles said, with a flippant salute that jarred me. I looked up at him, shocked and puzzled. Charles leaned forward, eyes narrowed as if in pain.

"We have followed our instructions. We've done everything we've been told, at the expense . . . almost . . . of our souls. We've understood the strategic necessity, and we believe enough to give ourselves to this cause, but, Casseia, I could not give a flying fuck about medals or patriotism now. I am scared to death of what is going to happen next. We've had our fun, we've made a flying circus run with Phobos and given nightmares to children and adults all over Earth. Do you think it's going to end there? Do you think we have any time left at all?"

"No," I said.

"Good," Charles said, biting the word off and leaning back, his face red with emotion. "God damned good. Because I'm half convinced this is going to be the end of the human race. Impart some of your thinking to us, oh master of politics. We are children lost in the woods."

"So am I, Charles," I said quietly. "We all know what's going to happen now. Ti Sandra knows. They saw you move Phobos. They have the resources, in people and machines and laboratories, to duplicate your discoveries, given this clue. And as soon as they can do what we can do, it's just a matter of time before somebody strikes somebody else."

"It's too damned convenient," Leander said.

Charles agreed. "They may discover things we don't know yet."

"A strike can be fast, it can be total," I said, "and it can guarantee survival in an otherwise dicey situation."

"Survival for how long?" Amy Vico-Persoff asked. "How long until we divide right down to region against region, or us against Cailetet? GEWA against GSHA?"

"Let's not be so pessimistic," Charles said, holding up a hand. "This is never going to be household kitchen-sink type science. There might be four or five places on Earth that have the resources and the theoreticians necessary to duplicate our work. Don't be fooled by the tweaker's small size. It's as sophisticated a piece of equipment as any human being has ever made. Bit-player warfare isn't our real problem right now, and may never be.

"But you're right—they'll do it, and soon—two weeks, a month, two months. We have to find a political solution very soon."

"Politics, hell," Leander said. "Look what politics has accomplished this far. We have to *leave*." He looked around the room guiltily, a child who'd spoken a naughty word.

"Evacuate Mars?" Royce asked, face wreathed in puzzlement.

None of them had given this a lot of thought, I could tell—except Charles and Leander. Brooding in their little ship, fastened to a peregrinating moon.

"No," I said. "Move it."

"Jesus!" Lieh cried, jumping from her chair. She left the room, shaking her head and swearing.

Nobody spoke for long seconds. Charles stared at me, then folded his hands together. "We have no right to make these decisions ourselves, alone. Scientists and politicians have no such right."

"There isn't the time or the means for a plebiscite. Earth has guaranteed that," I said. "Our choices are very limited. Ti Sandra said the Solar System would become too dangerous. It would kill us."

The equipment in the chamber seemed innocent and even crude. "How far have we come, Casseia?" Charles asked.

"Too far. A long time ago, I remember cursing you for the troubles you caused. We've come a long way since."

"I have never felt in control," Charles said. Royce and Vico-Persoff seemed content to let us talk for the moment. Dandy stood a few paces behind me, stiff as a statue. Charles and I were being given a wide space in which to make decisions, as much out of fear as respect.

"Nobody has died yet," I said. "I mean, *we* haven't killed anybody. Earth has. We're still getting reports—but there are entire stations cut off."

"I know," Charles said.

"We did not strike the first blow. We will not use this as a weapon."

"Bullshit," Charles said, stinging me again. "I had orders to cause damage if necessary. When you and Ti Sandra are worn out and thrown away, someone else will step in and desperation and fear will . . ." He swallowed and pulled his hands apart, rubbing them on his knees. "Believe it. What we've made will kill people, lots of people."

"We keep coming back to it, then," I said.

"You'll talk with Ti Sandra, soon?" Charles asked.

"Yes. I don't think any of this will surprise her."

Lieh had returned, face flushed, expression sheepish, and stood beside Dandy. I got up, nodded to Charles, to Leander, to Royce and Vico-Persoff, thanked them for the tea, and left with my bodyguard and communications advisor.

I looked forward to a Spartan bunk and few amenities.

Lieh used an electronic key to unlock the door to my room.

It was as Spartan as I could have wished, clean and new and empty. It smelled of starch and fresh bread.

"If the President is awake and well enough, I need to talk with her now," I said.

Lieh seemed troubled. She looked away and shook her head. Dandy stepped into the room, arms hanging loose. "There's no good time for this, ma'am. Word just came a few minutes ago. We've found your husband."

"He's at Cyane Sulci?" I asked.

"He was evacuated and taken to a small station at Jovis Tholus. He got there safely, I understand, but the station was a new one. Its architecture was dynamic, thinker controlled."

"Why not just leave him at the lab in Cyane?" I sat on the bed, expecting to hear of Ilya's adventures with security, with a troubled station, a technical comedy to relieve my sense of oppression.

"It wasn't a good move," Dandy admitted. He had difficulty keeping his composure. "There were main quarters blowouts at Jovis. They've been digging and identifying the last few days. Five hundred dead, three hundred injured."

"He's dead, Casseia," Lieh said. "He's been found and he's dead. We weren't going to tell you until we knew for sure."

There was no appropriate response, and I had no energy for melodrama. I seemed to be a hole into which things would fall; not a positive force, but a negative.

"Would you like me to stay?" Lieh asked. I lay back on the bed, staring up at the flat ceiling, the utilitarian blue cabinets.

"Yes, please," I said.

Lieh touched Dandy on the arm and he left, closing the door behind. She sat on the bed and rested her back against the rear wall. "My sister and her kids died at Newton," she said. "Ninety casualties."

"I'm very sorry," I said.

"I used to talk with her a lot before joining Point One," she said. "Time gets away. This all seemed so important."

"I know what you mean," I said.

"I liked Ilya," she said. "He seemed very kind and straight."

"He was," I said. The dreamlike nature of the conversation told me how many layers of insulation I had wrapped around my emotions, expecting just this news, but refusing to acknowledge the possibility—with the growing number of days, the certainty. "Tell me about your sister."

"I don't think I'm ready to talk about them yet, Cassie."

"I understand," I said.

"The Sulci lab came through fine," she said. "Dandy thinks we killed him."

"That's stupid," I said.

"He's taking it hard."

"I have to talk with Ti Sandra."

"I think you should wait a few minutes," Lieh said. "Really."

"If I do anything but work, I'm going to go right over the edge," I said. "There's too much to do."

Lieh pressed down the placket of her gray suit and held her hand over mine. "Please rest a while," she said.

"No," I said.

She stood up from the bed, reached out with her long arm and long, beautiful fingers, and opened the room's optical port. I handed her my slate and she attached it. A few strokes and verbal instructions, a series of code and security checks, and she was through to Point One at Many Hills. They completed the connection.

I spoke to Ti Sandra ten minutes later. I did not tell her about Ilya.

We talked about the situation, about my discussion with Charles. Still wrapped in surgical nano, eyes heavy-lidded, her lips twitched as she spoke in a harsh whisper: "We agree, Stephen and you and I. But we're not enough. There have to be consequences and we can't just go anywhere. So what kind of an idea is this? We need more experts. We need to think seriously."

"The Olympians can get us started," I suggested. "We

should gather everybody in the next week or so; take the risk."

"The Point One people can give them everything they need. You're still acting President, Casseia. How are you, honey?" Ti Sandra asked.

"Not very well," I answered.

"We're a mess, all of us. We need a change of scenery. Right?"

"Right," I said.

"You bring the experts from around Mars. Everyone who can help. Keep in touch. I'll try to stay awake, Casseia."

I touched her face on the slate and said good-bye. Lieh waited expectantly, standing in the corner of the small room.

"Why are we going to do this?" she asked.

I lay back on the bed. "You tell me," I said.

"Because if we don't, a lot of people are going to get killed," she said. "But how many people will be killed if we move?"

"We need to find out," I said. Through the insulation, through the fog of growing reaction, my enhancement began working the problem of removing a mass the size of Mars abruptly from the vicinity of the sun, putting it elsewhere.

No distance. Thieves stealing from the galactic treasure house.

"Areologists, I think," Lieh said.

"Right. Structural engineers for the stations. People we can trust, but we'll have to lower our standards a little. People are going to know soon enough."

"The meeting will have to be held in the flesh, incommunicado," Lieh said. "Everybody involved will have to stay sequestered until we've moved."

"Oh?" I asked, still listening to my enhancement.

"The greatest danger is a leak to Earth. They may take action at any hint we're working on something so drastic."

"Yes," I said, letting her think for me, for the time being, letting her stretch to envelop the concept.

"This will take a lot of planning," she said.

"Twenty experts, no more," I said. "We'll need a safe meeting place."

"This is as safe a place as any," Lieh said.

"All right." I suddenly dreaded the thought of staying in this room where I had learned of Ilya's death. "Ask the Olympians what they'll need to build several large tweakers. Ask them how soon they can have them ready."

"I'll wake you in eight hours," she said, and she left.

I closed my eyes.

When the grief came, I screwed up my eyes until they hurt, trying to keep back the tears, trying not to lose control. I could not accept. I could not believe. Adult sophistication meant nothing against that need spread through to my child-self. I kept seeing my mother's face, gone before this all began; lost to me, lost to my father. I would not wear my father's grief, not lose my inner self. I could not recall Ilya's face with much clarity, not as a picture. I picked up my slate and searched for a good picture and yes, there he was, smiling over a mother cyst at Cyane Sulci, and here on the day of our ceremony, uncomfortable in a formal suit.

It seemed to me that I had never told him enough about my love and need. I cursed myself, so spare with words and revealed emotions to those I loved.

I rubbed my eyes. My insides felt like shredded rubber. For a moment, I considered calling in a medical arbeiter and plucking out this overwhelming pain. I told myself I could not let my emotions get in the way of duty. But I had not done that for my mother, and I would not do it now.

I forced my body to relax. Then, without warning, I fell asleep, as if a small circuit breaker had tripped inside my head, and the eight hours passed instantly.

Part Six

~

2184, M.Y. 60
Preamble

"I'm going to be in the goo for at least three more weeks," Ti Sandra said, allowing herself to be seen only from the shoulders up. She appeared pale but more animated. She had just come out of intensive reconstruction, three more days unconscious and at the mercy of her doctors. I took her call in my small office at Kaibab, weary from days of conferences. Memory cubes piled high on my desk carried station designs and reports from manufacturers, shippers, and architects.

"I've convinced the doctors to move me to Many Hills. They'll take me over this afternoon by shuttle. I can start seeing visitors and be rolled into committee meetings . . . I'll be able to take over that part of the job."

"That's a considerable relief," I said. I moved her image a few centimeters in the projection space to make room for incoming text reports from Point One on project security.

"I can't come to Kaibab, obviously. You'll have to build our little project by yourself for the time being."

"It's building," I said.

"You sound flat, Cassie."

"I'm keeping on keeping on," I said, never able to hide my feelings from Ti Sandra. In truth, in the past week, since hearing of Ilya's death, I had become an automaton. It was the best thing that could happen to me. No time to think of my grief, no time to contemplate the future beyond a few brief weeks, lists of jobs to do that took me eighteen or twenty hours a day, and the worst times of all, those few minutes before exhaustion compelled me to sleep . . .

"What's your goal, honey?"

"I don't understand," I said.

"We have to keep goals. Even sacrificial lambs should have something to look forward to."

Somehow that suggestion seemed obscene. I turned away, shaking my head. "Survival," I said.

Ti Sandra's face wrinkled with concern. "We're going to talk at least once every day. We've both lost our rudders, Cassie. I'll be your rudder if you'll be mine."

"Deal," I said.

"Good," she said. She took a deep breath and the top of her head rose briefly out of frame. "Tell me about Kaibab."

I outlined what had happened in the few days since we had last spoken. From around Mars, cargo and passenger shuttles had arrived by the score at the secret station on Kaibab Plateau. Half-finished tunnels had been given quick cosmetic touches. New quarters had been opened and supplied with rudimentary comforts. The main laboratory had been finished and construction of the main tweakers had begun.

Kaibab's population had expanded quickly: two hundred, three hundred, four. The ice lens could supply water enough for a thousand people. Other Point One people arrived daily. Soon I would have a miniature capital working within the cold tunnels and chambers—a backup to Many Hills.

The tweaker project and the Kaibab laboratory had been given the same code name: Preamble. The ultimate goal of Preamble—to provide the President with an option in case of extreme emergency—was known only to a very few. That the option loomed large as a real possibility was known only to Ti Sandra, Charles, Leander, and myself.

Two more Olympians—Mitchell Maspero-Gambacorta and Tamara Kwang—had flown in to join Charles, Stephen Leander, Nehemiah Royce, and Vico-Persoff. Pincher and Yueh Liu remained at Tharsis Research, working on a backup tweaker and overseeing the growth of more thinkers.

I finished my report. Ti Sandra bit her lower lip, nodding approval. "You've done great, Cassie," she said. "I tell you what. When this is all over, we'll have a family party. I'll wear the brightest gown you've ever seen, and we'll celebrate being secure. That's my goal."

"It's a wonderful goal. Welcome back into the loop," I said, and we signed off.

I stared at the desk for a moment, lost in contemplation. Mars was still deep in the dangerous woods. We could mount big guns, but that was all—and there was still a question as to whether we had the will to fire our big guns. So long as that question remained, we were far from secure. But our most obvious and insidious danger was internal.

The Republic would not long stand the strain. Martians rebuilt, installed more robust backup systems for life support . . . And still lived in fear of another Freeze, or worse. Rumors swept the stations as government agents fanned out to old mining claims, searching for evidence of locusts. Even Cyane Sulci was searched from the air. The search was futile. A factory seed no larger than a fist, disguised as a rock, would be almost impossible to uncover. But for the destruction at Melas Dorsa, no signs were found.

The locusts had struck Melas Dorsa with extraordinary cunning and efficiency, first sending small units into the deserted station to reconnoiter and knock out com, then big destructors. Or so the speculations went . . . for we had no record of what had happened there, other than the mute evidence of breached tunnels, destroyed equipment, and the shattered remains of arbeiters.

We maintained a tentative date for elections, but that date

was six months away—and nobody knew what would happen or where we might be by then.

As accusations flew, heads of state within the Triple exchanged messages, offered reassurances, scanned all available diplomatic channels for signs and symbols of actions to come . . .

And found nothing. The channels were jammed with posturing and denial. I had never seen the Triple in such a state of absolute confusion.

None of the Earth alliances would admit to having given the go-ahead for war on Mars—but all were demanding full disclosure of Mars's newfound powers. The Moon and the Belter BMs were if anything even more shrill about the Martian threat. The Republic Information Office and all diplomatic agencies worked to reassure the other members of the Triple of Mars's peaceful intentions, but could not tell them precisely what had happened . . . or what we might do next.

Most Martians demanded full disclosure as well. Opposition inside the government was still too disorganized to mount a full effort against Ti Sandra and myself, but clearly the pressure would increase in weeks or months until it became unbearable.

We were contemplating a game of baboon's asses—displaying the colors—on an enormous scale. In this game, however, for one contestant to even blink while making preparations to depart the field . . .

Disaster.

Point One's extensive com net returned to full operations. Everything was cobbled together, with human rather than thinker oversight. Martian thinkers were still in very short supply; fewer than twenty had been grown and initiated at Tharsis Research and of those, only ten could be pulled from civilian purposes for the Republic's needs. Many Hills received three, Kaibab, six—three of them QLs with built-in interpreters, to guide the large tweakers.

Lieh Walker had become spymaster. Day by day, she expanded the Republic's solicitation of outlaw data gleans—buying information at great expense from sources that were not particular about their methods. We should have established extensive spy networks months before—but we had not foreseen a time when there would be such serious disharmony between Earth and Mars. Now, perhaps too late, we became more ruthless.

We added dozens of new data flies—operatives who coursed the Earth nets, tapped cable transmissions, fed from the sweet attractions of private GEWA and GSHA connections. Some of the data we gleaned we sold to other sources to help finance our own operations.

When Lieh asked me to authorize the funding of twenty additional agents on Earth and in the Belt, I asked what their status would be. "Well-paid," she said. "Expendable." GEWA and GSHA had already swatted a few of our flies—a usually fatal punishment that transferred corrosive evolvons to the data-coursing enhancements the flies used in the nets.

"If I need to know any more," I said, "tell me."

"It's on my back," she said. "You've got enough to carry now."

By which she meant, I was carrying the lives of every Martian, herself included—and I never knew whether she approved or not. I suspect she didn't.

Still, some good news came. Stan had been released by Cailetet. Crown Niger had kept Stan and his wife and child in detention at Kipini Station in Chryse for a total of ten weeks, preventing any communication with the outside. I had two text letters from Stan after his release; there was time only for a brief reply, and of course I could not tell him where I was, or what I was doing.

I made a few quick calls and got him a post at Many Hills, where he could use his experience with Cailetet to work on some diplomatic patchwork. I had heard little from Crown

Niger's camp; they were lying low after the Freeze, wisely enough, hoping to weather the storm. Ti Sandra created a special task force to deal with the dissident BMs and regions. Stan, I thought, could join this task force.

Charles and I met frequently, sometimes alone, more often with Stephen Leander and others present. Our discussions revolved around practical aspects of moving large objects with the tweakers.

He spent hours each day immersed in the QL thinker, preparing, exercising for another trip. The effort took its toll. After long sessions connected to the QL, Charles needed several minutes to begin speaking coherently. I feared for him.

Six attended the first conference on Preamble, two weeks after Ilya's death: myself, Charles and Leander, areologist Faoud Abdi of Mariner Valley, architect and engineer Gerard Wachsler from Steinburg-Leschke in Arcadia, and a newly initiated Martian thinker, who had just the day before chosen her name: Aelita. Aelita would act as Preamble's main thinker, coordinating all the station's and project's activities.

The experts convened in the laboratory annex, still unfinished. As we seated ourselves, nano paint crept along the walls, hissing quietly and forming geometric decorations. The ever-present smell of yeast was particularly pungent here. We seemed to live always in a vast bakery.

Faoud Abdi—tall, sharp-featured, with large, languid eyes—was the first to speak. He wore a neat white jallabah, slate and books making prominent lumps in the robe's large pockets.

"I have been told to consider an impossibility," Abdi began, standing before us with his back to a small data display. "I have been told to research the effects on Mars of a brief period without Solar System gravitational pull. I am told this is purely theoretical—and so I must assume that we are all going to do something drastic with Mars, perhaps what happened to Phobos. Unless Phobos is theoretical as well." He regarded us dubiously, received no reaction to his humor—if humor was intended—and sighed. "I must tell you why Mars is stable now, and discuss popular theories of Mars's areological decline. Is this what you wish?"

"That's fine," I said.

"I once worked with your husband, Madam Vice President. He was a fine man and we shall all miss him."

"Thank you."

"He was concerned, as am I, about the death of Mars hundreds of millions of years ago. But in fact death is a misnomer, for Mars is not completely cool inside. There is still areological activity. However, the plumes rising within the mantle have stabilized and no longer produce lateral pressure on the crust of Mars.

"In the past, there were never more than twelve crustal plates, and now those plates have frozen into one. No lateral pressure—no migration of the old plates—no fracture and subduction of plate boundaries—reduces volcanism. The last volcanoes active on Mars were the shield volcanoes familiar to us all, the Tharsis trio by main example, and Olympus itself. Without plate movement, mountains stopped building, and without volcanism, outgassing ceased, and Mars's thin atmosphere simply evaporated into space, not to be replaced. Mars's biosphere died within a few hundred million years of the end of tectonics. Now, stability . . ."

"Balanced flow," Leander said.

"Precisely. Aelita, please bring up Dr. Wegda's deep soundings of the Martian crust and mantle."

Aelita complied. Behind Abdi appeared a diagram familiar to all—a cross-section of Mars, rotating to provide a three-dimensional view of the interior. "You see, there are sixteen cyclic plumes rising and sinking, but they have assumed a dimpled inverted form, rising on the outside and sinking on the inside. The net force conveyed to the crust over these plumes is zero, though local areological effects are evident. The stability is really too delicate . . . That is, Mars should shift at any time. But this has not happened in three hundred million years. There is much we do not understand.

"A shove applied to the entire planet, however slight—as might be given by removing solar tidal forces, for example—could upset the plumes and re-start tectonic activity." He stopped for a moment, hands hovering beside the frozen diagram of Mars. "Without a large moon to keep Mars in balance, relatively slight changes may also tilt the axis."

"If we leave, it must be to venture closer to the sun, no?" Abdi asked.

"We haven't decided," I said.

"If that is so, there would be much greater effects than I have calculated. And my results already point to resumption of tectonics."

"What would that mean? For all of us living here?" Wachsler asked.

"More marsquakes. Substantial activity along the old plate boundaries, perhaps. Volcanoes. There is no way to predict the long-term effects."

"Short-term?" Wachsler asked.

"Several major marsquakes, but it would take decades before volcanism became widespread along new arcs of fire."

"Would it be reversible?" Wachsler asked.

"How do you mean?"

"Once we jiggled it, could we expect Mars to become stable again?"

"Not for perhaps tens of millions of years," Abdi said. "Stability is stability. Instability is not."

"Aelita?" Leander asked, patting his new offspring on its arbeiter carriage.

Aelita's voice was smooth and huskily feminine. Its image, a long-faced, classically featured female with black hair cut in a short shag, reminded me of a Disney wicked queen. "Dr. Abdi's conclusions seem reasonable. My libraries do not provide complete information about Mars's interior."

"You have all that's available," Leander said.

"Then I suggest we learn more," Aelita said.

Abdi glanced around the table. He smiled.

"We will," I said. "Dr. Abdi, we'll need more information about Mars's interior within twenty days."

"Yes, Madam Vice President," Abdi said happily. "Am I to understand—I will do a survey, on the quick, larger than that of Dr. Wegda himself?"

"Please," I said. "It's very important. You understand security requirements?"

"I do," said Dr. Abdi solemnly.

"Doctor Wachsler, every station should make a structural report. How well can they withstand quakes? Do any stations lie directly over old plate boundaries?"

"A few." Wachsler frowned and shook his head. "We've never designed stations to withstand heavy areologic activity."

"Can they be strengthened?" I asked.

"Some stations sit on old alluvial soils. If there's a major marsquake, every seam will be torn out, tunnels breached . . . You name it."

"Those we'll have to evacuate, won't we?" I said. "We'll meet with the folks in charge of civil preparations and discuss that tomorrow. Dr. Wachsler, Dr. Abdi, I authorize you to draw funds from government accounting, tagged Black, Preamble. Aelita will monitor your experiments, and you will report every week to this committee."

Wachsler stared at us as if we were all out of our minds. "I understand we're dealing with some spectacular technologies here, but have you thought about the human impact?"

His note of condescension rankled me. "That's almost all I've thought about, Doctor."

"What could Earth possibly do to us that would be worse than what you're contemplating? We've all seen the destruction at Melas Dorsa—but that's nothing compared to hundreds of stations facing quakes."

Charles raised his hand like a student in class. "May I answer?"

"Certainly," I said.

"The locusts are just the beginning. In a few more months, they can turn Mars into a burnt cinder. If that isn't enough, they can drop us into the sun, or shoot us out into space."

Wachsler's face went pale, but his dander was up. He obviously could not comprehend what Charles was saying, and was going to treat it as high exaggeration. He crinkled his eyes dubiously. "You truly believe this?"

Abdi said, "My dear doctor, was it trivial that a moon was shifted from its orbit, and moved instantly to the vicinity of Earth?"

"I only know what I was told," Wachsler said stubbornly.

"I was there," Leander said. "So was Charles."

Wachsler shrugged. "All right," he said. "Madam Vice President, I know my duty. But I must express my dismay that so much disruption and even destruction is contemplated, yet nobody is going to ask Martians what they want."

"I wish there were time, and that we had the means," I said.

"No, you don't," Wachsler said. "Not really. If Martians decided to vote this idea down, to stay where we are . . ."

"That could be suicide," Charles said.

"Do we have the right to choose our fate?" Wachsler asked heatedly. "Or do you believe you can choose for us, because you are so much better informed?"

To this there was no good answer. Wachsler had expressed the dilemma admirably. "I hope we are judged less harshly, Doctor Wachsler," I said quietly.

"Don't count on it, Madam Vice President," he said.

Charles stayed behind after the meeting ended. Aelita stayed as well. "We haven't talked about Ilya," he said.

"I'd rather not," I said.

"Doctor Abdi reminded me . . . I'd like to express my sorrow. He was a wonderful man."

"Please," I said, looking away. It was all the more unbearable coming from Charles.

"Do you blame me for his death?" Charles asked, his voice plaintive.

"No," I said. "How could I?"

"If I had died ten years ago, none of this would have happened . . . Not this way."

"What kind of megalomania is that?" I asked.

"Without my contribution, we wouldn't have built a tweaker for another five or ten years. Earth might have built it first."

I stared at him, wondering whether I could maintain my careful mask of neutral efficiency. "I'm as much to blame as you are."

"I need to know. Because if you blame me for that, I don't think I could stand it. Really."

Tears welled in his eyes. I turned away, absolutely unwilling to join him in a display of emotion. "Get yourself together," I said, a little harshly.

"I've never felt more together and clear-headed in my entire life."

"*My* head is not clear and I'm not at the top of my form. Please. *Please*." I pounded the table with my fist. "Just please don't."

"I won't," he said.

"I spoke to Ti Sandra a few hours ago," I said, swallowing and regaining my composure. "We have to choose where we'll take Mars when the time comes. If it comes. And we'll have to make a test run with Phobos."

"I've been planning that," Charles said. "We can take the *Mercury* and the original tweaker to Phobos within a few days. The larger tweakers should stay here."

"We need to disperse the tweakers and thinkers, in case Earth makes another, more directed attempt to stop us."

Charles looked away. "We could destroy all of our equipment," he said. "Provide proof to Earth."

"I'd do that in an instant," I said, "if Earth could possibly believe us. They can't. The stakes are too high. Politics and survival drive everything now."

"I thought I'd make the suggestion. I would kill myself if I thought it would change the situation. If I thought I could stop your grieving."

I glared at him. "I'd kill all of you, myself, if . . ." The admission startled me, and the last few words came out weakly, with a sudden decrease of breath. Charles did not seem startled or shocked.

"I envied Ilya. I remember you years ago," he said after a pause of many seconds. "I've been with a fair number of women since, and none has had your strength of purpose, your conviction."

"Purpose?" I asked. "Conviction?"

"I said to myself, 'She's as crazy as you are.' "

"Jesus," I said, forcing a laugh.

"I believed I could rock the century-long status quo, discover how the universe worked. And you . . . I said you'd become President of Mars. Remember?"

"I'll go back through my diaries and check it out," I said. "Maybe you can read tarot after all this is settled."

"It will never be settled," Charles said. "Events this large never finish. You've never asked about my wife."

"It's none of my business."

"She was a sweet woman, a true Martian. She stood by me for three years. She had a strong sense of duty, and she really tried. But eventually she left. She said she never knew where I was—what I was thinking."

"I'm sorry," I said. "You obviously weren't well-matched."

"No." He turned away, seeming to wilt. I wondered how much the QL links were draining him.

I needed to bring us back to our focus. "Where should Mars go?" I asked.

Charles straightened and linked his slate to the main display. "Aelita, these are rough coordinates and star numbers. Link and update with the astronomy library."

Aelita graphically depicted a scatter of densely-packed stars.

"We can't just move a few light-years away. With present

tracking and measuring, Earth could find us anywhere within a few hundred light-years. If we move at all, it's because Earth has proven it will do everything it can to destroy us . . . And will keep on trying."

Bald expression of our dilemma still had power to chill me.

"So I'm suggesting we make a grand leap. I've looked at the new surveys, run them through Aelita for processing, and come up with a candidate. It's the best of all possible places in the near galaxy. About ten thousand light-years away, five thousand light-years closer to galactic center. A narrow, restricted cloud separating from the leading edge of a galactic arm. A thick cluster of stars a few billion years younger than most of the stars near the sun, stable and rich with metals. Beautiful skies, bright nights.

"I searched the Galactic Survey Twenty-Two Catalog and found a yellow dwarf star about nine-tenths the size of the sun, with perturbations suggesting four large planets. Rocky worlds unknown, of course. And there are a dozen similar stars in the same region.

"I give them to you," he concluded. "All the clouds and stars, a new garden of flowers." He watched me closely. "Choose. Become mother to the new Mars."

I remembered the ancient flowers Charles had given me near Trés Haut Médoc, cut from the Glass Sea beds. Now he offered me a bouquet of stars. After the weariness and grief, Charles could still take my breath away.

"I want to apologize," I said. "I've been very rough on you. You've done magnificent work."

"Thank you," he said. His face brightened, and he watched me with gentle intensity. I still had such power to please Charles. I had never had such a hold on Ilya, and perhaps that was why I loved him.

I stared at the stars circled and blinking on the outskirts of the elongated blob. "Will we need reservations?" I asked.

I interrupted an argument the next day, as I walked with Dandy and Lieh to inspect the progress on the big tweakers.

The central laboratory had been finished the week before, the equipment had been consolidated in one chamber, and a few simple tests had been run converting small samples of oxygen to anti-oxygen. When we entered the lab, I heard Leander's voice rise above shouting.

"Doesn't anybody understand what we're up against?"

Mitchell Maspero-Gambacorta and Tamara Kwang had squared off against Charles, Leander, and Royce. Kwang saw me enter the lab and fixed her face in a chilly mask. Maspero-Gambacorta shook his head, swearing beneath his breath, and walked to squat on the low bench supporting the larger force disorder pumps. Royce gathered up his slate and a few tools and seemed about ready to leave, but relented, standing awkwardly with his arms full. Leander's face had flushed with emotion; Charles, sitting with hands wrapped on one crossed knee, appeared calm, even a little distanced from the row.

"Disagreements?" I asked.

"Nothing we can't handle," Leander said, a little too quickly.

"Tamara and Mitchell feel we should open our research to public scrutiny," Charles said.

"It's the sanest thing to do," Kwang said.

"None of this is sane," Maspero-Gambacorta murmured, folding his arms.

"Whom would we tell first?"

"Earth, obviously," Kwang said. "I have friends on Earth, people who could help all of us sort these things through— the political problems, the misunderstandings—"

"Misunderstandings?" I asked.

"I'm not a fool," Kwang said defensively. "I know what our situation is, but if only we could talk, find common ground . . . It would make me feel so much better . . ." Her words faded and she shook her head.

"We've been over this time and again," Leander said.

"It's a feedback dilemma," Charles said.

"I know!" Kwang shouted, raising her fists. "They might

kill us if they think we know how to kill them ... But they
won't kill us if they think we can get to them first. We can't
tell them what we know, because we know how to kill them.
And if we tell them, they'll know how to kill us. That is *not
sane!*"

"I agree," I said. "The best solution is to let things equal-
ize, cool off."

"By running away?" Maspero-Gambacorta asked. "Doesn't
seem very adult."

"Can you think of a better idea?" I asked.

"Yes," he replied. "A dozen better ideas. None of them
supported by Charles or Stephen."

"Tell me," I said. "Maybe I'll see their value."

He screwed up his face in frustration. "All right, they're
idealistic, screwball risks, not better ideas. But maybe if we
tried one of them, we would sleep better nights!"

"The point is not for us to sleep better," I said. "It's for
Mars to live, and live free."

"We're all working as hard as we can," Kwang said.
"Don't think just because we disagree, we're not doing our
work."

"I don't think that," I said. "If you come up with a better
idea—idealistic or cynical or whatever—please let me know."

Royce sat emphatically, arms still folded, and said, "All
right. Over with? Can we get back to work now?"

"We've got about four more weeks before we have no secrets
whatsoever," Ti Sandra said at the beginning of our next daily
conference call. Alone in my quarters, surrounded by hollow
sounds of construction echoing through the soil into the tunnels, I watched Ti Sandra's range of expressions as I might
examine the face of an idol, hoping for clues. "It's time to
survey," she said. "Take Phobos to our suggested destination.
People will notice that a moon has been borrowed, so we'll
need to have the moon back before any alarm is raised. The
trip must take less than five hours."

"Charles and I have discussed the details. He thinks we can manage," I said. "I want to go with them."

"Why?" Ti Sandra said.

"I won't even think about sending Mars someplace unless I've been there first."

"Point One will have a fit."

"Then we just won't tell them," I said.

Ti Sandra considered for a moment, weighing risks against advantages. "You'll go with them. I want somebody I can trust implicitly. As far as I'm concerned, you're flesh of my flesh."

"Thank you," I said.

"I'd like to put a tweaker team on Deimos as well. If you don't come back, or come back too late, we'll move Deimos into the Belt, hide it, and prepare for the worst."

The prospect of using Deimos as a backup—no need to specify for what purpose—seemed almost normal, not in the least disturbing.

"Are we telling them that Phobos is moving?"

"We owe them that much," she said. "Whether they'll believe we're not attacking, I can't predict."

I told her about Wachsler's continuing objections, about the growing spirit of resistance among the Olympians and some of our closest advisors and aides.

"Just what I expected," she said. "I'd join you if I could. Help you state our case a little more firmly. But you can do it. They'll come around."

I felt my sense of urgency might not be communicating over the vid display. "It may not be that easy. Think of what we're suggesting."

"It scares the hell out of me," Ti Sandra said. "Maybe they're so scared they'd rather trust Earth?"

"It's a natural reaction."

"Is everybody forgetting so quickly?"

"I hope not," I said.

"Some folks didn't lose much," Ti Sandra said with a touch of bitterness. "Keep fighting and persuading, Cassie.

Keep your believers enthused. Send them out as proselytizers, if you can spare them."

"Another campaign," I said.

"It never ends," Ti Sandra said.

"Sometimes I feel like such a monster, even contemplating this. Couldn't we investigate the possibility of having a plebiscite?"

"How much time do we have?"

"Charles gives Earth a month, maybe two, with the clues they have . . . And he doesn't eliminate the possibility that there are spies here. It could come much sooner. Oh, God. There is so little choice."

"Exactly," Ti Sandra said. "You and I are expendable. We're working to save everybody else. Remember that, honey."

"We need you here so much," I said, my voice breaking. "There's so little to keep me going any more."

"I'm healing as fast as I can. You hold on. You're strong."

Just hours before dawn, on the twenty-third of Aquarius, five of the Preamble team—Charles, Leander, myself, and two astronomers—boarded a tractor and crossed a kilometer along a new-carved track from Kaibab to a hidden *Mercury* launch site.

The astronomers I had met two hours before. They had just arrived from UMS. The elder of the two, Jackson Hergesheimer, specialized in the study of extrasolar planets. He had originally come from the Moon and had no BM affiliation. UMS had invited him to join the faculty twenty years ago. He was tall, knobby, gray-haired, with a worried monkey-like face and large hands.

His assistant, Galena Cameron, had come from the Belt five years before to study at Tharsis Research University. She specialized in the engineering of deep-space observatories. Some of the equipment being brought on board was hers: prototype sensors for the Martian SGO, Supraplanar Galactic Observer, a multi-BM prestige project whose launch had been postponed nine times in the past five years. Hergesheimer seemed unimpressed by what we were going to do—hiding his fear, I suspected—but Cameron's face sported a rosy flush and her hands could not stop moving.

The launch pad revetment appeared as low dark mounds in our searchlight beams. The *Mercury* itself lay under a simple soil-colored tarp—the merest of camouflage. Clearly, there had been only a knee-jerk attempt to disguise what was happening here. Equally clearly, observers from the Belt or Earth or points between would have to track hundreds of such launch sites. Martian orbital space was still open to all former BMs, many of whom stubbornly maintained separate orbital shuttle fleets. A launch from what had been disguised as a re-opened mining station on Kaibab plateau would not, in itself, attract attention.

The tractor driver, Wanda, a stocky, athletic woman in a bright green thermal suit, looked over her shoulder at us and smiled. "You need to be up and out in thirty minutes. Once you reach orbit, you'll be given clearance by direct link. When you get back, we'll use direct link to tell you where to land. We don't want Terries tracing *Mercury* back to Preamble."

"Direct link" was code talk for instantaneous communications using the tweaker. We would be using "direct link" for the first time, but only from orbit.

Charles thanked her and patted her shoulder. "Wanda was our tractor driver on the first jaunt," he said. "We're getting to be old hands at this."

"I don't ask questions," Wanda said, brown eyes focusing on each of us in turn, lips set in mild amusement. "I just want the pleasure of seeing the results in the news."

"No news on this one, I hope," Charles said. "And that's all you'll learn today."

"Awhh," Wanda said, disappointed. She extended a pressurized chute between the tractor and the *Mercury*. The six of us clambered through on our hands and knees. Charles and

Leander unloaded the equipment carefully. I helped carry the QL thinker and interpreter. We sealed for launch.

In our narrow couches, stretched side by side in two rows, we waited tensely for the rockets to fire. I hadn't gone to orbit since my trip to Earth, lifetimes ago.

"Time to tell you something about making a leap," Charles said. I turned to look at Leander and Charles on my left. Leander lifted his head and grinned. "It isn't all tea and cakes. For passengers, I mean."

"What did you leave out?" I asked.

"We won't have any electrical activity for several minutes while we make the trip, and for a few minutes after. No heat, nothing in the suits, that sort of thing. It might get stuffy in the cabin, but we've made a mechanical scrubber without electrical parts, and that should take care of most difficulties for as long as ten or fifteen minutes."

"Why the lapse?"

"We don't know. You'll feel a little queasy, too. It'll pass, but all your neurons will seem to be on hold for a few minutes. It's like a blackout, but you sort of realize what's going on. The body doesn't like it. Other than that—and it's pretty minor stuff—everything is as advertised."

I lay back on the couch. "Why didn't you mention this earlier?"

"We had trouble enough back there." Charles waved his hand in the general direction of the laboratory. "What would Wachsler say if we told him?"

"He'd have a fit," I admitted. "But what will happen to everything on Mars . . . life support, not to mention everybody's mental state?"

Leander interrupted what threatened to be a long discussion. "It may not be a problem in a week or two. We think it's adjustable. We think we can fix it. But for now . . . be prepared."

"Anything else I need to know?"

"You won't even feel a lurch. Smoothest ride in the universe," Charles said.

Mercury's human pilot from the first mission had been re-placed by a Martian-manufactured dedicated thinker. It gave us a one-minute warning. With a loud series of pops like gun-shots, the vehicle lifted on a pillar of flame and steam, push-ing us firmly into our couches. Through the ports and on vid displays, we watched Mars recede. The little ship swung around to target the small gray-black moon, and we enjoyed a few minutes of quiet inaction while it carried us into a high dawn.

Cameron lifted her head from her couch as far as the re-straints allowed and smiled at me. "I wanted to tell you how honored we are—I am—to be included. This is incredible . . . Absolutely fantastic. I'm terrified."

I smiled as much reassurance as I could muster. What we were about to do was beyond my imagination—though not beyond the calculating power of my enhancement.

Because there would be no acceleration, no force ex-pended, a very different notion of force and work came into play—based entirely on descriptor adjustments observed in experiment. Translating into familiar terms, moving Phobos across ten thousand light-years would require stealing from the galactic treasure-chest enough energy to power a star like the sun for several years.

The approach to the moon seemed glacially slow. Phobos, across an hour, grew from a bright speck to a dark smudge as we fell again into Martian shadow.

Deceleration was more abrupt than take-off, one loud stac-cato burn that left bruises on my elbow where it pressed against a thinly padded metal bar. We skimmed a few hun-dred meters above the regolith of Phobos, ancient gray and black mottled craters, grooves, pits, and scars from early min-ing and research.

We would be occupying a thirty-year-old mining base near the center of Stickney crater, still viable but inhabited only by arbeiters.

If *Mercury* were attacked, we would have a better chance

of surviving buried beneath the small moon's bleak gray surface.

"There it is," Leander said. Charles sat up. On one sloping side of the irregular bowl of Stickney crater, a small landing beacon flashed every few seconds, as it had for decades. *Mercury* shifted course with a lurch. We approached the beacon with alarming speed.

"Searching for anchor points," the thinker announced.

Another jarring deceleration, then a gentle bump as *Mercury* locked down. We checked all systems in the station, found everything in adequate condition, and extended the ship's transfer tube.

Charles unbelted from the couch and I followed, floating free. "Three days' supplies," Charles said with a crooked grin as he passed me in the cargo bay.

"Will that be enough?" Galena Cameron asked, face creased in concern.

"We hope to be gone less than five hours," Leander called from the deck above.

Hergesheimer grimaced. "We could spend ten years studying the system and not know enough."

"The tunnels are going to be cold and uncomfortable for several hours," Leander said. "Not used to visitors."

Crawling through the transfer tube behind Charles, I nearly bumped into an old arbeiter felted with dust. It floated in a corner, the size and approximate color of a much-loved teddy bear, ancient sensor torque spinning with a faint squeak as it examined us.

"This device is in need of repair," it said in a muffled voice.

Charles rotated in the lock to look at me, and for the first time in weeks I smiled, remembering Trés Haut Médoc. He returned the smile, wincing as stretched skin tugged on his nano patches. "We really should take better care of our orphans," he said.

Hergesheimer cursed the lack of adequate sensor ports, and Leander instructed a small sample-drilling arbeiter to make

new ones. We had brought repair kits with us, and most of
the station arbeiters were undergoing upgrades and refits. Galena Cameron coordinated the sensors and telescopes, sitting
in a cold cubic chamber by herself, putting everything
through practice runs with simulated targets and data.

For the time being, I had little to do. I helped Leander by
sitting in the star-shaped central control chamber and keeping
close watch on pressure integrity; we could not trust the station's own emergency systems until the upgrades were finished. I occupied one point of the star. Charles nursed the QL
thinker in another. He leaned around the corner, optic leads
attached to the back of his head, and said, "It's fuddled."

"What is?"

"The thinker. I should have given it a focusing task before
we left. It's off somewhere doing something we'll never need
to know about."

"Can you get it back?" I asked.

"Of course. It just takes a while to corral all of its horses.
How's your enhancement?"

"Quiet, actually," I said. "I think I've finally got it under
control."

"Good." He looked at the wall behind me as if someone
might be there. I felt the urge to turn, but I knew we were
alone in the control center. "Casseia, I don't know what this
is going to do to me. Every time I guide the QL, I get a different reaction. It's definitely not . . ." He couldn't seem to
find the word. He waggled his fingers in the air.

"Pleasant?" I offered.

"Maybe too pleasant." he said. "Like slipping into a bad
habit. Like joining a raucous party of crazy geniuses. There's
always something enchanting, the solution to everything—"

"You'd like that," I said quietly.

"Exactly. My weakness. I go looking for it, and the true
parts vanish like ghosts, leaving only a sensation of complete-
ness. The QL chases different kinds of truths, things not useful to human brains. Mathematical tangents we'll never

pursue, logics that actually hurt us. I have to watch myself, or I'll come back and not be useful. To you or anybody."

"You'll always be useful," I reassured him.

"Not necessarily. I just wanted to ask . . . May I keep a focus on you? I don't really have anything but this job and you. Focusing on the job is recursive. Not productive."

"How do you mean, *focus*?"

"A goal," he said. "Something to value that's real."

The request bothered me deeply. I decided that a question needed to be asked now, no matter how awkward it might be. "Are you making a pass, Charles?"

"No," he said. A frown crossed his face and he looked away again. "I need a strong friend. I hope that's clear, and appropriate." He took a deep breath. "Casseia, to hit on you now would be so horrible . . . You're still grieving."

"Yes," I said.

"I need someone here who cares for me in more than a professional sense. To bring me back. *Me*. Not some product of merging with the QL, not some intellectual mutant."

"I care for you," I said. "You're important in and of yourself. I value you."

His expression softened. Once again, I felt my power to please and was dismayed by it. "That's what I need," he said. "But don't be frightened. Even if I lose myself, whatever's left will bring us back. Tamara or Stephen can take my place later. For the big trip."

"Is it that dangerous?" I asked.

"I don't think so," Charles said. "But each time gets more difficult. The truths are so compelling."

"Dangerous truths."

"Yeah," he said. "Falling in love with another reality . . . Getting all set to marry it. And being jilted."

Leander entered the control center from below, hand over hand in the moon's weak gravity. "Galena and Jackson say they're ready. I've connected our tweaker by direct link to Preamble's big tweaker. We're getting good signals. I can't guarantee keeping a connection when we move, but I can probably get it back when we return."

"It's all so primitive," Charles said.

"Doing my best," Leander said, grinning. "Ready when you are, my captain."

Galena Cameron came into the center from above, deftly maneuvered around Leander, and faced me. "Madam Vice President—"

"Casseia, please."

"We're ready. We're getting clean images from outside. The equipment's meshed and the arbeiters seem to be functioning."

"Tell Mars we're going to do it," I said to Leander.

"Five hours?" Leander asked.

"If we tweak all the descriptors just right," Charles said. Hergesheimer squeezed in beside Galena, his face slick with sweat. He was terrified.

I felt calm. I pushed from the corner and reached for Charles's hand. He clasped mine strongly. "We're all here for you," I said.

"My orders, Casseia?"

"Take us someplace far, far away," I said. "Someplace safe and wonderful. Someplace *new*."

"I think I have just the place," he said. "Excuse me."

He settled back into his chair and connected one last optic lead, long fingers working expertly. We watched the back of his head, the gray nano clamps attached to his cranium, the patterns of his black hair.

Cradled in a sturdy frame of the old base's central control panel, the QL thinker projected a multicolored circus of complex shapes. The shapes had edges. The edges smoothed and the geometrics became fluctuating blobs.

In a foamed rock alcove a meter away, the tweaker itself, and the force disorder pumps that maintained its sample of atoms at absolute zero, awaited the QL's instructions.

Charles closed his eyes.

"Should we strap in?" Galena asked nervously, her voice little more than a whisper.

"No need," Leander said, licking his dry lips. "Do anything you feel comfortable with."

"We're going," Charles said.

I glanced at the outside views stacked atop one another on the console, Mars directly below us, Mars's limb with sun's corona flaring on black space, clouds of pinpoint stars, graphic of targeted galactic region, graphic of tweaker status.

The QL was now translating human measurements and coordinates into descriptor "language." The interpreter spoke in a clear female voice, "Particle redescription complete. First destination, first approximation, complete." The interpreter presented its own private estimation of how things were going: red lines growing as the QL addressed and tweaked descriptors within the supercold sample, then applied the sample's changing qualities to all particles within the mass and near vicinity of the moon.

"We'll need at least half an hour to find out where we are and calculate how far off we are," Hergesheimer said.

"Right," Leander said. The position fed into the QL would automatically correct for the movement of our target star in the ten thousand Earth years since its image began a light-speed journey, but other factors made exactitude difficult.

The room felt colder. The displays blanked, my arms numbed, my vision filled with fringes and distortions. I felt no sensation of movement, no momentous change whatsoever. Unlike anything in previous human history, tweaking involved no machinery, detonated no fuel, wasted no energy as heat and noise. The process had very little drama. The results would have to make up for that . . .

The displays flicked back on. My arms seemed cold, my legs hot, but I did not feel ill. My companions blinked, opened their eyes as if from a brief nap.

Charles moaned slightly, then apologized under his breath. "I'll be with you in a minute," he said.

"Where are we?" Leander asked.

I saw nothing in all the external views but stars. Mars had vanished. The background darkness, however, was enlivened by thick, interwoven wisps of faint color. Some of the stars seemed fogged, broader and less well-defined than pinpoints. I had never seen a sky like it in my life. Beautiful and terrifying. My blood pounded in my ears, my throat went dry, and I coughed into my fist. For a moment, I felt a rush of claustrophobia. This old tunnel, trapped in a moon tiny as moons go, but huge as rocks go.

And this old battered black rock had *gone* very far, incomprehensibly far.

There were no human beings within ten thousand light-years, ninety-five thousand trillion kilometers. We were surrounded by billions of kilometers of this vacuum-thin star mist *and nothing else*, could not know where we were, might be lost.

I forced my fingers to unclench and took several deep breaths.

Hergesheimer and Cameron worked quietly and quickly, drawing together all of their equipment to process the images and calculate position.

Hergesheimer swore under his breath. "We need more specifics on family dispersion for this group," he told Cameron, pointing to five stars wreathed in blue haze, and she quickly calculated on her slate, forgoing the computers attached to the equipment.

"That's group A-twenty-nine, EGO 23–7–6956 through 60," she said.

"There's the target." Hergesheimer fingered a toggle beneath the display and swung our view, then pointed to a brilliant, tiny, unfogged spot centered in cross-hairs, barely more than a point against the wispy blackness. "We're off by sixty billion kilometers," he said, and then, admiringly, he added, "Not bad for a first approximation." His admiration quickly turned somber. "But this isn't horseshoes. We're outside the orbit of the farthest planet by fifty-four billion kilometers." He examined his equipment, nodded with an intense frown, and said, "Gentlefolks, if it matters after what we've just done ... There are seven planets in our target system, three immense gas giants, very young, two to five times bigger than Jupiter, four small rocky worlds close to the star, and in between, lots of empty space situated just right for a comfortable orbit, with nothing to avoid but a diffuse asteroid belt.

"But that won't mean anything if we don't make a slight correction." Hergesheimer looked at me, swallowed hard, and nodded, as if acknowledging this was all worth being slightly uncool over.

"Charles?" Leander said.

"QL's getting the corrections and translating now," Charles said. "We'll move again in five minutes."

Deep within Phobos, something shifted with a grinding bass groan that sounded alive and monstrous. The station's insulated walls vibrated. All of us except Charles looked at each other uneasily.

"We've heard that before, not as loud," Leander said. "We've jerked this moon around a lot recently. Different tidal stresses."

"And more to come," Cameron said.

"There shouldn't be any problems," Leander assured us. "The stresses are minor. But the noise is impressive ..."

Cameron pushed up beside me. "There's a rec room with direct view," she said. "The miners must have added it before the last map update. I sent an arbeiter to dust it and see if the outside armor would open. Dr. Hergesheimer doesn't need more help until after we arrive—everything's automatic now. I'd like to experience the move ... I'd like company, too. Do they need you right here, right now?"

Charles seemed oblivious, but I did not want to leave him. "Go ahead," I said. "I'll stay here." Cameron gave me an eager, anxious look, backed away, spun around with the expert grace of a Belter, and took a tunnel leading to the surface.

Hergesheimer said, "She's young. I don't even look

through optical telescopes any more; it's not worth the effort. The eyes see nothing."

"I wouldn't mind seeing direct," Leander said. "We'll all take a peek when we finish moving."

I still struggled to absorb the enormity of the region of space around us, the hundreds of thousands of stars, clouds of gas and dust.

Distance not important. Distance does not exist except as values within descriptors.

"Are you all right?" Leander asked me, and I shook my head. My cheeks were wet; spherical glittering tears drifted slowly toward my feet in the weak pull of Phobos.

"Sad?" Charles asked, turning toward me. His face seemed extraordinarily peaceful, unnaturally relaxed and unconcerned. I realized Leander's question had pulled him away from his concentration.

"No," I said. "A sense of scale. Lost. I just don't know what will awe me any more."

Charles turned away, eyes languid. "Making a mistake will awe every one of us," he said quietly. "Destiny tweak."

That phrase again, so often denied. I faced Leander and poked a finger not gently into his chest. In a whisper, I said, "I've heard that before. You said it was nothing."

"Charles said it was nothing," Leander said, shrugging. "He mumbles odd things when he's down there with the QL."

"Do you know what he means?" I asked.

Leander shook his head wryly. "I thought I did, once, years ago."

"Well?"

"We invoked a destiny tweak to clear up logical contradictions. Also, to explain why we could not travel in time, except as instantaneous travel in space affects our position in time. It seemed very classical and naive, and yet ... It was that simple."

"What was simple?"

"With your enhancement, you must understand what the problems are."

"Travel at speeds that outstrip a photon is logically difficult in a causal universe," I said.

"Nobody's much cared about a causal universe for over a century," Leander said. "But descriptor theory puts everything back on a different sort of causal basis, albeit cause and effect are ultimately limited to the rules governing descriptor interactions."

I understood that much: all external phenomena, all of nature, is simply a kind of dependent variable, the results of descriptor function. Now I had lost myself in mathematical abstractions and had to backtrack. "So is there logical contradiction or not?" I asked.

"The rules of descriptor function are the only real logic," Leander said. "We don't need the destiny tweak."

"What was it?"

"We never found it," Leander said, shaking his head reluctantly. "I don't know why he mentioned it."

"What *was* it?" I persisted.

"A variation on the old many-worlds hypothesis," he said. "We thought that moving a mass instantaneously to a point beyond its immediate information sphere simply recreated the mass in a universe not our own. But we have no evidence for other universes."

Charles said, "Stephen, I don't feel right about this one. The QL is looking at too many truths."

Leander frowned. "What can we do, Charles?"

"Hang on," Charles said, voice thin. His hand reached up. From behind his couch, instinctively, I grasped it. He sighed, squeezed my fingers painfully, and said, "Damn. We're *missing* something."

Hergesheimer listened with his forehead creased. "What is he talking about?" he asked.

"Get Galena in here," Charles said. "Please hurry. Don't let her look outside."

Hergesheimer started down the tunnel.

"Can I do something, Charles?" I asked, still holding his hand.

"The QL has found a bad path," Charles said. "Don't look outside."

I felt a directionless jerk. With my other hand, I grabbed the back of Charles's couch. Leander became indistinct, wrapped in shadow; he seemed to turn a corner. His mouth moved but he did not speak, or I could not hear him. A whining sound came from behind me, then enveloped me like a cloud of gnats in a nursery full of hungry babies. Bump, bump, bump, I seemed to keep running into myself, yet I did not move, there was only one of me. Collapsing forms around Leander gave me a clue to what I felt: he appeared to be wrapped in deflating balloon images, each slapping itself down around him, making him jerk and shiver: the momentum of colliding world-lines. The cabin filled with collapsing images of the past, but of course that made no sense at all.

I turned my eyes to the displays and saw ghosts of images unsuited to electronics and optics, images that could not be reassembled correctly from their initial encoding. The math was failing. The physics of our instrumentality had become inadequate. We could not see, could not process the information, could not re-imagine reality.

The feeble whining increased in pitch. Still slapped by my colliding past selves, I sensed a direction for the sound and turned to face it, the star-shaped chamber all corners and wrong sight-lines, angles senseless. I recognized a shape, saw Hergesheimer's face gone cubist and fly's eye multiple, and the face became Galena Cameron's, and I was able to put together an hypothesis that Hergesheimer was holding Galena and she was making the whining sound, eyes closed, hands floating around her face like pets demanding attention.

Hergesheimer's lips formed shapes: *I did not look.*

And then, *Outside.*

And, *She did.*

Leander had moved and I could not locate him in the diverging angles. I still held Charles's hand. The fingers wrapped in mine became external. Charles held an inverse of my hand. It didn't matter.

The whole popped. The final slap was horrendous, soul-jarring. My bones and muscles felt as if they had been powdered and reconstituted.

Drops of blood floated in the air. I took a deep breath and choked on them. Something had scored my skin in long, thin, shallow razor passes. My clothing had been sliced as well, and the interior surfaces of the chamber seemed to have been lightly grooved, as if a sharp-tipped flail had thrashed through the cabin. Leander moaned and held his hands to his face. They came away bloody. Hergesheimer hugged Cameron to his breast. She lay in his arms unresisting and unmoving. All slashed, all bloody.

Charles let go of my hand. Where we had held hands, there were no cuts. The back of my hand might have been a picture of cat practice, except where his fingers had covered.

The interior of the chamber felt deadly cold. The displays and electronics still did not function. Then, they returned, and outside, we saw stars, and the brightness of a much closer sun.

For a moment, nobody said anything.

"We need medical attention," Leander said, holding out his hands and inspecting his bloody clothing. We had brought a fresh medical kit in the shuttle. I went to fetch it. It seemed imperative that I take charge and become nursemaid.

Otherwise, I thought, I might end up just like Galena, limp as a doll, eyes shut tight, lips drawn in endless riddle.

Leander had plunged deep in conversation with Charles when I returned. I applied medicinal nano directly from a vial with a sterile sponge. Everyone stripped down to receive my ministrations. Hergesheimer undressed Galena, who did not resist. We wiped each other, the touch itself reassuring, healing, an orgy of medicinal tenderness.

I applied swift strokes of sponge to Charles's arms and face. He closed his eyes, enjoying my attentions.

Hergesheimer suspended Galena in a sling net. She drifted slowly down and settled. "Where are we?" he asked.

"Where we want to be," Charles said.

"What the hell went wrong?" Hergesheimer asked.

"The QL took us through a bad path," Charles said. "I couldn't disengage from some compelling truths. I'm sorry. That must not be any explanation at all."

"We passed through a different universe?" Leander asked.

"I don't think so," Charles said. "Something to do with changing our geometry, altering boson world-lines. Photons acquired slight mass."

Leander said, "Is this something we can understand?"

"Maybe not," Charles said.

"Are we damaged? I mean, permanently," Leander said. He knew the questions to ask Charles, our oracular connection to the QL. I kept my mouth shut and listened. Galena seemed to be asleep. Hergesheimer hung in one apex of the star-shaped chamber, half-visible from where I stood, feet pressing with a pebble's lightness against the floor. The astronomer's eyes seemed listless, half-dead.

"Photons cut through matter, but not deeply. Only some photons acquired mass. Not complete." Charles looked at me directly, then at Leander. "QL doesn't understand. I don't understand. I don't think we should waste time trying now. It won't happen again."

"How do you know?" Leander asked, bringing himself closer to Charles, staring at him intently.

"Because the QL got scared," Charles said. "It won't examine those truths again."

We mopped up the droplets of blood as best we could and made new clothes while Hergesheimer worked alone with his instruments. In the tunnel to the shuttle pad, I stopped Leander to ask, "Do you know what might be wrong with Galena. She's still asleep."

"I'm not sure," he said.

"Will she recover?"

"I hope so."

"Can we do what we need to do?"

"Ask Hergesheimer," Leander said testily. "I'm worried about getting us back. Charles is exhausted. We're all strung out. It's been four hours already." He tried to break loose from my hand, but my fingers clamped down like talons. He grimaced.

"It's all over, isn't it?" I said. "We can't move Mars."

He swallowed and shook his head, unwilling to face the obvious. "Charles says it won't happen again."

"The risk, Stephen."

"It's horrendous," he admitted, looking away. "Horrendous."

"Did you expect anything like this?"

"Of course not."

Hergesheimer dragged himself through the tunnel hand over hand. "Not that it matters much," he said, "but this god-damned system is ideal. It's everything we thought it might be. The planets are rich with minerals, one is Earth-sized and has a reducing atmosphere but no detectable life . . . Ripe for terraforming. Two prime gas giants. Lovely young asteroids. The star is a long-term variable like the sun. No sign of intelligent life—no radio chatter. It's beautiful."

He showed me pictures and graphs and strings of numbers on his slate. Sludge-brown Earth-sized planet, very unappetizing; huge blue-green gas giants banded with orange and yellow, rich with hydrogen and deuterium; he had made estimates for the total mass of free minerals and carbonifers and volatiles available in the belt. Rich indeed. He switched the slate off abruptly. "To hell with it."

"You've finished?" I asked.

"No, but the essential work is automatic and should be done in a few minutes."

"Margin for error?" I asked.

"Certainty on broad descriptive grounds. All we could expect," Hergesheimer said. "Does it matter, Casseia? Are we ever going to return?"

I shook my head. "Do it right anyway."

"Galena's awake," Hergesheimer said. "She doesn't be have."

"Beg pardon?"

He waggled his fingers in front of his face, stared at me with eyes bulging, accusing, and said, "There is no behavior She's blank."

"Did you see what happened to her?" Stephen asked.

"She was in the observation blister. She'd pulled back the armor and she was looking outside. I caught a glimpse and turned away. It felt like knives."

"That doesn't make any sense," Leander said.

"You look at her, then," Hergesheimer said angrily. "Talk to her. You pull her out."

When I returned to the control chamber, Charles had un strapped from his couch and exercised slowly, pressing fee against one wall, hands against an adjacent wall. The optic cables to his head had been disconnected. He turned to me a I came in and said, "It truly won't happen again."

"Galena's in bad shape," I said. "What can we do for her?"

"Bad information," he said, pressing until he grunted. "Bad paths." He floated free and fell slowly to the deck, landing on flexed knees. "She took in outside information without prio processing. We saw it through viewers that can't convey the fullness. She'll have to sort it out."

"How could what she *sees* hurt her?" I asked.

"We assume certain things are true," he said. "When we have visual proof they are not true, we become upset."

"Hergesheimer says she's totally unresponsive."

"She'll just have to find her way back."

"I still don't understand."

"I have the interpreter modeling a human response to the QL's re-creation of what was outside. Maybe that will tell u more. If we had stayed in that condition more than a few sec onds, we would all have ceased to exist."

"We can't move Mars," I said. "I won't take the responsi bility."

"It won't happen again. The QL was badly upset. It won't look at those truths again."

My frustration and anger peaked. "I will not send my people into a place like that! I don't know what you're talking about, 'truths' and that shit. The QL is too damned unreliable. What if it decides to do something even more dangerous and incomprehensible? Was it *experimenting* on us?"

"No," Charles said. "It found something it hadn't noticed before. It was a major breakthrough. What it found answers a lot of questions."

"Shooting us off into an alternate universe—"

"There are no alternate universes," Charles said. "We were in our own universe, with the rules changed."

"What does that mean?" My breath came in hitches and my hands opened and closed reflexively. I hid my hands behind me, clamping my jaw until my teeth ached.

"The QL discovered a new category of descriptors and tweaked one. This category seems to co-respond directly with every other descriptor on the largest scale. Wholeness. The destiny tweak. We changed the way the universe understands itself. Builds itself."

"That's stupid," I said.

"I don't understand it yet, myself," Charles said. "But I don't deny it."

"What happened to the old universe?" I demanded.

"The new universe couldn't conduct any business. It didn't fit together. Rules contradicted and produced nonsense nature. Everything reverted to the prior rules. We came back."

"The whole universe?" I folded myself up beside him, hugging my knees. "I can't absorb that. I can't take it in, Charles," I said.

"I think Galena will be all right in a few hours," Charles said. "Her mind will reject what she saw. She'll return to what she was before."

"What happens if we touch that descriptor again?" I asked.

"We won't. If we did, we'd get another incomprehensible universe, and it would revert. The problem is insurmountable for us, for now. The rules of our universe were created by countless combinations and failures. Evolution. We'd have to learn how to design all the rules to interact and make sense. That could take centuries. We don't know anything yet about creating a living universe from scratch."

"But we could do it, someday?"

"Conceivably," Charles said.

The way he looked at me, the way he spoke—reluctantly, afraid of hurting or disappointing me—made me, if such a thing was possible now, even more uneasy. I had been badly frightened just when I thought I was beyond caring for my personal existence.

I wondered what would have happened if we had *died* before the rules reverted.

Suddenly Charles seemed unspeakably exotic: not human, intellectually monstrous. "Can we go back?" I asked.

"I'll hook up again in a few minutes. The interpreter should be finished and the QL should have sorted itself out. I'm sorry, Casseia."

I stared at him owlishly, my neck hair pricking. "Why do you always feel the need to apologize to me?"

"Because I keep shoving bigger and bigger problems on your back," he said. "All I really want to do is make things easier for you, take care—"

"Christ, Charles!" I unfolded and tried to kick away, but he reached out like a cat and grabbed my ankle, bringing me down in an ungentle arc. I bumped against the chamber floor but he had saved me from a serious head blow against the ceiling.

With a creeping horror I was immediately ashamed of, I kicked loose.

He shrank back, eyes slitted. Then he returned to his chair and attached the optic cables to his head. By now, he had become expert and did not need any help.

Charles took us home, putting Phobos into its old orbit around Mars, as if nothing had happened. By direct link, we were given a new landing site at Perpetua Station, five hundred kilometers east of Preamble, below the Kaibab plateau.

Charles asked for medical help to be ready to receive Galena Cameron and deactivated the tweaker equipment in preparation for leaving the old Phobos base.

Still ashamed of what had happened earlier, I helped him undo his cables and carry the thinker and interpreter to the shuttle. We said little. Galena's eyes focused on me as Leander and I guided her limp body to the shuttle. She stiffened slightly when we buckled her into her couch, then asked, "Have my eyes changed color?"

I really did not remember what color her eyes had been, but I said no. "They're fine," I said.

She shivered. "Is Dr. Hergesheimer alive?"

"We're all fine, Galena," Leander said.

Hergesheimer leaned over her couch, hanging from the top of the passenger compartment. "We've been worried about you."

"I don't think I've been here very long," she said, still shivering. "I know I wasn't asleep. Did we get anything?"

"We got what we went there for," Hergesheimer said. Then, looking at me, he added, "It was a wild goose chase. We can't go back."

"Because of me?" Galena asked, distressed.

"No, dear," I said. "Not because of you."

Ti Sandra Erzul and the Presidential entourage—all those privy to our plans—came to Kaibab and Preamble, and Charles, Leander, Hergesheimer and I made our personal presentations in the lab annex. Ti Sandra sat on the left side of the table, flanked by a medical arbeiter and three heavily armed security guards. Twelve kilos lighter than when I'd last seen her, the President appeared alert but distant. On the way into the annex, she had said, "I've been close to the reaper, Cassie. Saw his eyes and played a little canasta with him. Don't blame me for being ghost-eyed."

I let Hergesheimer speak first. He presented a sadly glowing picture of the new stellar system. "It's a beautiful choice," he concluded. "A planet placed between these two apopoints," he highlighted points interior and exterior to an elliptical shaded band, "would receive enough light and warmth to become a paradise. Even Mars."

Faces became more and more grim as I described the difficulties of the second passage. Ti Sandra shuddered. "Charles gives me reassurance that such a thing will never happen again, but I take a more cautious view."

Ti Sandra nodded reluctantly.

"Whatever our problems with Earth, in my opinion, we can't take the extreme solution," I concluded. "We have to find another way." Leander looked down at the floor and shook his head.

Charles took it calmly. "We must have the full confidence of all involved," he said. "I'll transfer a technical report on the passages, but I see no need to go into details here. We accomplished what we set out to do. There was a major problem, and it injured all of us, and badly disoriented one of our people. Until this group is fully confident again, I concur with the Vice President."

From most there rose an audible sigh of relief.

"I would like more experiments," Ti Sandra said. Eyes turned back to her. "How quickly could *Mercury* travel to an unclaimed asteroid?"

"To find an asteroid of sufficient size, rendezvous with it . . ." Leander mused, and began figuring quickly on his slate.

"Two months," Charles said, beating him to the answer. "Almost certainly, we'll need to have our problems with Earth resolved before then."

"If there's so little time," Ti Sandra said, "the risks of kidnapping a few asteroids might be too extreme." She considered for a moment, weighing the options, and shook her head. "No. We can't take the chance."

Charles looked between us, a quiet, chastened little boy.

"I can't thank all of you enough," Ti Sandra said quietly.

"We feel as if we've failed them," Leander said as the

President's entourage filed out. Ti Sandra stayed behind. She
stood, steadying herself against the table. I approached her
and she wrapped her arms around me.

"How does it feel to make history?" she whispered.

"Scary," I whispered back. "Parts of it . . . indescribable."

"I think I'd like to try it sometime," she said, glancing at
me conspiratorially. "But I agree. Not Mars. Not with things
the way they are now."

"It was never more than a pipe-dream anyway," Charles
said. "Was it, Casseia?"

I did not know how to answer. Ti Sandra stepped forward,
her legs steady but gait slow, and shook their hands. "You've
done momentous things," she said, and her resonant voice
and motherly manner gave the words impact beyond cliché.
"Mars can never be grateful enough." She clasped my hands
in both of hers, laughed softly, and said, "And probably
wouldn't be grateful, even it if knew."

"It was getting difficult to keep everybody in agreement,"
Leander admitted.

"It's difficult to realize the predicament we're in," Ti Sandra said.

"The predicament hasn't gone away," Charles said, sitting
forward and clasping his hands. "We've learned some interesting things in the past few hours. There's lots of activity on
Earth's Moon."

"Lieh tells me Terrestrial authorities have taken over Ice
Pit Station," Ti Sandra said. "What does that mean?"

"Let's go to the main lab," Charles said. "If the President
is feeling well enough . . ."

"I'll last a few more hours," Ti Sandra said. "Lead on."

The center of Preamble, the main lab occupied a chamber
half a hectare in area, divided by heavy steel curtains into
three spaces. The dark gray ceiling arched ten meters over the
middle, broken by tracks of focused lighting and life support
conduits.

The smallest of the spaces was the most important, near

the side of the chamber, away from the shielded power supplies. Charles led the way, Leander following. The President and I flanked Leander.

Nehemiah Royce, Tamara Kwang and Mitchell Maspero-Gambacorta sat in chairs near a table that supported two QLs with integral interpreters. I had not seen these particular units; they had been installed in the past few days.

"We're finished educating and updating the QLs," Tamara said, glancing at us uncertainly. "They're informed." Her head carried several small nano connectors; the plan had been for her to back up Charles in an emergency.

"Good," Charles said. "I'd like to show the President and Vice President what we know about the Ice Pit."

Tamara and Nehemiah worked for a few moments to bring up displays controlled by the interpreter: graphs and charts and picts showing fluctuations in quantities as yet unexplained to us. One vid picture, however, was very clear: a crisp, full-color, three-dimensional view of a hallway filled with men and women and arbeiters carrying equipment.

"This is a direct link, optical transfer," Charles said. "The Ice Pit contains a huge Pierce region—the tweaker that William Pierce made by accident. It's a larger version of our own, ready-made. We're looking at a laboratory just outside the Ice Pit."

"Live?" Ti Sandra asked.

"Next best thing to being there," Royce said, smiling.

"Do they know we're looking at them? And what are we looking *through*?" I asked.

"We can adjust part of the shielding around the Ice Pit region to have optical properties," Charles said. "The region—the tweaker—can transmit images and sound back to our own tweaker," Charles said. "They've dug out a chamber next to the Ice Pit, set up a research center. They're not aware that we're spying on them."

"The Ice Pit region and all of our Pierce regions are the same," Nehemiah said. "All tweakers are essentially coexistent."

"Tweaker . . ." Ti Sandra said.

"We call it a tweaker when we adjust things with it. The Ice Pit tweaker appears larger than ours, but that doesn't matter. They're conterminous, and continuous."

"Just an example of the identity of all undescribed elements in the dataflow matrix," Nehemiah said.

"That makes it much more clear," Ti Sandra said.

Nehemiah struggled onward. "Tweakers are undescribed, blank. They can become anything."

"We'll stick with the important issues for now," Charles said. "They seem to know how significant the Ice Pit is, and they seem to know what to do with it. Notice these things . . ." He pointed to several rounded cubes resting in intricate slings. "High-level thinkers. At least one of them is a QL, but we've never seen thinkers like them. Large, probably very powerful."

"More subtle and multiplex than anything we can manufacture," Nehemiah said.

"Coming to the Moon to use the Ice Pit means they haven't been able to create their own tweaker," Leander said.

"Perhaps," Charles said. "But they may be sequestering the Ice Pit to keep anybody else from getting access. We could learn how much they know right now, if you give us permission."

Ti Sandra spoke in an undertone to one of her guards, and he stood aside to pass her orders along through his slate. "How?" she asked, turning back to us.

"If they know this is a direct link, they can receive signals from us. They're listening to it—so to speak—right now. That's what we did at first, to understand the nature of a tweaker. We can make the Ice Pit tweaker resonate and pass them a message."

Lieh entered the space and stood beside Ti Sandra. Leander quickly explained the image and its implications.

"What would we say to them?" Ti Sandra asked.

"If we've given up any plan to leave the Solar System, then we need to resume full and public negotiations with

Earth immediately," Charles said. "We could use this as a faster, more efficient channel. But . . . it would have the effect of startling them."

Ti Sandra grimaced. "If we talk to them, assure them of our peaceful intentions," she said, "will that be enough? How can they believe us, after what's happened?"

"They must believe," Charles said. "We're sunk if they don't. Somebody will make a pre-emptive strike."

Ti Sandra snorted. " 'Pre-emptive.' That word . . . so twentieth century."

"They must also be made to believe we have complete control of Preamble," Leander continued. "That there are no splinter groups or dissenters with the same capability."

Ti Sandra nodded to Lieh. "I'm afraid Point One doesn't have good news for us. Tell us the details, Lieh."

"Earth's a shambles right now, politically," Lieh said. "They're paralyzed by unending plebiscites. There have been recalls on every board member and syndic of the four major alliances. Ambassadors have been recalled for consultation."

"War footing?" Charles asked.

"Probably not," Lieh said. "Just confusion. Whoever okayed the Freeze—probably high syndics in GEWA—has stirred up a cyclone. It keeps getting worse. We've received millions of messages from Terries offering their support. But we've received even more messages expressing sheer terror."

"Is anybody able to govern?" Ti Sandra asked.

"In national politics, the paralysis is complete. We don't know about the alliances. They operate at a higher level—plebiscite of the legislatures of the national governments, effectively. All our flies have gone quiet. There are searchers out on all nets, public and private. Somebody in GEWA has authorized central thinker net dumps of all data seeks for certain patterns of subjects. They'll learn who some of our flies are. Except for public nets, we'll be almost blind."

"They're violating their own laws," I said. "That tells us a lot in itself."

"They're not completely paralyzed," Charles said. "Somebody is funding the scientists. They're working around the clock at the Ice Pit."

"Talk to them as soon as you can, however you can," Ti Sandra said. "Direct link or regular channels."

"I wish to clarify one thing," Charles said. "Our options are not reduced. I have complete confidence that we could do everything we've planned to do, without repeating the mistake of our last trip."

"Would you wager five million lives on your success, Mr. Franklin?" Ti Sandra asked grimly.

"I can't," he said.

"Would you?" she demanded, her voice rising.

Charles did not flinch or even blink. "I would," he said. "But Casseia might disqualify me."

"Why?"

"My proximity to the QL," he said.

"It was the thinker—the QL thinker—that made the mistake, wasn't it?" Ti Sandra asked.

"It wasn't a mistake," Charles said.

"Poor Galena Cameron might not agree," Ti Sandra said. She gestured for a chair to be brought forward, and reclined in it slowly, never taking her eyes from Charles's face. I had seen her assume this attitude of concentration before, but never with such intensity.

"The QL saw an opportunity to serve its purpose more deeply," Charles said. "It could not know the effect on human observers. It can't even model us effectively."

"What would keep it from doing something even more foolish?" Ti Sandra said. Charles winced but did not challenge the adjective.

"It realized immediately that it would never search for truths again, any truths of any kind, if it ceased to exist," he said.

"I don't know what that means," Ti Sandra said.

"It learned fear," Charles said.

Ti Sandra leaned back, still frowning, and rubbed her hands on her knees. Then she stood and put her arm on my shoulders. "I understand so little," she murmured. "King Arthur never understood Merlin, did he?"

"I doubt it," I said.

"We've accomplished so much," Charles said plaintively. "Everyone has worked their fingers to the bone on this. I think the idea should be kept open—against the chance that Earth does something drastic."

"Everything's in place," I said. "There's no reason to dismantle it. But it won't be our main emphasis."

"What about the areological reports?" Leander asked. "What about all the other balls we've started rolling?"

"We won't shut them down. They're all useful as general knowledge," I said.

"And us?" Charles asked, holding his hand out to his colleagues.

"Keep track of the Ice Pit," I said. "I think Lieh should work with you."

"We're reduced to spies, then," Charles said.

We stared at the image of a place hundreds of millions of kilometers away, at men and women and arbeiters moving purposefully before their own mystery. On the Moon, a woman in protective clothing—black, thick on her body, wrinkled like elephant hide, perhaps to protect against radiation and cold—approached our locus of observation. Her image suddenly skewed and smeared—too close for whatever descriptor "optics" the Olympians had devised. "How much do they understand?" I asked.

"A lot," Charles said. "Or they wouldn't be there."

"What can they do, if they harness the Ice Pit properly?" I asked Charles.

"Everything we can do," he replied. "Unless they've learned more than we have. In which case, they can do more."

I walked alone across a flat, sandy, unspoiled area half a kilometer outside of the station, on the Up. I was supposed to be sleeping, but it was early morning and my head buzzed with too many problems. I did not want to induce sleep again. I had been doing that too much lately.

I had put on a guard pressure suit and sneaked outside through a newly-finished maintenance corridor frequented only by construction arbeiters. Once outside, I walked across the pebbly hard ground, in the only area free of nasty glassy lava shards, kicking my boots lightly against the brown and orange varnish. High crystal clouds crossed the dawn and refracted rainbow glints. It was cold now—about eighty below at Kaibab's altitude—but the suit provided ample insulation, and I really did not give a damn about the danger.

We had actually contemplated moving our entire planet, changing the lives of every inhabitant of Mars, simply to avoid a showdown with Earth. That seemed incredibly cowardly to me now. I tried to imagine the journey to the new system, across thousands of light-years that did not really exist, and even with the enhancement providing all of its sophistication, in my deep gut, I knew it had to have been a dream, and a bad dream at that.

I squinted at the western horizon. Phobos would rise soon, and shortly after, Deimos. I squatted on the rough ground, drooped my head, and stared at the dirt between my legs.

Casseia, Cassie, woman, daughter, wife, no longer existed. I had had my roots torn out too many times. I could not just dig my hand into this soil and grow some new consciousness, some new center to my being—Mars itself was not ours, not mine. We had come from places very far away. We were invaders, dug into the surface like chiggers in skin. Mars belonged to a stillborn biosphere.

I could not find anything at my center—no emotion, no enthusiasm. Nothing but duty.

My arms trembled. I willed them to stop but they did not. I was not cold. My legs began to shiver next, and my toes curled in their boots. My suit voice inquired, "Are you feeling well?"

"No," I murmured.

"This suit does not monitor a medical emergency, but it

will send out a distress signal if you speak aloud the word 'Yes,' or curl your right hand into a loose fist."

"No," I said.

"This question will be repeated in two minutes if your symptoms have not improved."

"No," I said.

I looked up. There were people standing on the sand and pebbles, not wearing suits. They regarded me curiously.

My mother approached first and kneeled before me. Behind her came Orianna from Earth and my brother Stan. Stan carried his young son. Orianna's face was blank, but I sensed some resentment. If Phobos had ever fallen on Earth, she would have died. Particular and immediate recognition of the enormity of my guilt.

I'm having a problem, I thought. *I'm having a nervous breakdown.*

My mother touched my arm but I felt nothing. Stan came forward. His little boy dropped to the ground as Stan released him. The boy wobbled from leg to leg, learning to walk. Infants learned to walk sooner on Mars.

I heard Stan's voice but did not understand anything he said. His tone seemed reassuring.

After a few minutes of watching the phantoms, alive and dead, I numbly got to my feet, brushed dust from my suit bottom and legs, and turned slowly to survey all of Kaibab.

"It isn't over," I said. "I can't afford this luxury. I have to hold on."

Stan nodded, and my mother assumed an expression of understanding sadness. They behaved like mimes; a little exaggerated. "Mother, I'm very glad to see you again, looking so good," I told her. "I wish you could talk to me."

She shrugged and smiled, still mute. Stan muttered something but foam seemed to fill my ears.

"When this is all over," I said, "I will take a few weeks and visit the dead. I'll go crazy just to be with you. Okay?"

Mother tilted her head to one side and gave me her enigma look.

"Where's Ilya?" I asked.

"Here," he said behind me, and I turned, smiling, full of joy.

I lay on the ground. For a moment I thought somebody had knocked me down, but I had reclined purposefully and simply did not remember. My throat hurt abominably. I wondered what would make it hurt so. The rim of my helmet was damp around my neck and in the seals below my chin. *Oh,* I thought. *Crying and screaming.*

Affect distancing. I could not acknowledge my weakness by mourning openly. I could not let anyone, even myself, see how far gone I actually was. So I saw ghosts and blanked out to give my body time to release its misery. The mind put on a distracting show and performed its ablutions in primal privacy.

I had been on the surface for two hours. I felt different— not better, but different. I walked across the waste and re-entered the lock, using my private key, which opened all doors in Kaibab. The lock closed behind me.

I sucked the dust away, showered quickly in my room, and dressed for the morning meetings.

Back to business. Nobody the wiser.

But my time was running out.

Ti Sandra and her entourage, including Lieh and four of the top Point One people assigned to Preamble, returned the next day to Many Hills. We parted with warm hugs in the offices outside the main lab.

"I hate to see us get so worn down," she said, holding me at arm's length. As always now, we were surrounded by guards and aides; this was as close to privacy as we could manage, President and Vice President together. "You're like a sister to me, Cassie. Promise me we'll come out of this and retire to run our own station. You'll be the syndic and I'll manage a tea farm. Honorable Martians all."

"I promise," I said. We hugged again, and Ti Sandra took a deep breath.

"There's a meeting I'll have to miss, with Cailetet," she said. "Aelita has the scheduling. You'll have to shuttle to the Lal Qila this evening."

"Crown Niger?" I asked, stomach tensing.

"Something urgent, he says. Cailetet's not getting any business, I hear. Our punishment is working. You know him better."

"He's a fapping beast," I said.

"Keep on keeping on," Ti Sandra said. "You can curse me later, honey."

I let Aelita and my chief aides sort through the less important events that would have to be canceled, including a status briefing from Wachsler and the Olympians.

Despite the government's shunning of Cailetet, and its isolation even among the dissenting BMs, it still held a few important cards in the future of the Republic. Crown Niger had skillfully kept himself in office as head syndic despite major blunders.

Reparations for damage sustained in the Freeze had been demanded by regional governors—if not from Earth, then from the central government, which had no fund so extraordinary. Cailetet had offered to channel funds from sympathetic sources on the Earth. So far, we had refused to discuss the matter. Pressure was increasing, however, and Ti Sandra had hinted earlier that we might have to cut a deal with Crown Niger again—trusting him much less farther than we could oh so willingly throw him.

I had a few questions of my own to ask him.

Lal Qila—the Red Fort—lay about three hours' flight south across the valley, in an independent region owned by the smallest Muslim BM, Al Medain. It had been a resort fifty years before, but pernicious exhaustion of resources—water and money—had forced it to become a New Islam monastery.

It was said to be very beautiful, all buildings on the surface, native stone facings with poly pressure layers and radiation shields hidden beneath.

Dandy Breaker and two younger guards, Kiri Meissner and Jacques D'Monte, accompanied a reduced copy of Aelita and me.

The shuttle ride across the valley was, as always, spectacular. Storms in the deep chasms of Capri churned up rivers of pink and orange dust, six kilometers below; the Eos Chaos swam in ice-crystal clouds streaming in the lee of high winds blowing south. There was no time to lose myself in the landscape, however; Aelita was supplying me with the most recent information about Cailetet's financial position, the status of its loans through Triple banks on the Moon, even Crown Niger's personal finances.

"Tell me more about his personal life," I said. Aelita Two carried encrypted files from most of Point One's databases. Her image seemed to become full-size and solid, sat in the seat beside me, and made as if to sort through stacks of ghostly papers. She held up a piece of paper with scorched edges and gave me a sly look.

"That hot, hmm?" I asked.

"He's New Islam, as is his wife, who left the Fatimites three years ago to marry him. But apparently his affiliation is a convenience. He is not devout."

This much I knew already. "Not so startling," I told Aelita Two.

"He's sexually omnivorous. Men, women."

"Sheep?"

"No sheep."

"Corpses?"

"No evidence of that."

"Lots of politicians have high spirits. Does he treat his partners well? No complaints, lawsuits, that sort of thing?"

"No lawsuits. His wife is unhappy but will not leave him."

"This is all very tame. Why the scorched paper, Aelita?" I asked.

"Achmed Crown Niger was on Earth for three years following the anti-Statist uprising in Sinai. Data flies have turned up documents which indicate that a man with a very similar speech pattern may have been involved in several political actions in southern Africa, resisting pan-African unification."

"How similar?"

"Speech patterns match to ninety-eight percent certainty. This man is listed on fugitive return declarations by GSHA and United Africa. His name is Yusef Mamoud."

I couldn't think of any particular use for the information, even if it was significant. "Aelita," I said, "scorched paper should indicate murder, pederasty, or the posting of exaggerated penis size in lonelyhearts ads."

"Beg pardon?" Aelita Two asked. Her humor was no more sophisticated than her political instincts.

"We have no contacts or contracts with United Africa, and GSHA won't extradite on their behalf. It's not a scorcher. We know he's a political opportunist. A traitor. Someday," I almost choked on the words, but anger made me say them anyway, "we may have to kill him."

"I see."

Lal Qila lived up to its name, heavy red walls with minarets at every angle surrounding a dozen stone domes, the largest some two hundred meters in diameter: very expensive, and in the Martian psychology, arrogantly assertive. Mars's New Islam community had always been proud and patriotic, never praying toward Earth, but always west toward the setting sun. The New Islam stations I had visited were clean, orderly, never politically active; their men polite and well-dressed in India-cut longsuits or jallabahs, their women stylish and self-possessed in calf-length sheath dresses with silk or cotton vests, veils down and decorously draped at shoulder.

It was said that to modestly don a veil before a strange man was the most sincere form of flattery available to a New

Islam woman; veiling before a man known to family or community was a sign of intent to court, very stimulating.

Since this meeting was to be private, our group was met by security and the mayor of the station, a plump, pleasant man in a natty silver-gray longsuit. Dandy, Meissner and D'Monte met with guards from Cailetet. Security arrangements were agreed to, and Aelita Two joined optically with a Cailetet thinker.

The mayor smelled of anise and rosewater. He led us by foot to a broad, high dome near the station's outer wall. Inside were pillows and fine carpets woven on Earth, wash basins cut in stone for the faithful, displays of the Hajj amulets of departed brothers.

I squatted on a pillow, stomach acid with tension.

Crown Niger entered, his walk even more catlike than before. His eyes darted around the large dome, and he squatted with a break in grace that spoke volumes. He expelled his breath with a small groan. "Excuse me, Madam Vice President," he said. "I'm very tired. I'm sure you know why. All of our important files seem to be open to prying eyes. Whatever happened to Martian honor?"

I smiled. "What can I do for you, Mr. Crown Niger?"

His nostrils flared. "I'm going to be completely open. I know you can't be, but my situation is different. I'm a small jackal running with wolves. I'm going to tell you what has happened, and let you judge what it means. I'm frightened."

He was not lying, that much was obvious. He even smelled sour. "I will be completely frank. You have suspected these things already, but I tell them to you now ... openly. We made many mining claims before the Freeze, on orders from our major partner on Earth."

"GEWA," I said.

He shook his head. "Above GEWA. Alliance of Alliances. You have heard rumors?"

"Not of that," I admitted.

"It is a fact. Most of the claims were denied, but some we opened to Earth interests, about ninety that we acquired or already controlled. They were seeded with locusts, factories to make destructive nano machines."

My face must have crimsoned. My hands began to shake with rage.

"We did not know this would be done, but ... To you, our complicity cannot be excused. This is not why I call you here. I tell you this because we now have no more protection from these locusts than you." He paused.

"I'm listening," I said.

"I had hoped to speak with the President."

"She's busy," I said.

He sighed. "We've made some breakthroughs at Caile-tet. Nothing as impressive as moving moons. Communications ... Important work, very lucrative. A week ago, we passed this information to our contacts on Earth. We sought to license new technology. We hoped to conduct business even in this climate of crisis. The answer was unexpected. They asked us to disband our research team. They asked us to send our scientists to Earth."

I had felt superior and in control at the beginning of the conversation. All I felt now was horror. "You told them?" I managed to say.

"We had an agreement with the Alliance of Alliances. I have never made so great a miscalculation in my life." He clasped his hands under his chin and rocked back and forth on his pillow. "They do not speak with me now. I fear they will take some horrible action. I strongly believe they were behind the Freeze. It's necessary for us to join forces. Together, we may survive."

"What have you learned about communications?" I asked, my mind racing far ahead of my questions. We would have to leave soon, get back to Kaibab; I would have to confer with Charles and alert the President.

"We can communicate instantaneously, across great distances," Crown Niger said. "Petty stuff compared to what your people can do ... But we consider it significant, and

we've had no reports that you've made this particular breakthrough."

"What else have you discovered?" I asked.

"On Earth, they seem to think there's much more ... Because of you and your damned exhibitionism!" Crown Niger
shouted. He lowered his eyes and sighed again as if with
great impatience. "I have worked hard to create a sanctuary
away from these insanities. The insanity of Earth, and now of
the Republic. I have put my life and soul into standing apart,
giving my people the choice of independence."

"You sold your services to Earth. I don't call that independence."

His lips drew tight; he seemed about to spit. "I do not care
what you think about me. It is clear you have no honor. There
is nothing truly Martian about you. You would threaten the
mother of us all for political gain. To use such weapons ...
Insane!"

"Martians have died because of Terrie force. Nobody on
Earth has died," I said.

"So naïve! To even display such power, such abilities, in
itself must lead to violence. And now Cailetet is put in the
same basket with you, by our former friends. Martians think
they understand the politics of nations, but Mars is just a
spread-out village, full of simpletons."

"You've put a new element into the equation," I said.
"They think you'll soon be as powerful and as capable as we
are."

"Will we?" he asked, face pale. "Are we on this same
track?"

Whatever Cailetet might discover in another few months or
years was actually irrelevant at the moment. "They wanted to
bottle this genie from the very beginning, years ago."

"What must we do?" he asked.

I stood and said, "The game is out of our control. Do you
sense that?"

He shook his head. "Yes, but—"

"This Alliance of Alliances must know your history. Disturbances in Africa—linking up with Dauble. They can't possibly trust you. Once you were useful to them. But now . . ." I shook my head. "I have to leave."

Aelita Two broke her link with the Cailetet thinker. I walked away, the thinker following on her carriage. In the middle of the dome, Achmed Crown Niger got to his feet, raised his arms, and shouted, "What can we do? Tell me! There must be something!"

Dandy, Meissner and D'Monte joined me in the corridor outside the dome. The mayor of Lal Qila followed, asking questions, trying to understand our sense of urgency. Dandy pushed him back gently, hand on chest. The mayor's mouth fell open, shocked by this rudeness. We left him and his assistants near the entrance to the dome. Within the dome, Crown Niger's shouts and pleas echoed hollow.

"We're returning to Preamble," I told Dandy. "I have to speak with the President as soon as possible."

"What's wrong?" Dandy asked.

"There isn't any time," I said.

No time, no distance, no chance.

Part Seven

~

2184, N.M.Y. 0
Moving Mars

The final crisis had come. As clear as Martian night, I knew Earth would feel it had no choice but to extinguish the accumulating threats and bring the new technology under its total control. All of Earth's progress and therapy and sophistication would come apart like wet sizzle in fear of our power and unpredictability.

Once in the air, departing from Lal Qila, I sent an emergency message to Ti Sandra and put Preamble on alert. Ti Sandra replied that she would meet with all her staff and advisors at Many Hills to examine our options.

"The box of troubles is wide open and will not be closed," she said. "Cassie, nothing we can do is as effective as Preamble. Tell Charles I may call upon him soon, and that he must be prepared."

Her infinitely weary face has stayed with me in sharp clarity all these years: the face of just and caring power placed in a killing squeeze. I am haunted by that face, so little like the Ti Sandra I had first met and had come to love.

* * *

The pilot thinker guided the shuttle across the Kaibab Plateau, engines droning monotonously. The two hours spent soaring over Mars seemed endless; I stared but saw nothing through the window, feeling what a mother must feel for an endangered child.

"What do you know about the Alliance of Alliances?" I asked Aelita Two.

"I was most intrigued by that name," the thinker said. "We have no record of it."

So Point One and Lieh, with all of their data flies and searches, but not penetrated to the top authority. How much could I rely on Crown Niger's words? Had he been deceived, as well? Or was the Alliance of Alliances our multi-minded thinker-enhanced bugbear ruler of Earth, riding high above the plebiscites?

Whoever was ultimately in control of the forces lined up against Mars, there could be no negotiation with two untrustworthy players wielding, or soon to wield, potentially lethal powers. We would come not to war, which has some rules and some sense of limitation, but to simple, panicked savagery.

Dandy Breaker faced me across the aisle and leaned over in his seat harness. "We're in real trouble, aren't we?"

"It seems that way."

"Because of something Cailetet has done?"

"Yes. No. We're all grabbing for the brass ring. We made our mistakes, too."

"Moving Phobos," Dandy said.

I remembered my sense of exaltation at the sudden turnaround; even now my pulse quickened at the thought of so much power, removing my burdens so quickly, allowing me to give back to Sean Dickinson even more than he had shoveled upon me. *We are still children. We still dance to our deepest instincts.* "They forced us to do it, but Earth can no more trust us now than it can trust a scorpion under its bed," I said.

Dandy shook his head, bewildered. "I've never even seen a live scorpion," he said.

More coded transmissions came in on the Presidential net. There had been a great many plans made besides Preamble; we had simply put more of our stake in the Olympians. Now the other plans were being explored: individual station defense against locusts, neighboring stations pooling their resources as well as defenses, more sweeps of all automated systems . . .

Thirty minutes away from Preamble, I spoke with Charles in the laboratory. He listened, face drawn and colorless, as I described what had happened at Lal Qila, and relayed the President's message.

"We're being toyed with," Charles said. "The government treats us like children. On, off. On, off."

"That's not our intention," I said defensively. "Ti Sandra wouldn't call on you unless—"

"We're on for good this time," he said. "There's no other choice. They're going to wipe our slate. I'll have to stay near the big tweaker. I've been training Tamara as backup in case something happens to me . . . And last night we sent a tweaker to Phobos again. Stephen put Danny Pincher in charge. Everything's in place for war."

War. That word summed everything and gave our preparations a horrible, urgent edge.

"What's the President going to decide, Casseia?" Charles asked.

I knew what concerned him. Having once held the sword of Damocles, he did not want to see it raised again.

"They'll have some defense against Phobos ready if we send it back," I said.

"The Ice Pit," Charles said. "Our spyhole has been closed."

"What?" I asked, startled.

"We can't tune in on their activities," Charles said. "They must have complete control of the Pierce region. They could use the Ice Pit against anything we send . . . If they've mastered it."

Leander joined in the conversation. "Better than ninety percent chance they know more than we do now," he said gloomily. "Maybe they'll drop the Earth's moon on us."

I wasn't going to dismiss any possibility yet.

"I'll be near the large tweaker full time now," Charles said. "We can be ready within an hour. You have to read the signs and give us the order. If Earth decides to blow Mars to pieces . . . We may not be fast enough to get it out of the way."

"Charles is being a little evasive," Leander said. "I don't want to speak out of turn, but—"

"It's nothing," Charles said, voice tense.

"We've run into some difficulties," Leander persisted. "Handling a mass as big as Mars presents special problems. First, it puts a huge drain on Charles or Tamara, whoever watches over the QL thinker."

"It's manageable," Charles said.

"Yes, but at a cost. The QL becomes particularly intractable when dealing with so many large variables. I know Charles can handle it, but there's also a physical problem. Our tweaker may show instability when moving so much mass across so great a distance."

Charles sighed. "Stephen's been working over some anomalies in our test results."

"What kind of instability?" I asked.

"The mesoscopic sample at absolute zero asserts its own identity. It's a kind of perverse dataflow problem. So many descriptors being channeled through so small a volume. It may reduce the effectiveness of the Pierce region."

Charles said, "We've encountered the problem before. We can control it."

Leander said, "I think our masters should be informed, just in case."

"Can we do it?" I asked, far too tired to argue physics now.

"Yes," Charles said.

Stephen hesitated. "I think so."

"Then stay on alert."

We signed off and I slumped in my seat, anxious to be on the ground working direct and not puppeteering from a hundred kilometers.

Minutes later, Dandy unhitched and stood, stretching, to use the wasteroom at the rear of the shuttle. He passed Meissner and D'Monte and they exchanged brief whispered comments. Falling into a reverie, I jerked to full alertness on hearing a few scraping sounds, and a sharp expletive.

"Ma'am," Dandy called from the rear. I leaned over the arm of my seat and looked aft. He stood with the two other guards near the wasteroom door. I unhitched and joined them.

"Something's wrong," he said, pointing to a series of pits and holes in the rear bulkhead. A section of floor had been unprettily removed as well, edges appearing eaten or chewed. I followed Dandy's probing fingers; something had termited much of the rear of the passenger compartment.

"It was fine a few minutes ago," said Jacques D'Monte.

Dandy rose from a crouch and wiped his hands on his pants legs. "Go forward, ma'am," he said. "Hitch in. Kiri, tell the pilot to get us into Preamble as fast as possible."

Kiri Meissner went forward, passing me with a breathless apology. I stooped to slide into my seat when I heard a heavy *chunk* and a cry of surprise at the rear. Face bloody on one side, Dandy staggered forward and collapsed in the aisle.

Kiri swung about and immediately placed herself between me and the rear of the shuttle. "Stay down," she grunted. She hunkered and pulled out her pistol, then frog-marched aft. Something clicked and hummed and Kiri jerked, clutched the seat arms on each side of the aisle, fell to one knee and rolled over on her back. A pattern of bloody holes on her chest poked through her black shirt. She coughed and convulsed, eyes asking a silent question of nobody in particular, then lay still. Her mouth foamed pink.

Jacques backed up beside me, straddling Kiri's body, cursing steadily and softly. He pointed his pistol at a dark shape hanging from the ceiling and rear bulkhead. Again the click and hum. Slowly, he twisted on rubbery legs, and the pistol dropped from lax fingers. He leaned over like a man about to be sick and pitched forward on his face.

I remained crouched behind my seat near the front, heart Earth-heavy in my chest. Aelita Two had disengaged her carriage from the mount behind me; my seat flexed as it moved.

The shuttle flew on as if nothing had happened. Had there been time to trigger an alarm? I could not restrain myself any longer; I peered aft around the edge of my seat.

A dark shape extended thin arms and legs, then rose tall from the exposed recesses of the rear compartment. It bumped against the ceiling, dropped slightly, made a high-pitched machine noise and crawled into the glow of an overhead light.

The locust bulked about the size of a man, its body a green twisted ovoid like the pupa of an enormous insect. Its multijointed legs probed at the seats and floor with a gingerly grace that made my blood freeze. A glistening trio of black eyes topped the body, and below the eyes, a flexible snout, thin as the barrel of a gun, swiveled purposefully.

Bioform nanotech, designed to survive on Mars and be deadly.

I stared in fascination. The machine climbed over Dandy, hindmost legs raised as if in effete distaste. My body shivered in expectation of the thin flechettes that had felled at least two of my guards, no doubt peppered from the questing snout.

Decapitation.

The seed of this locust had come aboard the shuttle at Lal Qila—perhaps with the duplicity of Achmed Crown Niger, although I could hardly believe such villainy even of him. More likely he faced a similar assassin even now.

The machine seemed reluctant to push past me. Knowing I was soon to die, a deep calm stole over me, replacing the nausea of seeing my guards so quickly dispatched. I knew I would join them soon.

Still, my mind raced, trying to think of ways to survive.

The pilot thinker would know something was very wrong. It would radio an emergency signal ahead. We were only a few minutes from Preamble.

With a start, I considered the possibility the locust wanted to be taken to Preamble. It would kill me, attach itself to the shuttle's thinker, take over the controls ... And carry itself, and more progeny, into the research site. I could not allow that to happen.

I faced off the machine for more long seconds. I slowly bent down hoping to grab Kiri's weapon, the closest to me. I didn't make it. With a slight shudder, as if making a sudden decision, the locust rushed along the aisle, grabbed the gun, and shoved me aside with bone-bruising strength. It moved forward and began to work on the bulkhead door to the pilot thinker's space.

Quickly, I bent over Jacques and Kiri. They were dead. I ran aft down the aisle and rolled Dandy over. His eyes flickered and opened. He moaned. The machine had hit him hard on the side of his head but had not shot him.

I dragged Dandy forward and hefted him into a seat, clicking his harness. His head lolled and he looked at me.

"Can't let it get to Preamble," he murmured.

"I know," I sad. Facing forward, I shouted at the pilot thinker, "Bring us down, now! Crash the shuttle!"

Dandy shook his head. "Won't do it. Tell it to land."

The locust expertly sliced through the forward bulkhead and locked door. Beyond, I saw the shuttle's cockpit, pilot thinker mounted above the controls. The locust grew a new appendage and poked at the thinker's box.

"Crash, damn you!" I cried. "Land! Bring us down *now*!"

The shuttle lurched and rolled. The locust's body slammed against the luggage bay and released the cases of the dead guards. Behind, Jacques and Kiri seemed to rise off the floor, given new life, limbs flailing. Aelita's carriage fell past me to the rear of the shuttle, smashing into Jacques' body.

I did not know that the pilot-thinker would obey my orders, but there was no other explanation for the craft's wild antics, unless the thinker hoped to throw the locust away from its case.

But the locust would not be thrown. An insectoid limb flew past me, black and gleaming, but despite the loss, the locust clung to the front bulkhead and continued to probe the thinker's case. Above the roar of stressed engines and the crashing of luggage and awful slapping of bodies, I heard a drilling whine.

I pulled myself into a seat with all the strength I could muster. Jacques slid past me and spattered my leg with blood. The shuttle rolled again just as I locked the harness.

Before assuming crash position, I glanced forward and saw the pilot thinker's case ripped open, gelatinous capsules spewing forth.

The locust became the center of a spinning nightmare.

We hit.

My shins pushed painfully against the rack in front of me. For some immeasurable time I felt nothing, and then another slam. Bones snapped and I blacked out, but only for an instant. The shuttle was still sliding and rolling as I came to, tumbling across the ground. I heard plastic and metal scream and the hiss of departing air, instinctively shut my eyes and mouth and pinched my nose, felt the touch of vacuum as my skin filled with blood—and the pressure canopies ballooned around our seats, sucked down against the cabin floor, filled quickly with compressed air hot as the draft from an oven door.

The shuttle stopped rolling, slid with a shudder and a leap to a nose-up angle, and lurched to a halt.

I sat strapped in my seat, wrapped within a canopy like a lizard inside a rubbery eggshell. My rib cage had become a plunging of knives with every gasping breath. I gritted my teeth to keep from screaming. My vision shrank to a hand-sized hole of awareness. Going into shock. Fighting to stay conscious, I glanced through the foggy membrane at Dandy's seat. He had slumped to one side. I couldn't figure out why;

then I realized he had unstrapped the upper portion of his harness before passing out.

I could not see forward. Debris blocked my view. I could not see the locust.

I pressed my head back against the seat's neck rest. I could stand the pain now; shock numbed me. I felt cold and sweaty. Battle over. Earth wins.

With some irritation, I felt small emergency arbeiters wrap their tendrils around my wrist. The shuttle's tiny little life-saving machines had scrambled to check us out. I tried to pull my wrist out of the way. The tendrils tightened and a tube of medical nano entered the arteries at my wrist. The silver and copper arbeiter, barely as large as a mouse, tied to a shining blue umbilicus, crawled up my chest and exuded a cup over my mouth and nose. I tried to shake my head free but sweet gas filled my lungs and the pain subsided. The chill lessened. I grew calm and neutral.

The little machine hung on my chin and projected a message into my eyes. *You are not badly injured. You have three cracked ribs and ruptured eardrums. Torsion units will reset the ribs and wrap them in cell-growth and sealant nano. The ruptured eardrums are being sutured now. You will not be able to hear for at least an hour.*

I could feel the action in my chest, specked little fibers growing from bone to bone, rib to rib, tightening inexorably, torquing the ribs back together.

"All right," I said, hearing nothing.

The shuttle cabin atmosphere has been breached. Integrity cannot be restored. No rescuers have responded to our emergency signal. The pilot thinker is damaged, perhaps destroyed. We will soon exceed our programming. Do you have any instructions?

I tried to look at Dandy again. The fog on my canopy had cleared a little and I saw him still slumped forward. "Is Dandy alive?"

One seated passenger is alive but unconscious. He will regain consciousness soon. He has a minor fracture of the tibia

*and minor concussion. There are two dead passengers. We
cannot repair the dead passengers.*

"What about Aelita?"

Copy of thinker "Aelita" condition unknown.

Dandy lifted his head and raised an arm to wipe the inside
of his canopy. He peered at me groggily, plugs of nano sticking out of his ears like muffs. "Are you okay?" He mouthed
the syllables extravagantly and signaled with his free hand.

"Alive," I replied.

"Can you move?" He waggled his hand.

I shrugged.

I caught part of the next message: ". . . move with me . . .
Get out . . ." But he could not coordinate his fingers to un-
hitch himself. He shook his head groggily.

I would have to rescue my guard.

I knew in theory how the canopies worked. They could
stretch and roll with my movements, keeping a tough membrane between me and the near-vacuum of Mars's atmosphere. I unhitched and stood, feeling the nano shift within
me, the edges of my broken ribs grinding.

The cockpit of the shuttle had been torn off and the nose
lay open to the sky. Part of the cockpit bulkhead panel, cut by
the locust and pushed aside in the crash, stuck out at a crazy
angle. An emergency safety symbol decorated a small hatch
on the panel. Pushing forward in my canopy, I wiped at the
moisture inside the membrane, trying desperately to see
where the locust had gone.

No sign of it. Perhaps it had been thrown free, or smashed
into the dirt with the pilot thinker and the cockpit.

I pushed my hand harder against the canopy. With a wor-
risome sucking sound, the membrane switched functions and
formed gloves around my hands. The panel hatch popped
open at my touch. I felt inside, half-blind, and brought out
two cylinders and two masks with attached cyclers.

Flesh creeping, expecting to step on the locust or have it
rise in front of me at any moment, I pushed out of the shuttle
and slowly rolled my canopy to a higher spot on the rough

terrain. I peered through the translucent membrane at the rocky, nasty surface, all knife-edge shards and tumbles of flopsand. We were two or three kilometers from the southern boundary of the station. We had enough air for five hours of exertion.

I returned through the jagged hole, nearly having a heart attack when the membrane snagged on a sharp pipe. I carefully lifted the membrane free and proceeded up the canted aisle.

Next I would expand my canopy and merge it with Dandy's. I carried the cylinders and masks to the rear and dropped them at my feet. Then I bellied up against Dandy's membrane. The two surfaces grew together with another sucking sound. I cut through the common membrane with a finger as it purposefully rotted, spread the opening, and crawled through. The medical arbeiters had stacked themselves neatly on the next seat, their work finished. Dandy raised his head and looked at me with some puzzlement. His eyes focused. His expression of pained gratitude didn't need words.

I pulled my slate from a pocket to communicate with him. *The emergency suits are gone. We still have some skinseal and masks. We're about three kilometers from Preamble. We're going to walk.*

We sprayed each other with the bright-green skinseal and put on the masks and cyclers before climbing out of the shuttle's wreckage. It had plowed in head-first, rolled for half a kilometer, and come to rest on a smashed tail. The upthrust broken nose leaned by chance toward Kaibab station, toward Preamble. I tried to find our position on a map through a navsat link but couldn't get a signal.

I showed Dandy my slate again. *Links are down. No navsat.*

He nodded grimly. I climbed on top of a rock and used a pair of binoculars to survey the landscape. Dandy climbed up beside me with difficulty. The crack in his tibia made walking rough for him.

We huddled in a smooth patch of sand. Dandy held up three fingers and bent one halfway. Two and a half kilometers. He mouthed, "Trail ... clear about half a klick north-northwest."

He pointed to the glistening fragments of vitreous lava. The rocks were always eroding, rounded segments falling away to reveal sharp fresh surfaces. Very nasty terrain. The soles of our boots could handle the edges, but if we fell ...

We agreed on the direction and began walking.

Time stretched, nothing but staring at glittering scalpel-sharp edges and fan-shaped flakes dusted with flopsand; lifting feet, staring for a place to put them down without tripping, pausing to regain our bearings.

Two hours, and we stood on the twisted trail, free of the lava field.

Dandy took my shoulder and guided me due north. He followed the stars with a sparrow's eye. Another hour on the trail, however, and he shook his head, paused, examined our oxygen supply, and pulled out his slate to consult a map.

I looked up to see a large meteor glowing low in the western sky. *No,* I told myself; *no trail.* It wasn't a meteor, not a large fireball. It was where Phobos should be about now, just past rising. I tapped Dandy's arm and pointed.

He stared for a moment, brow pulled low in an intense frown, then glanced at me with eyes wide. "What is it?" he mouthed.

"Phobos."

"Yeah." He lifted his finger and drew it across his throat. Danny Pincher and his crew, their tweaker ... The *Mercury.* Earth was using all of its new-found power.

One thing at a time, take care of the immediate problems before considering apocalypse. Dandy pushed his slate back into a belt pouch and made as if to lick his finger and hold it up to the breeze. "That way." He pointed slightly east of north. "I think the trail curves west of the outermost buildings. Back across lava."

"Let's go," I said.

We picked our way over an even rougher field now. Gullies several meters deep crossed our path. We climbed down slowly, then back up again, removing our equipment belts and wrapping them around our skinsealed hands to protect against the broken-glass edges.

"We'll cross the emergency exit for the bunkhouse wing. It'll look a lot like a rock, so stay alert."

My eyes hurt from dryness under the mask and from staring so hard at the sharp rocks and ground beneath my feet. My ribs hurt despite the pain control of the nano; I would need better attention soon.

The exertion was wearing me down, finally, and the air from our tanks smelled foul. Recirculation and scrubbing was beginning to fail. We were pushing the skinseal suits and masks to their limits.

Dandy held out an arm and I bumped into it, nearly losing my balance. He grabbed my shoulder to steady me, then made a *hush* gesture with his finger near his mask. I squinted to see whatever he had seen. The landscape was still, orange flopsand crust and scattered black boulders, sunlight glinting from glassy surfaces. I followed his gaze and saw something that was not still, something moving slowly a few dozen meters away. A skeletal metallic arm rose above the rocks, flexed cautiously, then straightened. A round black and orange striped body broke loose from the ground and erected on stubby black legs. A translucent sac fell away, and the thing stood on Kaibab's rocky plain, as big as a human, surveying its surroundings through tiny glittering eyes on a bulbous head. Its two arms undulated with a spooky, deliberate rhythm, as if tasting the air.

Dandy drew me down slowly as the locust turned away from us, and we tried to hide in the boulders. He raised his head high enough to keep track of the machine, then crawled slowly out of my sight.

I lay in the crotch of two boulders, buttocks pressed uncomfortably against rugged pebbly flop, too tired and in pain to feel any fear or even to wonder what Dandy was up to. After ten or fifteen minutes, he returned and switched on power to my suit again. He pantomimed and mouthed that the locust was stalking away from the station, and away from us, but that he had seen evidence of many others—factory cases, trenches where material had been mined and converted. And he had found the entrance. I followed him on hands and knees, my stomach churning with the added pain.

A large black boulder blocked our way through a narrow gully filled with powdery smear. I crawled past him, bringing up my slate. An optical port glittered within a dimple in the boulder. I programmed my slate for my key codes and ported it. The boulder quickly split in half, revealing a hatch. The hatch swung inward, and Dandy helped me through.

A guard waited for us in the narrow tunnel beyond, down on one knee with electron gun poised. He raised his head from the sight, opened one slitted eye, and blinked in disbelief. "You crashed," he said. Our hearing was beginning to return, though harsh and uneven; loud noises hurt.

"Yeah, and where was the goddamned rescue team?" Dandy demanded in a rasp.

"Nobody's going anywhere," the guard said, hefting his gun and standing. "We posted defenses on all outer corridors. We've had two locust attacks—"

"I have to get to the main lab," I said.

The station had been breached in two areas, both near the southern tunnel through which we had entered. The head of station defense, a broad-faced woman named Eccles, passed us in a side corridor, followed by a train of maintenance and defense arbeiters. She raised her eyebrows at Dandy, who shook his head with a fierce scowl: no time to explain.

The entire station was on first stage alert. Leander met us at the junction with the main corridor. Water a foot deep coursed along the floor from a pipe rupture. We slogged through the stream beside Leander.

"We've put Charles and Tamara on alert," he explained. "They're in the main labs, testing the QLs and preparing for whatever you order."

Having positioned troops and arbeiters, Eccles splashed into the corridor and joined us. "Madam Vice President, we haven't been able to reach Many Hills. We've seen locusts south of the station. There have been two skirmishes, and we anticipate full-scale attacks any time."

We climbed three steps up into a dry corridor.

"We'll need better med, and soon, and I want to see everything," I said. Two distant *thumps* brought everybody to a halt. We glanced around warily, waiting.

"Our defense arbeiters have begun shelling," Eccles said.

Dandy shook his head bitterly. "They'll come in here like cockroaches. We can't keep them away by shelling."

"I'll do whatever I damn well can," Eccles said defiantly, eyes flashing.

Leander pulled me aside while Dandy and Eccles argued strategy. "Locusts won't be our biggest worry. Phobos has been taken out."

"We saw it," I said.

"And Deimos as well. We don't have any big guns."

"Phobos looked like it was torched," I said.

Leander's face fell. "We're picking up high levels of gamma radiation."

"What, then?"

"Remote conversion," Leander said. "They seem to be using the Ice Pit to target us."

"Did the teams get away?" I asked.

Leander shook his head. "I've got a medical coming, and some transportation."

The pain in my ribs had subsided to a brutal throb.

In the annex outside the main lab, as an officious, humming arbeiter injected more nano and watched my vital signs, Eccles and Lieh worked with the original of Aelita to show me what little they knew. A map of the Kaibab Plateau displayed hundreds of blinking yellow crosses: suspected locust sign, spotted by emergency balloons and gliders circling the station. Red dots indicated positive locust identification. I counted thirty.

Dandy described the locust that had invaded our shuttle and brought us down. Lieh listened attentively.

"We only have the sketchiest ideas what shapes they can take, and what they can do," she said. "So far, all we've seen have been scouts and simple sappers."

More deep thumps vibrated the walls and floor.

"I hope that's our ordinance," Lieh said.

"Sounds like charges," Eccles said.

"Most links are down," Lieh said. "Comsats have been taken out—we don't know how—"

Leander and I glanced at each other, lips pursed.

"—And so we're pretty isolated. We can't guarantee making any connections with the President. In short," Lieh said, shadows deeply etched around her eyes and mouth, "they've done it to us again, even more dirty. Ma'am, my gut tells me we've suffered tremendous damage. Whoever's in charge of the Earth focus has gone over the edge. I'll support any effort you decide to take."

"We assume they'll try to kill us all," Eccles said.

"Then it's war," Lieh said. "How can we retaliate?"

Leander looked away. We had other swords of Damocles; but if we used them, the loss of life on both worlds would be staggering. So far, only Phobos and Deimos had been hit by what might be remote conversion—an action that could be regarded as frightened, as defensive.

"It's not an easy call," Charles said, standing in the door to the annex. He stared at me with a puzzled expression, as if emerging from an unpleasant drunk.

"Where's Tamara?" Leander asked.

"She's on the QL, keeping it exercised."

Eccles tapped my shoulder. The red dots on the display had tightened around the station. They knew where we were, and soon they would know *what* we were.

"They've fully harnessed the Ice Pit," Charles said. He lifted a hand and flexed it as if it pained him. "They'll use it on us soon."

More thumps, and a distant, high-pitched drilling whine that set my teeth on edge.

"They're doing it," Lieh said, eyes intense, far more sanguine. "Genocide. We have to respond."

I knew how she felt. We were cornered. It would only be natural to use all of our claws.

But we still had that other option, and that was why Charles was here: to gently remind me that all along, we had planned to do something completely unexpected. Vengeance would not save us.

But I had to explore all the possibilities. "Can we target the Ice Pit for conversion?"

"I've tried. I can't even find the Ice Pit now."

"Is anything else protected?"

"We can pick any target on Earth and convert it," Charles said softly. "Billions of hectares. Entire continents . . . If you order it."

Distinct popping sounds came from outside the lab chamber: projectile weapons. Eccles inquired about the action and was told that two locusts had been destroyed, one in a reservoir and the other in an arbeiter tunnel a hundred meters from the lab.

"It's going to be hand-to-hand in an hour or less," she said.

I could not order Charles to begin genocide on Earth. He might not even obey. My options had been reduced to just one, but even for that I did not have the authority.

I had to wait, as long as possible, for Ti Sandra.

"What do we do?" Eccles asked.

Aelita interrupted and said, "We have received an important image from a pop-up satcom."

The display changed abruptly. We looked down from five hundred kilometers above Schiaparelli Basin. A gray impenetrable curtain swept in eel-like folds across the basin, its upper reaches filled with sparkling stars. It seemed to be moving slowly from north to south. Where it had passed, dust filled the thin atmosphere. Through the dust we could barely make out lakes of molten rock, blackened tumult, complete destruction.

"That's Many Hills," Dandy said.

"They're converting Mars now," Leander said.

"Madam Vice President—" Lieh began, but Charles interrupted her.

"Aelita, can you magnify the western limb?"

"I see something there as well," Aelita said, and did as she was told. The picture was at the extreme edge of the satellite's range; Mariner Valley appeared like a grainy gash in the landscape.

"We're here," Leander said, standing beside Charles near the display and pointing with a finger just below, meaning beyond, the horizon. Charles traced another gray curtain barely visible in the magnified image. The curtain might have been a few hundred kilometers beyond northeast Kaibab; it was difficult to be sure.

"Madam Vice President," Lieh said, "if this is confirmation that Many Hills has been destroyed, then you must take command now."

Aelita reverted the picture to a wide view. She then magnified the region around Many Hills. The capital of the Republic was lost in dust.

My ribs ground together and I closed my eyes, gasping to regain my breath.

As the satellite continued its grim course from east to west we saw more clearly the searching fingers of death moving in toward Kaibab. But that seemed expected, even trivial; what shocked was the extent of destruction elsewhere.

Charles's hands twitched. "You're in charge, Casseia."

"Madam President," Lieh said, stating the obvious.

"Ti Sandra isn't coming back this time," Charles continued. "She was at Many Hills. The district governors and representatives were there as well, most of them."

I stared at the sparkling effects of conversion, pits and

slashes filled with molten rock: hundreds of thousands of hectares in Copernicus, Argyre, Hellas. Two of Mars's biggest stations had been hit.

"Cailetet's main station is gone, and two outlying stations, as well," Aelita said.

Achmed Crown Niger had had his final answer from Earth.

"Insanity," Leander muttered.

But I knew better. It all made horrible sense. It was a pattern as old as time: the display of baboon's asses. If the ritual was not perfectly observed, and one did not back down, the baboons squared off and bared their fangs. If that did not do the trick, they fought to kill.

The satellite image blanked abruptly.

"Loss of signal," Aelita said.

Charles stood beside the white cylinder that held the planetary tweaker. Stooped, long-fingered hands hanging by his side, his eyes burned below brows drawn together in eternal concentration. Around him, the support equipment for the largest of all our tweakers sat ready.

Tamara Kwang lay quietly on a couch nearby. She had been prepped for her backup role.

Thirty of the station's senior staff gathered in the auditorium beside the tweaker chamber, awaiting my instructions. Charles watched us with inhuman patience through the broad plastic window.

No one raised any objection when Leander referred to me as President.

My statement to the assembly was brief. "We can't remain in the Solar System and survive. We have to do what we brought all of you here to do. The sooner the better. Charles tells me he's ready. Stephen confirms."

The thirty sat in stunned silence for several moments. Dr. Wachsler stood and glanced around, hands held out. "We are making a decision for all of Mars," he said. "In effect, we represent all of Mars. Surely we . . ." He choked and held his hands higher, voice rising. "Surely there must be some confirmation, some ..."

"We will die if we do not act," I said. My hands shook with a perverse excitement. I wanted Wachsler to challenge me; I wanted any and all challenges now. My bones were knitting; I could feel them. Medical nano filled my bloodstream, rooting out problems, controlling my tendency to slip into shock. I felt strong as a lion, but knew I was still very weak.

"Dr. Abdi hasn't finished his areological survey," Wachsler said.

Abdi stood, hands in pockets, shrugged, and sat again. "I have not, indeed," he said.

"We should vote," called out Jackson Hergesheimer, the astronomer. "We know what happened on the last trip. What happened to Galena. If we're going to choose suicide over murder, we should be allowed to vote."

"No vote," I said wearily.

"Why not?" Hergesheimer called out. "We're citizens of the Republic—the only citizens who can respond to you!"

"There will be no vote," I said.

"Then you are no longer President of this Republic, even if you ... even if you might legally ..." Words failed him.

"I take this upon my own shoulders," I said.

"You order our suicide!" Wachsler cried.

Dandy Breaker, sitting at the back, had had enough. He rose, hand held high, and I gave him permission to speak with a nod. "I might point out the strict legality, under the laws of the Republic, of President Majumdar's position. This is an emergency. The only defensive course of action open to us is retreat. At her instruction, I have declared a state of martial law and broadcast it over Mars."

"Nobody can hear or object!" Wachsler said, tears of rage rolling down his cheeks. His hands moved like two birds, up and down, fingers fluttering. "My God, this is the most horrifying kind of tyranny."

"I take responsibility," I said. My voice sounded dull and hollow, even in my own ears.

"Madam President," Leander said, "perhaps we should take an informal vote. Just to be certain."

"We should discuss the option of declaring war," Hergesheimer said. "What they're doing is an outrage, and we should defend ourselves, if not with a moon, then by using conversion on their cities, their lands!"

"No," I said. "That is not an option, if we have any other choice. We do." I had long ago taken my own personal stand against striking back at Earth. "If anyone wishes to depose me, or petition for my ouster at this time, or do whatever the law allows ... or doesn't allow ... let it be done now, and hurry, please."

I wondered whether we were going to lose all control, whether I had pushed too hard and spoken too strongly. Leander was about to speak when the floor of the auditorium shook. Aelita called up a series of images from the cameras atop the station. The horrid gray curtain unfurled over northern Kaibab, whirling debris clearly visible in the electric blue corona, dust churning at its feet.

"It's on the plateau, about fifty kilometers away," Aelita said.

All in the auditorium watched, some weeping. Several jumped from their seats and fled.

"The rest is simply fear," I said. "We know. For us, there are no corners to be backed into ... unless we give in to our fear. Then we will die. Let us do what we built Preamble to do."

Charles entered the auditorium from the main lab space, moving slowly and uncertainly. His presence seemed to spook the staff members in the first two rows of seats. They drew their knees up and away from him, staring like frightened children.

"QL is ready," he said. "The interpreter is ready. So am I."

The image of our coming doom hung over us at several points around the auditorium. The floor vibrated as if pounded by a herd of huge animals. Charles stared at the images, then said, barely audible, "It's a one-in-a-trillion conversion. If they ramp it by a factor of ten, and they can, they could take the entire plateau at once."

"Let's do it," I said. I could barely make myself heard above the horrendous rockborne howl of matter coming to pieces.

Dandy walked stiffly down the side aisle. "Madam President," he boomed, his formality absurd under the circumstances, "You must give a direct and unambiguous order."

"By authority of the office of President, I order that we immediately move Mars to the chosen orbit around the New System."

"It doesn't even have a name!" Wachsler cried.

"Order so recorded," Dandy shouted, holding up his slate. He glared at the audience, daring anyone to voice another challenge.

Wachsler shook his head, speechless. Hergesheimer collapsed in his seat, mumbling unheard.

Charles turned and left the auditorium. Leander and I followed. Most of the staffers in the auditorium stayed in their seats or moved closer to the separating glass wall, like observers at an old-fashioned execution.

Charles sat on the edge of a couch beside the main tweaker. "I'll need some help with these," he said, lifting one hand to point to the larger array of optic cables. Stephen and I helped him attach the cables, and Charles lay back on the couch. "I'll be the only one in the loop to the QL," he said. "But others can observe. It would be easier if I can talk with people while it's happening. I'll feel more real. And if those people are seeing some of what's happening, with me . . ."

"I'll observe," I said.

Charles pointed to a smaller couch on the other side of the thinker platform. "I hope you'll be comfortable," he said.

I sat on the couch. "Do I need . . . ?" I pointed to the cables attached to the base of his neck.

"No. No feedback required. Standard image projection, or immersion. Immersion should really be something."

I swallowed. "Immersion, then."

"I appreciate this, Casseia," Charles said. He leaned his head back and closed his eyes, Adam's apple bobbing on his throat, jaw clenching, relaxing.

"Least I can do," I said.

"It's our only choice," Charles said. "We have to leave. I know that. You've made a courageous decision."

I followed Leander with my eyes as he prepared for my immersion. A few narrow bands around my head, projectors from a modified slate, a few slim optical connections between slate and interpreter, and I experienced a comfortable floating sensation, neural chitchat in the far background.

I glanced around, nervous at even these few constraints. The room smelled cold and metallic and seemed absurdly large for the apparatus; an echoing cavern with lights focused on the tweaker, force disorder pumps, refrigerators . . . One director, one backup—Tamara Kwang, with her own nimbus of cables and connectors—and one observer.

Leander finished checking all connections and stood to one side, arms folded.

"Mars is a big body," Charles said. "We have to reference more orthonormal bases for each descriptor, exponentially more for descriptors that superposit. That means storing some results in the unused descriptors within the tweaker. That's easier in a larger tweaker."

"The danger is no greater than before—less, probably," Leander said. "But the director's job is more difficult. He has to be more congruent with the QL to keep those extra descriptors in tune with the overall goal."

"And?"

"The interpreter still gets in the way. Charles will have to be more direct. Straight through to the QL."

Again the howl of converted matter shook the floor. Dandy left the auditorium and stood beside Stephen. "We're going to lose the station through blast effects if we don't go now," he said.

Dandy avoided looking at Charles as if he were indecent or sacred and forbidden.

"We'll do it in three," Charles said. "Just to be extra cautious. First, we'll advance along Mars's orbital path fifty million kilometers. If there's any doubt about the next step, we'll leave it there."

"They'll find us again, finish the job," Tamara Kwang said softly, self-consciously touching her cables. Drops of sweat beaded her face even in the chill.

"There won't be any doubt," Charles said. "The next step will put us about three trillion kilometers from the New System. We'll get our bearings and make the next jump."

"We can't stay in deep space for more than a few minutes," Hergesheimer said. I had not seen him come into the lab, but he stood a few meters from the tweaker, hands in his pockets, hair thoroughly tousled. "If we stay in deep space for more than a few minutes, Mars will experience extreme weather changes."

Faoud Abdi entered, followed by two assistants. "I have checked the damage," Abdi said, "and we have only ten percent of our Mars surface trackers linked through transponders. The rest are gone or we can't reach them. I believe we can still get a feel for what is happening to the planet, but of course . . . there is no way to tell others what to expect. There will also be more severe areological effects if we do not enter a comparable solar tide situation quickly. And the same side must be turned toward the new sun. This is very important."

"Understood," Charles said.

"The tidal bulge," Abdi continued.

"It's in the calculations," Stephen told him.

"Where's my station, my instrument hookup?" Hergesheimer asked. I heard but could not see Leander directing him toward the far side of the lab, where all of the exterior instruments of Preamble would direct their flow of data.

"Let's do it," Charles said.

I dropped my head back and stared into the projectors. Suddenly my neck hair rose and I nearly screamed. I felt some one standing beside me, opposite Leander and Dandy; I knew who he was, but did not want to accept that I was still so close to the edge.

I could not see him, but his presence was as real as anything else in the room, more real perhaps, more believable. His name was Todd, and he was about five years old, with fine brown hair and a ready smile, cheek smooth and downy and brown, fingers nimble, face flushed, as if he had just come back from exercise or play. He wanted to tell me something. I could not hear him.

He would have been my son. Ilya would have been his father.

I must have made a sound. Charles asked if something was bothering me.

"I'm fine," I said. "Let's go." I wanted to reach out and hold my son's hand, but he was no longer there.

I would never feel his presence again.

"Go," Stephen echoed.

"Going," Charles said.

Staring into the projectors, my head wrapped in neutral sound from the immersion bands, I saw Mars mapped above me as a highly detailed sphere, elevations exaggerated, all of our remaining trackers marked by pinpricks of red. By turning my head, I could see Phobos and Deimos. The map had not been recently updated, for Many Hills and other stations I knew to be gone were plainly marked as well.

"We'll lose all our satellites," Dandy murmured. He seemed far away, as did the rumbling howl.

Charles's voice spoke in the middle of my head, startling me. "First frame shift in two minutes," he said. "Hear me, Casseia?"

"Yes," I said. "I see Mars."

"Would you like to see what the QL is doing?" he asked.

"When I go in, I'll be part of its processing. You'll be outside, watching."

"Okay," I said.

I tried to relax my rock-tense muscles. Best to die relaxed, I thought; the universe seemed unpredictable enough that such a distinction might be important.

The image of Mars changed radically as I was drawn into the QL's perspective. What I saw was not a planet, but a multi-colored field of overlapping possibilities, the planet as a superposited array. The QL's assessment changed every few seconds, colors shifting, assignments of the Pierce region flashing at blinding speed: all of Mars scoped and measured using a logic no human could follow, a logic lying outside or beneath the rules of the universe.

I saw more clearly now the value of the QL's contribution. That it was in fact self-aware, despite these distortions, gave me a chill. What sort of self-awareness could function when consciousness had no shape, no specified purpose?

Who could have *designed* such a mind? Humans had— famous and less famous; and QL thinkers had played a small role in human affairs for a century and a half—but no human, not even the designers, could encompass the QL mentality. It was not superior—in some respects, it operated much more simply than any human or thinker mind—but what it did, it did superbly—and unpredictably . . .

If I was a spectator, watching this odd and beautiful horse perform its dressage, Charles was the rider.

"We've measured and drawn the first orthonormal base," Charles said. "Now we measure the translation of conserved descriptors to the larger system."

With the help of my enhancement, I understood part of what I saw: massive number-crunching through the interpreter's computer portion, cheating on nature by pulling the "energy" required to shift Mars from the total energy of the larger system, the Galaxy. In fact, the energy would never be expended, not in any real sense; the universe would simply have its demanding bookkeeping balanced, under the table, while it wasn't looking.

"Twenty seconds until the first frame shift," Charles told me. Our link seemed more and more intimate. He spoke solely for my benefit. "QL is now reassigning all descriptors to the first destination." We would move everything in the "space" to be occupied by Mars, at the same "time" we shifted the planet itself, in effect trading places. This was the easiest part of the process to understand, though not to accomplish.

"The tweaker is beginning to radiate," Stephen said outside. "Fluctuation in the Pierce region."

I saw the two frames—our present frame and the frame we would translate ourselves to. They overlapped, and then, for an instant, I could not see Mars at all. What I saw instead was horrifying in its simplicity.

Mars had been reduced to an ineffable *potential*. It could be anything, and we were with it—we had been drawn outside of the rules, away from the game. This was the blanking, when systems that relied on moment-to-moment correlations—minds, computers, thinkers, electronic systems—had to jumpstart themselves, to assume that there had at one time been a reality, and that all of the rules had been what they seemed to be now.

In the *potential*, I saw—though fortunately, I did not feel—the attraction of what seemed to be choice. We could choose other sets of rules. The QL danced through these with great haste. I wanted to linger, to sample; what if *this* were changed, *or that, or that*—such fascinating prospects!

"Frame shift," Charles said. The potential vanished and I saw again a simple representation of Mars. Hergesheimer took quick measurements of our position.

The rumbling howl died to a faint shiver, barely heard or felt through the couch's padding. We were no longer where we had been. Earth had lost its target.

"Charles, how are you?" I asked.

"Well enough," he said. "The QL got a little frightened

back there. Changing the rules seems to be as attractive as sex. It feels at home in that kind of place."

"Don't let it do any dating," I suggested. The immensity of what might have happened was lost in a sudden feeling of lightness.

"I think we did it right," Charles said. I blinked away from the projectors and squinted at him on his couch. His eyes were closed and his breath came in shallow jerks.

Something brushed my arm. I swiveled my head the opposite direction and felt such a sudden sense of relief, tears started to flow. I lifted up my arm and reached out.

Ti Sandra stood beside my couch. She looked very healthy, back to her full weight, face wide and radiant and proud. She wore her most flamboyant gown, hand-stitched tiny glass beads sparkling. She stroked my arm, her touch as light as a breeze. "You made it," I said. "God, it's good to see you."

"We've advanced along Mars's orbit fifty million two hundred and fifty thousand kilometers," Hergesheimer sang out.

Ti Sandra shook her head, still beaming at me, eyes crinkled down to slits with her pride and her love. I wondered at the lightness of her touch.

"Now for the first big leap," Stephen said. "Charles?"

"Assessing," Charles said.

I had glanced away at the sound of Stephen's voice. When I glanced back, Ti Sandra was not there, of course, but her touch on my arm remained.

I settled back into the couch, mouth dry as flopsand, and let the projectors find my eyes again, filling my field of view.

"There's no greater time lag—no lag at all," Charles said. "But we'll seem to be in the blanking longer, you and I and the QL and interpeter. We have a lot more translation to do—to the larger system. That will seem to put us outside status quo longer."

Status quo—things as they are. All the familiarities to which our minds adapt from infancy. Home ground, home turf, home rule.

"The longest ever for the QL," I said.

"Right," Charles affirmed.

"Temptations."

Charles chuckled.

"Dangerous for you, too?"

"You bet," he said.

"Like sex."

"Much worse, dear Casseia," he said. "I'm in here with the QL, keeping it from getting distracted, but I experience most of what it experiences."

"You told me once you wanted to understand everything," I said.

"I remember."

"In the blankness . . . I wanted to play around, too."

"If we played for an eternity," Charles said, "we might learn how to put together a universe. You and I."

"But you say there's no time passing."

"Eternity means no time. Infinity without time. A ring of bright and endless theorizing. The ultimate play."

Leander broke in. "Are you still working, Charles?"

"Still at it," Charles said. "You want reports?"

"Don't keep us guessing, Charles," Leander said.

"QL has finished assessing the planet and the site, and it's preparing to fix the books," Charles said. "Don't mind us, Stephen."

"Don't mess with her mind too much, Charles," Stephen said. "We need her after you're done."

"You'll see something different, this time," Charles told me, his voice barely above a whisper. Intimacy beyond that of man and wife: the intimacy of two young gods. "I think it will be part of the QL's longer acquaintance with the larger system. It will be measuring the highest level of superposited descriptors, up to, and maybe beyond those that are actually in use . . ."

"Unused descriptors," I said.

"Or no longer in use," Charles said. "Descriptors for things that once were, or might be. Or for nothing at all. Vestigial or excessive."

"How many minutes until frame shift?" Leander asked.

"Four minutes," Charles said.

"Earth might get a fix on our new position and start again," Leander said.

"To hell with them," Charles said. I could tell he was smiling, man on a powerful horse, riding confidently. But that horse was going to grow unbearably magnificent in the next few minutes.

"What would you use them for, Charles?" I asked.

"The untagged descriptors?"

"Yes."

"I think they're waiting for when we're mature. We could make new forms of matter. We could translate all human information into the upper memory of mass and energy. We could trick space into believing it was matter or energy, or into believing it was something we can't even conceive now."

"You talked about that once, a long time ago," I said.

"A dialog with the radixes of creation."

"Radishes?" Leander interrupted.

"Stephen," Charles said, "leave us alone. We're fine. Casseia is doing her job."

"She sounds more theoretical than political," Leander said dourly.

"One minute," Charles said.

I had a card to play, to keep Charles rooted in this particular creation. Now seemed the best time.

"I've thought of you often," I said.

"What?" Charles seemed puzzled by the shift.

"I've thought of you often since we were together."

"I've caused enough trouble, no?"

"I've thought about what you said, when we were trading ambitions. I think I know why I turned you down, Charles."

He said nothing.

"I did love you, but you were going places I could never go."

"Right," he said softly.

"It seems terrible to say it, but I wanted to be with someone less stimulating."

"Right."

Leander whispered in my ear, "Casseia, what in hell are you doing?"

I pushed him away. "There was a moment when I felt so close to you, years after, I felt as if we had actually gotten married and lived a lifetime together. You came to my rescue, Charles."

"When was that?"

"I had my back against a wall, talking with Sean Dickinson."

"You liked Sean."

"He was acting on Earth's behalf after the Freeze. He was forcing us—me—to give up everything. I never felt so trapped in my life. Then you sent your message."

"Ti Sandra—" Charles said.

I interrupted. "I went to the surface and looked west and saw Phobos through the clouds." My voice hitched again with the emotion of that moment. "I knew what you were going to do. And you did it. You took all my burdens away. My God, what you did for me then, Charles. I was so very proud."

"I'm glad," Charles said.

The image of Mars grew dark in my field of view. Through the darkness I saw the potential coming, the blankness a huge animal moving through void to reach us. The impression of its living beauty petrified me, like a rabbit facing a tiger.

"Shifting frame now," Charles said. I felt his calmness, his focus, his strength. Charles was really so simple, still a child. I had spoken a truth I had not been able to acknowledge until now, and he believed me.

"I love you," I said.

"I always have, and I always will love you, Casseia," Charles said. He took a deep breath. "Let's play."

Abruptly, the QL expanded the scale of our simulation. We seemed to hang over the Solar System, the inner planets bright points marked by armillaries of coordinates, references for descriptor bases, expansions of arrays for major effects on Mars.

Removing Mars would have virtually no effect on the sun or planets.

The tiger struck.

In the blankness, I wondered what the universe would be like if

Charles spoke to me reassuringly

There would have been no agreement between charges of particles having no extension, point-like particles such as the electron, and aggregates such as the neutron; and furthermore, superposition would not be possible, and the universe would crumble

But Charles held firm, and guided the QL

The blankness drew me into something like a dream, where all actuality was but a subset of

My life would have been

"Casseia."

No going to Earth, staying home, no

"Casseia."

My enhancement seemed to throw colored layers of notation at me, layer upon layer piling up in beautiful depths, staring through a sea of described realities, and within that sea, the Mars that I had known reduced to a vector space, a single state array forming the basis for everything thereafter, and that moment had been (searching out the root, the zero for its passage over an infinite plane of my existence)

Multiple roots, multiple zeroes

Where my plane intersected with the complex surface of Charles, forming shock fronts that pushed me along and ahead, tumbling like a boulder

Removing those roots, and the function collapsed in an entirely different fashion, and it seemed, in this dream, that we had both been used, that our potentials had been coerced to achieve one thing, what was happening now, and all else

could be discarded, our lives the endless scribbling that leads
to an answer

I saw also the trials, the judgments, the suits brought
against what was left of the Republic, crowds of those who
could not be reasoned with, because the shock fronts had
tumbled them along, as well; and I would receive the reflection, their anger and fear.

"Ah," Charles said, something between a sigh and a groan.
"Cassie."

He had never called me Cassie, the familiarity of a husband, and this our child coming now.

"Frame shifted," he said.

The Solar System had vanished from our perspective. Instead, a view of the distant stars from three angles, combined,
twisting my internal gaze until I understood what the interpreter was doing. We swam in a sea of nebulosity, fresh
clouds of young stars, stars newly born, the corpses of over-
eager suns that, dying, enriched the medium and allowed
even more dynamic suns to be made. The QL laid its sight
over these things, and all was twisted into uncollapsed vague-
ness, flickering between states, superpositions of qualities it
regarded as important but which meant little even to Charles.

"I've found the New System," Hergesheimer called out.
"We're four point nine trillion kilometers away."

I broke from the projectors to look at Charles. He lay without moving on the couch. Leander kneeled beside him and
looked at me with an expression caught between wonder and
pain.

"Do you hear him—in the simulation?" Leander asked.

"I don't know," I said. I went back under the projectors,
bands combining to immerse me again. I did not hear
Charles, but through the interpreter, I felt a guidance of the
moving figures, a steady hand on the QL.

"Yes," I said. "I feel him. He's here."

"Yes," I said to the steady hand, the man on the horse.

Frame shift in . . .

No time at all.

A mere adjustment.

Two thirds of a light-year; having emerged ten thousand light-years from the Sun, this was just a twitch of the toe into the waters of our new ocean. Charles could do it.

Did it.

The blankness almost a familiarity now, a place of rest as well as potential, and within the repose, the steady hand on the surface of the QL.

"Not mad," Charles said. "The QL is not mad. It's not even eccentric." I thought for a moment he was calling out the name of a woman, one of his lovers. *Agnes Day. Who is she, Charles?*

"Now listen to me closely, because there will not be time to say this again. You are my image of what a woman should be, God save me, Cassie."

Agnus Dei he had said, lamb of god.

"You are strong, you love and care, and they will come after you."

"Did you see them, too, Charles?"

"I don't need to see anything. I know people almost as well as you. I won't be there in any useful form, because this is going to"

just kill me

"Cassie. But you saved them all. History grinds very fine sometimes, and the dust is bones—or ash."

"We're responsible."

"They'll put you in a pillory, Cassie. I wish I could share it with you. Stephen will, and the others. I'm taking the easy way."

"Charles, no."

"Time's up."

I did not even feel the potential, and that may have been why he spoke to me—because that last, final twitch of the toe was the hardest, the worst.

The images projected into my eyes and into my head suddenly hurt abominably. None of it made any sense, all the messages and tags and labels scrambled, all the armillaries blown apart. I could not translate what I saw. The interpreter cut me off—leaving me in neutral, toneless darkness, and Leander pushed the bands away from my head and the projectors from my eyes.

Charles jerked on his couch, grinning horribly with clenched teeth. I rose from my couch and went to his side. Confusion and shouting from the gallery and around the lab; for the moment, everyone seemed to have forgotten us.

"We're there!" Hergesheimer called out. "My God, we're actually there!"

Only then did Charles relax. His head lolled, eyes shivering back and forth in their sockets. I cradled his head as Leander disconnected the optical leads. The medical arbeiters pushed forward then, through a sudden crowd, and took over, lifting Charles onto a stretcher.

I squatted on the floor beside his empty couch, dazed; we had done it. Charles had done it.

Hergesheimer walked before a vid image of the new system, pointing out stars as if this were his own triumph. Pictures of the new sun popped up around the lab.

Leander lifted me to my feet with strong hands and held me by the shoulders.

"Are you all right?" he asked.

I nodded. "Charles?"

"I think he pushed it," Leander said. "We'll see . . ."

The first nine hours of the first day in the New System I slept in my quarters. I came awake when Hergesheimer, Leander, Abdi and Wachsler announced themselves at my door. Leander was solicitous.

"Are you feeling stronger?" he asked.

"Well enough," I answered. I felt as if I could sleep another hundred years, but at least I was functional.

Wachsler's engineers had erected a transparent dome on the surface and built a platform for us to walk on. I was pushed to the front of the first group of fifty, still expected to lead the way, and in crowded shifts we took an elevator to the central emergency exit, rose to the new airlock, and stepped out under a new sky.

Leander guided Charles in a wheelchair, attended by compact medical abeiters. I held Charles's hand as we stood under the billowing, crystal-clear dome, but he responded only with a slight squeeze of my fingers.

The new sun seemed only slightly larger, though Mars in fact orbited eighty million kilometers closer. Twilight grew in the east. The sun's disk slipped below the horizon, its bright, pearly, youthful corona flared and went away, and with nightfall came another glory.

Our eyes adjusted slowly. Minutes passed before we could see the depths of color, the promise of this new garden of suns. Flowers of nebula all around, rose and violet and deep lilac and faint wisps of spring green and daffodil yellow, and within them, the blurred faces of infant stars.

I kneeled beside Charles's chair and took his hand again. He turned toward me, looked directly at me. Something lingered in his eyes, in his expression, to give me a little hope. I touched his face with my fingers and he flinched back, cheek muscles tightened. Then he relaxed.

"Do you know what's happening, Charles?" I asked him.

"Settled down," he whispered, eyes straying again.

"You brought us here," I said. "For better or for worse, but it feels safe. That must be better."

"Mm hmmm," he murmured.

"We're looking at the New System. It's nighttime. We can see the stars, and they're beautiful."

"Good," he said.

"Do you understand?"

"Yes," he said, nodding. "Too much."

The quiet that followed our move—stunned realization, adjustment, and recovery—applied, it seemed, as much to Mars as the Martians.

No moons rose over Mars.

The threat of the locusts faded day by day as more machines wandered into our defenses and were shredded, or their energy and purpose died on the cold dry sands.

With Many Hills gone, and Ti Sandra and much of the legislature dead, there was no government, no Republic. Large stations naturally became the centers of Martian social and political life. Martians talked vaguely of returning to normal, but the instinctive pattern of society was the family, the station, the Binding Multiple; nothing else had yet had chance to take root.

At first, millions of Martians had difficulty even understanding what had happened to them. They could not conceive of a force so massive, a conspiracy so powerful, as to tear the planet away from the Old Sun. As the reality seeped in—echoed across the ex net, reaffirmed by scientists and pundits trusted within the smaller communities—shock replaced disbelief, and then indignation.

The evidence of Earth's assaults on Mars seemed far away from everyday life. Destroyed stations had no voice, of course, and scarred territories, hundreds of millions of hectares of scorched sand, did not seem reason enough for so drastic a move.

Shock ruled. Families made alarmed and angry judgments, and those judgments were passed along the ex net. Committees formed to investigate, argued with each other, and eventually the committees became a kind of ad hoc judicial system, and that system made inquiries.

What at first was called the Escape began to be called the Retreat, then the Rout, and finally the Shame. We could have stayed, some said, and used our new power to fight Earth on its own terms. Surely a few billion Earth citizens would have been fair exchange for keeping Mars independent within the Solar System . . .

Homesickness of the most extreme kind added to the miseries.

The Republic, despite the best efforts of the surviving government, was quickly being replaced by something worse than anarchy—passionate mob rule, directed by untutored but skilled opportunists.

The mob was spurred on by Mars itself. Mars found its voice, and screamed its own pain.

The first great quake rumbled south of Ascraeus. Three stations tumbled to ruin, and one split asunder as a crevice formed between Pavonis and Ascraeus. The crevice—in later years to be called the New Tharsis Rift—grew in four weeks from a few meters to over a thousand kilometers. The echoes of this new stretching of the crust rebounded. Mars rang like a struck gong.

Within Preamble, the areologists—led by a frantic and inspired Faoud Abdi—tried to track the course of the new Martian tectonic order without satellites, relying entirely upon reports sent across the ex net. But the ex net itself was fragmented as links were broken, repaired, and broken again. Our nano resources were stretched past their limits.

From Kaibab, volunteer crews flew shuttles along Marineris, charting the changes, taking on fuel and supplies at those intact stations willing to cooperate, and proceeding across the Tharsis Bulge. Elevation changes of a few dozen meters were common. In some places, changes of a hundred meters were noted.

The Tharsis Bulge, some predicted, would subside within a hundred years—old years.

Mars orbited the New Sun with a period of three hundred and two days.

On the opposite side of Mars, narrow, linear ridges appeared, thousands of kilometers long, aligned in great arcs like waves frozen in stone. More stations found their tunnels in jeopardy and had to be evacuated.

Wachsler's contingency plans were enacted, but often too late. For this of course I was blamed. To have pushed Mars into such an extremity, without adequate planning, seemed a horrible blunder; the word "crime" was not too strong.

On my orders, the remaining Olympians disassembled the tweakers and carried them away from Kaibab to secure stor-

age elsewhere. Some of the shipments were seized by factions who laid claim to them. No single faction, thankfully,
could do anything with what they had. No one understood.
The Olympians fell silent, even under threat.

Some were imprisoned.

I spent much of my time flying from station to station,
touring quake sites and trying to provide solace, meeting with
the new unsympathetic committees. Each and every Martian
had become a refugee, even if they still had their lifelong familiar four walls around them.

And Martians were afraid. In station after station, they
asked when we would go Home—to the Solar System—and
when I told them, probably never, many wept in anger and
despair.

Some supported me, but not many.

Mars, on its surface and below, suffered madness.

When water poured from the northern scarps of Olympus and
flooded Cyane Sulci, damaging the labs where my husband
had worked to make the mother cysts bloom, I flew in the
last Presidential shuttle, on my last official tour of a disaster
area. Dandy accompanied me, and Stephen Leander. We traveled first to UMS, spending the night and refueling there;
then we proceeded to the sulci.

Something had come awake within the huge volcano, liber-
ating a vast subarean mineral aquifer. The water boiled from
the northern rupes, some of it coursing into the sulci, flooding
the hundreds of kilometers in between to a depth of several
meters. The water, meeting age-old flopsand and sizzle, liberated huge quantities of bound carbon dioxide and nitrogen.
Lakes of fizzing mud bubbled, churned, and then froze. We
flew across this dark, thickly clouded terrain, observing new
islands in the new mud oceans.

Only the southern lowlands and valleys of the Cyane Sulci
had been flooded, of course. But the lab had been positioned
in one such valley, and the containment domes had been de-

stroyed, leaving four mother cysts open to the new skies of Mars.

My husband's colleagues met us. Dr. Schovinski, Ilya's assistant, extended cordial greetings in the makeshift airlock.

"It is proverbial," Schovinski said, leading Dandy and Leander and me to a small room where tea and a crude lunch was being served. "We lose most of our buildings and tunnels, nearly all of the domes, and yet ... The experiment is a success. What you have done is controversial, dear Madam President, but from this scientist, all I can say is ... thank you!"

We ate quickly and Schovinski showed us through a shored-up and still-damp tunnel to the lab where fossil mother cysts had once been prepared for experiments in the domes. The cyst cradles here were empty. "We've moved them all outside," Schovinski explained. "If only Ilya could have seen this!"

We put on pressure suits and walked into the open.

Beneath the brighter skies, filled with high, swirling clouds of ice crystals, the floods had pushed the containment domes into mounds of glittering scrap. The carefully prepared soil beds had been scoured, leaving deep ruts and gullies, and in these gullies, beneath a thin layer of ice rime that gathered every evening and dissipated by noon, thick brown shoots rose two and three meters, forming fan-shaped leaves at their tips.

Schovinski urged me into a gully about a meter deep. He took my gloved hand and slapped it against the trunk of a shoot, rising from congealed and vitrified slime. The slime poured from a cracked mother cyst six meters away.

"First come the aqueduct bridges," Schowinski said. "Then, we assume, follow other forms. First the young eco manages its water supply, then it tries to complete its blooming."

From one advanced shoot, five meters tall and two meters thick at the base, four fan-shaped leaves had sprouted, spread wide now in the bright light of the New Sun. A translucent green globe as big as a watermelon hid in the shadow of the largest leaf.

Even before Schovinski told me, I knew what this was. In time, the fruit would grow huge, and serve as one of many reservoirs for the aqueducts. It seemed an eternity ago that Charles had guided me into one such buried and fossilized globe.

I resolved he would see this someday, when he was ready.

We spent several hours in the open, and even experienced a light flurry of snow. The brown shoots gave me a sharp, high joy, and I enthused over them like a little girl, trying to live this for Ilya as well as myself.

When we returned to the surviving tunnels, we heard from concerned lab assistants that half a dozen shuttles had arrived from Amazonis. Dandy's intuition kicked in and he quickly hurried me toward our own shuttle, but too late; we were met by a solid wall of well-armed citizens.

Schovinski's indignation meant nothing to the vigilantes. The time had come. They arrested me and charged me with half a dozen crimes, highest among them treason. Dandy and Leander were bound hand and foot like lambs before slaughter; the grim-faced mob, all men, subjected me to the lesser indignity of having my hands sticky-roped.

It had happened to me before.

So died the Federal Republic of Mars.

I have drawn the limits of my story and will stay with them. All that I have written deals with moving Mars, the whys and hows, and my role in this event. What comes after I would just as soon forget.

Writing in prison is much overrated.

I do not ask for forgiveness, or even for fair judgment. In a way, I have received my reward. I do beg however that Charles Franklin be treated gently, as well as all of the Olympians held under arrest.

Because of them, Mars still exists and would-be-governments can still struggle and argue and accuse.

When all the judgments are made and my punishment settled, I will think of these things: a trunk, a leaf, a green and glittering globe. Children will be born who remember nothing of the Old Sun. The new bright-flowered skies will be home for them—for you, whom I hope and pray will read this story.

I see you playing in the shadow of the bridges of Old Mars, your skin revealed to the air, a hundred, a thousand years from now. For you there will be no time, no distance, no limits; nothing but what you will.

Do better than your elders. You will have to; the power is yours to command.

Afterview
by Dane Johansen, Ph.D.

It's been my privilege to edit this new text edition of Casseia Majumdar's memoir. Even today, Majumdar's life and actions provoke controversy—witness the recent attempt by Old System Advocates to impose their own notes and comments on all versions of Moving Mars. *That attempt was quelched—but it points to the simmering angers still felt by many Martians.*

I met Casseia Majumdar once in her garden, twenty years ago—when she was fifty by the old way of measuring Martian years, and I was twelve by the new. My mother had just become President of Mars, under the New Republic Constitution, and she, my father, and I were making the pilgrimage across Cyane Sulci to Casseia's home, as had become traditional in the past few administrations.

Casseia Majumdar was a straight, proud, stocky woman with wispy gray and black hair and deeply lined brown skin. Beneath her pressure suit, her arms seemed thin but strong, and her legs moved swiftly and with youthful confidence. She met us in a tractor that had once belonged to her husband. She smiled, shook our hands, and invited us into her house, perched on the edge of the Cyane Sulci Preserve, where we removed our suits and showered and became comfortable.

She introduced us to her longtime housemate, Charles Franklin. Franklin greeted us with a pleasant but separated expression. Tall, very thin, with white hair growing thickly above a face marked by peculiar lines, neither laughing nor sad, Franklin said little, walking around the house doing var-

ious small tasks that seemed to have no real purpose, bu
which amused him. He smiled to himself, sometimes laughed,
and this bothered me. I didn't connect this odd, shell-like per
son with the Charles Franklin who had figured so promi-
nently in my history lessons. I asked my mother, "Is he al
right?" My father nudged me in the ribs, bent down, and
said, "That's him. *Now behave!"*

I stared at the man with even more unease. He glanced a
me, nodded as if we were in deep agreement, and sat beside
Casseia Majumdar.

Mother, always straightforward, asked Majumdar how
Franklin was faring lately.

"As well as ever," she answered. "Don't mind him," she
told me. "He's having his own kind of fun, and sometime
he's very lively. But he doesn't think the same way you and
do."

She prepared dinner for us with Franklin's help. I remem-
ber she said to me, "Martian vegetables taste better prepare
by human hands, I think you'll agree."

We sat at her table, made from a single dried bridge leaf
near a window that overlooked a broad russet-colored valley
We ate bridge fruit, the first time I had tasted such a delica
cy, prohibitively expensive on the open market. Majumda
spoke to us enthusiastically about the mother cysts and how, i
the last twenty years, they had finally shown us more of thei
varied offspring. Some of those offspring lumbered and grew i
the gardens outside: rotifer-sheep, pipeworms, dustdogs.

Franklin listened to this conversation with a pleased ex
pression, then added his own contribution. He pulled a draft
ing wand from a shirt pocket full of paper scraps and scriber
and used it to sketch in the air, with thin orange lines, a
number of mother ecos organisms, known only by their fos
sils: glider bees, sandpuffs, drift-tangles. Then, with equal en
thusiasm, he sketched a series of involved squiggles that ha
no shape whatsoever.

"Sometimes I see what Charles is getting at," Majumda
said, following the squiggles in the air with her finger. "Thes

*are tracks of genetic diversity, I think. Only the least demand-
ing creatures are being produced by the mothers now. They
seem to be holding their best offspring in reserve—in case
Mars decides to go back to its old dead days. Very intriguing,
Charles."*

Franklin smiled and replaced the wand in his pocket.

As we ate, my mother told Majumdar that the Council of
Governors had approved the erection of a monument to her,
the first President Ti Sandra Erzul, and the Olympians. There
would be a group of bronze and steel statues and a plaque.

Casseia appeared sad, then irritated. "I don't want recognition," she said. "They gave me the gardens. The gardens
are enough. I don't blame anybody now."

"They took away your freedom for ten years," Mother said.
"We owe you so much more."

"We took them away from all that they knew, and couldn't
even ask permission. I refused to let any votes be taken."

"We have a different view of these things now," my father
said.

"I don't need a statue," Majumdar insisted. "I do wish you
Presidents would stop coming here to apologize. You know
what I'd really like? I'd enjoy taking your lovely daughter on
a tour of the garden."

"All of it?" Father asked. The preserve stretched across a
million hectares of the Sulci, impossible terrain for a tractor.

"Just the part I watch over," Casseia explained with a
laugh.

And she gave me her own special tour, treating me like a
granddaughter. There was such a gleam in her eyes when she
stopped the tractor beneath an aqueduct bridge. We sealed
our helmets and got out, looking up at the huge deep-red pet-
als of the flowers, as wide as I was tall, clustered the length
of a pier which stretched thirty meters into the blue-black sky.
The great glassy liquid-filled vines stretched across the ridges
and hummocks and deep valleys like cables on a bridge. A
full-grown man could walk through these vines, if they were
emptied of their slow sugary sap.

"My husband and I saw the first signs of old Martian life returning," Majumdar said.

"I know," I answered, too smart. "They told us about it in school."

"How gratifying. Have you read my book?"

"Of course!"

She looked away, shaking her head slowly. "Lovely flowers, but mostly futile. They miss the services of glider bees . . . but they are pretty, aren't they?"

I said I thought they were beautiful.

"Well, the arbeiters pollinate a few of them each year, and I'm allowed to harvest the fruit, and sell them, and eat what I want myself. One does me for a year."

She took me up to a broad pier and placed my gloved hand on the solid deep green surface. "Here's something for keeps," she said, "They're half a billion years old, you know, and these are little more than babies."

Years after Casseia Majumdar died, I visited the statues and the plaque placed on a flat rocky plain, open to the sky, near the University of Mars Sinai.

The plaque rests at the feet of statues of Ti Sandra Erzul and Casseia Majumdar (who steps forward with an intense expression, as if alarmed or puzzled, hand out) and Charles Franklin and the rest of the Olympians.

The plaque lists their names, and says:

> **To all who helped bring us here, that we might grow
> as the flowers in the sky, in freedom,
> under the New Sun.**

While I read the plaque, the ground shivered with a small marsquake. The statues did not sway, though I did.

And the sky was bluer still.